W9-AWG-204

THE

GREAT
PRETENDER

THE
GREAT
PRETENDER

MILLENIA BLACK

NEW AMERICAN LIBRARY

New American Library
Published by New American Library, a division of
Penguin Group (USA) Inc., 375 Hudson Street,
New York, New York 10014, USA
Penguin Group (Canada), 90 Eglinton Avenue East, Suite 700, Toronto, Ontario, M4P 2Y3, Canada
(a division of Pearson Penguin Canada Inc.)
Penguin Books Ltd., 80 Strand, London WC2R 0RL, England
Penguin Ireland, 25 St. Stephen's Green, Dublin 2,
Ireland (a division of Penguin Books Ltd.)
Penguin Group (Australia), 250 Camberwell Road, Camberwell, Victoria 3124,
Australia (a division of Pearson Australia Group Pty. Ltd.)
Penguin Books India Pvt. Ltd., 11 Community Centre, Panchsheel Park,
New Delhi - 110 017, India
Penguin Group (NZ), cnr Airborne and Rosedale Roads, Albany,
Auckland 1310, New Zealand (a division of Pearson New Zealand Ltd.)
Penguin Books (South Africa) (Pty.) Ltd., 24 Sturdee Avenue,
Rosebank, Johannesburg 2196, South Africa

Penguin Books Ltd., Registered Offices:
80 Strand, London WC2R 0RL, England

First published by New American Library,
a division of Penguin Group (USA) Inc.

First Printing, September 2005
10 9 8 7 6 5 4 3 2 1

Copyright © Millenia Black, 2005
Readers Guide copyright © Penguin Group (USA) Inc., 2005
All rights reserved

NEW AMERICAN LIBRARY and logo are trademarks of Penguin Group (USA) Inc.

LIBRARY OF CONGRESS CATALOGING-IN-PUBLICATION DATA:

Black, Millenia.
The great pretender / Millenia Black.
p. cm.
ISBN 0-451-21648-2
1. Triangles (Interpersonal relations)—Fiction. 2. Fathers and daughters—Fiction 3. Married people—Fiction.
4. Mistresses—Fiction. 5. Adultery—Fiction. 6. Secrecy—Fiction. I. Title.
PS3602.L325225G74 2005
813'.6—dc22   2005009358

Printed in the United States of America

Without limiting the rights under copyright reserved above, no part of this publication may be reproduced, stored in or introduced into a retrieval system, or transmitted, in any form, or by any means (electronic, mechanical, photocopying, recording, or otherwise), without the prior written permission of both the copyright owner and the above publisher of this book.

PUBLISHER'S NOTE

This is a work of fiction. Names, characters, places, and incidents either are the product of the author's imagination or are used fictitiously, and any resemblance to actual persons, living or dead, business establishments, events, or locales is entirely coincidental.

The publisher does not have any control over and does not assume any responsibility for author or third-party Web sites or their content.

The scanning, uploading, and distribution of this book via the Internet or via any other means without the permission of the publisher is illegal and punishable by law. Please purchase only authorized electronic editions, and do not participate in or encourage electronic piracy of copyrighted materials. Your support of the author's rights is appreciated.

ACKNOWLEDGMENTS

I thank God, first and foremost. Without him, for me nothing noteworthy is possible—thank you, God. I offer heartfelt thanks to the friends and family members who continue to help and support me in significant ways.

No man is an island. Behind every great accomplishment stand great people. I have to take this opportunity to thank the great people behind this great accomplishment. To all of you—thank you. Your support will always be remembered. . . .

A special heartfelt appreciation:
To Roberta Austin, Sara Camilli, Ruth Caron, Kara Cesare, Arlene Connolly, Angie Dixon, Gladys Fackler, Richard Love, Nicole Outen, Nancy Rivero, Judith Henry Wall, Pamela Whitmire, and Zane, I offer enormous gratitude. Despite the fact that I've never met some of you in the flesh, you've all made efforts to offer much needed help and support, sound advice, and valuable guidance. Thanks, and love to you all.

To Mina Anderson, Marcia Crawford, Patricia Heath, and Tanya Stevens, I want to say the help and opinions you offered after reading the drafts will be treasured, now and always—lots of love and thanks.

And finally, because of his unyielding and unwavering belief in me, because of his investments, perseverance, and caring, this was possible—to my father, Timothy Aldred. You're the best father a person could ever have. This accomplishment, and all it represents, is for and because of you. . . . Love to you, Daddy!

PROLOGUE

ORLANDO WAS NO LONGER what it had once been to Reginald Brooks. For years he had made the central Florida city a home that camouflaged him, symbolizing refuge and protection. . . . But lately, something unusual was happening.

Overtaking a white sedan, Reginald glanced at his Rolex and knew he was going to be late for dinner. The procurement meeting for Disney's new advertising campaign had run over the allotted time, and he hadn't had a moment to call Renee. She would be pissed.

The fact that tonight's delay was legitimate would be of no consequence, since Renee was never able to decipher the truths from the lies. He thought about calling her now, but changed his mind. His hand stopped in midreach for the cell phone.

Driving past their town home community, Reginald headed for the local Blossom Bloom and bought flowers instead.

That would do the trick. It always had.

AT HOME, RENEE was *indeed* pissed. Looking at the clock on the stove, she noted that it was six thirty-five. She practically threw the tiny strips of pork chops onto a Barbie plate.

She worried when Reggie was late getting home and didn't call. Hell, she worried even when he did call. One would think that she'd be accustomed to the late meetings by now, but Renee Jameson was *far* from accustomed. Given his schedule, it seemed that Reginald's work was just as important to him as his family. He already spent the last two weeks of every month at the Miami offices, which was a huge thorn in her side. His time at home was so limited, why make it worse by coming in late the entire two weeks he was home?

Year after year, she became more and more preoccupied, nursing the growing resentment.

"Denise, for the last time, bring your little butt down to this table now!" Renee shouted as she poured Kool-Aid into her daughter's favorite Barbie cup.

"Okay, Mommy, I'm coming!" Six-year-old Denise Brooks came running down the stairs and almost tripped in her haste. Renee placed her dinner on the table and yanked out the chair.

"Mommy, how come Daddy's not home yet?" Denise asked. Her inquisitive eyes were big and bright. "He's going to bring ice cream tonight—he promised!"

Renee looked at her daughter. "Daddy is always making you promises he doesn't keep. Why do you even listen to him? I wish you'd learn. I'm really tired of hearing you whine whenever Daddy breaks his promises." Renee slid into her chair and irritably began devouring the tender pork chops.

Denise sulked. She picked at her food and remained silent. She waited to hear the door open, for Daddy to come in with the ice cream. This time Mommy would be wrong. Daddy *does* keep his promises . . . sometimes.

REGINALD QUICKLY MANEUVERED his Land Cruiser into the driveway. He told himself to relax, but the truth was that he dreaded walking through the front door to face Renee. He could no longer ignore the obvious. After six and a half years, this lifestyle was actually beginning to tax him to the point of distraction.

A very tall and handsome man with a striking face of prominent features, Reginald looked much younger than his forty-one years. The presence of Reginald Brooks awe-struck men and women alike—it was a strength in which he arbitrarily allowed himself to indulge. Lately, though, he felt a distinct disconnect from his charismatic appeal.

Reginald was tired—desperately tired.

He walked up the winding sidewalk, put the key in the door, and let himself in, happy to see his daughter. Denise was always a sight for sore eyes. He always found much needed comfort in her animated, effervescent spirit.

Denise had heard the key in the lock and was up and running as the door opened.

"There's my angel. Come give Daddy a kiss!"

She ran toward her father but stopped abruptly when she saw his hands. "Daddy, where's the ice cream?" she demanded, her bottom lip protruding as the eyes filled. "You didn't buy it. You promised me ice cream today! You let Mommy win again! Mommy was right again!" Denise ran back to the table in tears. She picked up her little fork and shoved buttery mashed potatoes into her mouth. She wanted to finish and go play in her room, away from Daddy. She didn't like it when Mommy won.

"Oh, sweetheart, I'm sorry." Reginald placed his snakeskin briefcase near the table and knelt beside his daughter. "Daddy worked late and forgot all about your ice cream tonight, but I promise I'll bring it for you tomorrow night. Okay?" Without waiting for a reply, he dropped a kiss on her forehead, then stood and faced Renee. Denise would be fine.

"Hey . . . I'm sorry I didn't get to call. The Disney meeting ran over, but I shot out of the building the minute it ended. I brought you these as a peace offering." He extended a dozen soft pink roses. "Call it male intuition, but somehow I just *knew* you'd be furious when I finally made it home."

Renee said nothing. Taking the flowers, she put them on the counter and placed a gentle kiss on his mouth. "Knowing you feel bad is enough. . . . Especially bad enough to bring my favorite flowers. Thanks." She grinned, seeming placated.

They then fell into their routine. They sat down to dinner while Reginald watched CNN, and Renee playfully coaxed Denise into eating her vegetables.

All was well in Orlando.

*   *   *

LATER THAT NIGHT, after fifteen minutes of what had long since become mundane sex, Reggie waited patiently for Renee to fall asleep—then he fell into his six-year-old routine.

He expertly manipulated his way out of their king-sized waterbed and descended the stairs to use his cell phone. If she awoke and came downstairs, he'd be caught in the refrigerator and the phone would disappear into the cupboard. . . . However, in the last six and a half years, he had never needed to enact this subterfuge. Knock on wood.

Reginald called his wife in Miami.

The phone rang four times before Tracy Brooks picked up, her voice laced with sleep. "Hello?"

"Hi, Trace—just got in. What's up down there tonight?"

He heard a yawn, and the sound of her voice varied as he imagined her shifting the phone from one ear to the other. "Not much. I've been trying to wait up for your call. . . . Just dozed watching *Howard Stern*. How'd it go today?"

Reginald kept a vigilant eye on the staircase. "It was good. Roger is one happy CEO since the numbers were more than we'd projected for this quarter. And that reminds me. . . . I keep telling you that I can probably persuade him to put someone else on this Orlando division, Trace. Then I won't have to come up here for more than a day or two at a time, like I used to. This traveling back and forth is getting to me. . . . And I'm beginning to hate being away from you and the girls for so long every month. . . . Especially you-know-who. I just can't stop thinking about the effect my being away has had on Olivia. I can hardly get her to look at me for more than two seconds at a time. . . . Almost ten years of living like this is taking its toll, Tracy. Don't you think?"

They'd had this conversation several times, and Tracy never gave an inch. Nevertheless, it had served as an essential front to support Reginald's "life insurance"—up until now. Of late, he found himself wanting her to relent, wanting her to want him home.

"Reggie, I've said it before and I'll say it again—no way. You rake in way too much money with the perks you get for doing it. We may not need the money, but we'd definitely notice if it suddenly stopped showing up in the bank account." He sighed as Tracy settled into her seductive voice. "Besides . . . if you're missing me more than usual, I can always fly up more often when you're there. You're not the only one who's"—she sighed—"inconvenienced by this arrangement, you know."

Reginald closed his eyes. He should be at home, in that bed beside his wife. He'd even been craving Tracy more than usual lately. "I'll tell you one thing: You'd better be prepared for my arrival tomorrow, because you're making me as hard as Chinese algebra right now and I'm wishing that I was on the next flight home."

She chuckled and said, "Ready for tomorrow? I'm ready right now. . . ."

He opened his eyes and looked back at the stairs. "I'll see you tomorrow when I get home. Love you."

"Love you too, Regg. I'm sure you can make it through one more night in that lonely apartment without me."

Reginald chuckled. "Well, I know home is just another day away, so I'll manage. 'Night, honey." He pressed the END button on the phone and slipped back upstairs. After a quick check on Denise, he returned to his bedroom.

As usual, Renee was still sleeping soundly. He slipped back into the waterbed and got comfortable. He closed his eyes.

All was well in Miami, too.

PART ONE

1

MIAMI, FLORIDA

AFTER HANGING UP THE TELEPHONE, Tracy Brooks bolted off their king-sized bed and slipped into the blue, knee-length dress that she'd selected earlier that evening. She had nodded off while waiting for Reginald's nightly telephone call, but if she hurried she could get there in fifteen minutes, tops.

Frank got on her case whenever she showed up after ten. He worked for the UPS corporate offices and liked to be in early, so he wanted to be in bed and asleep by eleven. Besides, Tracy didn't enjoy it when they had to rush things. It was bad enough that Reggie spent so much time out of town, so she liked to take her time when she was with Frank. Just thinking about the forthcoming pleasure made her move even quicker.

ON THE WAY back up to her bedroom, Valerie Brooks saw her mother practically running down the stairs, toting her gigantic Donna Karan shoulder bag. "Mom, Ginger Ledford, from across the street, just stopped over to tell us her grandma was taken to the hospital. She's having kidney problems."

Her mother barely stopped to look at her. "What? Oh, that's awful! We'll have to go visit her. You'll have to tell me more about it tomorrow, honey; a friend's waiting for me at the Ivory." Then, Tracy was through the doorway and Valerie heard the ascension of the electronic garage door.

SHE MUST THINK we're stupid, Valerie thought, heading back upstairs. As if an idiot wouldn't know that she was up to something. Valerie had suspected for quite some time that her mother was involved with another man. She didn't know who on earth it could be, but she knew there was definitely somebody. When she reached the top of the stairs, Valerie walked past her own bedroom and went into her parents' room.

At seventeen, she had grown into quite a snoop. She was habitually slinking into her parents' and her older sister Olivia's bedrooms to dig into their belongings for information. It had become a regular habit of hers since she was about twelve, and a lucrative habit indeed. As a result of her shuffling and digging, Valerie discovered many, many wonderful bits of information.

She knew when Olivia had started her period. She knew when she had gotten involved with her first boyfriend—her first *real* boyfriend. She knew things Olivia would never have told her at the times that they'd happened.

It was this practice that had planted the seed of suspicion about her mother.

Now as she conducted her routine inspection of her parents' large bathroom, Valerie was convinced that her mom went to see a man. The distinctive fragrance of Realm lingered in her mother's wake, and her favorite lipstick was left opened on the marble vanity table. Valerie shook her head and went down the hallway to her own bedroom.

As she entered her room and closed the door, she thought, *Damn it . . . how can I find out who he is?*

2

"ARRRRHHHHAAAA!" ROARED Franklin Bevins as his back slowly arched into a perfect C. Tracy could always drag a deliciously primal roar out of him. She had the sweetest nest he'd ever had—and he'd bedded quite a few.

Once he recovered, he rolled from her body, slipped off the condom, and went into the bathroom to wash. Frank gazed at himself in the full-length mirror. Thanks to regular workouts, his body was cut in all the right places. He kept his hair well groomed and visited his barber weekly. Standing six feet tall, his striking features and enigmatic eyes were what most women found utterly irresistible. . . . Including Mrs. Tracy Brooks.

When he left the bathroom, she was fast asleep. "Bitch," Frank muttered to himself. It never failed. She knew he didn't like her to spen the night, but she didn't seem to get the hints. *She sure is lucky that s Mrs. Reginald Brooks,* he thought. He actually didn't believe in scre married women, but Mrs. Brooks here was a major exception. Sh *Reginald's* wife, and that made all the difference in the world cially in light of Reginald's Orlando "business."

Franklin quickly went over to his bed and tapped Tracy's up, up. It's time to go home." It was already after one in th damned if he'd get any sleep tonight. "Come on, Tracy, g from now on, if you can't make it before ten, just stay ford to go to sleep at one thirty in the morning wher

Once dressed, Tracy wiped sleep from her eyes, found her purse, and walked to the door. "You know I have to wait for Reggie to call at night. I can't risk him becoming suspicious if I'm not home at that hour."

Lying in the bed, Frank pulled the sheets up and turned his back. "I need to get to sleep."

Tracy stared at Frank's form under the covers. When had he begun to treat her like some common whore from a brothel? And why? Unbeknownst to Franklin, she'd grown to value this relationship far more than her resilient pride would allow her to disclose.

She opened the door. But just before it slammed, she threw over her shoulder, "Watch it, Frank. One of these days, I won't come back at all."

But they both knew she would.

THE FOLLOWING EVENING, Reginald landed in Miami just as the heavy rain began to fall. He was exhausted. The years were definitely not being kind to him. In fact, they had practically been mean. Between Renee and Tracy, he wasn't sure whom he wanted to find out about what first. For the past few months, he'd actually been thinking of coming clean—of telling both women that the other existed.

Could he do it?

He'd thought he never would, but somehow, more and more with each passing month, he desperately wanted to. . . . Hell, it felt like he *needed* to. The compounding lies and covering up had created a wall that blocked him from the prospects of happiness. Reggie didn't know how much longer he could continue to successfully hold everything together—and that potential was frightening.

As he made his way to the airstrip's parking lot for his Lincoln Navigator, he made yet another attempt to pinpoint the ultimate catalyst for his torment. When exactly did this start happening?

Reginald Brooks was virtually unraveling.

No one would believe that could ever happen. Not Reginald Brooks. Not the man who always had everything under control. And he'd *always* kept things under control.

Neither woman had ever suspected a thing. But many a night had passed when he lay in bed with one, and scenes would act themselves in his head about how she would react if she ever knew the truth.

This has to end, Reggie thought as he dodged a puddle. He was not fully conscious of it, but a decision had been made. He drove home, feeling the weight of the lives on his shoulders.

ONCE HE WAS in the house, he went straight up to his bedroom, dropped everything, and stretched out on the bed.

He would try sleeping off the melancholy mood. . . . But he knew it wouldn't happen. When he awoke, he would still have the disturbance in his chest.

Deep down, Reginald Brooks knew the end was near. He himself would ultimately bring everything crashing down around both families.

OLIVIA BROOKS WAS depressed.

The moment she turned her Toyota Camry into the driveway and realized her father was home, she cringed.

At twenty-one, Olivia was a very sharp and perceptive young woman. As such, she knew that relative to her father, there was much more than what met the eye. He was always very guarded—maybe even surreptitious—and he'd been that way for years. Her father's presence always made her uncomfortable, and she found it especially taxing to be around him when he returned from Orlando.

Now as she opened the garage door, Olivia prepared to have his presence in the house. *Oh, boy,* she thought. *Here we go. . . .*

But to her surprise, neither her father nor anyone else was anywhere in sight.

Good, she thought. *I get to go straight to my room.*

WHEN REGINALD AWOKE, he could hear water running in the bathroom. He smiled as he rolled over and stretched his powerfully built body to its full height.

Tracy was home.

He left the bed and went into the bathroom to find his wife bent over the tub. She was drawing a bath. Saying nothing, he walked up close and wrapped his arms around her. His palms settled over her breasts.

Tracy had heard Reginald enter the bathroom, and she mentally prepared herself for his attentions. She only wished she'd had time to do so physically. They were going to make love, and she was already tender from an encounter with Frank that afternoon. She knew it was foolish to see him on the very day Reginald was due back, but when Franklin was determined, he was difficult to resist.

"You're home?" she said.

"Yeah," Reginald replied. "Do you remember what I told you last night?"

"Of course I remember, babe." Tracy kept her back to him but smiled in spite of herself. "Has it been like Chinese algebra all this time?"

Reggie chuckled. He pressed against her. "It would appear so. . . ."

They made love in the large roman tub.

Afterward, they showered, and Tracy wanted to faint. She ached beyond belief. She vowed to glue her legs shut for a solid month.

Later, when Reginald went downstairs to the kitchen for food, she lay on the bed and phoned Frank to set up their next interlude. She was disappointed when she got his voice mail. . . .

DOWNSTAIRS, AS SHE slipped a plate into the microwave, Olivia smelled her father enter the kitchen. He never wore anything that wasn't made by Escada, and for that, there wasn't a scent in the world she recognized more.

"Hey, Liv, what's up?" Reginald tapped her shoulder.

"Nothing much," Olivia said. She set the microwave for a minute and a half and then turned. "How long have you been home?"

"Not long—a few hours. I was beat. . . . I was practically asleep before I hit the bed."

Olivia crossed her arms. She willed the microwave to heat faster.

"What's for dinner?" Reggie glanced at the stove top.

"Leftover salmon." She rubbed her palms on her sleeves and gazed at nothing in particular. . . . Their kitchen's wallpaper was nice. . . . The copper pots that hung over the countertop were very . . . copper. Olivia faced the microwave again.

"You won't believe what I managed to pull off," Reginald said, checking out the saucepan of salmon. "I can hardly believe it myself, and I haven't even mentioned anything to your mother yet, but after this next trip to Orlando, I'm going back to my old schedule. I know I've been saying it for years, but the time has come. . . . And the first thing I'd like us to do is plan a vacation. We all really need to spend some time together. It's long overdue."

Olivia avoided eye contact. "What was your old schedule? I don't remember anything but this."

"Well, I fly up once or twice a month for meetings and for oversight, and that'll only be for a night or two each time. It'll be rare that I'll need to stay any longer than that. It's going to be wonderful. We can make big plans. . . . I figure we can take a long vacation to spend solid family time together. . . . You know, make up for all the lost time." Reggie spooned some rice.

How can you make up for ten whole years of "lost time"? Olivia thought.

"Well, Dad, I have a lot of things to get done in the next few weeks. You know, with school and all."

"Oh, hold on there, Olivia. Are you telling me that you won't be able to find two minutes to spend with your family? We haven't really been able to spend much time together—me, you, and Valerie—in years. You've got to make the time, Liv. You can even do some homework and studying on vacation, if need be."

"I don't know, Dad. I'm seriously busy. I have quite a few projects to do, and I have to spend a lot of time at the library doing research. I just won't have the time. You should be able to understand, right?" With that, she took her plate from the microwave and left the kitchen.

Reginald watched her go. As usual, he almost called her back, wanting to have it out with her, but he was afraid to. He feared the litany of accusations that may come out of her mouth if he broached the subject of her attitude toward him. He knew why Olivia avoided him—and she did avoid him.

Up until now, Reggie had resigned to leaving things the way they were, to accept the change in Olivia. What was the use in trying to make things better when one day they could easily become so much worse?

He looked out the kitchen window and noticed that the rain was still coming down in sheets. The weather mirrored his mood. . . .

He needed to see Franklin. He needed to unload some of this on him, bounce his plans off of someone he could trust. *I'll call Frank first thing tomorrow.*

3

<hr>

THE FOLLOWING MORNING, Franklin Bevins decided to take a personal day from work. He needed a break, a day with nothing to do and no obligations. He just wanted to stay home and relax.

He thought about calling Theresa but changed his mind. *Why be bothered with anybody?* he thought.

He watched some of the morning talk shows and then called his office around ten a.m. to check messages. There was one from Reginald, saying he was back in town and needed to talk.

After listening to the other messages, he reclined in his favorite beige chair and thought about Reggie. . . .

LAUDERDALE LAKES, FLORIDA
SEPTEMBER 1982

SIXTEEN-YEAR-OLD *Franklin Bevins paced the sidewalk outside Brooklyn's pink-and-white apartment building on Twenty-ninth Street. He was livid. He had been dating Brooklyn for the past three months, and had just found out that she was dumping him for his best friend.*

"You and my goddamn best friend! You're gonna start screwing Reggie! I don't fuckin' believe this shit!" Frank screamed.

They were attracting too much attention. Two little old ladies opened their front doors and peeped out, a couple of guys hanging out under the stairs to avoid the sun stopped talking to watch and listen, and a young married couple looked on from the window of their '75 Ford.

"I'm sorry, Frank!" sixteen-year-old Brooklyn Speights screamed. "I'm sorry! I really like Reggie. You knew all along that Reggie was the one I really wanted."

"Oh, so you've just been fucking me as a one-way ticket to Reggie?" Franklin's voice dripped with anger.

Shit! This can't be happening, *he thought*. Not Brooklyn, Reggie—any girl but Brooklyn!

Frank mentally calmed himself down. He could not lose Brooklyn; she meant everything to him. She was the first girl that he had ever felt this way about, and he felt like he loved her more than anything—even his idol, John Lennon! When he and Reggie first met her in the neighborhood diner, he had noticed that she'd shown more interest in Reggie, but he thought that had all changed these past few months. He and Reggie often sampled the same girls, but Reginald should've known that Brooklyn was off-limits!

Obviously feeling bad for Frank, Brooklyn began to cry. "Frank, I like you a lot—I do. But I'm not about to pass up on Reggie Brooks. I've been waiting for him to notice me for months. . . . And now he has!"

Nervously, Frank babbled, "I—I thought you liked me, Brooklyn. We've been having such a good time together. What happened? How did you and Reggie end up getting together, anyway?" Frank was desperate to keep her outside, to keep her talking to him. As long as she doesn't walk away, I've got a chance, *he thought*.

"Look, Frank, it's over, all right?" Brooklyn seemed embarrassed that all the neighbors were watching, and Frank knew that news of the show would definitely get back to her mother. She seemed eager to get back in the house. She started to back up, away from the sidewalk, away from Frank.

He panicked. Franklin ran up to her and grabbed her arm. "C'mon, Brooklyn, give me another chance. We've been all right together. C'mon. Reggie has a whole bunch of girls, so you're only gonna get used if you get mixed up with him, anyway!" He was desperate. He was prepared to say or do anything to keep from breaking up with Brooklyn. She was one of the prettiest and most sought after girls at Byrd High, and he didn't want to let her go. He'd die if he lost her. He'd just die, he knew it. Oh, God, don't make me start crying in front of her, *he prayed*.

"Oh, Frank, I'm really sorry, but I gotta go. My mom'll be home soon."
She tried to slide her arm from his grasp. Then she drove her point home.
"Bye, Frank. I'm Reggie's girl now."

At that moment, Frank saw red. He let go of her arm, pulled back his
fist, and punched the shit out of her.

All hell broke loose.

The little old ladies screamed and came running out, the married couple jumped out of their Ford, and the guys under the stairs ran over and
two of them grabbed Frank.

"Hey, man, what are you doin'?" shouted the tall one as he shook Frank
like a rag doll.

"Oh, is he crazy?" said the other one.

Brooklyn—holding her jaw and sobbing—jumped off the sidewalk and
ran into her apartment. The door slammed behind her.

THE NEXT DAY when Reginald and Franklin were walking to school, Frank
decided not to be the one to bring up Brooklyn. He didn't have to wait long,
though, before Reginald did the inevitable. . . .

*"So, I heard you got really upset with Brooklyn yesterday, Frank. What's
up?"* Reggie asked.

*"Oh, you know . . . the bitch got disrespectful with me. She said she'd bet
some other dude had a bigger dick than mine. Bad joke. Man, I just lost it. I
mean, what right does a whore like her have talking to me like that to my face?"*

"Hold on," Reggie said, coming to a halt. *"She told me that you punched
her in the jaw because she broke up with you."*

*"C'mon, are you really gonna believe that crap? The bitch is lying, Reg-
gie. You really think she'd tell anybody that she said something that foul? I
wouldn't count on it, hell no."* Frank couldn't let anybody—especially not
Reginald—think that he turned into mush over some girl, even if the girl
was Brooklyn Speights.

As expected, Reginald believed him and forgot all about it. However,
Frank did not.

His birthday came just a few days later on September seventeenth; he
turned seventeen. His mother and his aunt Bertha threw a party for him,
and he should have been happy, but he wasn't. In fact, it took Frank more
than a month to stop crying himself to sleep at night.

Losing Brooklyn to Reginald hurt Franklin more than anything else ever had. He missed spending time with her, talking to her on the phone, skipping school so they could sleep together—he just plain missed her. Now Frank not only had to sit back and watch Reginald with Brooklyn when they hung out, but he had to listen to his details about screwing her, since they always shared each other's juicy experiences. And the worst part of it all: He had to pretend he didn't care.

The situation with Brooklyn Speights set the tone for the rest of their friendship, and as time went on, Frank lost several other girls to Reginald. Reggie was taller and older, and they found him more attractive, dubbing him the best-looking guy in school. Since Frank and Reggie were best friends, some of the girls only hung out with Frank to get Reginald interested in them. Frank's jealousy festered. He began to resent Reggie quietly— but so passionately it scared him at times. He could not let it show, though, because then he would seem weak. So he played it cool and hid behind a cloak of indifference.

He started exercising and working out, determined to be buff. He even started keeping his hair groomed, cutting it short. But as the years passed and they grew older, Frank began to believe he would always come up short against Reggie.

That is, until he managed to rope none other than Mrs. Reginald Brooks herself.

FRANKLIN PULLED HIMSELF out of the past and sat up in his recliner. Over the years, he had nurtured those malicious feelings. They became irreversible. Reggie was too damned selfish and he never considered anyone else's feelings but his own. For that—and for all the years of losing girls, and later even women, to Reggie—Frank felt more than justified in sleeping with Tracy. Therefore, he would go right on banging her until he'd had his fill and no longer wanted to be bothered.

Frank smiled, thinking how willing Tracy was to be with him the minute her husband left town, while he wanted her only because it was the best way to privately stick it to the almighty Reginald Brooks. Having this clandestine relationship with Tracy filled Frank with a deep, quiet satisfaction. It symbolized well-earned retribution for years of enduring Reginald's countless triumphs over him.

Frank went into his all-white kitchen and got a Budweiser from the refrigerator. As he savored his first sip, he focused on the television and settled back into his chair. He thought again about calling his ex-fiancée, Theresa, and decided he would—but later. Right now he was going to call his buddy Reggie and find out just what the next "crisis" was going to be about.

Ever since the seventies when they were teenagers, Franklin and Reginald shared everything with each other. Their parents had been neighbors in the same duplex, and they'd raised them as brothers. Over the years, though, Reginald's dilemmas had gone from incredibly entertaining to utterly ridiculous, and eventually their lives had begun to take different paths. When Frank was ticked about not getting the model car he wanted, Reggie was plotting the best ways to cover up cheating on his wife.

Frank grabbed the cordless phone from the coffee table. He dialed Reggie's direct line at work.

"HART-ROMAN, REGINALD Brooks speaking," Reggie answered the phone just as his secretary, Dana, walked into his office.

"Hey, Regg, I just got your message. Welcome back," Frank said. "So, how's the ever-so-sexy Renee?" Franklin had met Renee on several of her brief trips to visit with Reginald at the Fontainebleau, where she believed he lived while in Miami.

"No, Frank." Reggie held the phone between his ear and his shoulder as he handed Dana the invoices he'd just initialed. Keeping his voice low, he said, "You know I'm not talking about her over the phone. . . . But we do need to talk. It's about lunchtime, so what do you say we meet? How does Pollo Tropical sound?"

"I didn't go into the office, so I'm at home," Frank replied. "I just didn't feel like being bothered with any UPS bullshit today, you know?"

When Dana was gone, Reggie exhaled and said, "Frank, I'm drowning. I've got some heavy decisions to make, and I need your help, friend."

"Well, why don't you shoot over with some lunch and we can talk about it." He paused before adding, "You sound serious. Are you all right?"

"No. I'm not. That's the problem." Reggie stood, already slipping into his jacket.

"Okay, come on over. I'll be home all day."

"I'm on my way right now. What do you want from Pollo?"

"Uh . . . get me two chicken sandwiches, boiled yucca with garlic, and a Pepsi," he said.

"Roger that. I'm leaving right now."

"Hey, and don't forget . . ." Frank began, but he was reminding the dial tone.

FRANKLIN PLACED THE phone in its cradle. *This should be interesting,* he thought.

4

REGGIE FELT A great relief as he made a left turn onto Fontainebleau Boulevard and then into Frank's complex, San Marco Apartments. He knew that once he unloaded on Franklin, he'd have a better perspective on things.

Getting out of his Navigator, he set the alarm and walked up the two flights of stairs to apartment 210. He pressed the small, lighted button twice.

After about ten seconds, Frank opened the door. "Hey, get in here, because I've been dreaming about those sandwiches."

Reginald handed the food over to Frank, walked in, and took off his jacket. He loosened his tie and sat in his usual armchair by the window. He leaned forward, propping his elbows on his knees and resting his chin on his hands. He was ready to unload.

After stuffing it with yucca, Frank took a bite of his first sandwich. Then with a mouthful he said, "So, let's hear it, man." He sat straight up in the recliner as he chewed, fully attentive.

Reginald got straight to the point. The story came out like a plea. "Frank, I'm planning to come clean. I just don't know who to tell what—now, wait, let me finish." He raised his hand when he saw the incredulous look on Franklin's face. "Olivia practically hates me and that's bad enough, but it seems to be getting even worse—she leaves a room within two minutes of my entering it, and I don't even know if Valerie's coming or going. . . . I'm completely in the dark about her life.

Tracy's grown a bit distant. We used to be a couple that finished each other's sentences. . . . I miss that. Now it's like we're rotating in different orbits. And most of all, I'm just plain tired, Frank. I'm *really* over this life. Deep down I knew this would happen eventually, but I never really planned an exit, did I? I can't keep this back-and-forth arrangement going any longer. . . . And I really just don't want to live like this anymore."

Reggie dropped his arms, depleted. "The question is: What do I do? How do I end it? Tell me what to do so that no one gets hurt and it all works out in the end." He looked over at Franklin for a response. "Right now, I think I'd take all the advice I can get."

Totally unaffected by Reginald's speech, Frank took a sip of Pepsi and looked him directly in the eye. "Which one do you want to be with?" he asked, starting on his second yucca-stuffed chicken sandwich.

"What?" Reggie asked, taken aback.

"Which one do you want to be with?" Frank repeated in the same tone.

"I guess that would be a fair question, wouldn't it?" Reggie looked out the window onto Fontainebleau Boulevard. After an extended pause, he said, "Tracy. There's no life without her." It was a lot for him to admit to anyone.

Frank soaked up that deep, quiet satisfaction. *Perfect.* He looked at Reggie. *That's just perfect.*

When he finally spoke, he said, "So it's simple. You tell Renee the truth, and you tell Tracy nothing. It shouldn't be that hard to figure out, Reggie."

"What about Denise?" Reggie said as he pressed his thumbs into his eye sockets.

Frank thought for a moment. "Work something out with Renee."

"What could I possibly work out with Renee beyond very *brief* visits while I'm in Orlando? I can't bring Denise here. . . . I could never explain her to everybody."

"Well, then, you can go up there from time to time to 'oversee expansions' or 'oversee acquisitions' and visit Denise that way." Frank balled up his sandwich wrapper. He had devoured the sandwiches in record time.

"Could I really do that, though? I mean, Denise is not even seven years old yet. I *should* be a consistent part of her life because she's still so young, Frank. She needs me." He smiled. "Right now I'm hearing her ask me how long she'll have to miss me this time."

"I don't see any other way, Reggie. How else do you think you can work something like this out?" Frank sat back in his recliner, full and content. *Those were really good sandwiches,* he thought.

Reggie left the chair and stood by the window, deep in thought. Almost to himself, he said, "I called Renee this morning and she's her usual self—she can't wait for me to get back. How will she respond to the fact that I have a wife and two practically grown-up kids?"

"Why are you worrying about Renee?" Frank asked. "Over the years, she's proven to be like clay, and can be molded to complement any situation."

After a long silence, Reggie turned and faced Frank. Frank was absently stroking his mustache and looking at the television, where Dan Rather was reporting live from Capitol Hill.

"Tell Renee and not Tracy, huh?" Reggie mused. "What if I tell them both?"

Frank himself wondered how Tracy would react if she was told about the existence of Renee and Denise. He really wasn't sure if she would leave Reggie or not. . . . But he decided that it was something he would find out.

"You can't tell them both, Reggie, not unless you want to risk losing them both. If it's Tracy you want, you'd better make damn sure you don't tell her anything, because I'm almost certain that she'd leave your ass." Frank didn't think he wanted Reggie and Tracy to have problems. That would make his secret so much less satisfying.

"But what if Tracy finds out from someone else, Frank? Like if Renee flips out and decides she wants to get up close and personal with my wife? I can't have that happen, either, Frank. If Tracy has to find out, it has to come from me—it definitely has to come from me."

Frank stared at Reginald. *Look at him—the almighty Reginald Brooks.*

When Frank finally spoke, he said, "Who says Tracy has to find out? Do I have to do *all* the thinking for you, man? C'mon, all you have to do is orchestrate it so that Renee isn't upset with you. Make up a rock-solid story, Reggie. Tell her you're sick and you can't go on hiding it. . . . Or tell her your wife was missing for years and just showed back up out of nowhere." Frank stared down at the coffee table, thinking. "Tell her . . . tell her you just found out you're still legally married because your divorce never went through. Be creative."

When he finished throwing out his ideas, Frank looked over at Reggie, who had also sat down, listening intently to every word. He could see that Reginald meant what he'd said. He'd take just about all the advice he could get. He was determined to put an end to the charade.

Reggie slowly ran his hand down the length of his face, mulling over Frank's words. "Yeah . . . I think something like that would work, but it would have to be something really plausible. Renee may be gullible, but she's no idiot."

"Well, at least now you have an idea of how it has to be. If she's not upset with you, you'll have a better chance of keeping her from contacting Tracy. You might even set it up so that she'll end up feeling sorry for you in some way. . . ."

"Well, I have to come up with something fast because after this next trip, it'll be a while before I head back up there."

This surprised Frank. His eyes bulged. "What? You mean you plan to do all this right now? Why the rush?"

"The rush is for my sanity, Frank. It's for Tracy. It's for my girls. All these years I've robbed myself of being a regular part of their lives, and now one of them practically hates me for it. I just want to have a normal life with my girls and with Tracy, you know? Whatever *normal* is."

"Okay. So when will you plan to be a regular part of Denise's life? I don't see how you think you can work this out so quickly without getting burned somehow, man." After a lengthy pause, Frank added, "You just might have to tell them both."

"No way. Tracy would leave me if she knew, and you said as much not five minutes ago. Then what would I have? No, Frank. I can't tell Tracy. I'm taking your advice. . . . I just need to figure out a way to keep Renee on good terms with me when I tell her that I'm married. That way, there's no reason Tracy and the girls would have to find anything out."

"So how exactly do you think Renee will react when you do tell her?" Frank asked.

"All I need to do is come up with an ironclad story, just like you said, a believable one, and Renee will be handled." After a pause, he said, "You know, the more I think about it, the more I realize that Renee is actually the least of my troubles. She really *has* always been like clay. . . . If I continue to play my cards right, she won't be a problem at all." As he spoke, Frank saw him transform into the cocky, egotistical man that had gotten himself into this ridiculous mess in the first place.

"Okay, so you don't have to worry about Renee. What about your little girl? How are you gonna stop her from ending up like Olivia?"

"Man, I don't know. When all is said and done, I think I need to work on my primary responsibilities before I worry too much about the secondary, don't you? Besides, Denise is still young yet. There's plenty of time."

"Nope. Like you said before, that little girl needs a father. How do you think you're gonna feel when Renee finds another man and Denise starts calling *him* Daddy? I know that would piss me the hell off."

Reggie shook his head. "I'm the only man Renee sees. There won't be another. After all these years, I can't believe that you of all people don't see what I've come to mean to this woman."

Frank put his hands up in resignation. "All right, all right . . . I guess you know best. But hypothetically, *what if* she does meet someone else? I mean, you aren't gonna be around nearly as much anymore, right? Love or no love, buddy, a woman can get lonely and—"

Reggie cut him off in midsentence. "Look, it won't happen. I know Renee, and I'd bet everything I own that I'm it for her."

You're that sure of yourself, huh? Frank thought. "Would you say the same about Tracy?" Frank watched him for a reaction. This was where he would have the *most* fun.

Reggie stood in front of the window again, gazing out at traffic. His words were so low that Frank strained to hear them. "That's part of the reason I want to be home, isn't it?" He paused. Then in a practical whisper he added, "Of course . . . I should just admit it."

The look in Reginald's eyes spoke volumes of the truth: they were somber, his expression grave. Franklin didn't doubt that Reginald loved Tracy. He'd kill for Tracy.

Frank got up from the recliner and turned toward the kitchen before he smiled. He couldn't help it. He smiled the wide, ear-to-ear smile that continued to melt the hearts of many women. *This couldn't be more perfect,* he thought. "Want a Bud?" he called out from the kitchen.

"Yeah," Reggie absently replied from his spot at the window. Reginald turned just as Frank returned to the living room with two Budweisers. He tossed one at him as he slumped into the recliner. They sat in silence, sipping beer for quite some time, each preoccupied with his own thoughts.

Finally, Reggie said, "I'm gonna head back to the office before Dana puts out an APB on me." His stab at humor didn't work. He couldn't even laugh. He put his empty beer can on the coffee table and grabbed his keys.

"So you're sure you're all right? I mean, you're sure you've got all this stuff straightened out?"

"Well, I've got another week or so to figure out what I'm gonna say to Renee. I hate to say it, but it looks like I'm gonna have to sacrifice raising Denise for a while in order to salvage my relationship with Olivia and Valerie. I mean, let's face it . . . they were my first priority. If I have to choose—and right now I really need to choose—it's definitely Tracy and the girls."

"That's a really fucked-up way to look at it, Reggie. It's not that little girl's fault she wasn't your firstborn." Frank managed to keep the bitterness out of his voice. *This conceited prick! When does he ever think about anybody but himself?* Frank shrugged. "All right, buddy. Keep me posted."

"Yeah, I'll call you. We're thinking about having a barbecue on Saturday, so make sure you don't plan anything, all right? And bring Theresa with you." Reggie was out the door before Frank could respond.

The almighty Reginald Brooks, Franklin thought again. *Well, let the games begin.*

FRANKLIN KNEW THE DAY would come when the invincible Reginald would come tumbling, slipping, and sliding off his high horse. He recalled the night Reggie called him from Orlando, saying that he had unintentionally gotten a girl pregnant. Renee Jameson had refused to have an abortion, and although he tried, Reginald couldn't convince her otherwise. Renee had only been a warm body for him while he was on his brief stints working in Orlando, but before he could say *birth control,* she'd gotten pregnant. Then, taking Frank's counsel, Reggie softened to the idea of being a father again. Frank convinced him to embrace the challenge of leading separate, clandestine lives.

Denise Rose Brooks was born on March 11, 1998. By then Reggie had bought an illustrious town home and moved Renee into it. He told Renee that he'd move up to Orlando and they'd be a happy family— the first two weeks of every month. Renee didn't like it, but what could she do but accept it? He wasn't about to tell his wife about her, nor did he plan to tell *her* about his wife and kids.

Frank chuckled as he remembered how he'd helped Reginald manipulate everything to perfection. . . .

First, Reggie went to his boss, Roger Roman, CEO of Hart-Roman, Inc., and proposed management of the Orlando division on a very absolute basis, personally overseeing the promotions for the Disney World account they had recently acquired. Despite the fact that Reginald had been the driving force behind landing Disney, convincing Roger that it would be beneficial to have him there as a permanent fixture was no easy feat. But in the end, Roger conceded.

Next, Reggie simply told Renee that his moving to Orlando would come at the expense of having to spend the last two weeks of each month in Miami—for Hart-Roman.

Finally, he told Tracy that Hart-Roman was offering him a ridiculous sum of money to spend the first two weeks of each month in Orlando as head honcho—an offer he simply couldn't refuse. She didn't like it, but what could she do but accept it?

Roger leased him a luxury corporate apartment just off Osceola Parkway and allowed him a ridiculous raise in salary to go with it. That's how he got Tracy to calm down; he just showed her a direct deposit pay stub, which was nearly half of his actual earnings, but still a substantial sum. She never knew about the funds Reginald had automatically sent to an account in Orlando to support Renee and Denise.

Once she got used to the supplementary money, Tracy never complained again. Renee, on the other hand, did nothing but gripe about the situation. She tried many times over the years to get him to stop traveling back and forth, even for a few months, but of course, she never succeeded.

Since Reginald had conferred with him before making any major decisions over the years, Frank often felt as though he were the one living two lives. In fact, he could even say he was responsible for Reggie getting himself into this catastrophic mess. But he sure as hell didn't feel the least bit guilty about it—not the *least* bit guilty. He took pleasure in the fact that Olivia was likely closer to him than to her own father. Too bad Valerie didn't feel the same way.

Valerie, Frank thought. Now, she was a piece of work. She was a sly, scheming little girl, and Frank had a feeling that one day she would be big trouble for Reginald and Tracy. He pictured her getting caught shoplifting or getting some poor guy charged with statutory rape. *I'm surprised it hasn't happened already,* Frank thought.

Now, Olivia was the total opposite. She was subtle, but woe was unto the person that pushed her too far. She was a tough cookie, and she pretty much kept to herself. The only thing Frank was certain of about Olivia was that she was head over heels for some idiot named Sean and her relationship with him came before anything else—including her family. Frank noticed that the girl was totally oblivious to the goings-on in the household, and she really didn't seem to care what they did or didn't do.

Who could blame the poor girl? Look how unstable that home's been for the last ten years! It's no wonder she seeks stability from a man. And it certainly didn't take long for Tracy to find love in all the wrong places. Well, I'm just gonna sit back and enjoy the show, because the curtain is definitely going up, Frank thought, reaching for the telephone.

He was finally ready to summon Theresa.

5

ALTHOUGH HE WAS TIRED and tempted to pack up and call it a night, Brent Stone continued doing what he was being paid to do.

He'd been tailing the man since five o'clock that evening. It was now ten, and he was still unimpressed with his subject's activities since landing in Atlanta.

Brent knew this guy's story. Rich, married chap—had money to burn. In his line of work, he saw it repeatedly, and this one was a textbook case; no more exciting than the rest.

He parked his rental at the end of the block and made his way toward the house he'd seen his subject enter. It was an average-sized residence, nothing to write home about. The neighborhood wasn't one that Brent would've guessed this guy would be visiting. It left much to be desired. Brent wasn't going to stay long, anyway, just long enough to get a couple pictures, and then he would be on the next flight back to Miami. He wasn't crazy about flying, despite the fact that his work usually required lots of it.

He wanted to get the goods, compile the final report on this guy, present the information to his client, and return to his easier, less extensive cases. Those where the poor, unfortunate chaps were of the average working class and kept their mistresses local. Naturally, they didn't pay nearly as well as wealthy cases such as this, but Brent preferred them nonetheless.

Later, as his plane raced down the runway, Brent closed his weary eyes, thinking, *She can definitely hang him out to dry with these pictures.*

MIAMI, FLORIDA

THE FOLLOWING MORNING, Brent Stone was prepared to present his findings to his client. After telephoning her with this information, they agreed to meet at his office within the hour.

When she arrived, her presence and her beauty took Brent aback. He had never met her before, since their only contact had been by telephone. She had been forwarding all fees and expenses by messenger. She made all payments by check, drawn on a joint account, which she shared with her husband. Brent didn't doubt that she was tying a noose around this guy's neck, using his own money.

The woman walked into his office with rigid shoulders, wearing what appeared to be an expensive beige linen suit, high heels, and a broad-rimmed hat. Brent guessed she was deeply disturbed by her husband's philandering. Unlike many of the wives he worked for, she seemed to be the type that was still emotionally attached to her husband. Usually, by the time they decided to hire a PI, wives had already disconnected themselves emotionally and only wanted leverage to use against their double-crossing husbands. Brent sympathized with them all, but he was cautious not to wear it on his sleeve. He remained aloof and delivered the news—good or bad—in the most professional manner possible. He had learned that it was the only way to survive in this line of business.

They exchanged greetings and made small talk about the indigo décor of his office, while he positioned everything in the file as he would present it to her. Then he began.

"As you know, we began official surveillance on March fifteenth. I'm going to go down the list, reading relative dates of activities and then the corresponding activity. Once I've completed that, I'll be happy to answer any questions you may have." Brent paused. "Are you ready?"

The woman quietly cleared her throat. "Yes, Mr. Stone. I'm ready."

Brent slipped on his reading glasses. "Good. Then let's begin."

*   *   *

FORTY-FIVE MINUTES LATER, Brent rose and went to the window of his fifth-floor office. He watched the woman exit the building.

She had politely asked several questions and appeared to take the news rather well, but then her eyes had been hidden behind dark sunglasses, which she had never removed. After writing a check to satisfy her final payment, the woman had informed Brent that she may need to retain his services again in the future. Then she had quietly left his office.

Her demeanor had given away nothing, yet Brent sensed that she was wounded. He wished she had removed the sunglasses. Perhaps he would have learned more about her if he could've looked into her eyes.

Brent ran his fingers through his blue-black hair. Sighing, he returned to his desk. No client had intrigued him after only one meeting quite like this one.

Maybe it was the tone of her voice or the rigidity of her shoulders, but something . . . *something* about her kept her on Brent Stone's mind long after she had gone.

HER MERCEDES CRUISED along I-95 as she reached for her gold cigarette case. She swore when she discovered that it was empty. Just when she needed a drag the most, the damn case was empty!

Exiting the interstate prematurely, she drove east to Bal Harbor. After purchasing a package of Virginia Slims and taking the much needed first drag of her cigarette, she walked along the boulevard, window-shopping the boutiques that she had come to know and love. As she moved along, she was stopped by a number of acquaintances, and she offered polite greetings. By the time she reached a small outdoor café, she was much more relaxed than when she'd left Brent Stone's office.

He was fucking half the United States. He had his whores scattered all over the damn globe! The pictures had come as a shock. To *see* him, actually *see* him, together with so many different women turned her stomach.

She had questioned Stone extensively about the women, and as a result, she had extremely useful information about each and every one of his little sluts—and she intended to use every bit of it.

When a waiter came, she ordered a cappuccino and sipped it as she mourned the loss of the last eighteen years of her life. She hadn't needed any black-and-white pictures to tell her what was going on. She'd known. The photos only served as tangible proof of the infidelities, proof that could never be denied, proof that told the truth and nothing but the truth.

Tears came . . . despite her resolve not to get emotional. She removed her dark shades and swiped at them quickly with a napkin. She actually felt her heart muscles constrict as she sat there under the table's large yellow umbrella and sipped from her cup.

She needed help. If she was going to go through with her plans, she would have to get some help. She slipped her cell phone from her silk purse and placed a very important call.

6

"MOM, GUESS WHAT? Reggie and I are getting married." Renee held her breath, waiting for the reaction. She'd called her mother just to give her the news, but they ended up talking for almost an hour before she got the nerve to bring up Reginald.

Seconds passed. She heard nothing. "Mom? You are still there, aren't you?"

"Yeah, I'm here. . . . And I heard what you said."

"So?" Renee felt one of their disagreements coming on. She clutched the cordless phone and got off the kitchen chair, preparing for it.

"Honey, what do you want me to say? Congratulations? Well, I'm sorry, but you won't ever hear that from me," Beatrice Jameson said, her tone cross. "And don't even think of inviting me to the wedding—if there is a wedding."

"Why not? What is so wrong with Reginald? We've had this discussion many times, and you have yet to tell me *why* you hate him so much! I'm sick of it! It's time you got over it, Mom!" Renee began pacing back and forth on the tiled kitchen floor. She needed to vent her frustrations. *What kind of wedding day will it be without my mother?*

Bea sighed. "Renee, you're wrong. I don't hate Reginald. I'm tired of repeating myself. I just don't think he can be trusted."

"*Why?* Why can't he be trusted? You won't even get to know him! You won't give him a chance. In all the years I've been with him, you hardly ever want him around, and it shows. You're not exactly subtle about your feelings, are you?"

"Well, that's probably because he's *hardly ever* around to begin with," Bea said in a venomous tone.

As it was intended, her point hit home with Renee. It hurt. That was indeed her sore spot—Reginald's two weeks in Miami. She wandered dejectedly into the living room and sat on the peach-colored loveseat.

"His job takes him away, and you know that." Renee calmed herself. She tried another strategy. "Do Denise and I want for anything? Do you? Let's not forget that if it weren't for my *untrustworthy* man, you wouldn't be getting your hair and nails done once a week, you wouldn't be eating food in fine restaurants, and you certainly wouldn't be driving around in a brand-new Lincoln!"

"How dare you throw what you do for me in my face. Don't . . . you . . . dare! I'll do without before I allow you to throw your help in my face, Renee!"

"I'm sorry, Mom." Renee knew she had gone too far. "I'm sorry. It won't happen again. . . . It's just that I love this man, and it seems like you hate him. How could I be happy without you at my wedding? What kind of day would that be for me? I mean, to know that you're alive and well, but you're not at the wedding . . . I think it would be one of the worst days of my life instead of one of the happiest."

Bea sighed again. "I'm so sorry, Renee, but I want to see you happy, and that is why I can't agree with this." After a long silence, Bea said, "Renee, dear, I think you chose the wrong one. . . . I really do. I mean, how can you trust a man who lives in two places?"

"What are you talking about, 'lives in two places'? Reggie lives here. He moved from Miami to live with me before Denise was even born. You know that."

"Is that right?" Bea said ruefully. "Come on, Renee. . . . Benjamin and I didn't raise you or your brother and sister to be fools."

Renee sat up in the loveseat and panicked. "What is that supposed to mean? Do you know something that I don't?"

"No, but I think I can pick sense out of nonsense a little better than you can."

"Oh, Mom, just get to the point! What are you trying to say here?"

"I'm trying to say that Reginald spends just as much time in Miami as he does here in Orlando, dear." Bea paused to let her words sink in. "I mean, what makes you think that Reginald didn't leave some old flame in Miami? You can't honestly tell me that the possibility has never crossed your mind."

Renee closed her eyes. Oh yes. The possibility had crossed her mind more times than she cared to admit.

"And how come," Bea continued, "after six years he is just getting around to asking you to marry him? Recently divorced, maybe? Come on, Renee, surely you can understand why I'm doubtful about this man. Whenever he comes around, he's hardly ever able to look me in the eye. He always seems preoccupied and unsettled. Never really seems to fit in with the rest of us, never goes out of his way to get close to us."

"All right, enough. Reginald loves *me*. *We are happy.* He doesn't have anyone in Miami—trust me, okay? Mom, can't you just be happy for me?" Renee balled up her legs. She brought her knees under her chin. She wiped at tears on her cheeks. "I can't be happy if you're against this. Please, I'm begging you to please try to get over this suspicion you have where Reggie is concerned.

"When I got pregnant with Denise, he stood by my side. I know it was unexpected, but Reggie didn't dump me or start sending me checks from Miami like you all said he would, remember? No, he bought us a place, and he moved five hundred miles to be with us. Now Denise has just turned six, and we're still together. If that's not love, I don't know what is." Renee waited, but Bea said nothing. "Mother, please . . . say something."

"All right, honey . . . because you'll always be my baby and I love you, I will come to the wedding. I will try to be happy for you," After a few moments, Bea added, "I just want you to be happy, Renee. That's all. . . . I just want to see you happy."

"I am. Reggie does make me happy. He loves me." Renee hesitated and said, "Mom, you know what you said before about Reggie not asking me to marry him sooner?"

"Yeah?"

"Well, I have to admit that I've always worried about it."

"I told you Ben and I didn't raise fools," Bea said conceitedly.

"I thought about it, but I had to believe that one day he would realize that that's what he wanted. I made sure I never hinted or insinuated at it. . . . And now I'm certain he's ready to ask me to marry him."

"What?" Bea exclaimed. "You mean he hasn't asked you yet?"

Renee hesitated. She began to twine her shoulder-length hair around her forefinger. "Uh . . . well . . . no, he hasn't exactly asked me yet, but I just know that's what he wants to talk about when he comes home tomorrow." Renee braced herself. "When he called this afternoon, he said that when he gets home, we have to talk about something that's very important to both of us."

"And you think it's gonna be about getting married?" Bea deadpanned.

"Yes, I do. I really think that this is it." She paused and said with a chuckle, "I got the distinct impression that we aren't going to be 'living in sin' for too much longer. Most mothers would be overjoyed at that prospect."

"Honey, I'm happy as long as you're happy," Bea said. There was a brief silence before she added, "Having said that, I don't think I'm gonna be happy too much longer."

Another lengthy silence. Finally, Renee broke it. "I'll call you tomorrow. I'm gonna go pick Denise up from Helen's. It's getting late."

Once she hung up the telephone, Renee left the kitchen and went upstairs to the bathroom. She had to blow her nose and clean up her face before she went to her sister's house to get Denise. Once in the bathroom, she stood in front of the mirror and stared at her reflection.

Renee was not a traditionally pretty woman, but she had a body that gave married men plenty of reason to cheat on their wives. It's what had attracted Reginald in the beginning. She had been working as an attendant at the Mobil gas station on Osceola Parkway and Seventeenth Street, where Reggie stopped for gas regularly when he came to Orlando. When she noticed he was a regular, Renee began flirting with him. She almost fainted the day the unbelievably gorgeous, over-six-feet-tall, broad-shouldered man began to reciprocate her interest. And that's when it all began.

He'd told her he lived in Miami and came up to Orlando two or three times a month for business. Renee had just celebrated her twenty-first birthday when she and Reginald began their affair. Seven months later, she was pregnant.

Now almost eight years after we met, we are finally gonna be married, Renee thought. She continued to gaze in the mirror. She smiled. *Finally . . . and everything will be perfect.*

STILL DAYDREAMING ABOUT her future with Reginald, Renee turned onto Helen's block in Springsdale. She'd tried to get her sister to keep Denise until Sunday, but there was no such luck. She hoped that she and Reginald could be alone when he got back so they could celebrate their engagement. She envisioned a nice long weekend of lovemaking and lying around in bed, only leaving it to eat and use the bathroom. She could have asked her mother, but after their last conversation, she decided against *that* alternative.

We'll just have to make the best of it with Denise home, she thought, smiling.

When she rang the bell, she was surprised to see her eight-year-old niece, Ashley, open the door.

"Hey, Ashley! What are you doing here? Helen said you were going over to your father's." Renee stepped into her sister's modest home and gave Ashley a kiss.

"Hi, Aunt Renee. Daddy called and said he couldn't make it again," Ashley replied. She held her head down.

"Oh, Ash, cheer up. I'm sure you'll see him this weekend. Come on now, cheer up!" Renee gave her another big hug. Just as she was releasing Ashley, Denise came running toward them from the direction of the kitchen.

"Mommy! Mommy!"

Renee bent and scooped her up. She kissed her briskly on the cheek. "Where's your auntie Helen, Pooch? We gotta get going."

"But Auntie Helen just made us dinner, Mommy, and I'm hungry!" Denise whined.

"Helen, what'd you cook for dinner?" Renee shouted as she headed toward the kitchen. She found Helen and her fifteen-year-old son, Brian, sitting at the dining table eating dinner—baked chicken, mixed vegetables, and white rice. "Hi, Brian! What's up?"

"Hi, Auntie Renee. Nothin' much. Just chilling out," Brian replied in a voice that was already giving James Earl Jones a run for his money.

"Hey," Helen greeted. "I just baked some chicken. Want some?"

"Oh yeah. Now I won't have to rush home to throw something together. I should've cooked earlier, but I was feeling lazy," she said as she put Denise on her feet. She went over to the stove and helped herself to dinner. Ashley and Denise returned to their places at the table. Since the table had only four chairs, Renee took a seat on a barstool and ate at the counter.

When they finished, the kids went into the den to watch *The Wizard of Oz*. Denise and Ashley loved to see Judy Garland and her friends skip down the Yellow Brick Road. Brian went up to his room to call his friends on three-way—a nightly ritual Helen couldn't get him to break.

When they were alone, Renee helped Helen with the dishes. "So, Ashley says Lonny called and canceled again, huh? What the hell is wrong with that man? *Where* the hell did you get him? I mean, what kind of father lets his kid down ninety-nine point nine percent of the time?"

"Okay. Here we go. You just got here, and already here we go with the blame. Just blame me for everything, Renee. It's *my* fault that I have two kids with two different fathers. It's *my* fault they're both deadbeat dads. It's *my* fault Ashley's unhappy. Just blame me for everything," Helen said, slipping into her martyr act.

"Come on, Helen. That's not what I meant! Why do you have to take everything the wrong way? I'm just tired of that poor child having that brokenhearted look on her face every time Lonny brushes her off!"

"Whatever. It sure sounded like you were implying that this is my fault," Helen retorted. She shoved Renee a handful of soapy silverware for rinsing. She knew she was overreacting, but she felt like being touchy, though she did mind her blood pressure problems by keeping her voice calm.

"It's not your fault, but you should at least *try* talking to Lonny. I mean, doesn't he even care about how much he's hurting her?"

"Did *talking* to Reginald stop him from going to Miami every month? I mean, doesn't *he* care about how much he's hurting you and Denise?" Helen fired back.

Renee paled. "Why do you have to go there, Helen? Why do you always have to bring up Reggie? What does he have to do with this?"

She had taken the dig rather hard, and it showed. Helen knew how fragile she was on the subject of Reginald.

"You never could take a dose of your own medicine, baby sister," Helen said, wiping water from the counter.

"Look, leave Reginald out of this. I'm just trying to help Ashley. I hate seeing her so sad. She's a kid. She shouldn't be so sad all the time, Helen." Renee busied herself wiping the kitchen table and cleaning the placemats. She was trying to shift the focus off Reggie and back on Ashley and Lonny. But as usual, when Helen was determined, there was no such luck.

"Now you think he's gonna ask you to marry him. Well, I'll have to see it to believe it," Helen said softly.

Renee's jaw fell slack. "The words didn't even have a chance to leave my mouth before Mom jumped to call you, huh?"

"Yeah, I got off the phone with her not long before you got here," Helen said. "Anyway, I think you'd be a fool to marry a man that lives in two different places," she said matter-of-factly.

Renee had had it! She was sick of everyone harping on Reggie's time in Miami. Why couldn't they just let it alone? He loved her! Why wasn't that enough? She wanted to hurt Helen as much as Helen was hurting her. She went for her Achilles' heel. "At least I will be *marrying* a man! That's more than *you* could ever say, isn't it?" She watched Helen's short-lived smugness drain from her face. "That's it, isn't it, big sister? Jealousy. You've always been jealous of Reggie and me. From day one, you've just been pea green with envy. Admit it!"

Visibly offended, Helen said nothing. She sat in a chair at the dining table and clasped her hands. She tried to remain calm. "My pressure," she muttered, "I have to mind my blood pressure. . . ."

Renee took the seat across from her. She didn't enjoy punching below the belt, but she certainly didn't enjoy hearing about the flaws in her relationship with Reginald, either. "When I got pregnant, what did you say?" Renee recounted Helen's words of the past in a babylike pitch. " 'Oh, he's gonna leave, Renee. Go have an abortion, Renee. He's probably married and he'll just send you money every so often, Renee.' " She smacked the table. "Well, he surprised you, didn't he? And you never recovered! Denise and I don't want for anything. For the past six years, I've been living the good life with a good man and you . . . just . . . can't. . . . stand it. That's why every single time we have it out, you have to bring up something about Reginald! You're just jealous!" She pounded her fist on the table with each word.

Helen looked up, tears now standing in her eyes, and said, "Get out. Get your little bastard and get out of my house, Renee. I resent every word you just said to me, and one day you'll choke on 'em. Who would be jealous of a woman whose man spends half a month with her and half a month down in Miami with God knows *who*? And make no mistake: I'd bet the farm that there is somebody else. . . . And it's probably somebody as dumb as you. You think he just goes down there and sits around, waiting to come back to you? Or sits around, waiting for you to fly down so you can shack up in a plush hotel room for a night? *I don't think so.*"

Helen's words stung. She was shining light on Renee's biggest insecurities. But Renee would rather die than show her pain any further.

With a knowing smirk, Renee rose from the table without replacing the chair. "Denise, where are you? It's time to go!" She grabbed her purse and headed for the den. When she walked in, Dorothy was helping the Scarecrow dislodge himself from the post. "Come on, Denise. You can finish watching it at home. We have to go." Renee reached for her tiny hand. "Ashley, we'll see you later. Try not to be so sad. You'll see your daddy soon, okay?"

"Okay, Aunt Renee," Ashley replied, never taking her eyes off Judy Garland and Ray Bolger following the Yellow Brick Road to Oz.

After quickly gathering Denise's things, Renee clasped the little girl's hand and nearly dragged her to the Mitsubishi Eclipse. She drove home in silence. She nearly took Denise's head off whenever she made a sound.

* * *

THAT NIGHT, RENEE lay in bed reliving every word of her argument with Helen.

I can't wait to see the look on their faces when I am finally Mrs. Reginald Brooks, she thought. *Hurry home, Reggie. Hurry home and propose to me . . .*

She finally drifted off into a troubled sleep.

7

MIAMI, FLORIDA

REGGIE AND TRACY were bowling at the Dolphin Lanes on the corner of Bull Run and Ludlam when Tracy thought she might have a stroke. *No, no, no . . . he's not saying this . . . not now.*

" . . . Very little time together as a family, Trace," Reggie was saying. He posed for his next throw.

She had tuned him out after he said, "After the next trip, I'm going back to my original schedule. I talked to Roger, and we both agreed that things are stable enough for me to revert to visiting the Orlando office two or maybe three times a month. I'm going back a little early to finalize some issues. . . ."

Now she just stared at him as he sent the ball whirling down the alley. "But . . . but what about the money? The stipends are too sweet to give up. What about—"

Reginald cut her off. "It's just not worth it anymore. I don't think you realize how much strain I've been under all these years. . . . Do you even appreciate how much time I've lost? No, you probably don't. Because of this schedule, I've lost the love of my daughter. . . . And I can't deal with that anymore. Olivia is twenty-one years old now, and I want to right things with her before she gets any older.

"I want to try to give her some semblance of a normal family life, and Valerie, as well. They'll be getting older and moving out, and I

don't want them to go out on their own and all they remember is this."
He waved his hand. After a pause, he placed his hands on Tracy's hips
and turned her to face him. "Besides, the two of us need to spend more
time together, too."

Tracy looked into Reginald's eyes. *Frank . . . what are we going to do
now?* She realized it was unlikely that Reginald would change his mind.
Especially since he'd already made arrangements with Roger. What
could she say? If she pressed her objections, she'd be running the risk of
making him suspicious, so she ultimately had to relent and be supportive. She and Frank would just have to find ways to work around
it . . . somehow.

"Reggie, the girls are grown up now. They understand that you had to
work. Don't worry about Olivia. I'm sure she'll come around now that
you'll be home more. I'll have some talks with her. . . . She'll come around."

THEY WERE SILENT for most of the ride home in Tracy's Grand Cherokee. Both were haunted by the uncertainty of the immediate future. Finally, as Reginald made the turn onto Miami Lakes Drive, Tracy said,
"You know, it's probably good that you'll be here to help me get Valerie
back under control. She's been so disrespectful lately."

Reggie pressed the garage door opener and spun into their winding
driveway. "Disrespectful how?"

"You know . . . sassy with the mouth, quick to talk back. I'm not sure
exactly what's going on with her, but you know what I've been thinking, don't you?" She looked knowingly at Reginald.

"What? Sex?" Reggie said incredulously.

"Yeah, sex. That's usually what it is when they start getting rude like
that."

"No, I don't think so, Trace. She doesn't look like it."

"Look like it? Well, how exactly does a sexually active seventeen-
year-old look?" Tracy asked, settling into the leather seat and crossing
her arms.

"Well, you know what I mean. She doesn't act like it to me," Reggie
replied, not able to picture his little Valerie as sexually active. It wasn't
that long ago that she was still in pigtails.

"I'm telling you that I think she's doing it, and I think she might be doing a lot of it! But don't take my word for it. You'll be home now to see for yourself," Tracy said as she got out of the Jeep.

Reginald got out and closed his door. "See, that's what I'm talking about. If I had been around more often, I would've been able to pick up on something like my little girl starting to have sex. I've been in and out of their lives for so long, I feel like I don't even know my own children." He pressed the lighted button next to the kitchen entryway. They made sure the garage door was secure before going into the house. Reginald held the door open and allowed Tracy to enter before him.

INSIDE, THEY FOUND the subject of their conversation in the den, watching television. Valerie looked up when she heard them come in. "So who won?" She smiled.

Tracy laughed. "Do you always have to ask? You know I can barely bowl a sixty!" She flopped onto the leather sofa across from Valerie.

"You know your mother can't bowl to save her life. After all these years, she'd be lucky to bowl a sixty!" Reginald said, sitting next to Valerie. They all laughed.

Tapping her knee, Reggie said, "Val, run upstairs and get Olivia. Your mom and I want to talk to you two about something important."

Tracy gave him a questioning look as she swept up her short, dark hair and retied the bow.

"Olivia isn't here, Daddy," Valerie said.

"But her car's outside," Reggie said, his forehead creasing.

"Well, Sean probably came and picked her up," Tracy guessed. She looked at Valerie to confirm. Valerie nodded yes while still keeping an eye on a rerun of *The Cosby Show*.

Reggie turned to Tracy and said, "Who is Sean?"

Hearing this, Valerie lost all interest in Theo Huxtable and turned her attention to her parents.

"Sean Johnson's her boyfriend," Tracy said. "They've been dating for a few months now. Is this the first we've mentioned him? I could've sworn you knew about Sean."

"Yeah," Reggie said in a low voice. He took a deep breath. "But that's all about to change."

"What do you mean, Daddy?" Valerie asked.

"Well, that's what we wanted to talk to you girls about. I'm going back to my old schedule at work." He slipped a lock of Valerie's hair behind her ear and pinched her chin. "No more of this two weeks here, two weeks there arrangement. From now on, I'll only fly to Orlando on an as-needed basis, for meetings and such. Two or three times a month, max."

Valerie covered her mouth. She let the information sink in. "Daddy, tell me you're not joking. Really? You'll be working out of Miami most of the time now? You're actually gonna be home more often?" She glanced at her mother. Valerie was thrilled that her father would be home more often. . . . But there was a bit more to her excitement.

"Well, I'm going back tomorrow to wrap things up," Reggie replied. "Hopefully, it won't take too long to finalize everything with the management team, and then, yeah, that's it." Reggie turned to Tracy. "Things have gone on far too long. I need to be more involved with my family, closer to all of you, so if one of my daughters is seeing someone for months, I'll know about it." Inside, Reginald was mortified. He knew so little about his own daughters.

"Oh, come on, Reggie. Don't be so hard on yourself," Tracy said, walking over to him. She sat across his lap and pulled his head to her chest. "I thought that you knew about Sean, or I would've mentioned him before now."

Reginald locked his arms around her waist. He relaxed in the embrace. This was why he loved this woman and no other. She was especially thoughtful and remarkably considerate. She always sensed his need for a soft place to fall, and she'd always been right there to catch him—the way only she could. This was why he'd fallen in love with her all those years ago. . . . And this was why he loved her still.

Valerie looked on from her seat on the sofa. *Let's see how she runs out to see her boyfriend now,* she thought.

Valerie was the first to break the silence as she rose to go to bed. "Well, I'm glad you'll be here, Daddy. For as long as I can remember, you've only been around half the time and gone to work the other half. It'll be wonderful!" She paused for a moment, slipping into her bed slippers, and then she bent to kiss his cheek. "G'night . . . g'night, Mom."

" 'Night, honey," said Tracy.

"Good night, Val," Reggie said.

They watched Valerie leave. Then Reggie whispered, "You really think she's doing it, huh?"

"Oh yeah—a lot," Tracy said.

"You don't seem to mind very much, Trace," Reggie said raising an eyebrow.

"Well, it's not that I don't mind, but I figure they're gonna start doing it some time, right? What can we really do about it? If we keep the leash too short, they'll just rebel and break away and do exactly what we *don't* want them to do." Tracy rubbed her eyes. "If I dwell on it, it'll kill me. I mean, imagine Valerie getting pregnant. They're gonna do it whether we like it or not." After a pause, she added, "We did, re-member?"

"Uh-huh, I remember," he said. His eyes darkened. He kissed the line of her jaw.

"You're getting horny," she said. It wasn't a question.

"Umm," Reginald replied.

She began running a light trail of kisses from his temple to his smooth lips. She settled there for a kiss.

Reggie ran his hand from her waist to her thighs, settling it on her sex. He felt himself rise as the kiss deepened. He unbuttoned her jeans.

"Come on," she said against his lips. "Let's go."

Turning off the television, they left the den and made their way up the staircase to their bedroom at the end of the hallway. Once inside the privacy of their room, Tracy removed her shirt and jeans and lay back against the silky sheets. Reggie turned on the CD player and undressed as Nat "King" Cole filled the room. He joined her in bed.

Tracy reached down and caressed him.

Reggie groaned.

They kissed deeply, and she used his penis to stroke herself. . . . Back and forth, up and down, around and around . . . then his tip slid to-ward her opening. . . . Reginald held his breath. He shuddered in an-ticipation.

When he finally slipped into her, Tracy felt a cloud of ecstasy settle over her, and she let out the exquisite sigh of pleasure that was like music to Reginald's ears. He buried his head in the crook of her neck and suckled the tender skin there as he ground circular motions against her. Matching him thrust for thrust, she felt the familiar tremors shimmering through her pelvis and contracted her vaginal muscles at just the right times, bringing him the most pleasure.

"Hmm . . . I missed you, Trace," Reggie said huskily as he caressed a breast and covered her mouth with his. He slipped his arms under her legs and held them wide, raising her pelvis. He sank deeper and deeper with every plunge.

Reggie felt his climax coming. He reached down and cupped Tracy's soft buttocks and squeezed in time with his shudders.

When it was over, he relaxed his body and lay his head next to hers on the pillow. He was still tightly nestled inside her.

"I missed you, too," Tracy said breathlessly. She wiped sweat from his brow. It wasn't long before her thoughts turned anxious and drifted to Frank. "So, when exactly do you think you'll be back?" Humming along with Nat, she raised her legs and wrapped them around Reginald's waist.

"Hmm . . . you mean, you're missing me already?" he said, giving her a soft thrust.

Moaning, she kissed his nose. "Oh yeah. We have a lot of time to make up for, you know." She contracted her muscles, gripping him.

"Ahh . . . I'm not sure when I'll be back." He turned his head and licked a nipple. "I think I'll shoot for a week at the most. . . . Depends on how smoothly things pan out. There's one particular meeting I've been putting off, but it's unavoidable now. . . ." His voice trailed off. Renee had invaded his thoughts.

A week, Tracy thought. *That should be enough time for us to figure something out. . . .*

Wanting to have a little more fun before drifting into sleep, Tracy continued to tighten her muscles. She felt Reggie grow hard again. She nibbled on his earlobe and ran her palms up and down the back of his thighs.

With an incredible kiss, Reggie sank himself deep and nestled inside her for a second time.

Damn it, he thought. *I've been such a fool.*

8

FRIDAY NIGHT FOUND Olivia Brooks speeding northbound on I-95 toward Miami Gardens Drive. She'd paged Sean more than eight times in the last two hours.

Where the hell was he?

She hated when this happened. It only meant that he had to be with that bitch!

Sure, as usual he would have the perfect excuse, such as he'd left his pager at home, or the batteries had died and he hadn't yet replaced them, or the biggest whopper of all—he simply never got the pages. He always had excuses, and they were making Olivia suspicious—very suspicious. She suspected that Sean was still seeing his ex-girlfriend Jacquelyn Henderson, since she apparently never really left the picture at all. . . .

SEAN JOHNSON WAS twenty-eight years old and shared a dilapidated apartment in North Miami with his older brother, Vincent. Olivia first met Sean in an algebra class at Barry University almost two years earlier. He was a charming character who amused everyone, including Olivia. Everyone knew about his live-in girlfriend Jackie, since she shared his car and was usually in the parking lot, waiting for him after class each day. Some days Jackie was late and Sean would be left waiting for more than half an hour. Everyone got a kick out of teasing him about it when he groaned and complained.

One day, word spread that Sean and his girlfriend had broken up and she had even moved out of his apartment. Everyone noticed that Sean was different somehow. He wasn't the zesty Sean everyone had grown accustomed to. Olivia attributed it to the big breakup she'd heard rumors about.

There was no initial attraction when she first met Sean. He was tall, but rather lanky and not quite Olivia's cup of tea. She saw him as the class clown, never having a thought of a romantic relationship.

Several months after the conclusion of the algebra course, they met again in economics. Sean seemed to be back to normal by then, and each night they'd converse about this issue or that, until he began flirting with her and asked her out. Lacking interest, Olivia spent weeks feigning fatigue or scheduling conflicts to avoid a coffee date, but still he persisted. She finally agreed to a date. One date turned into two and two became three, and before Olivia knew how it happened, they were officially a couple.

Sean explained that things hadn't worked out with Jackie because she was pressing for marriage and he wasn't even ready to propose. Jackie spewed ultimatums and threatened to leave. He helped her pack.

For a few weeks, things were wonderful between them. Olivia had fallen in love. But one Saturday she stopped by to see Sean—unannounced. She'd been at the library and thought it would be nice to visit him on the way home. She usually called first, but that morning she'd forgotten her cell phone.

When she arrived at his mediocre apartment complex, The Woods, she saw Jackie's red Honda in the parking lot. She climbed up the grimy stairs with a queasy sensation in the pit of her stomach. When she reached his door, she knocked five times with no response. *What the hell is going on?* she thought. *God, don't let it be what I think it is. . . .*

Reluctantly, she turned away from the door and went back down to the parking lot. Olivia noticed that both Jackie and Sean's cars were there, but Vincent's was not. That meant they were up there alone! What the fuck was going on? Olivia drove away enraged.

Just as she was about to enter the highway and head home, her pager chirped. It was Sean. She made a swift U-turn, pulling into the nearest gas station. She drove up to the pay phones and hurriedly dialed his number. He had given some excuse about Jackie being over to visit his brother, Vincent. Sean claimed that he'd been asleep in his bedroom and didn't realize that they'd gone out to the store. That explained why Vincent's car was gone and Jackie's was not.

At the time, Olivia believed his story without doubt. However, such peculiar incidents continued: pages ignored for hours, Jackie always "visiting Vincent," and once Sean even drove Jackie's car for more than a month while his own was in the shop. Olivia ended their relationship on numerous occasions, but Sean always managed to win her back. He sent flowers, showed up on her doorstep, and persuaded others—like her mother and sister—to feel sorry for him.

NOW AS SHE continued to speed along I-95, Olivia prayed it wasn't happening all over again. They'd had such a remarkable time Wednesday night. Sean had taken her to see a movie starring two of her favorite actors. The movie was spectacular. . . . And afterward they'd gone back to his apartment and made love until they were weak. Sean loved it so much that he begged for an encore Thursday night.

And now this, Olivia thought. Why did he always have to screw everything up?

She exited at Miami Gardens Drive and drove east to Dixie Highway. When she reached his street, adrenaline began to shoot through her veins. Olivia braced herself for the worst. *This is it. If that nasty whore is there again, Sean can shove his excuses up his ass.*

Sure enough, when Olivia made it to his building, there sat the infamous red Honda, yet again, with the all-too-familiar Mardi Gras beads dangling from the rearview mirror.

She haphazardly threw her Camry into the parking space beside it—ignoring the fact that it was reserved for handicapped drivers—and slammed the door in haste.

Reaching Sean's door, Olivia pounded on it repeatedly with the usual result—there was no answer. But she decided not to give up quite so easily this time. She crossed her arms and leaned against her car to wait until Vincent got home. It was Friday, and she knew he left work at eight.

At approximately eight twenty-five, Olivia spotted Vincent's Mercury. When he parked near her, she jogged over to meet him before he even removed his seat belt.

"Vinnie, what's going on? What's Jackie doing here with Sean, and why won't anyone answer the door?" she beseeched. Anxiety filled her.

Vincent released the seat belt and motioned for Olivia to step back, giving him room to open the door.

"Vincent? Come on . . . tell me what's going on! I need the truth. Is he still seeing her?" Tears welled up in her eyes despite her will to keep them at bay.

"Olivia, I don't want to get involved in this confusion with you and Sean," he said, moving around her.

"I'm coming in with you," she said, falling in step beside him. "I'm coming in to find out what the hell is going on."

"Look," he said, coming up short, "I'm going to be honest with you here, okay?" He gave her a rueful look.

"Please, Vinnie, that's all I want. Is he still seeing her?" Olivia didn't know how much longer she could keep from letting the floodgates open. Her twenty-one-year-old heart was pounding like a sledgehammer as she waited for his next words.

"Don't do this to yourself anymore. It's been my experience that if you suspect something like that, it's probably true." Vincent looked her directly in the eyes.

Olivia felt like her insides had been hollowed out. Of course. He was telling her that it was indeed true.

"How long, Vinnie?" she asked quickly. "How long has Jackie been back in the picture?"

"Olivia, go on home now, okay? There's nothing here for you but more grief." He turned and walked away.

Olivia caught up with him just as he started up the stairs. "I'm coming in with you. I want to hear what he's got to say to me now."

"Did you hear what I said? Why do you want to continue hurting yourself? I'm telling you in plain English that you're wasting your time with Sean. Our entire family knows that he's only loved one woman and one woman alone, and that's Jackie. It's always been Jackie. You just need to take this as a learning experience and move on, dear." Vincent shook his head. Pity.

"Vincent, after all he's put me through these last few months, he owes it to me to look me in the eye and tell me the truth. Now, I'm going in with you!" She climbed up the stairs ahead of him and waited in front of their door.

"Fine, but don't say I didn't warn you. You'll just learn the hard way," Vincent said, joining her at the doorway. He shuffled with his keys and opened the grimy door. Olivia followed him inside.

There was no questioning that Sean and Vincent were horrible decorators. The living room consisted of a ghastly mahogany-colored sofa and a hideous blue pinstriped loveseat that Olivia assumed were hand-me-downs. No piece of furniture in the room matched or complemented any other. To the right of the doorway was a tiny dining area that barely accommodated the two-chair Formica dining table. On the left was a slightly larger, all-wooden kitchen.

As she passed, Olivia noticed two empty wineglasses on the counter. Her adrenaline spiked again. Before she could get any farther, Vincent stepped ahead of her and knocked on Sean's room door, to the left side of the two-bedroom residence.

"Sean, you awake?" he called, trying the knob. It was locked.

"Yeah, I'm up. . . . What's up?" Sean said from the other side.

"Come on out here and talk to Olivia. She's here to see you," Vincent yelled before turning back to Olivia, who was right on his heels.

"Now, I'm going to my room and I don't want to hear the racket, so please take it outside."

"Thanks for letting me in, Vinnie. You know I respect you very much. I will take it outside." Her eyes never left Sean's door.

Vincent walked to the opposite side of the living room and closed his bedroom door behind him.

Olivia stood rooted to the spot, waiting for Sean to open the door. He never did. She stood there, listening and waiting. When she came to the hurtful realization that he was not going to come out at all, she banged rapidly on the door.

"Open the door, you bastard! Open the door and face me!" She screamed and pounded away. "I don't care if you have your slut in there with you, Sean! Just open the fucking door! Now!" Olivia yelled. She beat the door for nearly ten minutes, but Sean was ignoring her. He didn't even acknowledge that she was there. She finally gave up and stormed out of the apartment without even closing the front door. So much for respecting Vincent. Fuck Vincent.

Olivia descended the stairs two at a time and ran to her car. She recklessly backed out of the handicapped space and almost hit an approaching Buick. The floodgates opened as she drove out of the complex. She made her way, dazed, along Dixie Highway. Unable to see the road clearly, she pulled into the parking lot of a deserted Bank of America.

"Oh, my God! Oh, my God! Oh, my God!" Olivia chanted. He'd been making a complete fool of her all this time. Lying . . . and cheating!

It began to pour. Olivia was remotely aware of the pellets hitting her car. "Damn you, Sean Johnson! Damn you for making a fool of me! Oh, my God, oh, my God! Damn it!" she sobbed. "How could he do this to me? *Why* did he do this to me?"

Over and over she beat the steering wheel with her fists, which were already tender from the pounding she'd given Sean's bedroom door. She bawled and screamed in an attempt to lessen the agony, but there was no stopping the painful sensation. There was an invisible dagger lodged in the pit of her stomach.

"I trusted you. . . . I believed in you!" she screeched at the top of her lungs, but the screams only bounced off of her car's interior.

FORTY-FIVE MINUTES LATER, Olivia raised her head from the steering wheel. She removed tissue from her glove compartment. Once she cleaned her nose and face, she started the car and headed home in the pouring rain. She just wanted to get into bed, and when Sean called—because she knew he would—he would find that she had activated the call-block feature on her private line.

She tried her best to stop the incessant flow of tears when she turned onto Miami Lakes Drive. Although she was no longer wailing, the tears poured uncontrollably down her cheeks, and she knew she looked like death itself.

Pulling into the driveway, she pressed the garage door opener. She was relieved to see that her mother's Cherokee was not there, but prepared to encounter Valerie as she entered the kitchen from the garage.

As luck would have it, Valerie was there in the kitchen, taking a slice of pizza from a Papa John's box. "Hey, where'd you go? I ordered a fully loaded pizza," Valerie said, not looking at Olivia long enough to notice her agitated state.

"I'm not hungry, Val. I'm turning in early," Olivia replied in a drained tone. She rushed for the stairs, not giving Valerie enough time to comment.

Secure in her cozy pink room, she let the tears run again. She rushed over to the caller ID, checking to see if Sean had called yet. . . . Although she knew he hadn't, because he would have paged her first.

How come he hasn't called yet?

She went over to the boom box and put on a Color Me Bad CD. Then she dragged herself back over to the double doors and flipped the light switch, plunging the room into darkness. Finally, Olivia crawled into her bed, curled into a fetal position, and sobbed into her pillow.

9

TRACY BROOKS HELD HER HAND in the air and scrutinized her well-manicured nails. Her nail tech, Josie, had polished them in a light, glittery brown, and she was happy with the result. She hadn't thought that she would like the color, but once applied, it was beautiful. It went perfectly with her highlights.

"See? Didn't I tell you this color would work?" Josie said with a smug grin on her face.

"Thanks, Josie. It's an excellent color. I guess you're better with colors than I am," Tracy said, laughing.

Josie worked in the Nail Haven at the Miami Pines Mall, and Tracy, Olivia, and Valerie were three of her most faithful customers. She often gave generous discounts on all the services, and they in turn tipped her extremely well.

Gazing at her nails, Tracy's eyes fell to her wedding bands. Lately, she tried to avoid looking at them. Her involvement with Frank made noticing them a bad omen. *You are still Reginald's wife,* they seemed to say.

Everything was going to change now that Reginald would be home regularly. She and Frank were accustomed to being together nearly every night for the entire two weeks Reginald spent in Orlando. What would they do now? She'd never needed to lie to Reggie about her whereabouts as long as he was away, but now that would certainly be changing. She would definitely have to lie. She would have to lie a lot.

Tracy wondered if she could handle it. . . .

She thanked Josie, said good-bye, and moved over to the fan to dry her nails. At that moment, she knew she would go back on her word. She would telephone Frank. She'd promised herself that she wouldn't be the one to call this time. She wanted Frank to call her for a change. He always knew when Reginald left for Orlando.

However, it had been two days and he had not called her, even when he must've realized she wasn't going to call him. Therefore, she was going to swallow her pride and call. They had lots to discuss.

She needed to feel him out, discover exactly what his intentions were. Why was he attentive and tender one minute, yet scornful and rejecting in the next? Why hasn't he ever mentioned the prospect of her leaving Reggie? The possibility of a future together? They'd been seeing each other for nearly four years, yet Franklin had never referenced anything beyond the present. But then again, neither had she.

And why should she? She's a woman. The man should initiate such a step, right? Tracy also wanted to find out what Frank thought about Reggie's newfound urgency to be a family man.

When her nails dried, Tracy gathered her purse and keys from the table where Josie had placed them, and headed for her Jeep.

Her mind drifted to that haunting night. The night it all began . . .

REGINALD HAD BEEN away in Orlando, and Frank had come to their rescue when Hurricane Donna was barreling down on the east coast of South Florida.

Frank's seduction had actually begun a few weeks prior to that night, with arbitrary and subtle romantic insinuations. Never one to cheat on her husband, Tracy had chosen to laugh, treating his attentions as innocuous teasing. Though she had always thought Franklin an attractive man, he was Reginald's oldest friend, and she'd never had a romantic thought about him.

The day they met, he'd been introduced as Reginald Brooks' best friend. There'd never been any questioning the jurisdictional nature of their acquaintance. Some doors were closed for a reason and should never be opened.

But on that rainy Saturday evening when Tracy and the girls couldn't install the hurricane shutters on their own, Reginald had sent Frank to the rescue.

Reaching category-five strength, Hurricane Donna packed winds in excess of 170 miles per hour, and Dade County was in the forecast track, facing the possibility of a direct hit. Reginald couldn't get a flight in time, and the roadways were impossible due to the numerous mandatory evacuations. He told Tracy he would phone Frank and a couple of their neighbors to ask that they come over to the house to help her secure the shutters.

With the neighbors' help, they all labored in the strong gusts of rain and wind to secure the entire house. The weather had worsened so quickly that Frank wound up staying with her and the girls to ride out the storm. Luckily, they never lost power, so for the next two days they watched lots of movies and ate lots of food, and then they watched more movies and ate more food. It was an enjoyable time.

The house was dark since shutters covered every window and glass door. The rain came down in torrents; the thunder clapped. But they were all safe inside and having a good time together. . . . Until the night Frank had touched her.

At first Tracy had been startled. She was in disbelief.

She'd gone into the kitchen to put a bowl in the dishwasher, and he'd followed her with a glass of his own. With Valerie and Olivia laughing at Jim Carrey in the den, she and Franklin had been alone. Isolated.

"Tracy," he'd said, voice low.

She had glanced over her shoulder, surprised anyone had followed her into the kitchen. "What's up? Haven't had enough to eat yet?" she'd laughed.

Frank said nothing. He'd put his glass down and closed in on her. Taking the bowl from her hands, he gently pinned her arms to her sides. "Tracy." He slipped an arm around her waist, bending close to her ear. "I can't take this anymore. You know what I'm feeling. . . . And I know you feel it, too."

She pulled away from him, so hard she nearly tripped. From a safer distance, she stared Frank down. Minutes passed in silence.

Then she slapped him—twice. "Don't ever touch me like that again."

She turned and left the kitchen.

Hurricane Donna had eventually veered to the north, grazing them with outer bands of heavy rain and tropical storm–force wind gusts.

But an even deadlier hurricane had hit Tracy that night. . . . And its name was Frank.

NOW AS SHE made her way home from the mall, she thought, *Would I actually leave Reginald?*

She imagined Frank asking her to be with him . . . permanently. Would she do it? *Yes. Yes, I believe I would. I'd miss him. . . . But, I hardly know him anymore. . . .*

In supplying the answer to her own question, Tracy realized that she would do it because it seemed like she had fallen out of love with Reginald. The love and passion she had for him before he took that Orlando assignment . . . they'd been stripped away by the last ten years. Who could blame her for accepting comfort elsewhere?

Although she occasionally flew up to Orlando to see Reginald while he was there, she'd grown into a woman with extraordinary needs, and he'd no longer been around to meet them. Years of that lifestyle had taken its toll on their intimate bonds, leaving Tracy to eventually gravitate toward Frank, who had lured her into open arms.

The incident in the kitchen had lit a flame that still burned inside of Tracy. Frank knew it. He preyed upon it. And Tracy succumbed.

She had felt like an adulterous slut the first time they'd made love at his apartment. She avoided him for weeks thereafter. But as weeks turned into months, Frank reasoned and inveigled his way back into her bed. No one had to know; they were simply fulfilling each other's needs . . . for the time being.

That was four years ago.

And there was still one question that Tracy could not answer as she thought of her children and maneuvered her Cherokee along Ludlam Road: *What kind of mother does this make me?*

TRACY WAS GLAD to see Olivia's car in the driveway when she got home. She had hoped Olivia hadn't gone out with Sean. She'd been meaning to talk to both Valerie and Olivia about their father's decision to change his schedule. Tracy knew that Olivia nursed resentful feelings toward Reggie, but she was confident that in time, that would amend. The last thing Tracy wanted was for the girls to resent their father—on top of everything else.

In the kitchen, she noticed the pizza. Upon opening the box, she discovered that they'd left her zilch. *Great . . . now I'll either have to cook or order out,* Tracy thought, taking the empty box into the garage.

Back in the house, she found Valerie in the den with the cordless telephone tucked between her ear and shoulder.

"Hey, Val," she said, getting her attention. "Listen, call your friend back later. I need to talk to you and Olivia about something. Is she here?" When Valerie nodded, she added, "I'll go up and get her."

Valerie watched her mother leave. When she was sure Tracy was gone, she whispered into the telephone, "Listen, Debbie, we'll finish talking about it when I call you back." After a pause, she said, "Yeah, she said she wants to talk to both of us about something. I'll tell you about it later. Bye." Valerie placed the handset into its cradle.

Upstairs, Tracy knocked for the second time on Olivia's bedroom door.

"Olivia, are you there?" She waited a moment and called again.

"Yes, Mom, I'm here. I was sleeping," Olivia said, barely audible.

"Well, I'm sorry I woke you up, but I want to talk to you and Valerie, so come on out."

"Mom, I'm really tired. We'll talk tomorrow, okay?"

"Are you sure? I don't want to wake up in the morning and find you gone. This is important."

"Okay, Mom . . . tomorrow."

Tracy descended the stairs and rejoined Valerie in the den.

"What's the matter with Olivia?" Tracy asked.

"I don't know. You know how she is. She came in and just went straight into her room. She didn't even eat any of the pizza I ordered, and it was fully loaded," Valerie replied matter-of-factly. "She probably had another fight with Sean. You know she only acts like this when they've had a fight."

"Speaking of pizza, how come you didn't leave any for me?" Tracy asked, sitting on the sofa beside her.

"Well, I didn't know *when* you'd be coming home tonight," Valerie replied with mock innocence.

Tracy's hands itched to wring her neck. *When in the hell did she get so forward?* Tracy asked herself.

"Look, I want to talk to you guys about your dad going back to his old schedule."

"Yeah? What about it?' Valerie asked with interest.

"I want to know how you feel about it."

"What do you mean? I'm glad Daddy'll be staying home now! We'll be able to be a real family and go on vacation like we always talked about."

"I know *you're* okay with it, but—"

"But you're not," Valerie said, cutting her off. "Mom, I hope you don't mess this up and make him change his mind!"

"Valerie, what in the world are you talking about? Make him change his mind? Why on Earth would I do that?"

"Oh, I don't know, Mom. Maybe you're used to not having him around anymore or something," Valerie said with an eyebrow raised.

"Okay, cut the bull, little girl, and say what you mean. I've had it with your lip! You obviously have some kind of hidden implication. What is it? And don't you dare forget who gave birth to whom here," Tracy demanded, staring intensely at her youngest daughter.

"I don't mean anything, Mom," Valerie answered. She stared down toward the rug. She didn't want to push her mother too far—not yet, anyway. "I'm just happy that Daddy will be home now, and I hope nothing comes up that would make him change his mind. That's all. I don't mean anything." Valerie turned her attention to the television set.

Tracy rose from the sofa and stood between Valerie and the television. She treated her daughter to one of the infamous glares that always put both she and Olivia in their places when necessary. "I already spoke to your father about that insolent mouth you've developed, so we'll see just how long you'll be happy to have him home, young lady." With that, Tracy stepped from the room.

Oh, Mother, we'll see just how happy you'll *be to have Daddy home,* Valerie thought.

Rising from the sofa, she went upstairs to her room. Once she had locked the door behind her, she fell onto the bed and reached for her bedside telephone.

Valerie placed a call to her cousin Deborah.

"Yeah, Debbie," she half whispered into the receiver. Although she had her own phone line, Valerie couldn't risk being overheard.

"Okay," Debbie replied. "So you want me to follow Aunt Tracy?"

"Yeah, tomorrow night."

"What makes you think she's seeing somebody, anyway? And why do you think she'll be going to see him tomorrow?"

"Look, Deb, I know my mom. She runs out of here almost every night when Daddy's in Orlando, and nobody's ever up long enough to know when she comes back," Valerie replied. "Plus, a couple of times we've caught her coming in at like seven or eight o'clock in the morning, trying to pretend like she got up early and went out. She's doing it, all right. . . . Trust me. And she's stupid enough to think nobody's figured it out," she said in arrogance. "Just come at around seven tomorrow, because she never leaves before that. I think she waits for Daddy to call her before she goes."

"Okay, I'll be there, but I'll kill you if I waste my time following Aunt Tracy to a friend's or to a club or some place innocent like that," Deborah said with doubt. She hesitated and added, "Why are you so interested, anyway, Valerie?"

"Please just be here, Debbie. I just want to know."

"Okay. See you tomorrow," Deborah said, reluctant to concede.

"Bye."

When Valerie hung up, she smiled. *This is the perfect way to find out who this mystery man is. . . . How come I never thought of this before?*

AFTER HER SHOWER, Tracy settled into bed and dialed Frank's number. She felt a twinge of doubt, considering the fact that he hadn't called her at all since Reginald left. However, she pushed the hesitancy aside. She had no idea when Reggie would be returning home and they would be out of time.

The telephone was answered on the third ring. Tracy was stunned to hear by whom.

It was Theresa Parker.

"Hello?" Theresa said for the second time.

Tracy replaced the receiver. *What's she doing there? I thought they were over.*

She reached for the telephone again and punched in Frank's pager number.

ACROSS TOWN, THERESA Parker replaced Frank's bedside telephone just as he reappeared from the bathroom. The wonderful, soapy-clean smell of masculinity emerged with him.

"Tell me that you did not just answer my telephone," Frank demanded as he vigorously ran a towel through his damp hair. His muscular chest and shoulders glistened with tiny beads of water from his recent shower. Theresa couldn't resist lowering her eyelids to follow a water trail on his torso that disappeared into the white towel he had wrapped around his sexy waist.

"Yes, I answered it, but the person hung up on me. Why? You have a problem with me answering the phone now?" Theresa questioned irascibly.

"Look, we only fucked, all right? We didn't get married. So I'd appreciate it if you weren't so damn presumptuous," he said as he strode from the room.

Theresa lay back on the fluffy pillows and gnawed on her lower lip. Why did she keep coming back to see Frank?

They had been engaged for only two short months when one day out of the blue, he broke it off. He'd given her some cockamamie story about not being ready and having cold feet, but instinct told Theresa that stories like that only meant one thing—another woman.

It had been a few years since the breakup, but occasionally he would call on her if he needed a date for a social gathering or a disengaged roll in the hay. Why she was always willing to drop everything to accommodate him she would probably never know. He treated her like yesterday's kindling and she despised it, but she chalked it up to a good strategy. If she stuck by him long enough, one day he would realize that she was all he needed, and things would be the way they were before he broke off their engagement.

She was daydreaming about the future when Frank strode back into the room. He had gotten a Budweiser from the refrigerator and was taking a long sip from the can when his pager began to chirp.

"Time for you to go, babe." Frank walked over to the left side of the bed and retrieved his pager from the nightstand. Once he checked the display and recognized Tracy's number, he automatically reached for the telephone. He now knew for certain that she'd been the one to call and hang up when Theresa answered.

The last thing he needed was to have Tracy pissed off now that Reggie was feeling like a semifaithful husband. She believed Theresa was out of the picture and that he only showcased her for the benefit of Reginald and their mutual friends. Well, he would be damned if he was going to make any excuses and grovel at her feet about it. So what if she knew? She'd get over it.

He pulled himself out of his thoughts and realized that Theresa hadn't moved from her place under his sheets. She was treating him to an intensive, lust-filled stare that he was more than familiar with.

Before he could utter a word, she used her legs to pull the sheet off and bared her naked body. Theresa then raised her knees to her chest and spread them wide apart, exposing her femininity. Next she slid her index finger into her mouth, extracted it, and brought her hand down to massage her clitoris. "One more for the road?" she invited, continuing to rub herself enticingly. She let out a soft, restless moan and threw her head back as her finger brought on a tidal wave of pleasure.

Frank strolled over to the armchair where her clothes had been discarded and gathered them up. "Look, we already did it three times tonight. I don't have the time or the energy to do it again." He walked over to the bed, where she had ceased her tease show in shock and, no doubt, embarrassment. He took her by the arm and effortlessly pulled her from the bed, shoving her garments toward her bare chest. "Here, get dressed, and I'll see you later."

Humiliated, Theresa grabbed her clothing from Frank and swiftly made her way to the bathroom. She wasn't about to demean herself any further.

Once alone, she wept silently as she dressed. *He'll wake up one day, Theresa. Be patient.*

*   *   *

TRACY WAITED AN annoying ten minutes before Frank returned her page.

"Why is Theresa answering your phone?" she inquired in place of the traditional hello. Thanks to caller ID, she knew it was Frank.

"Don't question me about my interests. . . . I certainly don't question you about yours," he shot back, locking his front door behind Theresa.

"So you're still sleeping with her, huh?" she asked tentatively.

"As a matter of fact, yes. What of it?"

Tracy thought quickly. If she slipped and disclosed her jealously, he would run away with it. So she spoke with her usual facade of indifference. "Think nothing of it, honey. I was just caught off guard when she answered, is all. You know, we can't risk having her find out about us. . . . That's why I hung up on her."

After a brief pause, she decided to pursue another tactic. It was a risky idea that took root and had been blossoming in Tracy's mind for some time. Knowing it could mark the end of their relationship, she'd been debating her own rationale. But now . . . it was an area she felt compelled to explore. The realization that Theresa was back in his bed pressed against her.

She continued, "You know, it's interesting that this happened, because I've been thinking a lot about what we're into here. . . . Especially in light of Reggie's decision to go back to the old schedule. I think it would be best if—wait a minute, I assume you two have discussed this already, right?" she said as an afterthought.

"Yeah, he told me about it the other day when he first came back. I was expecting you to get in touch sooner to talk about it. What happened?" Frank asked.

Good, he's helping me out, Tracy thought, glad that he was throwing her a line to reel him in on. "Well, I didn't call sooner because I was conflicted, to be completely honest. Reggie gave me quite a bit to think about, and in the end I realized I had to make a decision." She paused for effect. "I can't see you anymore, Frank. Since Reggie's going to be home more, it's too precarious, and I don't think I could handle sneaking around." She unconsciously stopped breathing.

Frank sat upright in his recliner, stunned. What in the hell did she just say? He must have heard incorrectly. She doesn't want to see him anymore? No way; that would mean . . .

Frank chose his words carefully. "Why such rushing to *that* decision? Of course we can find ways to work around that, if we wished to. We'd just have to make sure we were careful, and we wouldn't get together as often. No problem."

Tracy shifted her weight on the bed and persisted. "No, Frank. He'll be home all the time now. I won't be able to do this anymore and sleep at night. I mean, seeing you while he's out of town is one thing, but I don't think I could be seeing you right under his nose. He was away and I grew lonely. . . . But you're his oldest and dearest friend! I just know I'd never be able to look him in the eye . . . nor either of my children. Moreover, Reggie really doesn't deserve this from us. Can you fathom him finding this out?" Tracy shivered.

"Listen, you don't have a clue about what *Reggie deserves*," Frank spat. His voice was laced with bitterness. He was treading on thin ice, but he wasn't about to let Tracy have the upper hand here. This was his show.

"What is that supposed to mean?" Tracy asked, bewildered.

"Nothing. Nothing. I just meant that you shouldn't worry about him finding anything out. We'll manage to sneak a rendezvous in here and there. Don't worry about it." Frank did not overplay his hand. He could not let her suspect just how passionately he needed to keep the affair alive. He certainly didn't want her misconstruing his reaction, interpreting it as love or anything of the kind.

Tracy was simply a secret weapon—a weapon of retribution. Being with her was therapeutic. . . . Not to mention the great sex they had together. What would it mean if she stopped seeing him in the name of Reginald? She would be no different from the hordes of other bitches that had consistently chosen Reggie instead of him.

No, that was not going to happen. He could not be left out in the cold yet again, while the mighty Reginald Brooks continued living happily ever after.

Tracy yawned. It would be great for effect if she ended the conversation at that very moment. "Look, Frank . . . we knew it would have to end one day, didn't we? We couldn't keep this going on forever. Now is obviously as good a time as any to stop." She paused, and then added, "It's been a good time for me. You filled a void that I didn't even realize I had at the time. But now I have to give my husband and my kids my full attention. . . . In fact, the phone's beeping and that's Reggie calling on the other line. I'm gonna answer it, Frank. I have to go. Talk to you later?"

Frank rushed to say, "I need to see you. Why don't you come on over after you talk to him?" If he could just get her face-to-face, all this talk about ending it would disappear.

"Hold on a minute. Let me get him on hold." Tracy pressed the FLASH button on the base of the cordless phone and waited several seconds. She glanced around her bedroom, uncertainty in her chest. Finally, she flashed back. "Okay, he's holding. You were saying?"

Frank's voice lowered seductively. "Come over when you finish talking to him so we can have one last night together, for old time's sake."

Oh, Tracy was tempted. From the beginning, Frank had always been difficult to resist. But if she wanted to win this gamble, she had to play it through. "No, I'm already in bed and I'm too tired to leave it. I'll try to come by tomorrow." *Let him have a night to mull it over. . . . Then maybe he'll decide he wants something more definite. Right now it has to be all or nothing,* she thought.

"I have to go—Reggie's waiting. Good night." She pressed the FLASH button again, then she replaced the receiver.

THE DIE WAS cast. Tracy would soon find out just how serious Franklin actually was about this relationship. After all, it was imperative that she know the extent to which he wanted her in his life.

Confident that she had baited Frank, Tracy decided to call and find out just how quickly things were progressing in Orlando. It would not be favorable for Reggie to show up right now when she was spinning a neat little web for Frank. *No,* she thought, reaching for the phone again. *It could be disastrous.*

10

ORLANDO, FLORIDA

REGINALD REMOVED HIS cell phone from his pocket clip, brought it to his ear, and said a terse hello. He was surprised to hear Tracy's voice on the other end. They had spoken the night before when he got home, and he had promised to call again tonight.

When he was in Orlando, he made sure he called home often enough to prevent her from having to call him. All calls to his corporate apartment were forwarded to his cellular—so if they called too often, it could cause dire consequences.

Maybe there was a fateful reason, after all, that he felt compelled to put an end to this madness.

"Hey, there. What's up?" Tracy greeted.

"Hi. Is something wrong?" he questioned, his palms moistening.

"No, no, everything's fine. I'm just eager to find out when you'll be back at home, that's all. Make any substantial headway today?"

"Well, I think I'll be working straight through the weekend with the department VPs on a few particulars, but I'm probably here until at least Tuesday. The largest accomplishments are still pending." He glanced over his shoulder at Renee.

"Well, take your time and do what needs doing—no sense in rushing and risking Roger's wrath. We'll have plenty of time once you finally get home. But the girls and I really do miss you."

"There hasn't been any change, has there?" Reggie asked, sounding panicked.

"Change? Change with what?"

"Well, I just thought that since you called, maybe something had happened on that end."

"No. Everything's status quo."

"Okay, I'll call tomorrow to check in. G'night." Reginald pushed the END button on the cell phone. He turned back around, ready to continue his conversation with Renee.

"That was my wife, Tracy," he stated quietly. He resumed his seat on the peach armchair, adjacent to the loveseat she occupied.

Renee lifted her hand and wiped away salty tears. Her hand was shaking. She'd been crying for the better part of an hour; tears were streaming down her cheeks. She said nothing. She simply gazed at him; her body was stiff with anguish.

"She called to find out when I'd be back, because there are consent papers that we both need to sign for Valerie to continue her treatments." Reginald kept his eyes downcast and studied the design of the Oriental rug beneath his socks.

He felt an urge to rush his performance and flee, but common sense prevailed. He had to be extremely careful with this—his life with Tracy depended on it.

He waited a few minutes, and they sat in silence. He studied the rug. She stared at him.

He kept his eyes on the rug when he finally broke the silence. "Roger has made some arrangements for me to stay in a corporate apartment out on the Parkway. Renee, all I ask is that you let me see Denise whenever I can." He looked up then and saw that she was about to interrupt, but he rushed on, saying, "I understand that you probably won't want much to do with me after this. I never told you that I was a married man—that I've been married for years—and that I have two other children. No, no," he said when she attempted to interrupt again. "Please, just let me finish. I couldn't tell you about Tracy and the kids for fear that you'd leave me, Renee. I was afraid I'd never see Denise again. I didn't think you would believe that we stayed married only for Olivia and Valerie's sake. That's a classic 'other woman' cliché, isn't it?"

"Reggie—" Renee began, unable to stop the tears.

Reginald raised his palm, stopping her. "Please . . . just let me get this all out in the open. I have to get it out before I lose the nerve. Please."

Swiping more tears, Renee slumped backward in the loveseat.

Reginald's eyes glistened with tears of his own, and he continued. "Tracy and I haven't gotten along for years. To make a long story short, many years ago, she had an affair with a man she worked with, and I found out about it. My first instinct was to file for a divorce, but then my sister, Thelma, got me thinking about the impact on my kids and reminiscing about how *we* grew up with no father, what his absence meant to our lives. I didn't want that for Olivia and Valerie, so I agreed that Tracy and I could continue raising them together, until they were of age.

"Now that Valerie's almost eighteen, my freedom seemed to be approaching. . . . And then this happened. Once the girls were grown up and the divorce was final, I had planned to ask you to marry me. I was planning to move to Orlando permanently. I don't know how I was gonna tell you about my children. I honestly hadn't thought that far into the future. I just planned to play the cards as they were dealt and take it from there.

"And to be absolutely candid, I never planned to tell you that I had actually been married all these years. I hoped I would never have to confess that, not only because it would be hard for me, but also because I could only imagine how much it would hurt you." He paused and glanced over at Renee, assessing the damage. She had remained silent, but the crying had not stopped.

Reggie wiped his own face dry and took a deep breath. When he spoke again, his words were choked. "Renee, I couldn't blame you for hating me now—no one could. You made a home here with a man you trusted, and now it's broken." Then he added with passion, "*I am so very sorry, Renee.*" He paused, letting the words penetrate the disturbed air, a soothing balm.

"Please understand," he whispered. "I never wanted to hurt you and Denise. That's why I kept my marriage a secret all these years. I should have told you I was married from the very start, but I did not." He held her gaze. "I cared about you so much that I risked everything to buy this house and stay here with you. Lord, if Tracy ever found out, she could take me to the cleaners when we get the divorce."

They sat in another lengthy silence. Finally, he went on. "Now I have to spend every possible moment at Valerie's side. So I had no choice but to tell you the truth. I can't rest until they find a match for her. Until then, Tracy and I will continue making things seem as whole as possible, so there's nothing to distract her from fighting this thing. Her oncologist says the mind can be a powerful healer. . . ." He turned his head, appearing too choked up to speak any further.

Renee had begun hugging a fluffy throw pillow. She clutched it and squeezed her eyes shut. He was married? Actually married? He had a wife. Two kids. Girls. One was twenty-one and the other was seventeen and recently diagnosed with leukemia. . . . Reginald is married. *Her* Reggie was married to another woman. With two daughters. All these years he'd been married. . . . He'd been going to Miami to a wife and two kids for half the month. He'd been sleeping with . . . "Do you have sex with her?" she asked suddenly.

After a brief stillness, Reginald rose from the armchair and knelt before her. He took her trembling hands, held them between his, and rooted her to the loveseat with an intense stare. "Tracy and I haven't shared the same bed since the day I discovered she was sleeping with somebody else. Look at me, Renee—say you believe that." His eyes commanded a reply. "Say it."

She raised her wet lids, searching his face for any sign of dishonesty, but she found none. "I believe you," she murmured.

He brought her hands to his lips, kissing them. "I'm sorry. I know that you may never be able to forgive me, but please believe that I *never* wanted to hurt you or the baby. I wish to God that I didn't have to do this now. I hate hurting you like this, but it's the only thing I can see my way clear to doing right now."

He rose from where he knelt and dried more tears from his eyes and face. He exhaled, moving toward the staircase. "I'll go pack a few things and get going. I don't want to make this any more difficult for you." After a beat, he added, "You do know that I love you, Renee. . . . I have always loved you." Then he jogged up the stairs to pack up and walk out of her life.

I CAN'T LET *him go! I just can't lose him,* Renee thought in anguish.

But she could wait. That's it; she'd wait. She could wait for his daughter's recovery, and when he finally got divorced, he'd marry her. She could forgive him being married. He didn't sleep with his wife; Renee had been the only one.

It certainly could not have been easy for him to tell her all this now, but his daughter's life was in danger and that had to come first. Renee understood. This news, in and of itself, proved that Reginald Brooks had a conscience; he was a decent man. No . . . she could not let him go. She would not let him leave. *I'd be crazy if I let him walk out that door.*

At that moment, Renee leapt from the loveseat and ran up the stairs, sopping her nose and face with her cotton sleeve.

When she reached their bedroom, Reggie was taking a handful of silk ties from his marble bureau. Walking over to him, she gently turned his face toward hers. "I can forgive you. Don't leave. Don't go anywhere. I forgive you." Placing her hands on either side of his face, she perched on tiptoes and kissed him.

"I can't believe this," Reginald whispered. He brought his strong arms around her waist and hugged close. Her body racked with sobs. In that moment, he couldn't hold back tears of his own. He'd succeeded. . . . So why, then, did he still feel so awful?

When they broke apart, he searched her eyes, asking, "Are you sure? I mean, have you had enough time to think this through? You . . . you really think you could forgive me?"

Renee wiped her face and smiled up at him. "Reggie, I love you and I know I can trust you." She paused, adding in a labored voice, "You proved it tonight when you told me all this. I know this must've been one of the hardest things in the world for you to admit. I think most men would've made up another lie or game, anything to avoid having to tell the truth, but you told me the terrible truth. . . . And you were willing to walk out of my life without adding more insult. You didn't expect understanding or forgiveness. Most men would've kept me in the dark, but you? You're a decent and conscientious man, and because of that, I can accept this.

"I'll wait for you, Reggie—as long as it takes. Right now, it's obvious your daughter's health is the most important thing. You go be with her. Denise and I will be here for you whenever you need us. We'll be waiting for you to come back home." She stretched her arms around his waist, holding tight. "We'll wait for you forever. I love you, Reggie. How could I hate you for telling me the truth? I could never hate you."

Reginald felt relief, but he couldn't avoid the pressing guilt. This had played out better than he ever could've anticipated. He'd never imagined she'd come around so quickly. Without a doubt, Renee loved him. Tonight certainly proved it, and now more than ever, he needed to protect that love and ensure it never turned bitter.

Tracy had his heart. She always had, and he'd come to realize that nothing could ever change that—not even Renee and Denise.

In light of tonight's progress, Reginald was confident he would not have problems seeing Denise in the future. . . . Which brought to mind another potential problem. He decided to settle it now. Holding Renee away from him, he said, "Would you agree that Denise never has to know about this? I mean, I don't think it's something she needs to know about."

"No, I won't tell her anything. Once your daughter gets well and we get married, Denise won't even know anything was wrong." Renee moved out of his arms and walked over to the large window that overlooked the grounds. "What about your kids? How will they handle you moving away from Miami?"

"Well, they're considerate girls. They'll learn to accept it. I'm sure they won't warm to it much at first, but they'll eventually adjust. Besides," he said, moving up behind her, "they do have their mother. Even when they find out about Denise, I'm sure with a little time, they'll love her just as I do. She is their sister, after all. Tracy won't be too happy about it, though. She'll be kicking herself for not finding out soon enough to clean me out."

Renee continued to gaze out across the moonlit lawn. Reginald was cuddling her from behind, burying his face in the crook of her neck.

Married . . . as he stands here holding me, he's a married man, she thought. He was married to a woman named Tracy. Dear God, would she ever really be able to digest it? The man she had been living with for six years!

Turning her damp face into his chest, she whispered, "Reassure me, honey. Reassure me that you'll be back and we'll be getting married."

Reginald bent and lifted her off her feet. He carried her to the waterbed and gently laid her across it. Tears continued to wet her face. Slowly, he used his tongue to dry them as they fell. He whispered words of love, of comfort, and most importantly, of reassurance. He promised her a future filled with happiness, when deep inside he knew it would never be with him.

Reginald made love to her most of the night. Reassuring her. Comforting her. Begging her for forgiveness that she swore was already his.

All the while, his spirit was elsewhere. . . . Miles and miles away in a city called Miami where Tracy was waiting for him to come home. He couldn't wait to get back home to her. It was a long time coming, but he was finally going to do right by her. Him, Tracy, and their girls, finally a normal family. It's what they all needed after all these years of chaos.

As he stroked Renee for the last time before dawn, Reginald thought, *Father . . . forgive me.*

SATURDAY MORNING, REGINALD awoke to find Renee's side of the bed empty. After listening for a moment and hearing no movement from the bathroom, he panicked. Perhaps things had gone a little *too* well last night. Perhaps she awoke and realized she didn't want to sweep his lies under the rug so quickly after all. Perhaps she'd decided to take Denise and run away. Perhaps . . .

Before his mind could wander any further, their bedroom door opened and Renee strolled in carrying a breakfast tray. She was clad in a white terry cloth robe and wore a glowing smile that stretched from ear to ear. *Relax,* he thought. *She isn't going anywhere.*

"Good morning," he said, eyeing her sexily.

"Good morning. I made breakfast," she said, placing the tray over his lap and extending the retractable sides. "I called the McDuffies, and Denise is fine. Then I labored over ham and cheese omelets, filled with everything you like: green onions, bacon, tomato, and bell peppers. I even toasted bagels and covered them with Philadelphia cream cheese. . . . Just the way you like it."

"You didn't have to, Renee," he said solemnly. He covered her hand with his larger one. "Despite what you've said, I know it'll take some time for you to get used to what's happened."

"Listen, I understand. And as I said, I'll wait for you. As long as it takes." She bent and kissed him lightly on the lips. "I love you so much."

As Reggie took the first bite of the delicious omelet and sipped his orange juice, he allowed himself to breathe for the first time in nearly twenty-four hours.

All was well again in Orlando.

HELEN JAMESON SQUEEZED Crest onto her toothbrush and began brushing her teeth. This Saturday morning found her in the same mood she'd been trapped in for the last two days. The altercation with her younger sister had upset her terribly, and left a cloud of despair that she couldn't seem to shake.

Once her teeth were clean, Helen gargled with Listerine until her mouth was on fire. Satisfied with her oral hygiene for the morning, she decided to talk to her mother about the situation. It was safe to assume that Renee had not yet beaten her to it, because knowing her mother, she would have long since called to analyze every detail. Beatrice loathed times when any of her three children quarreled among themselves. Even in their adulthood, she continued being a dedicated mediator in an attempt to preserve the well-being of the Jameson family.

After making Cream of Wheat for Ashley and Brian, Helen settled back into bed with a bowl of her own. She reached for the remote control and decided on Cartoon Network's Saturday morning lineup. Lowering the volume, she reached for the bedside telephone and dialed her parents' number.

Bea answered on the second ring. "Hello?" she said, voice singing.

"Good morning, Mom! Long time no talk."

"Good morning, honey. I know, I know. Ben and I were planning to stop by last evening for dinner, since you're the only person we know who cooks on Fridays, but Dean and Pat invited us over for a game of cribbage, and we didn't leave until almost midnight! I'm surprised I'm awake this early. . . ."

The last thing Helen wanted was to listen to her mother ramble about the cribbage game, so she cut to the chase. "Mom, I need to talk to you. Renee and I had it out on Wednesday evening, and it's just killing me."

For the next few minutes, Helen abridged the details of the spat. She purposely omitted the portion where she had called her niece a bastard, since she was certain her mother would only spend the remainder of the conversation berating her.

"Oh, Helen! Why did you have to say anything at all to her? You couldn't wait to tell her you knew, could you?" Bea demanded. Helen could picture her mother wagging her index finger in midair.

"Oh, forget that. I can't take this silence. I mean, we both said some mean things, and I just feel awful about the whole thing. I feel even worse because I just have a gut feeling that she's pushing us away so she can reach for something that isn't really even there. You know what I mean?"

"I know what you mean. . . . But don't you think she has a point where Lonny is concerned? You really *should* talk to him, Helen. Ashley is a fragile child. You can't keep letting him disappoint her like that. She'll probably grow up hating men or something."

"I know, Mom. I just don't want to deal with Lonny any more than is necessary. . . . But I will have a talk with him about it. If it happens again, I just won't make arrangements with him to come pick her up anymore—simple as that."

"I think that'd probably be for the best. I agree with Renee—that little girl spends too much time feeling sad, and she's too young for that!" Bea paused. "I also agree with you about Renee and Reginald. The man is trouble. Big trouble. You can see it a mile away."

"What can we do?"

"Honey, we can't do anything. All we can do is butt out and let her make her own mistake," Bea said in a concerned tone. "I just hope I can bear it when she's hit with reality. You know how Renee is."

"Well, in the meantime, I'm gonna call her and try to fix this mess, and I'm prepared for an uphill battle. I'm all too familiar with Renee's temperament. I already miss her, Mom, and I miss Denise, too. I know Ashley does. She asked me about her this morning."

"That's right, you call her. You know she won't be the one to make the first step, seeing as she likes to give herself pious airs."

"Yeah . . . I'm sure it'll be all right." Helen finished off the last of her cereal and attempted to get the conversation on a lighter note. "So, did Daddy finally get his fishing rods from Dean?"

RENEE LOOKED THROUGH the peephole. *I don't need this right now,* she thought. Helen was on the other side of the door. *What the hell is she doing here?*

She breathed a sigh and opened the door, but offered no greeting.

When it became apparent that Renee would sooner let her bake under the rays of the afternoon sun than invite her to come inside, Helen cautiously brushed past her and stepped into the tiled entryway. She glanced around briefly, looking for Reginald. She'd seen his silver Land Cruiser shining out front and knew he was home.

Moving over to the loveseat, Helen sat, crossing her long legs and smoothing her pleated skirt. She rested her purse on the coffee table and waited.

Closing the door, Renee followed her sister into the living room, but did not take a seat. Instead, she leaned against the column of the archway, folded her arms, and remained silent. She simply stared at Helen. She prayed to high heaven that her sister hadn't come over to cause trouble, especially in light of what happened the night before.

"I'm sorry," Helen said after a brief pause. "I miss you and Denise, and I'm sorry," she said quietly.

Taken aback, Renee's arms fell and hung at her sides. If the wall had suddenly turned into a cobra and bitten her on the butt, she couldn't have been more surprised. An apology was the last thing she'd expected from her sister.

Overwhelmed, the hostility left her.

"I'm sorry, too," Renee murmured, her eyes filling. She didn't want to start crying before Reginald left. He'd suspect that she'd immediately run to her sister with the news. So she simply rushed over to the couch and put her arms around Helen—desperately.

Equally surprised by Renee's reaction, Helen returned the hug, but she said, "Something else is wrong. Something other than our last quarrel. What is it?"

They pulled apart just as Reginald descended the stairs. He was dressed in business-casual beige khakis and a polo shirt that Renee had just ironed. Perfectly groomed, he was striking. He brought the captivating fragrance of Escada down the stairs, and the mere sight of him evoked an erotic reaction from both women.

Renee gazed up at him, remembering how sweetly he'd made love to her the night before. She noticed that Helen shifted her eyes toward the bright, sunny sky on the other side of the living room window.

Renee had always been aware of her sister's attraction to Reginald. His presence made Helen visibly tense, whether she herself was aware of it or not. She, like most women Renee knew, found him to be distractingly attractive and damn near irresistible—and there was no exception on this Saturday afternoon.

The man was gorgeous, and Helen had always been covetously aware of it.

"Hello, Helen," Reginald greeted, snapping his watch into place.

"Hello, Reggie. How you been?" Helen said, fixing her gaze on the little blond girl riding her tricycle across the street.

"I've been well, thanks," he replied, moving to the closet for his briefcase. "I'm heading to the office for a few hours to tie up some loose ends. . . . I'll be going away a little longer than usual. I'm sure Renee will fill you in." He glanced up. "By the way, how are the kids doing?"

"Oh, they're doing great." She watched the little girl struggle with her tricycle.

Renee patted her sister's hand. "I'll be right back." She rose to walk Reginald out.

Out in the driveway, Reggie buckled his seat belt and then turned to face Renee, who was leaning in the window, awaiting a kiss. He dropped a light kiss on her mouth, and taking her hand, he kissed her knuckles. "I'll be coming back as soon as I can, okay? And I'm gonna spend as much time with you and Denise as possible before I leave." He pinned her with his sincere stare.

"Reggie . . . I'm worried about how Denise is gonna react to you being gone away for so long."

"Don't worry about it—we'll talk to her together. I hope you know I'd never leave that burden on you alone. Denise will be fine." He kissed her hand again quickly and released it.

But I will be alone, she thought, as she watched him disappear around the bend at the end of their block.

The high-pitched laughter of the children riding their bicycles across the street alerted her that she was standing barefoot on the hot pavement of the driveway. She ran back inside and cooled her feet on the fluffy doormat in the entryway. Then, closing the door, she slumped dejectedly into the living room to find that Helen had helped herself to a carton of strawberries and whipped cream.

When Helen looked up and saw her face, she set the carton down, concerned. Her initial reason for being there was forgotten. "Sis, what's wrong?"

Renee needed to unload on someone, and her sister was going to be that someone. She couldn't keep it to herself; it was too overwhelming. She ran over to Helen and burst into tears.

"Oh, my God, Renee. What is this? What's wrong? What happened?" Helen cried, unprepared for this outburst.

Renee buried her head in her sister's lap and went into a crying jag the likes of which she knew Helen had never seen. "He's . . . married. Helen . . . he's married! Oh—my—God!"

"Married?" Helen repeated. "He's married?" Her head snapped up and she looked to the door, as if Reginald were still standing there. "Married to whom?"

"Oh, Helen . . . he's married . . . all these . . . years . . . he's been married!" Renee sobbed.

"Um . . . I need you to calm down for me, okay? Just calm down and tell me what happened." Helen tried to raise Renee's head from her lap. "What happened?"

Half an hour later, Renee was finally calm enough to raise her head and focus on Helen. Helen had simply been smoothing her hair and rocking her like an infant. She had never seen Renee like this before. It was unsettling.

Renee went into the kitchen for a tissue and blew her nose. She returned to the airy living room and resumed her position in Helen's lap. She needed to let it out, and right now she didn't care if Helen ran to their mother with the news; she needed her sister. Hell, she needed her family.

Renee sat silently for several more minutes, and Helen waited patiently for her to begin. Helen was obviously quite eager to hear all about this marriage, and she wasn't going to leave until she did.

"This has always been my biggest fear," Renee began calmly, into the pleats of Helen's skirt, though tears continued to streak her face. "I'd be a hypocrite if I denied that in the back of my mind, I've always had that fear, you know? That maybe there was someone else in Miami. I mean, he does spend just as much time there as he does here at home, right? But it never occurred to me—not even once—that he might have a wife! *A wife!* W-I-F-E, wife! A wife, Helen! A wife! And two children!"

Helen's eyes bulged. They looked as if they would soon pop out of their sockets. "Kids? *Two* kids? Oh, God . . . that son of a bitch!"

"Yes," Renee said on the breath of a sob. Her chest rose and fell with each word. "Two . . . grown-up . . . daughters. One's twenty-one, and the youngest is seventeen." Even as she spoke the words, it was as if someone else was saying them. Her entire life had been viciously torn straight down the middle, and her heart had never gotten the chance to escape the split.

"Where's Denise?" Helen questioned, looking to the archway. It suddenly occurred to her that the child might be in the house.

"She's at the McDuffies'." Renee blew her nose.

Helen gently nudged her head. "Sit up. Come on . . . sit up so we can talk about this, okay?"

Renee raised her head slowly; it had begun to pound.

"Now, how did you find out about this?"

"Oh, God! He told me! He—" Renee became hysterical.

"Sis, you're gonna have to calm down," Helen interrupted, wiping the flow of tears from Renee's face. "Come on, now, calm down and talk to me. It's all right. Take some deep breaths. . . . Yeah . . . inhale . . . exhale . . . good. Now, start from the beginning."

"Okay. Okay." Renee attempted to relax the tense, aching veins in her head. They felt like they were tied in knots. Five minutes passed before she calmly said, "He told me last night. He started by saying that he had no choice but to tell me . . . what he was about to say. He said he knew that he was about to change my life forever, but that it couldn't be helped."

Helen leaned in closer, her face full of anger.

"And then he said he was married." She threw her arms up and let them fall heavily into her lap. The tears poured once again. "He's married to a woman named Tracy. He was married to her when we met, but they've only stayed together for the sake of the two girls." Renee saw the disbelief in Helen's face and rushed on. "But once they were both of age, they planned to divorce and he was gonna propose to me. He said he found out Tracy was cheating on him with some other man and he wanted a divorce, but his sister, Thelma, convinced him to stay with Tracy for the sake of the kids. So they wouldn't grow up without a father."

"Renee, surely you don't believe all that gibberish?" Helen exclaimed. Her voice was saturated with suspicion.

Renee blew her nose again and rose from the sofa to stand before the window. She closed her eyes and let the rays of the sun rest on her face, a warm stimulant.

"Renee, *please* tell me you don't believe that gibberish," Helen demanded from the sofa.

"Hel, I can't lose Reginald. He's the best thing that's ever happened to me. I love him! Now, he says he had to tell me this because the seventeen-year-old has leukemia, and he has to go be there with her. They want her to feel that everything is normal, you know, so she's not at risk for any unnecessary stress or anything. But once they find a marrow donor for her, he's gonna get his divorce and marry me." She paused and then added, "And I told him I'd wait for him."

She saw the astonishment on Helen's face, but ignored it. "I told him that I could forgive him since he'd been so honest, and that I could wait for . . . Valerie . . . to get better." Renee toyed with the lapels of her robe. She opened her eyes and moved out of the sun, back to the sofa. "God help me, Helen, but I love him. I can't lose him."

Helen sighed. She felt for her sister. This was exactly what she and their mother had been afraid of. She remembered her earlier conversation with her mother and chose her words carefully. She didn't want to fight with Renee anymore. After all, they were sisters, and from what she could tell, Renee needed her now more than ever before.

"So you're saying that you're willing to wait indefinitely for his divorce. Is that really what you want? Is that gonna make you happy?"

"Of course it won't make me happy, Helen, but what else can I do? I can't lose Reggie." She clenched her fists. "I'd just die if he weren't in my life!" Her eyes darted, looking around the house. "What would anything mean if he was gone?"

"You would not die, Renee. You'd move on just like everyone else that has to." Helen paused and then said carefully, "Look, I know you don't want to hear this right now, but for the record, I don't believe it. I don't believe that he and this—this wife—are planning on getting divorced. Renee, it just sounds like this is his way of getting you on the back burner for a time. I wouldn't be honest if I didn't say so, and I'm positive Mom's gonna agree. Everyone already knows how *she* feels about Reginald. I mean, I hate to say 'We told you so,' but we did."

"All right, you told me. But just the same, I can't turn my back on him. . . . I just can't let him go. I won't lose him, Helen."

"Well, we can't live your life for you, but I know that I hate to see you like this. And if you want my advice, I think you should cut your losses before the other shoe drops."

"Why do you say that? When his daughter recovers, we're gonna get married. The worst that can happen is that it takes a while to find a matching donor, but I believe in him, Helen. He didn't have to tell me the truth, did he? He could have made up some lie and then just left. But he didn't do that. He loves me enough not to tell me any more lies." She paused. "Yes, it hurts like hell, and it'll be a while before I get used to the fact that he's hidden this from me all these years, but I know his intentions and I trust them. And that's what's gonna get me through this."

Helen stared at her sister. *You fool* was written all over her face. How could she be so stupid? Just listening to her logic was baffling. Perhaps she would have a little tête-à-tête with Mr. Brooks before he took off to reunite with *wifey* down in Miami.

Renee went upstairs to shower and change, and Helen stayed to keep her company. They spoke no more of the situation with Reginald, and both preferred it that way.

They walked arm in arm over to the McDuffies' town home to fetch Denise. They then picked up Ashley and Brian and spent most of the afternoon perched on the bleachers of Water's Edge Park, watching the kids play volleyball.

They discussed the children's various schoolteachers, upcoming report cards, and plans for summer vacation, but for the rest of the day neither woman voiced the one topic that remained first and foremost on her mind.

WHEN REGINALD DROVE through the Hart-Roman gateway that afternoon, he felt more optimistic than he had in months.

The way was paved for getting his life in order. When he returned to Miami, they would all finally be what they should have been all along—a close family. A happy unit. Even as he sat at his marble desk in his plush fourteenth-floor office, his brain racking over projections and evaluations, his thoughts were of home. Miami.

He couldn't have imagined anything would make him question his newfound resolve—until he returned to the town house. He saw the sadness on his daughter's face and felt shame. He was leaving her to grow up without him, without a father to love and nurture her, the way only a father could.

"You didn't even bring me my ice cream last time, Daddy. Who's gonna bring me ice cream when you're gone?" Denise pouted. Her round, bright eyes were questioning.

Reggie rose from the wicker chair and knelt in front of Denise. He and Renee were in her lime green bedroom, tucking her into her sleigh bed.

"Listen, sweetheart, I'm pretty sure Mommy will buy you plenty of ice cream, so don't you worry." He smiled. "And I'm gonna try to get back home and see you as much as I can, okay?" He brushed her nose. "Oh, and I promise not to show up without ice cream for my little

Denise, so don't worry. But"—he raised a finger—"remember, now, bad girls don't get ice cream, so if you're not a good girl for Mommy, no ice cream. Is that a deal?"

"But, Daddy," she whined, "you know how she says I eat too much ice cream all the time. You and Grandma are the only ones that give me my ice cream any time I want it. . . ."

"Okay," Reggie laughed. "I'll tell you what. I'll call to make sure Mommy's buying ice cream. You just have to behave and be good, all right?" Reggie glanced up and winked at Renee, who had remained silent until then.

"Oh, she'll be good." Renee joined in smiling. "My little Pooch is always good. And she'll get all the ice cream I can buy. . . . If she's a good girl."

"See?" Reggie said, standing and ruffling Denise's unruly curls. "Ice cream problem solved."

Denise giggled and fell back on the fluffy bed. "Oh, Daddy, I'll be good! I'm always good."

"That's Daddy's angel." Reginald bent and kissed her.

"Daddy?"

"Yes, angel?"

"How long will I have to miss you for?" Her eyes were bright, begging for an answer.

Uncertainty filled Reginald. "Oh, honey . . . I promise I'll try not to make it too long, okay? I'll be back as often as I can to see you. But it all depends on how my work goes. Can you understand that?"

"Uh-huh. I just don't want to have to miss you too long, because then I won't get to prove Mommy wrong about you all the time." She glanced at her mother mischievously.

"Prove Mommy wrong? Prove her wrong about what, sweetheart?"

"You know . . . when you promise to bring me stuff home on the way from work. Mommy always says I shouldn't listen to you 'cuz you always break the promise and she gets really mad—"

Reginald interrupted, "Is that what Mommy says?" His eyes cut to Renee.

"Yeah," Denise continued, "so if you're gone too long, I'll miss showing Mommy how many times you can keep your promise—see?"

"Well, in that case, I'll just have to make sure Mommy loses from now on then, right?"

"Right! Because sometimes I think she wins too much, and it makes me sad when Mommy wins."

"Okay, little angel, like I said, don't worry about a thing while Daddy's gone." He ruffled her hair again. "I'm gonna take care of everything—even while I'm away—and that's a promise, all right?"

"Promise?" she questioned eagerly.

"Promise," he answered. "I love you, sweetheart."

"Love you, too, Daddy," she smiled.

"All right, now. It's time for bed, Pooch," Renee chimed in. Clearly, she'd been embarrassed by the turn in the conversation.

ONCE DENISE WAS tucked in and secure for the night, they returned to the living room where they'd all been watching *Snow White and the Seven Dwarfs*. Reggie removed the tape from the VCR while Renee set about fluffing the sofa pillows.

Reggie thought it best to ignore his daughter's comments about the win-lose game between her and her mother—at least for the moment. With his retreat to Miami only days away, he needed another confrontation with Renee like a hole in the head. It did bother him, though, in spite of this resolve, that Renee had apparently been venting her frustrations with Denise. . . .

I'm bathing the wrong woman, he thought twenty minutes later as he lathered peach-scented bath gel on Renee's back.

He regretted the thought almost instantly.

Shit. He didn't think the guilt could get any worse.

They had retreated to their bathroom to take their nightly shower—an event rarely missed when they were together. Renee would never have stood for it.

Over the years, sex with Renee had become so predictable that Reginald wondered what was taking her so long to make the move tonight. He wanted to get it over with; he could barely look her in the eye.

Finally, Renee turned around in the middle of the back rub and began stroking him. He managed to harden under the pressure of her fingers. His eyes grew cloudy. He pinned her to the wall and slid his hand under her thigh, propping her leg on a gold faucet. He was being unusually hurried, but couldn't seem to stop himself.

Without warning, Reggie lifted his full penis, bent low, and thrust forward, plunging every inch into her.

Renee was stunned. "Oh—" she exclaimed, wincing at his harsh entry. He must have known she hadn't been ready for the penetration. Puzzled, she pulled her head back to look at him, but he had buried his head into the crook of her neck; his hands were braced against the shower wall, and he'd begun moving inside her.

What's going on? she thought, as he skillfully ground her.

It was never this way. Reginald loved to kiss her. . . . To lick her . . . to rub her until she thought she would die if he didn't slip inside.

So what was this tonight? Why was he making love to her as if he was in some kind of hurry?

She kept her puzzled eyes open, watching the steady stream from the shower head, for the duration of his swift lovemaking. When he climaxed, he slumped against her like a two-hundred-twenty-pound running back.

Renee didn't know what to say. She was afraid to say anything at all, since things between them were so delicate. . . . But if she said nothing, she would never know what was going on in his head. She hesitated. "Reggie . . . what was that?"

Reginald raised his head from her neck. He looked into her eyes.

Renee never really did have a chance, Reggie thought. He had truly done her an injustice.

His breathing was labored as he slid from her body. Unable to speak, he bent to rinse, then turned off the taps and stepped from the stall.

The silence that followed was as loud as the preceding torrent of water.

11

SATURDAY MORNING FOUND Sean Johnson pinned to his bed by Jackie Henderson's possessive left arm. When he awakened, one glance at his bedside digital clock told him it was half past eleven. "Fuck!" he cursed, almost to himself.

He was careful not to wake Jackie when he silently removed her arm from his chest and disengaged their legs. After dragging a pair of boxer shorts over his lanky hips, he stumbled his way to the rickety door, flipped the lock, and headed to the bathroom.

As he brushed his teeth, he was only mildly concerned about Olivia's unexpected visit the night before. He had fully intended to call her first thing this morning, but had unfortunately overslept, thanks to the many glasses of Chardonnay he and Jackie had consumed.

In the kitchen, Sean poured himself a glass of grapefruit juice and prepared his story for Olivia. He was very hungry, but he knew Jackie would find her way to the kitchen when she awoke.

He dialed Olivia's number and discovered that she had already blocked him from calling. "Shit—now I have to go over there," he said, pressing the FLASH button and shaking his head. He knew she wouldn't respond, but he paged her several times for appearance's sake. He had just replaced the handset when his brother, Vincent, emerged from his bedroom dressed in an off-white muscle shirt and a pair of faded khaki shorts.

Eight years his senior, Vincent's physique far surpassed that of his younger brother. Regular visits to the gym complemented his appearance. He had always tried to encourage Sean to join him, but Sean was too busy chasing skirts. His brother said quite often that he couldn't believe that Sean *still* hadn't outgrown that boyhood phase.

"I can't believe you did that, Vinnie. Why'd you let her in? You knew Jackie was here." Sean flopped onto their ugly mahogany sofa and reached for the remote control. He wasn't as annoyed with Olivia being upset as he was with the fact that Vincent's stupidity had caused it.

"Look, she was waiting for me outside, and I let her come up. I'm getting tired of always ending up in the middle of your games. You need to make up your mind, Sean—seriously."

Vincent crossed over to the far end of the apartment and pulled open the soiled verticals. "I wonder what it's like outside today," he murmured, as he slid open the glass doors and stepped out onto their porch. "Another gloomy day. The sky's full of gray clouds. That means more rain. When are we gonna get the sun to stay around for more than a minute at a time?"

Sean flipped to ESPN2 and found two suited men discussing nothing that interested him at all. He left the television on and joined Vincent on the porch, standing alongside him. "I don't know how to make up my mind, Vinnie," he said, running his hand over his bony stomach.

Vincent looked over at him. "Sean, grow the fuck up. It's time you plucked your head out of the sand and realized there's a time when a man should stop playing with young girls' emotions." He paused, and added, "So until you do grow up, keep me out of it. That means no more using me as an excuse for having Jackie here, you understand?"

"Yeah, I understand," Sean replied, not really understanding why Vincent was being so hard on him. His own brother!

Vincent turned and headed for the kitchen. "Hey, I'm heading out. Don't forget to take that foot powder to Mom—it's on the table in the bag." He motioned toward the dining area. "I went by there last night, and those toes look like they're getting worse." He grabbed a water bottle from the fridge and made for the front door.

Sean moved over to the table. He pulled the Tinactin powder from an Eckerd Drugs plastic bag. "Is this stuff any good? Will it help?"

"Well, I asked around, and most people say that's the best you can get over the counter."

"All right," Sean said, replacing the powder. "I'll have Jackie take it over there when she leaves."

"Whatever," Vincent said, rolling his eyes. Just before he closed the door, he said, "Sean, leave Olivia alone. That poor girl's had enough of you." Then he was gone.

Sean headed for his bedroom and changed. It was time to go see Olivia. He didn't plan to heed his brother's advice. He couldn't leave Olivia alone. She was a sweet girl—not to mention way out of his league—and he liked her a lot. *What's wrong with that idiot?* he thought. *I've never told him to drop somebody he cared about.*

Dressed in blue jeans and a white T-shirt, Sean left a note about the powder for a sleeping Jacquelyn—who was draining mouth water all over his pillow.

It was time to go to work. *That's what it is, after all,* he thought, climbing into his old, beat-up Skylark. *Work.*

A SOFT, CONSISTENT pounding on the bedroom door awakened Olivia early Saturday morning. She raised her head and glanced at her marble wall clock. It was only eight thirty. The knocking was followed by her sister's uncharacteristically low voice calling her name. Why didn't she just use the telephone?

"Liv, wake up and let me in," Valerie stage-whispered, not wanting to rouse her mother at the end of the hall. She knocked again. "Liv . . ."

A puffy-faced Olivia pulled the double doors open. "Why didn't you just call me? At least I wouldn't have had to get up." She padded back to her cozy bed.

Still in pajamas, Valerie rushed into the room, hastily closed the doors, and flipped the lock. "I wanted to see you. What happened with Sean this time?" Instinct told her it had to be about him. They all knew he was one of the only people that made Olivia behave so strangely. "And don't tell me it's nothing, because I know something happened."

Olivia rolled over and squeezed a fluffy pillow to her chest. "Val, he's still seeing that bitch. Can you believe it?"

"Yes. I can believe it." Valerie fell onto the bed. "Liv, don't you think it's time? Huh? I mean, don't you think it's just time to drop him already?"

"What? This from one of his most faithful defenders?"

"Yeah, but, even *I* can see that it's time. . . ." Valerie replied.

"I guess, but . . ." Olivia paused. "Valerie, I love Sean. Do you think if someone had told me that things would turn out this way, I'd have gotten so involved with him? No. Never in a million years. But unfortunately, no one told me, so I *did* get involved—way too involved."

"So how did you find out this time?"

"You mean besides the fact that Vincent practically spelled it out for me? I went by there, and she was locked up in the room with him. He wouldn't even come out and speak to me after I banged on the door and screamed at him. Can you believe that? I'm still wondering if I imagined the whole thing."

"Damn—that is bad." After a pause, Valerie tried to comfort her. "Look, Liv, you'll get over Sean. What does Grandma Rhoda say? 'There are plenty of other fish in the streets,' right?" Valerie giggled at their maternal grandmother's fudged cliché.

"Yeah, I guess," Olivia said, not really caring to find another fish. "Anyway, Mom wants to talk to us about Daddy quitting his job in Orlando."

"Yeah, he told me that he was gonna be home more often now, that he was going back to his old schedule." Olivia couldn't shake the sudden wave of emptiness that enveloped her. All it took was the subject of her father. "So, what does Mom want to talk to *us* about?"

"I'm not really that sure. . . . She says she wants to know how we feel about it. And just to let you know—since she'll probably blab to you, anyway—we kinda got into an argument."

"What did you say to her?" Olivia asked, turning to face Valerie.

"Nothing. I just kind of . . . sort of hinted that *she* probably wouldn't be too happy to have Daddy home." She saw the disapproval on Olivia's face and rushed on. "And even you must know that it's true, Olivia."

Olivia propped herself on her elbows. "Oh, Valerie, don't tell me you still think Ma's seeing some other man. Gimme a break already!"

"Stop acting like you don't see it, Liv!" Valerie raised her hand and counted off on her fingers. "Does she ever go out at night by herself when Daddy's home? No. Does she sneak into the house early in the morning when Daddy's home? No. Is she panicking now that Daddy's changing his schedule? Yes. I rest my case," she said smugly.

"Well, I don't think so. But even if she is, so what? Daddy's never home, anyway."

"Well, I asked Debbie to follow her later. It's about time we found out where she runs off to at night."

"You told Debbie to *what? Follow her?*" Olivia sat up in the bed. "Okay, Valerie, that's just a bit much. You're taking this too far." Olivia threw her hands up. "You're only seventeen. Why are you so concerned with this? What are you gonna do if she *is* seeing somebody? Steal him?"

"Oh, come on. Doesn't it upset you just a *little* to know that Mom's running around on Daddy?"

"Look, it's none of our business what they do. And how do you know your precious *Daddy* isn't doing the same thing to Mom?"

Valerie's forehead crinkled. "I never thought about that. I can't picture him with another woman." She shook her head emphatically and added, "Daddy wouldn't do that! He loves Mom too much. You know that."

"The only thing I know about Daddy is that he's more of a mystery to us than Mom is. We hardly even know him anymore."

Valerie reached over and shoved her on the shoulder. "You always say that! Daddy is not a mystery. Where do you get that from?"

"Well, just the way you have a hunch that Mom's having an affair, I have a hunch that Dad's a mystery. . . . Fair enough? Let's just forget it." Olivia lay back against the pillows and closed her eyes. What was Sean doing right now? And why wasn't her beeper chirping nonstop with pages? Her eyes stung and fresh tears formed.

He was still with *her.*

"Well, I know that tone. I see this conversation is over—at least for now. Getting you to listen to me anymore is as likely as getting a signed confession from Mom." Valerie sighed and joined Olivia under the covers. Within a few minutes, she was back to sleep.

Olivia lay there, studying the popcorn on the ceiling. The tears slid from her eyes. Her heart muscles ached again. He was still with *her.* Sean . . . locked up in that room with *her* . . .

Did he whisper the same words of love to Jackie? Did they have sex in the same positions?

Oh, Olivia, don't do this to yourself. Stop it now . . .

"CREAM CHEESE, MILK, bread, orange juice . . ." Tracy scribbled the items on a notepad as she intently watched a man lift at least thirty hideous-looking snakes with his bare hands. It was amazing that he still managed to speak animatedly into the video camera.

Still in her airy nightgown, she had trotted downstairs with an armful of dirty whites to do laundry and to write the grocery list. The cleaning service came in twice a week to make the house spotless, but Tracy had never been comfortable with the idea of a stranger doing her laundry. For her, that was too personal.

She had tossed the whites into the washing machine and returned to the kitchen to watch Animal Planet on the built-in television set. It was one of her favorite cable stations. Not that she cared for animals, for she had never wanted pets, but the documentaries had always been intriguing.

It was now twenty past ten; much later than she would have liked. She was usually up before eight on Saturdays, but this morning she had slept in. After her bizarre conversation with Reginald the night before, Tracy lay awake, thinking about the odd tone she'd heard in his voice. He just hadn't sounded like himself, and if she knew anything about Reginald, that meant something was wrong.

Oh, Lord, she thought. The last thing she needed was another surprise from Reggie. Her life was complex enough, what with Frank and his lack of interest in something respectable. Tracy shuddered at the thought of what everyone would say when she and Reginald separated. And what's worse? She'd be leaving him for his oldest—and closest—friend.

She left the barstool and went over to the refrigerator to scout for more necessities. But as thoughts of a divorce intensified, Tracy could not actually comprehend a life without Reginald. They had been together for so long. She was accustomed to all that he was. Reggie was an essential part of her. He was her husband. He was her friend. He was her everything. . . .

Until Orlando, she thought with a full heart.

Just as she closed the fridge, Tracy spotted Olivia walking toward the foyer. "Good morning, sleepyhead," she called out. Olivia was still in her pajamas, complete with tangled hair. Tracy smiled and added, "I'm certain you aren't going anywhere dressed like that."

"Yeah, right, Mom," she chuckled. "I was just opening the blinds. It's too dark down here." She joined Tracy in the kitchen. "It looks like we're gonna get more rain."

Tracy took one look at Olivia's puffy face and said, "Okay, what's happened with the infamous Sean this time?" She slipped back onto the barstool.

Olivia fell silent. She set about seeking food for her starving stomach, padding over to their walk-in pantry. She had awakened not only to find Valerie still sound asleep beside her, but also to the sound of a growling tummy. Finding nothing in the pantry that she wanted, she closed the wide door and went to the refrigerator, deciding on bacon and eggs.

"There's nothing there, honey. I'm doing the list now," Tracy supplied. "Now, tell me what happened." She reached up and turned down the animated chatter of the animal hunter.

Olivia took the stool next to her mother, and a fresh pool of tears managed to build up in her eyes. "Mommy . . . oh, Mom . . ." She laid her head on Tracy's shoulder. "Jackie. He's still seeing Jackie." She paused and wiped her tears. "I went over there last night, and they were locked up in his room together. He didn't even open the door after I screamed and pounded on it for bloody murder. And what's worse, his brother, Vincent, basically told me straight out that Jackie never actually left the picture." She sniffled and blew her already sore and tender nose in a napkin. "He said the *whole family* knew that Jackie was the only girl Sean's ever really loved." She sobbed.

Her mother let her weep, remaining silent for several minutes. Finally, she quietly said, "I think I know where this is headed, but I don't think there's anything I can do about it." She placed a soft kiss on Olivia's forehead. "Hon, you've got to be smart about Sean. It's obvious that he cares a great deal about you, and that he's a fun guy to have around. But what's that doing for you, Liv? At the end of the day, you're left with this broken heart." She laid her cheek on Olivia's head. "Has it been worth it? Would it be worth it to continue holding out hope for this relationship?"

"Mom—"

"Hold on, wait a minute," Tracy cut her off. "It's also painfully obvious that he's still tremendously wrapped up with Jacquelyn. I mean, if his own *brother* is tipping you off . . ." She fell silent, shook her head. "I'm not telling you it's gonna be easy, but just think about the facts and make a solid decision, because, honey, I hate seeing you in so much pain."

Tracy chose her next words carefully. "In light of all this, what do you want to do about the baby, Liv?"

"Oh, Mom, what *can* I do?" she sobbed. "That's what's *really* eating me raw!"

Tracy raised her shoulder, forcing her daughter to look at her. "Have an abortion, Olivia," she said simply.

Olivia closed her eyes. Then she really bawled.

She had known two weeks ago, the very day she missed her period, that she was pregnant. She went to the doctor's office only to confirm it. The first—and only—person she had told was her mother. She had wanted to share the news with Sean, but at the perfect time and place. She had yet to find either. "When can I get it done? Daddy's supposed to be home this week, and I don't want him to know anything, Mom. You understand?"

"I understand," Tracy said, smoothing her hair. "You know I won't tell your father if you prefer he didn't know. I'm just so relieved that you're making this decision." They hugged, and Tracy held her tight. "The last thing you need to do now is ruin your beautiful youth by becoming a single mother at such a young age. It would break our hearts to see that happen to you." After a pause, she added, "Thank God I never had to raise you two alone, without a father. I can't imagine what being a single mother would've been like for me—I certainly don't want that for you or Valerie."

"Well, you know, you practically have been a single mother for all the time we've seen Daddy in the last ten years. But look at what happened. I think it's so weird. We leaned on you, and you leaned on Uncle Frank," Olivia chuckled through the tears.

"Shhh," Tracy put a finger over her lips and quickly glanced toward the doorway. "Watch it, now. . . . Don't say that too loud, Olivia. Your sister's got big ears, you know. Is she up yet?"

"No. I left her in my room, fast asleep. She woke me up so early this morning. . . . Which reminds me . . ." She sat straight up, touching her mother's arm. "Mom, you've got to be careful. Valerie's getting ridiculous—"

"Tell me about it! Can you believe she flat out insinuated that I didn't want your father to make his schedule change?"

"Uh-huh, she told me that. But listen to me. She told Debbie to follow you later on to see where you run off to every night when Daddy's in Orlando."

"She what?" Tracy practically shrieked. "*Told Debbie to follow me?* Oh, my God." She covered her mouth. Seconds passed. Finally, she said, "You know what this means? If she's filling Deborah's head with her nonsense, what's to stop Debbie from telling her mother? Maybe now Reggie's entire family suspects I'm seeing another man. . . . Oh, my God!" she said in a sudden panic. "Damn it."

"So what are you gonna do? Besides, it's not nonsense, Mom. She just doesn't know who to put at the end of the equals sign, but Valerie's got the equation down to a T."

Tracy rubbed the side of her head. "I feel helpless," she murmured, more to herself than to Olivia. "My hands are tied. How can I scold Valerie in a situation like this when I'm up to my elbows in wrongdoing myself? What in the world can I possibly say to her without feeling like a hypocrite the size of Mount Rushmore?" It was impossible.

Tracy closed her eyes and shook her head. "Oh, Olivia, make sure you never get yourself into a situation like this. I'll tell you now from experience, it's completely avoidable. Damn! I should have seen this coming. No wonder she's become so cheeky." Tracy rose from the stool and reached for the kitchen telephone.

"What are you gonna do? Who are you calling?"

"I'm gonna call Deborah and give her a piece of my mind. She's old enough to know better. She should've called me the *instant* Valerie came to her with such a disrespectful proposition."

"Wait, wait, wait . . ." Olivia reached for the phone and put it back in the handset. "If you do that, Valerie will know that I told you and she'll be highly upset. She'd never tell me anything again. Can't you just wait till Debbie's following you? Catch her on the road? Then you can take it from there."

Nodding her head, Tracy replied, "Yeah . . . yeah, you're right. That's a better idea. And I'll also be giving Thelma a call to set the record straight, because I'm betting that Debbie's already spread the news to her mother. I couldn't imagine her sitting on something like this."

Thelma was Reginald's only sister and three years his senior. They were extremely close, and she and Olivia both knew that Thelma wouldn't waste a millisecond in phoning Reginald with a suspicion.

"Anyway, Mom, back to me. When can we get this done?"

Tracy pushed her own woes aside and focused once again on Olivia. Her eldest daughter. Their firstborn. Their pride and joy. Oh, what a happy time it had been when she was born! And now Olivia was pregnant with her own baby. Unfortunately, the timing—and the father— just weren't right. Tracy grieved. "Call Dr. Gabriel first thing on Monday and set up a morning appointment. We'll have to do it one morning when your father's at work and Valerie's in school."

"Okay." Olivia hesitated. "And what about you and Uncle Frank? You know, with Daddy being home and all? I'm sure you've been worrying about that a lot. . . ."

Tracy expelled a long breath and ran a hand through her hair. "Olivia, have you ever thought about your father and me splitting up?"

"Splitting up? You mean divorce? Is it that serious with Uncle Frank, Mom?"

"I think so. I mean, there's still a lot to sort out before it comes to that, but the truth is that things just aren't the same with your father and me anymore. I won't go into details, but things have really changed for me in the last few years. . . . And for him, too, I think." Tracy remembered the strange tone of Reggie's voice last night, though she wasn't prepared to share that with Olivia, knowing how she already felt about him.

"Well, you know what I think. God would have to come down out of the sky to tell me that Daddy doesn't leave a pack of heartsick women in Orlando when he comes home to work. Well, he must," she added quickly, when Tracy tried to interrupt. "Half my friends want to date my dad—women go gaga over him. I'm sure he's not beating them *all* off with his wedding ring."

"Listen, true or not, that's not for you to be concerned with—you're getting to be just as bad as Valerie." Tracy rose and snapped off the television set. "Things happen, Olivia, and we may not always make the right choices, but we are still your parents, and both you and Valerie better not ever forget it."

Olivia fell silent.

"Go up and wake Valerie, and let's go out for breakfast. I'm starving, and I know you are, too." Tracy stepped toward the stairway. "We'll get dressed and go have brunch at Brixel's. Then we can stop for groceries." She paused at the door and turned back to Olivia. Softening her tone, she said, "And honey, I know it's hard, but try not to worry about this thing." She cupped Olivia's jaw. "It'll be fine. Just call on Monday, and we'll take care of it. It'll all work out for the best." She hugged her close. "And like I said, get wise about Sean."

Tracy released her slowly and left the kitchen.

12

AFTER CHECKING HIS e-mail, Franklin signed off the computer and took the last sip of his black coffee. He'd been irritable all morning, so he hadn't bothered to visit the gym as he normally did on Saturday afternoons. Instead, he stayed home with his thoughts.

I've been doing that a lot lately, he thought matter-of-factly. He grabbed his mug and left the spare bedroom, which served as his work-at-home office.

His thoughts were full of Tracy. Her talk of ending their affair had really sobered him. He had always fancied the notion that she was smitten with him and couldn't get enough, in spite of her fronts to suggest it was purely physical. Perhaps she really *was* cavalier about their affair. Maybe, in all actuality, he was simply a stand-in for Reginald's absence in her bed. . . .

TEN MINUTES LATER, as he laced his Reeboks, Franklin felt his temper brewing. He didn't like these thoughts he was having. He didn't like them at all. Was she truly serious about calling it quits? What if she really meant it and it was all over? The frustration mounted.

I sure as hell can't slip quietly back into the role of supportive friend, he thought, leaving his apartment, *just casually watching them live happily ever after.*

Downstairs, he climbed into his SUV. Since his servicing was long overdue, he decided to take the car to the dealership. Then he'd head over to see Tracy. They needed to talk more about this whole thing. If he could only see her face-to-face, get her alone.

He wasn't ready to do away with her just yet. It would end when *he* decided it was time—and not a moment sooner.

THE BRIXEL'S ON Miami Lakes Drive was packed. With its airy, pastel décor and excellent cuisine, it was their favorite place to have breakfast. The walls were pinstriped in lime green and beige wallpaper, and throughout the restaurant there were heaps of hanging greenery and standing plants. The pleasant setting, coupled with the trademark cuisine, was more than likely what kept the customers out of the Waffle House across the street.

After dropping the car off with the valet, Tracy, Olivia, and Valerie entered Brixel's, hoping for a good table. They were disappointed when the hostess seated them in a booth near the buffet carousel. Hordes of hungry patrons, incessantly spouting mindless chatter, shuffled past them. The restaurant was abuzz with chatter, so to be heard, they spoke with slightly raised voices.

Over a breakfast of scrambled eggs and buttery pancakes, and despite the restaurant's Saturday morning noise, Olivia managed to hear her pager chime.

"That'd be Sean," Valerie announced, salting her hash browns.

Olivia's heart dripped with relief. It flowed from her mouth on a sigh, but she said nothing. It had been a long, abysmal night not hearing from him. She unclipped the beeper from her waist to verify that the page was indeed from Sean. It was. Her chest rose and fell on another tidal wave of relief.

"Don't dare call him, Liv. Just forget him," Valerie advised around a mouthful of hash browns.

Tracy noticed the relief that crossed her daughter's face as the pager chimed. Poor Olivia. She sensed what was ahead; she had a premonition that they had not seen or heard the last of Mr. Sean Johnson.

Over the next ten minutes, while they were engrossed in animated chatter, Olivia received several more pages. Tracy saw her resolve to stay angry slipping away with every chirp.

Olivia reached for the carafe, refilling her orange juice. Sean was trying to get in touch with her, no doubt wanting to explain, to apologize. She found herself suddenly eager to talk to him, to hear his explanation. *If he didn't care, he wouldn't even bother,* she thought, swallowing orange juice. She felt better now—much better. He was calling. He was calling. She wanted to fly.

Fingering her coffee cup, Tracy decided it was time to raise the subject of their father. "Your dad says he wants to take a vacation soon. You girls know where you'd want to go?" She eyed Olivia carefully and brought the mug to her lips.

Olivia groaned as she chewed the last bite of her sausage link. "I already told Daddy I have to pass on the vacation—too much schoolwork. You should know better, Mom." Olivia wiped her mouth with a napkin and sat back in the booth, folding her arms. "You guys can go ahead, and I hope you have a great time. But I'll pass."

Valerie drank the last of her orange juice and, obviously annoyed, reached to pour more from the carafe. "You know, you really tick me off when you talk like that, as if you're some sort of outsider and you only look down at the rest of us from the bridge of your snooty little nose. You need to cut it out, Liv. You *politely* act like you're not part of this family sometimes, and it's really starting to make me sick," she said, disgusted.

"Yeah, well, excuse me if I'm not so good with charades. I don't just sit around waiting for the man of the house to put in an appearance. If I'm busy, I'm busy. You guys will just have to launch the perfect family show without me." Olivia paused and bit her cheek. "I'll tell you what's starting to make me sick. . . . Having you jump down my throat whenever Dad's brought up. That's what's starting to make *me* sick," she shot back.

"Okay, I've heard enough," Valerie said, slamming the carafe back on the table. "What's your real problem? Daddy's always gone out of his way to coddle you, but you never give him lunch, Olivia! What's wrong with you?" After a pause, Valerie added, "You act like he's some stranger off the street that you don't even want to see! It's like he's not even your father!" Her voice had raised a few decibels.

Five Hispanics at a nearby table peeked at them curiously.

"You know, come to think of it, that really isn't all that far from reality, is it?" Olivia said matter-of-factly. "After all, in the last ten years, I'm lucky if I've seen him for all of ten minutes. Who is he, really? The tall man who pays all the bills, buys all the clothes, and strides in and out of the house the whole two weeks that he's home. *You* can pretend you grew up with a father if you want to, Valerie, but leave me out of it. If he really cared anything about us he would've raised us!" She clenched her teeth. "He would've been here when we were sick, he would've been at all our softball games, and he would've showed up for our school plays. I don't know if you remember him being at any of yours, but I only saw Mom or Uncle Frank at mine."

"But you're making it sound like he's been neglecting us or something! Like we've never had a father that supported us. Like he wasn't out there workin' his butt off to keep us living like queens— *like queens*!" Valerie's eyes were blazing. "All I want to know is how long you're gonna hold this petty grudge against him? How long do you think you can avoid him?" She turned to Tracy. "Mom, don't you think she acts like she doesn't even want him in the house sometimes?"

Total disbelief on her face, Tracy just stared at them. "Is this what it's gonna be like when Reginald comes home?" she said, shaking her head. "Oh, no."

Olivia had had enough. She couldn't listen to Valerie defend their here today, but gone tomorrow father any longer. She raised the palm of her hand toward Valerie's face. "I've heard enough. I've said enough. This conversation is over."

Valerie swatted Olivia's hand to the side. "Oh, no you don't!" Not nearly finished, she seemed oblivious to the nosy Hispanics drinking in every word from their table. "You really make me sick about this! *You're* never home half the time either, Olivia! And you don't cut him any slack when he *is* home. All you do is talk about him like he's a fifth cousin twice removed—like he's neither here nor there! And the guy you *should* be talking like that about gets all the love and attention! How come you don't condemn Sean the way you do Daddy, huh? How come he gets forgiveness for the stunts he pulls, but Daddy serves a life sentence for going off to work? Explain that one!"

"Valerie, you better shut the . . . you better shut up!" Olivia threatened through clenched teeth. She bit back an expletive since their mother *was* present.

"Truth hurts, doesn't it, Olivia? Sean is a saint, while Daddy's nothing more than a stranger! But who's the *real* stranger? The one who's out working to feed you and keep a roof over your head, or the one who's out humpin' Jackie Henderson—and God knows who else—to bring your stuck-up ass AIDS? I bet—"

"Valerie, that's enough!" Tracy stage-whispered. "Am I the only one of the three of us that's aware we have an audience?" She leaned closer. "This is disgraceful, you two. This has to stop."

"No, Mom, let her talk. She's the woman of the house now, after all, isn't she? Hell, she's sure acting like it. Seventeen years old, and she puts a tail on her own mother!"

Suddenly, as though a bucket of ice water had been thrown at her, Valerie's frustrated rage died. She fell back as if shoved, hitting the soft cushioning of the booth.

"Yes, I found out all about that, Miss Valerie Brooks. And make no mistake, your father's gonna get an earful first thing when he returns— you can take that to the bank. It's high time you were cut back down to size. We'll talk about it—in detail—when he gets home."

Valerie glanced at her sister. Filled with a dreadful foreboding, she was close to wetting her pants. There would be hell to pay now. Pure hell. She would have to call Debbie. . . . And soon.

Olivia glanced around, and still seething from Valerie's hurtful tirade, noticed their spectators for the first time. She was amazed that they had managed to draw such attention in the already noisy and crowded restaurant. She gave them a dirty look, and all five pairs of eyes averted, as though they hadn't heard a thing, suddenly becoming most intrigued by their steaming breakfast plates and shiny silverware.

"Okay, now listen to me, both of you," Tracy began quietly. She leaned even closer to the table. "This has got to stop, and the two of you have got to find a way to resolve this war about Reginald. He *is* your father and he wants to make up for lost time, so the last thing we should do is give him grief about it, okay?

"His heart's in the right place, girls. True, Orlando has kept him away a lot of the years, but it was only because of his ambitions to make sure we were all well provided for. And he's done an excellent job of that, hasn't he? Look at the restaurant we're eating in." She extended her arms, indicating the table. "None of us can complain that we've ever been in need of anything. Whether it was food, clothes, shelter, enter-tainment, or anything else. We've had it all. We've needed nothing."

The table fell silent.

Finally, Olivia said, "We've needed nothing, huh?" She glanced left, out the large window, overwhelmed. "Nothing . . . except him."

Her words set in—intensely. The sky was overcast, and murky clouds seemed to be itching to release a torrent of rain.

No one said a word.

They each knew the truth. The long-ignored truth. All the table's passion and energy had been reduced to three words.

A smiling waitress appeared then, her smile so bright and cheerful it cracked their table's cocoon like a rock. "More coffee, ma'am?" she of-fered Tracy, poised to pour the steaming liquid.

Tracy cleared the lump from her throat. "Um, no, thank you. We're fine." She reached into her leather purse for cash, eager to leave the crowded restaurant. "We'll have the check now."

They waited quietly, in emotional ambiguity, for the waitress to re-turn with the change.

When they left Brixel's, it was in a cloud of silence as deafening as the boisterous chatter within.

SEAN RESISTED THE urge to crank his engine and head back home. Maybe Jackie was still in his bed. . . .

The middle-aged couple next door had just returned from wherever they had gone, and he was still sitting there feeling like an idiot. He'd been there when they'd left more than two hours before.

He was parked alongside the lawn in the circular driveway of the Brooks' illustrious home in Miami Lakes. Having listened to one entire side of a cassette, he was growing restless and cramped in his car. He was also feeling ill at ease, as he always did, in Olivia's wealthy sur-roundings. Oddly enough, though, this was why he kept her close. She was a special girl, far different from Jackie—and far more valuable, he acknowledged regrettably.

He jumped up, catching himself snoring, just in time to see Tracy Brooks' Cherokee entering the garage. It had also begun to rain again.

He climbed out of the car, slammed the door, and then sprinted up the long driveway, hurrying to take shelter before they brought the door down.

The first person to acknowledge his presence, to his surprise, was Tracy. She shut the door of the Jeep and walked toward the open garage door where he stood. Her eyes dared him to come any closer. The rain came down in light sheets, blowing into the garage and wetting him, but he didn't move any closer.

Tracy stared at Sean. *Look at him,* she thought. *Olivia can do a thousand times better than this—there's no way in hell she's gonna have this creep's baby.* "I want you to listen to me, Sean, and I want you to listen with both ears." Tracy spoke slowly, careful not to raise her voice. "You are no longer welcome in this house or on this property. Liv doesn't care to see you right now. . . . Neither do the rest of us. After what—"

"But, Mrs. Brooks." Sean raised his hands. "It's all just a big misunderstanding, and I can clear it up if she'll just listen to me!" By the look on his face, Tracy knew that he was definitely full of shit. He was a horrible liar.

Olivia, leaving the Jeep, headed for the doorway that led into the house without even bothering to glance at Sean. Reaching the door, she slung over her shoulder, "You heard my mother, Sean. Go away. It's over. . . . *And don't bother coming back.*" She let the door slam behind her, completing the act. Valerie followed suit, clearly preoccupied, without a word of greeting to Sean, whom she'd always been fond of.

Sean's shoulders slumped and he shifted weight, looking uncomfortable. "Oh, come on, what's all that for? Did she really say 'don't ever come back'? She doesn't mean that. She's just upset. I'll be back."

"You heard her, Sean," Tracy said, turning toward the door. "Leave. Go find someone else's daughter to toy with." She placed a finger on the garage door button, ready to press it. She looked right at him. "My garage is getting wet."

Undeterred, Sean shrugged and sprinted back to his Skylark, only to find that he had left his windows down.

*   *   *

FROM HER ARCHED bedroom window upstairs, Olivia watched Sean drive away, muttering and cursing in his water-soaked car. After slamming the door on him downstairs, she had hurried up to her room, wanting to ride out the assault of conflicting emotions before anyone noticed. She had an overwhelming urge to call him, make him fill her head with apologies, but she suppressed it quickly. *No, no,* she thought. *He should work hard to get me back this time. Then he'll think twice about that Jacquelyn bitch.*

OLIVIA RETURNED DOWNSTAIRS to help Tracy and Valerie unpack the groceries. Just as when they had left Brixel's and headed for the grocery store, no one spoke.

The telephone rang as Tracy was stacking meat in the standing freezer. Olivia, standing closer to the stationery nook, reached for the cordless and tossed it to her mother. She was not in the mood to speak to anybody.

Tracy caught the phone and balanced it on her shoulder. "Hello?"

"Hi, honey." It was Reginald.

"Hey!" she said cheerfully.

"I'm in the office—busy as hell—but I wanted to hear your voice. What's going on down there?"

"Well, we just got back from the grocery store, the three of us," Tracy replied. She resisted an urge to fill him in on the situation with Valerie. That could wait until he came home. "We went out for breakfast first, though."

"Went out for breakfast, huh?" Reggie sighed. "I know this may sound a little pointless and irrational, but . . . I regret that I wasn't there." After a pause, he added, "I'm sorry I missed breakfast, and even doing groceries. . . ."

Tracy heard longing in his voice. She wondered what had sparked this change in him. "Oh, honey, let it go now. Stop beating yourself up. We'll have our quality time—things will improve. It's all right." She paused and closed the freezer. "So, any idea yet when you'll be home?" She remembered her unfinished business with Frank. To her surprise, she hadn't thought much of him all day. *Too much going on right now with the kids,* she thought.

"I'm almost a hundred percent sure that I'll be ready to leave before Wednesday. I don't expect it can be any sooner, with all the meetings that have to take place between now and then. Right now I'm drafting some memos that need to be disseminated, and then I'm outta here. Roger's in town, and we're gonna do some golfing down at The Bay Club."

Tracy laughed and said, "Are that Springer woman and her husband still members of that club? Because whenever you run into her there, make sure she knows that you're still *my* husband." Tracy had met the elegant Eunice Springer on one of her brief visits to Orlando. Despite the fact that she was *very* married, it was obvious that Eunice would be more than willing to bed Reginald in a room full of people. Tracy had even suspected, although she never voiced it, that the attraction was mutual.

Reginald laughed. "Hey, listen, none of that jealousy stuff. Eunice *is* a married woman, and besides, I only have eyes for you."

"Yeah, yeah, yeah. Well, you just come on back home and prove it. I miss you. . . ." She was mindful to endear him. The last thing she needed, on top of everything else, was for Reginald's eyebrows to be raised prematurely. Everything had to happen at the right time—whenever that was going to be.

By the time she hung up, Olivia and Valerie had both finished unpacking and left the kitchen. She breathed a long sigh. *He can't come home and find them like this,* she thought. *I have to make them iron out this mess. . . . And there's no time like the present.*

TRACY HAD JUST emptied the dryer when she heard Franklin's distinguished voice in the foyer. Valerie had let him in.

So it's working, she thought. He had heard her words last night— loud and clear.

"Hi, Uncle Frank!" she heard Valerie saying. "We hardly ever see you anymore. Where have you been?" After a pause, Valerie digressed. "Uncle Frank, your hands are empty. . . . You didn't bring us any gifts?"

Franklin laughed. "Oh, no! How dare I show up here empty-handed?" He shook his head. "Bring something ninety-nine times out of a hundred, and they act like you never brought anything at all!" He smiled. "Next time, honey." Footsteps sounded toward the kitchen as Frank asked, "So, are you glad your dad's changing that lousy Orlando schedule?"

Valerie hesitated for only a second before she replied, "Of course I'm happy. I can't wait! It's gonna be so different and exciting. I mean, it's been so long since he worked like normal people, you know, without all that traveling. . . . It'll be great for a change."

"True, because I know it hasn't been easy for him, basically living in two places," Frank said, nodding. "Where's your mother? I left her a message about that sprinkler system problem, but she never called me back, so I stopped in to take a look at it."

"I don't really know where she is," Valerie replied. "The last time I saw her, she was in the kitchen talking to Daddy on the phone. Maybe she's in her room."

Frank fell silent and waited as Valerie backed out into the foyer, paging her parents' room from the built-in intercom. He had stiffened at the mentioning of Reginald. Since when did hearing that he and Tracy spoke on the phone disturb him?

Tracy made her presence known then, carrying an armful of whites. "Hey, Frank, what's up? I did get that message, but I just haven't had the time to get back to you. You're right, though—something's got to be causing the pump to shut off as soon as it hits that third zone." Heading for the staircase, she said, "Give me a minute, okay? I'll put these away, and we can go take a look at it."

She hoped, while heading up the stairs, that this visit would be a productive one.

THEY WERE OUTSIDE, heading for the side of the house, with umbrellas to shield from the rain, when Tracy said, "Why did you come?"

"I came because . . ." Franklin hesitated. Why had he come? "I came because I'm not ready to call us off yet, Tracy. I mean, so suddenly . . . just like that?" He snapped his long fingers. *Just like that?*"

She looked offended. "Well, what else would you have me do? I mean, seeing you now—" She glanced around and moved in closer to the sprinkler pump, as if to make certain that if anyone happened to notice them, it would look like the subject of their deep discussion. "It would be a very different offense with him at home, Franklin. I mean, I just can't do the creeping around and the lying right to his face, day in and day out. I just can't! So it's really best if we call it quits." Tracy paused, and then added casually, "What's the big deal, anyway? It's just good sex. . . . And Theresa's around to keep up with you there."

"No, you're wrong, Tracy," he said seriously. "It's *great* sex—there's a big difference." Then he smiled.

If she was further offended, it did not show. "Okay, great sex. But just the same, it's run its course—we're done."

"Well, can I still expect you tonight?" He raised an eyebrow enticingly. "We should at least have a grand finale, you know."

Tracy filled him in on Valerie's scheme to have Deborah follow her.

"I don't know what you two are gonna do with that little busybody. I suggest you lock her little ass away in that room until she's eighteen, and then you pitch her out and let her be little miss grown-up over on that sidewalk." He pointed towards the road.

"You just wait until Reggie gets home. Let him deal with her for a change. She's getting to be too much for me," she said, twirling the handle of her umbrella. "Anyway, that means things have certainly gotten far too dangerous for us—all the more reason for us to end this. I mean, let's suppose she had gotten away with it? Deborah would have followed me straight to San Marco, and that would have been a fatal disaster."

Frank could not believe, as he gazed down at her from under the large umbrella, that she was being so cavalier about doing away with him. It hurt his pride—not to mention his huge ego, with respect to the attributes of his lovemaking. "Well, what did Deborah have to say about it?"

"I haven't spoken to her yet. I figured I might as well lay low and let Reginald come handle the whole mess. You know how Thelma is. If *I* confront Debbie, then I may end up looking as guilty as they probably think I am. It's best if Reginald handles this one."

Using the umbrella to block them from the view of any onlookers, Franklin stooped over the sprinkler pump and looked up into her face. "Come by tonight. No one's gonna follow you now that they've been called on the carpet. Just check your rearview to be certain. . . . And come see me tonight." She looked about to object, and he rushed on. "Baby, we haven't done it since before Reginald came back. It's been a while. Come on, one last time . . ."

TRACY HAD CAVED. She'd agreed to meet later that night for one last . . . fuck. Clearly, that's all it was to Franklin, after all—fucking.

She put off talking to Olivia and Valerie, nursing a resentful mood, until the following day. She resented that Frank did not want more— more than just sex. She resented the years she'd spent thinking they should ever have more. But most of all, she resented the fact that she was looking forward to being with him that night.

She would give him one more night. She would give in to him one more time, but it would be the last time—no more. Pride would not allow her to risk disclosing what he obviously didn't realize. Tracy had known the risk she was taking when she advised him she wanted to end the affair.

It had been a gamble. . . . And it was disturbingly obvious that she had lost.

13

LATER THAT EVENING, Tracy dressed simply in a black cotton strapless dress with matching sandals. She secured her hair with a large barrette, allowing a few tendrils to hang free around her face. Her stomach felt light. This would be her last night with Franklin. She felt uneasy at the thought. . . . And she had to shake it before Reginald came home. It seemed everyone in the house had issues to deal with where he was concerned.

She had confined Valerie to the walls of her bedroom, ordering her not to come out. Tracy made certain, reminding her of Reginald's wrath, Valerie didn't doubt the fact that he would hear about her behavior as soon as he walked through the door.

She still couldn't believe Valerie's presumptuousness! Trying to have her followed? The kid was totally out of order.

She selected a fine pair of knob earrings, surveyed her appearance, and headed out for her night of bittersweet pleasure.

FRANKLIN WAS WAITING patiently for Tracy's arrival.

For the sake of his sanity, he had resolved his unexpected—and overwhelming—feelings of hostility. If she wanted to end it, fine. He wasn't about to make a fool of himself begging her for sex as he'd done earlier that afternoon. He had cursed himself savagely on the drive back home. What had he been thinking? *She* should be the one begging *him,* not the other way around!

Well, he would show her tonight. He was gonna lay her, and he was gonna lay her really good. He'd give her something to think about, and then he'd sit back and wait for her to run back for more. . . . And he knew it would only be a matter of time. But *she* had to do the chasing.

He had taken a shower, brushed his teeth, and dabbed Eternity on his skin. Now he sat in his recliner, absently watching an old Bruce Lee flick, waiting patiently for her arrival. His mind drifted to the last time they had been together. She had met him for lunch in his office, and they had ended up panting and dripping sweat all over his leather sofa.

Franklin grew hard at the memory. He became restless, losing all patience, waiting for Tracy to ring the doorbell.

AS SHE NEARED the San Marco Apartments, Tracy had a sudden desire to weep.

What had she really done with her life? She was willing to leave her husband, who had always meant the world to her, for Franklin, who was his best friend, not to mention a notorious womanizer. And now, on account of her guilty conscience, she felt like a hypocrite for reprimanding her own child.

How had she gotten into this chaos? And more importantly, how was she going to get out of it?

Their conversation earlier that day had been a rude awakening. She now knew that it would be foolish to continue sleeping with Frank after tonight. She wasn't willing to throw her marriage away for a man that was only using her for sex—especially when that man was Franklin Bevins.

This will be it, she told herself, parking the Jeep. Tonight would be the last chapter in their clandestine book. Ambivalence consumed her, though. There was an odd awareness surrounding her. Was she disappointed . . . or relieved?

Tracy climbed the stairs slowly, not wanting to rush. As an aside, she wanted tonight to be memorable, since it *would* be the last. She reached the door, about to ring the bell, when it was jerked open suddenly. She gasped.

FRANK TOOK IN her short, sexy dress and beautifully wholesome face. He grew even harder.

He stepped aside, saying nothing, and allowed her to move past him, then locked the door. He backed her into the sofa. She fell backward, and he went down with her.

Grazing her thighs, Frank inched the dress up to her waist and slid off her silky panties, tossing them to the floor.

Parting her thighs, he lowered his head.

Tracy froze. He was going down! In the four years of their affair, Franklin had *never* gone down on her before. *Oh yes,* she thought.

Slowly, Frank's tongue began moving back and forth over her clitoris. She moaned.

Several minutes passed, but she could not climax. His performance was less than adequate. He had managed to lubricate her, however, so he raised himself, rolled on a condom, and pressed himself into her. He groaned with pleasure as Tracy's body enveloped him with a firm grip.

Bracing himself on the sofa's edge, Frank rode Tracy for as long as he could before she manipulated that familiar—and mind-blowing—surge of release. He hollered, as he always did when she made him climax. He fell on top of her, out of breath.

Tracy was even more confused than before. She had had no release, and he'd even gone down on her for the first time! Suddenly ashamed, she found herself wishing she had Reginald to go home to. *You truly are a slut,* she thought.

Frank rose up, pulling himself out of her. They chuckled at the pop of suction as he did so. He went to the half-bath across the room—he had a habit of washing himself immediately after sex—and then rejoined her in the living room.

"What was your hurry?" Tracy asked from her place on the sofa. She had retrieved her underwear and was smoothing down her dress.

"I was hard."

"Um," she replied. She felt like a fool for being there, and she was irritated for not having had her own release. "Well, now that you've had your grand finale, I have to go." She moved to stand.

"Not so fast, Tracy. You think I'm gonna let you leave without . . . you know . . . coming?" He grinned, approaching her. "I'm not that out of touch, you know. I know you didn't make it."

"Oh," Tracy said sarcastically. "You noticed?"

He picked her up, carrying her to his bed. He removed her dress and kissed his way down to her femininity. He proceeded to lick and suck, only succeeding at teasing her. Just when she reached the edge of a climax, he would weaken the pressure of his mouth and she would lose the high. When more than ten minutes had passed, she thought, *It's no use.*

She faked the orgasm.

Satisfied that he had blown her mind, Frank rolled on another rubber and plunged into her a second time. He groaned once again in utter satisfaction, this time stroking slow and easy. He gritted his teeth, trying to fight the orgasm, but it was no use. It was never any use. Tracy always won.

AFTERWARD, FRANK GOT a beer and sat on the edge of the bed. "So this is it, huh?"

"Yeah, this is it," Tracy said. She felt awful. She had never had to fake an orgasm with Frank before tonight. It was a bad omen.

There was a heavy silence.

"What would you do," Frank said, breaking the quiet, "if Reginald had another woman?"

"What?"

"What would you do if Reggie had another woman?" He watched closely, appearing eager to see her reaction.

Tracy was speechless. How could she discuss that with Frank of all people? At a complete loss for words, she joked, "Why are you asking? Do you know something I don't?"

"No, I was just wondering. . . . Would something like that upset you?"

"Well . . ." she groped for words. "Sure I'd be upset. He's been my husband for almost twenty years. I'm sure I'd be a tad upset."

"You wouldn't think he was entitled to it? Under the circumstances?"

"You know, Frank, I don't really think we should be having this conversation. Can we just drop it, talk about something else?" Why was he asking her this all of a sudden? She was very uncomfortable.

"Okay, it's dropped. . . . But no more talking." He set aside his beer can and moved over her. "One more for the road?"

They had sex again, and it was no different for Tracy than the two times prior. In fact, it was worse, since he had brought up Reginald.

She left the apartment, feeling the same as she did when she arrived—like a lost floozy.

THE FOLLOWING DAY, Tracy tried to get her daughters to listen to reason. Gathered around the kitchen table, Olivia and Valerie nearly began another heated altercation over their father. Valerie remained protective and sympathetic about Reginald, while Olivia was equally blasé and critical.

Stressing that she did not want Reggie coming home to find such an atmosphere, Tracy finally gave up. Olivia was not going to mitigate. Clearly, there stood a wall of resentment toward her father. It disturbed Tracy immensely. She pondered over it most of the day and into the night, unable to reconcile the situation in her own mind.

That night, as she drifted off to sleep, Tracy wept.

What was to become of their family?

14

ORLANDO, FLORIDA

REGINALD SPENT HIS entire Sunday at home with Renee and Denise. They watched movies, munched popcorn, and ate ice cream. Denise was deliriously happy.

Despite his efforts, he sensed that Renee knew something was amiss. Sure, he was there with them, spending as much time as he had promised, but he had changed. Though she tried, Reggie noticed that she couldn't quite conceal her worries.

He knew he was not leaving things with Renee as secure as they could be, but he simply couldn't help himself. His spirit had left him, gotten a head start to Miami. . . . And he couldn't keep the need to catch up with it out of his eyes.

LATER THAT NIGHT when they were in bed, Reginald decided it was time to leave. There was no need to stay past tomorrow. He would surprise Tracy and the girls by flying in early.

Paperwork could be faxed, phone calls could be made, e-mails could be sent; his physical presence in Orlando was no longer essential. He said as much to Renee now.

"So, what time is your flight?" Renee asked in her low voice.

"Not until late. I have meetings throughout the day and Roger's going to be present, so I'm not really sure how long they'll be." He turned away from her, rolling to his side and pulling the sheet over himself.

Renee stared at his form under the covers. He was obviously very worried about his daughter. He seemed so distant. *It's like he's already gone,* she thought sadly.

She moved up against his back. "When can we expect you back . . . for a visit at least?"

Reggie turned and faced her again. "Listen, sweetheart, don't worry. I'll be in touch. Things are so uncertain right now that I can't, in good faith, give you a date when I'll make it back. But I'll keep in touch—I promise. I'll keep you posted about what's going on, and I *will* try my best to fly back up here and see you as much as possible." He pulled her against him.

"I'm gonna miss you so much," she whispered, hugging him close.

"I know, honey, I'm sorry. . . . I'm gonna miss you, too, and Denise." He paused briefly before saying, "Hey, I meant to ask you about Helen. How did she react to the news?"

"She was quite upset and, of course, she thinks you're lying about everything." She paused, waiting for his reply.

"I guess I was expecting that. I thought a lot about discussing this with your family—especially your parents—but with all that's going on right now . . ." He sighed. "I just can't see defending myself to anyone else. You do understand that, don't you?"

"Yes, of course I understand that, and don't worry about it. I'll handle them."

"I can only imagine how John's gonna react," Reggie said. John Jameson was Renee's older brother. He had always been in strong agreement with their parents' and Helen's opinion of the relationship.

"Did you hear me? I said don't worry about it, Reggie. Everything will be fine on this end. You just go and look after your daughter. Then hurry back home." She snuggled closer to him and kissed his cheek in the darkness.

He knew what that meant. Reginald moved over her and obliged.

MONDAY EVENING, ROGER Roman saw Reginald off on the Hart-Roman private jet. Roger was a broodingly attractive man of medium height and was often told he resembled a shorter version of Tyrone Powers.

Despite his marital status, he managed to maintain a very clandestine string of mistresses. Reginald had always assumed that over the years, Roger's willingness to support him could be attributed to his own elaborate misconduct; he empathized with Reggie.

Roger Roman was more than just a boss; he was a valuable friend, much like Franklin, and Reggie could not have survived the past six years without him. Roger had covered for him on many a risky occasion. He had even gotten him memberships to two very separate golf clubs so none of his and Renee's acquaintances would ever rub shoulders with any of his and Tracy's.

LATER, AS HE settled into the leather seat of the jet, sipping Scotch, Reginald said a prayer. He closed his eyes and asked God for forgiveness. He confessed that he had not told Renee the truth, but he feared losing Tracy—and that could never happen.

He prayed for Denise, asking God to protect her, to forgive his absence in her life. Somehow he'd make his mark on her from a distance, but for the time being, he had to break away.

He was heading home. . . . And this time, he was heading home for good.

PART TWO

15

TRACY AND OLIVIA WERE taking advantage of the fact that the rain had let up considerably since Saturday. Monday evening found them in their bathing suits, taking a leisurely swim in the pool. Tracy was trying once again—and failing once again—to get Olivia to lighten up on her father.

"All I'm asking is that you give your father a chance, Liv. Just let him try to make up for lost time." Tracy backstroked to the far end of their gigantic swimming pool.

Olivia pulled herself up to the edge, dangling her legs in the cool water. "Mom, you just don't get it. Dad's just trying to save face. And the only reason for that is that he must have something to hide." She paused. "I don't know. . . . I just don't think we mean as much to him as he wants us to believe."

Tracy pondered that. It wasn't true. Granted, Reggie had his moods, but she had never doubted his love for them. She told Olivia so now.

"By the way, I've been thinking a lot about getting my own place. I feel like it's time for me to go out on my own. You know, buy a condo or something. What do you think?"

"I think I want to know why you feel the need to run away from this house."

They both jumped, turning at the unexpected sound of Reginald's deep voice. He stepped from under the cupola, which extended several feet from the house.

"Honey! You're home!" Tracy was the first to recover, and she shot a glance at Olivia, terrified that perhaps Reginald had heard too much of the conversation.

"Yeah, I thought I'd surprise you guys. Now, Olivia, what's this talk about moving?"

Tracy groaned inwardly. This was exactly what she'd hoped to avoid.

Olivia stood and reached for her towel. "I just think it's time for me to get a place of my own—that's all. I'm not getting any younger, you know." She began toweling off, planning to make a quick retreat to the house.

Reginald flinched. "We're going to talk more about this later, okay?"

"Sure, Daddy, whatever you want," Olivia replied, skirting past him.

Reginald shook his head; his shoulders sagged as he looked down at Tracy.

She swam over to the edge, returning his gaze. "You know, Regg, if she wants to move, we can't really stop her," she said quietly. "She has her own money."

Reginald loosened his tie and sighed. He had arrived home to find Valerie by herself in the den, watching television. After hugging and chatting a bit, she told him where he could find the others.

Once he'd put away his traveling bag and briefcase, he headed out to the pool area just in time to hear Olivia declare that she was thinking of moving out. As he had approached, he'd heard their voices, but that was the only part of the conversation he was fully able to discern.

From the looks of it, he had an especially steep climb to repair his relationship with Olivia. But he welcomed the challenge. Nothing, from now on, would come between him and his family.

He removed his socks, trousers, and shirt, and joined Tracy in the pool with a huge splash, sending water everywhere. Underwater, he swam over and tickled the bottoms of her feet.

Tracy squealed, trying to get away from him. When he surfaced, he grabbed her head, pulling it to meet his kiss. He slipped her his tongue, and she gently wrapped her legs around his waist.

God, he had missed her. He didn't quite understand the sudden awareness of something that had been his own for years.

As the passion of their kiss increased, he made his presence felt between her thighs. Breaking the kiss, Tracy arched her neck; he buried his head, suckling the smooth skin there. Reggie ran his hands down the length of her back, cupping her buttocks. He rubbed her against his hardness. "Hmm," he moaned. "I missed you. . . . I want you."

Tracy moaned in agreement, her eyes glazed over with desire. Then common sense took over and she said against his lips, "It's too early, Regg. What if one of them comes out? It's . . . too . . . early." He was driving her mad, grinding against her sex. The water splashed around them.

"They won't come out," he whispered. "Besides, does it feel like I can wait?"

She chuckled through her desire. "You're right. But, let's go into the pool house. . . ."

Ignoring her, Reginald reached down and slid the bathing suit cloth to the side.

Tracy shuddered, held her breath.

He pushed his boxer shorts down and released himself—full, long, and pulsing in the indigo water. Guiding himself toward her beneath the surface, he probed her opening with the tip of his penis. Tracy pressed against it, eager to feel him inside her. With ease, he slipped into her body. They both moaned the pleasure. He sealed their lips together, and once the initial wave of pleasure subsided, began bouncing her lightly in the water.

Tracy came almost instantly. She moaned into his mouth and then threw her head back as he continued to stroke her for his own release.

Reggie slowly moved them over to the edge, resting his back against it. He stared into her drowsy eyes. "Ride me," he said hoarsely.

And she did. She rode him until they came together in the water.

16

VALERIE SAT IN her fifth-period biology class, making useless attempts to give Mrs. Lyman her undivided attention. She'd had the same problem in her previous four classes. As the white-haired teacher droned on about crustaceans and amphibians, Valerie could only think about the situation at home.

Her father had been home nearly a month now, and she was still paying for trying to have her mother followed. Reginald had blasted both she and Deborah for the scheme—a blasting they would not soon forget.

Valerie hated it when her father was upset with her. He had reproached her behavior and told her to remember her place as a child. He had also been outraged that she could spread such utterly dreadful speculation about her own mother.

He just doesn't understand, she thought. Valerie was certain that her mother was seeing someone else. She wondered if it would stop now that her dad was home. She resented Tracy for doing that to her father. How dare she be out sleeping with somebody else when their father had to be away, so hard at work! And Olivia was just as bad. She still wouldn't give him the time of day.

To Valerie's surprise, Olivia had not yet taken Sean back. He'd been by the house on several occasions, but Olivia refused to see him. Given their history, she had thought for sure they would've gotten back together by now.

Despite Reggie's attempts to engage her in conversations about a family vacation, Olivia remained noncommittal and distant. She only left the house to attend her day classes at the university and to view condos and town homes. She was now determined to find a place of her own.

At times, Valerie thought about going with her, but she didn't think she could live with Olivia. Olivia intentionally distanced herself from their father, and Valerie didn't appreciate that.

Instead of improving, the tension in the house only mounted, until now it was anyone's guess when an explosion would occur. . . .

AS THE BELL rang, signaling the end of fifth period, Valerie gathered her books and headed into the hallway. Her friend Lydia was waiting outside the door, as usual, to walk to their last class together.

"So, what do you say we hit the mall and then go to the movies tonight? Ron and Joe wanna meet us there." Lydia, who was the same age as Valerie, had promised to set her up with Joseph Ellison, the cutest guy Valerie had ever seen. All the girls were after him. Now Lydia was telling her that it was done! He would be meeting them at the movies!

"What? How did you do it?" Valerie questioned, as kids noisily rushed past them in the hallway.

"It wasn't me—it was Ron. Turns out they have weight training together, and Ron told him he knew a girl he could hook up with."

"Oh, my God, Lydia! You gotta help me find something to wear!" Valerie giggled.

"Of course! That's why we have to hit the mall!"

At that moment, reality settled around Valerie like an unwelcome relative. She was grounded! She was expected home right after school. "Damn, Lydia, I can't go! I forgot I'm still grounded! Shit."

"What? You're still grounded? Damn! Hasn't it been, like, a month now?" Lydia's forehead crinkled.

"Almost four weeks—can you believe it? He won't let up!" When they reached their lockers, Valerie leaned against hers and sighed heavily. She stomped her foot against the bottom locker. "Shit, I have to go! I'm gonna go home and beg him to let me go. It's been four weeks now. It's about time he lightened up on me, don't you think?"

"Hell, yeah," Lydia agreed, shaking her head. "I've never heard of anybody being grounded *that* long."

LATER THAT AFTERNOON as she made her way up the driveway, Valerie felt her palms moisten with every step.

Gripping her heavy backpack, she prayed her father would relent and let her go out. After all, it *was* Friday, and she *had* been grounded for nearly a month now. . . .

"THEY SQUEEZED ME in at nine o'clock on Monday," Olivia informed Tracy, after practically begging the nurse at Dr. Gabriel's office for an appointment change.

Her original appointment had been scheduled for a week from Tuesday, but she needed it done as soon as possible. She insisted she did not want to carry the baby another minute, let alone another week. She was nearly six weeks along.

"Okay, nine o'clock is good," Tracy said from her closet. She was shuffling through her designer outfits, looking for something to wear to the play at Parker Playhouse that she and Reginald were planning to attend with Roger Roman and his wife, Justine.

"I tried to get it for tomorrow, but no luck."

"Well, Monday's fine, Liv. You'll make it through the weekend." Tracy pulled out a jade wrap gown and studied it. "Just be prepared, because this isn't something that can be taken lightly. Say a prayer and you'll be fine. No, not this," she said, replacing the green gown and pulling out a navy pinstriped pantsuit. "Nope, too businesslike."

"Where's that cute little skirt outfit you bought the other day?" Olivia said from the loveseat just outside the oval-shaped closet. "Wasn't it silk? That would look nice."

At the back of the closet, Tracy pulled out the silk Yves Saint Laurent ensemble. It was a solid red with curvy black wisps all over. "Yes, this is perfect. You know, I'd forgotten all about it." She set about finding shoes and selected a stylish pair of black suede sandals.

As she left the closet, Tracy noticed Olivia's glum expression and joined her on the sofa. "Oh, sweetie, you'll get through this. You know, even though it never feels that way at the time, it *will* pass. I promise."

"I know, I know. It's just that I can't seem to think about anything else, Mom. I wish I could just wipe the idiot completely from my mind!"

The night her father had returned home, surprising them out by the pool, Olivia had gone upstairs to shower and wash her hair.

Thinking he had suffered enough, she decided to call Sean. When she got his voice mail at home, she tried his cell phone, only to have none other than Jacquelyn Henderson answer.

When she asked to speak to Sean, she was told that he was unavailable at the moment. What in the world did that mean? Unavailable? Why the hell had he been unavailable?

She had hung up without saying another word to the scrawny bitch.

Now she sighed heavily and said, "I just want to forget about him, and it would help if I weren't carrying this baby."

"Honey, don't let it break your spirit, okay? I mean, you've got so much going for you with school and everything, so just put everything into its proper perspective and take it one day at a time. Before you know it, you'll be saying, 'Sean who'?"

"Yeah, I guess so." At the moment, Olivia could not imagine having a minute go by that didn't include a Sean-related thought.

Sean. His laugh, his smell. His hair, his funny little words and remarks. And last but certainly not least, his awful betrayals.

"Well, I've got to get ready," Tracy said cheerfully as she headed for the bathroom.

Olivia watched her mother as she glided across the floor toward the bath. How did she manage to do it? How could she seem to be so happy with their father now, while seeing their Uncle Frank at the same time? Well, Olivia didn't exactly know if they were still seeing each other, but she assumed they were. She decided to ask.

She entered the bathroom just as Tracy was stepping into the shower stall. She'd always marveled at how shapely and toned her mother was. At thirty-nine, thanks to Jane Fonda and Denise Austin, Tracy was in admirable shape.

"Mom?"

"Yeah, honey?"

Olivia perched on a stool by the dressing table. "What's going on with you and Uncle Frank now? Anything?"

Tracy cringed. She had a flashback to the afternoon three years earlier when she'd been lying across her bed, having an uncensored phone conversation with Franklin. She had been alone in the house and she hadn't heard Olivia come in from school, climb the stairs, and stand in her bedroom doorway.

Oh, there were times when Tracy so regretted that she hadn't been much more cautious; times she so regretted having had to admit such a thing to her own daughter. This was one of those times. She said, "Why do you ask, honey?"

"I don't know. . . . Curiosity, I guess."

"Well, no," Tracy said, lathering her washcloth. "I haven't seen him privately since your father got back this last time."

"Well, what does that mean? Is that a good thing or a bad thing?"

Tracy stilled her movement. "Liv, honey, where are you going with this? What do you mean, good thing or bad thing?"

"Well, you seem really happy. I mean, since Daddy came home, you seem *remarkably* happy. You're going out all the time, your bedroom's a regular rose garden. . . . And *you* were the one that said you were thinking of divorce. I was just wondering what was going on, that's all."

Dazed, Tracy stood still. It was true. Having Reginald home had not turned out to be at all what she had anticipated. She was indeed happier—*so much happier.*

How could she not be? For the past four weeks she'd been treated like royalty. Their bedroom was filled with dozens of beautiful pink and red roses. He had been taking her out on dates, and the destinations were always some wonderful surprise. His gazes at her were so intense that Tracy felt she was consuming his mind. She didn't know what had come over Reginald suddenly, but whatever it was, she liked it. She liked it a lot.

One afternoon, they'd spent time at an exclusive spa where he'd booked a couple's package and surprised her. Afterward, he'd arranged for them to be picked up by limousine and driven to the beach.

"I love you so much," he'd said, handing her a beautiful rose. His gaze was so passionate she'd had to look away.

"Reggie . . ." she had begun. *What's going on with you? What's happened suddenly?* She'd nearly blurted her thoughts. Then she reconsidered. Should it matter *why* he was suddenly so attentive and loving? Did she really need to ask? Why not just continue to enjoy and embrace this new course their marriage was embarking on? Just appreciate it? "I love you more," she had said instead, touching his cheek lightly. "You know, all this love and attention is getting to be extremely attractive. I'd be content just to stay in bed all day long with you at my beck and call."

"Honey, your father and I are just getting along, that's all," Tracy replied to Olivia now. "And that's a good thing. . . . Because I decided it was best to put an end to that other matter."

"Are you okay with that, though? I mean, can you just stop it without feeling anything?"

"Well, of course it's an adjustment that I have to make, but it's all in perspective and I can handle it." Tracy stepped under the spray of the water. "I love your dad, Liv. I always have. But sometimes emotions can lead you astray, and although we know better, we still end up making the wrong choices, you know?"

"You're asking me? With the mess I'm in? Please."

Tracy laughed as she turned off the taps and began drying off. "Never mind. After Monday, everything will be fine."

"MAKE SURE YOU fax a copy of that expansion proposal over to Jim Spaulding at Darden before noon tomorrow. They're opening a couple more Olive Garden chains in a few months, and we've got to get all the preliminaries behind us."

"Sure thing, Mr. Brooks. Anything else before I leave?"

"Hmm . . . no, Dana, that's all. Have a good weekend."

Once his secretary had left the office, Reggie placed a call to Roger's private line, hoping to catch him still in the building.

"Roger here."

"It's me. I was just checking on the time for tonight. When does the curtain go up?"

"Come on, Brooks, you know I'm bad with times," Roger Roman laughed. "That's Justine's specialty. And I'm sure Tracy knows, doesn't she?"

"I'm sure she does, but I thought I'd try you first if you were still in the building. I'm heading out of here now. We'll see you later, okay?"

"Yeah, okay. Hey, Brooks?"

"Yeah?"

"Everything okay? You have that 'something's bothering me' tone in your voice, and I can't help but wonder if it's gonna end up costing me money this time. . . ." Roger chuckled.

"You don't miss a trick, do you, Roger? What perception. Yes, something's bothering me, but no, it won't cost you any money." Reggie shut down his computer and prepared to leave for the day.

"Well, let me have it. What's up?"

"Well, it's mainly Olivia." Reggie sighed. "There's now ten years' worth of distance between us, and I'm not quite sure how to close the gap. I'll tell you more about it later on tonight when the ladies are otherwise occupied, okay?"

"Sure. See you later, then. Hang in there."

JUST AS HE was walking through the office door, Reginald's private line rang. It was Valerie.

"Hi, Daddy!"

"Hey, Val, I was just on my way out the door, coming home. What's up?"

"Can I ask you something? Just promise you won't get upset."

"Well, now, that depends on what you ask me, right? What is it?"

There was a hesitation before she said, "Am I still grounded?"

"What did I tell you when I grounded you, Valerie? I said you were grounded *until*. This means until *I* say you're not. And I don't recall saying 'You're not.' So yes, you are still grounded."

Valerie whined miserably. "But Daddy, it's been a month now! I've learned my lesson. Please let me go to the movies tonight with Lydia and some friends. Please?"

What the hell? Reggie thought. She had been on a pretty tight leash since he'd been back. "Hmm . . . let's see . . . ask your mother. If she's forgiven you for what you tried to do to her, then she'll let you go. But if she says no, it's just no."

"I don't know what to expect from Mom. It's not like we've gone out of our way to speak to each other lately." When he didn't respond, she rushed to say, "Okay, okay, Daddy. Thank you. At least I have a chance now. . . . But for the record, I really am sorry . . . for what I did."

"All right, now. If Tracy says yes, you have to be in by ten thirty tonight, okay? I'll see you later. Tell your mother I'm on my way."

After hanging up, Reggie leaned against the edge of his desk, contemplating calling Renee. It was his habit to call her before he left the office, in a direct attempt to avoid having to call from home.

He had come to dread each call. Aside from the fact that he enjoyed speaking with Denise, the calls were pure torture and he wasn't sure how long he could keep them up. Maybe he hadn't thought his story through well enough after all. She believed that Valerie was awaiting a marrow donor. How long could he really keep that pretense going?

He decided to attend to that later. He had more pressing issues to think about, such as the situation with Olivia. How do you reach out to your own child? He wasn't sure how to get through to Olivia. She never looked him in the eye, and avoided conversation with him at all costs. And in the rare instances when he did manage to engage her, she looked about as comfortable as a plucked turkey. It was as though she wanted to completely erase his presence from her life. Reginald was extremely concerned.

The peace he had felt, heading home on the jet, had been diced when he arrived only to hear Olivia say she wanted to move out. Move out? Just when he was coming home to make things right? His little Olivia. Where had the time gone?

Then there was Valerie. Little Valerie, always so sharp and observant, picking up on a change in her mother. She had driven a nail right into Reginald's plank of suspicion.

Tracy had been seeing another man.

He had suspected it for months, and having it validated by Valerie's own suspicions had hurt. Somehow, Tracy had given herself away. He knew her—at least he thought he did—and he had heard the slip of interest in her voice, sensed it in her demeanor whenever they were together. Although she remained the same superficially, he had sensed a difference underneath. It was just like the way a good warrior could sense danger from a shift in the wind current.

When he had returned home, he'd gone out of his way to sweep her off her feet. His ultimate goal, now that he was home, was to put an end to whatever relationship she had gotten herself into. Thus far, he was certain she had put an end to it—and he intended to keep it that way.

After months of speculation, Reginald decided that the other man's identity was irrelevant. If she ended the affair, that was good enough for him. She had been on her own for the better part of ten years, alone to handle all the ups and downs that occurred while raising Olivia and Valerie. Had he really expected Tracy to remain faithful all those years? Yes, he had. But just the same, he acknowledged that he had no more right to point blame in her direction than she had to point it in his.

As for Olivia, something had to be done to rectify the relationship. To have his own daughter turn into little more than a stranger was increasingly upsetting, and Reginald wasn't going to humor her much longer. He was losing patience with Olivia's behavior.

He knew one thing for sure: Reginald Brooks would stop at nothing to keep his family together. There was nothing more important at this stage of his life.

TRACY SAT AT her vanity table, carefully applying makeup. Thanks to the *The Greatest Hits* by Nat "King" Cole playing in the stereo, she was mellow and looking forward to the evening ahead. She was especially looking forward to returning home and being alone with Reginald.

Just as she was smoothing her eye shadow, thoughts of Frank invaded.

His presence in their lives had not turned out to be as awkward as she'd been anticipating, although she couldn't deny that she was never completely comfortable when she saw him.

Whenever he came by the house, she behaved normally, as though nothing was amiss. To his credit, Frank did the same. There were no hidden glances or furtive telepathy. It was almost as though they had never been lovers at all.

Operative word being almost, Tracy thought. Unfortunately they *had* been lovers. Thank God it was over now and there would never be a reason for Reginald to find out.

Just then, there was a knock at her bedroom door. "Come in," she called out.

She was surprised to see Valerie enter. They hadn't exactly been a model mother-daughter duo lately. Tracy wondered what she wanted. . . .

VALERIE WAS ENCOURAGED when she heard Nat "King" Cole. Her mother was always in a good mood when she listened to his music. "Mom, I just talked to Daddy. He said to tell you he's on the way home now."

Silence.

Valerie shifted from one foot to the other, searching the room for a spot to fix her eyes on before continuing. She settled on the bright florescent light of the stereo display.

Tracy waited, fastening a diamond bracelet to her wrist.

"He, uh . . . he also said that I had to get your permission to go to the movies tonight. He said if it was okay with you, then it was okay with him." She fell silent.

"Did he, now?" Tracy suppressed a smile. "Who are you going to the movie with?"

"Lydia and a couple other friends from school. Can I go?"

"Yes, you can go. I think you've been cooped up in the house long enough to learn a lesson. Just be back by ten."

Valerie's eyes swung to her mother. "But, Mom, Daddy said ten thirty."

"Well, okay, ten thirty. But not a second later, understand?"

"Yeah—thanks, Mom."

Valerie turned to leave when Tracy added, "I assume Lydia will be driving?"

"Yeah, she's using her dad's car."

Tracy nodded and resumed putting on her jewelry.

When Valerie closed the door behind her, she ran to her room excitedly and called Lydia to confirm their plans.

WHEN REGINALD ARRIVED, Tracy was on the telephone with her mother. He signaled to her that he was going to take a shower, and went into the bathroom.

"I know you don't agree, Mom." Tracy kept her voice low despite the fact that Reggie had left the room. "But it's what's best for her. Do you realize how drastically it would affect her life if she went through with this pregnancy?"

"Call me old-fashioned, Tracy," Beverly Russell declared, "but there is no reason for Olivia to do such a thing. I'm sure that child wouldn't want for anything. Between you and Reginald, that baby would be very well cared for."

"Mom, you know better than that. There are endless reasons for this abortion—good reasons. This boy is absolutely worthless, and Olivia can do better. She's still very young and in school, and I really believe that having this baby would ruin the potential she has at a bright future." Tracy paused, shifting on the settee. "This was an accident that should never have happened to begin with, and I'm so relieved something can be done about it."

Beverly sighed. "Tracy, abortion is not to be used as birth control. Olivia knew what she was doing when she laid with that boy, so she should be made to handle the consequences. She will have plenty of support."

Tracy gave up. She had confided in her mother for lack of anyone else to discuss the issue with. Her mother was the only person she trusted enough. Knowing that she was against abortions for the most part, Tracy still hoped for her mom's understanding, since this concerned her granddaughter's future. She realized now that she would get no such understanding from Beverly Russell.

"Well, I'm going to see to it that she's started on the pill right after this is taken care of. Please understand that I am not trying to encourage abortion as some morbid form of avoiding responsibility—I'm simply encouraging it as a *much needed* solution to this dilemma. Can't you at least try to understand where I'm coming from?"

"Trace, I see where you're coming from, but I just can't agree with that option under the circumstances." Beverly paused. "Does Reginald know of this?"

"No, he doesn't, and I'm not going to tell him because Olivia doesn't want anyone to know—particularly her father. And I know you won't agree with that, either, but just let it be. He really doesn't need to know."

"Tracy! He's the girl's father. You can't be that far gone from looking at this objectively!"

"Mother, he doesn't need to—"

"Bite your tongue, Tracy Russell! Put the shoe on the other foot. It would be bad enough if a stranger kept a secret like that from you, but to have your own daughter hide something like that from you. How would that sit with you? How do you think it would make you feel to be left in the dark about something concerning your own child? Honestly?"

Tracy sat transfixed at the thought. How *would* that make her feel?

Beverly continued in a soft tone, "I know you think you're looking out for Olivia's best interests here, but Reginald is her father and he has a right to know that this is happening to her. He has a right to be a part of this decision. Surely you can see that? You think I could've kept something like that from your father? Good heavens, no."

Her mother was right. Tracy had to relent. Reggie did have a right to know. She closed her eyes and breathed heavily. "You *are* right. . . . You're right. Yes, I do see that. It would kill me to be left out of anything concerning the girls." She paused. "I don't know, Mom. It's kind of funny. Since Reggie's been away so long . . . I guess it became natural to keep things from him." A wave of shame shot through her at the full implications of her words. "Anyway, we're due at Parker Playhouse in about an hour, so we'll talk tomorrow. I've got to finish getting ready. Love you."

"Promise me you'll tell that man about this baby before Monday, Tracy. Do you promise?"

"Oh, I'll definitely tell him now that you've shamed me into it. I just hope I can convince him to keep it to himself and not mention it to Olivia. She would have a stroke if she ever found out that he knew."

"Can't something be done about that situation, Trace? Olivia can't go on feeling that way about Reginald forever, you know. You all need to work that out, as well."

"Oh, boy, believe me. I'm trying my best to make things better around here. I guess it's just gonna take some more time, that's all."

"Well, you have a good time tonight, honey."

After the conversation ended, Tracy sat there on the sofa for several minutes, lost in thought. She barely stirred when Reginald left the bathroom and moved about, getting dressed. She responded absently as he remarked about the good things he'd heard around the office about the play they'd be seeing that night. She sat, worrying once again, about the direction their family was headed.

Tracy would have given anything for a magic wand.

17

"DAMN, THAT WAS A GOOD MOVIE!" seventeen-year-old Joe Ellison said as he threw his arm around Valerie's shoulder. They were exiting the movie theater.

Valerie had a cheek ache from smiling at Joe. If his attentions were any indication, he seemed to be incredibly interested in her. That gave her plenty to smile about.

"Yeah, it was good. I could've sworn that girl was gonna end up dead at the end!" This was from Ron, who was holding Lydia possessively.

The couples made their way through the theater's parking lot toward Lydia's car. As they walked behind together, Valerie felt Joe's hand slip over the mound of her right breast. He squeezed it through the cotton of her blouse.

She shivered.

Bending close to her ear, he whispered, "So, can I take you home?"

Turning to see if Lydia and Ron were watching, she answered, "Yeah, sure. I don't see why not."

Just then, Ron turned. "Hey, let's go to IHOP or Denny's. Lydia and I are hungry. You guys wanna eat?"

Smiling mischievously, Joe squeezed Valerie's breast again. "Uh-uh, you guys go ahead. Don't worry about Valerie, Lydia—I'll get her home."

"Okay, then. Catch y'all later." Ron and Joe did their "cool man" handshake, and Lydia smiled at Valerie knowingly. Valerie had just enough time to return the furtive smile before Joe pointed her in the direction of his car.

Once they reached it, Valerie was shocked to see that he drove a late-model Pontiac Grand Am. "Wow! Is this your car?"

"No, it's my Mom's car. She lets me hold it sometimes," he chuckled, "when she's in a good mood."

Valerie couldn't stop smiling. She thought surely she must look like a smiling idiot! She really liked Joe. He was so very polite, different from all the other boys she'd gone out with at school. Joe was much more polished and definitely smoother in his approach. His voice was low and mellow, and she loved the way he bobbed when he walked. It was so sexy.

"So, are you hungry?" Joe asked as he started the car. "Wanna get something to eat, go down to the park and hang out for a while?"

Valerie looked at the small clock display on the dashboard; the digits read 9:18. That meant she had just a little over an hour to get home. . . . But subconsciously, she knew her parents were out and wouldn't be home to know what time she arrived. "Yeah, that sounds like a plan. Let's get some McDonald's. We can stop at the one by Stoneman Douglas Park."

PARKER PLAYHOUSE HAD been packed to capacity for the production of *Henry VIII*. Theatergoers were now making their way to the strategically placed exits located all around the circular building. The place was abuzz with chatter of the production as everyone leisurely descended balconies and stairways.

Reginald suggested they remain in their seats until the crowd below had dwindled.

"I agree. Besides, it's probably going to be a hell of a wait out there with the valets," Roger said, running a hand through his hair.

"No, not really. They're pretty quick here," Justine Roman said. "When we came to see *Othello* we waited, what, five, ten minutes, Tracy?"

"Yeah, not even ten minutes," Tracy answered with a brief nod. "But we can still wait until the crowd's out of here, so we don't have to stand in these lines for the next decade."

As Roger and Reginald got into deep conversation about profit margins and quarter projections, Justine and Tracy exchanged conflicting opinions on *Henry VIII*.

Justine appreciated the style in which the story was presented, giving great praise to the overall tone of the play, whereas Tracy criticized the dreamy, fairy tale–like presentation. In nearly twenty minutes of debating, the only thing they could both agree on was the obvious talent displayed in the unique cast of players.

Once the building had virtually cleared, the foursome made their way to the valets, agreeing to meet at The Ivory Estate for drinks.

SPEEDING ALONG DIXIE Highway, Reggie and Tracy chatted about the play before Tracy grew serious. "Can we skip The Ivory tonight and go on home?"

"Ouch. That would be rather rude, wouldn't it? We just told them we'd meet them there! Why, is something wrong?" Reginald's eyes left the road briefly, shifting in concern.

"Well, there's something we need to talk about. . . . Privately. It's about Olivia."

"Oh," Reggie said, refocusing on the road. "Sounds serious. Well, if it's that important, I guess we can call and let them know we changed our minds. Do you have your phone on you?"

Tracy hesitated, apprehensive. She finally shook her head. "No, on second thought, let's go ahead and pop in for half an hour or so, at least. It actually has been a while since Justine and I got together. We can talk when we get home."

"You're sure?"

"Yeah . . . it can wait."

THE IVORY ESTATE was an exclusive, members-only recreational club. For a mere forty-eight hundred dollars per month, members enjoyed all manners of luxuries ranging from full-body massages and treatments to private, all-inclusive dinners and galas.

When they arrived, Reginald maneuvered the Navigator up the winding entrance, which resided at the top of a foothill elevation from the main road. "We'll just have one drink and take our leave," he said.

Turning the car over to the valet, Reggie slipped his arm around Tracy's waist, and she snuggled against him in kind. They made a striking couple as they walked into the building.

THE IVORY, as they made their grand entrance, was a flurry of activity. Several groups and couples were enjoying the chic atmosphere, jazzy music, and mouthwatering cuisine.

Jack, the host, knew them on sight and promptly escorted them toward Roger and Justine, who had just taken their seats.

Justine spotted them first and discreetly signaled Roger to cease his recitation of Reginald's current dilemmas. He was filling her in on what little they had been able to discuss in hushed tones while she and Tracy had been busy debating the play, back at Parker Playhouse.

When they were all seated and their drinks ordered, they laughed and bantered about current affairs and gossip. People stopped by the table to offer greetings, some coming over to congratulate Roger for winning the bid on an exquisite antique bureau.

Charity auctions were frequently held at The Ivory, usually at the request of its members. Knowing how his wife valued period detail and antiques, Roger had people keep tabs on forthcoming items so he could surprise Justine with trinkets and such. Although the nineteenth-century chiffonnier had cost him fifteen grand, he knew it was worth it just to see her eyes light up when she saw it. Seeing the tender appreciation with which she accepted such gifts warmed Roger's heart.

JUST OVER THIRTY minutes into their sitting, Tracy announced she was tired and that they would be leaving.

"But we just got here—you can't go yet!" Justine exclaimed, sipping a martini. "We didn't even have a chance to have our girl talk, Tracy, and it's only quarter past eleven."

"Oh, I know, darling, but how about we meet here tomorrow morning for tennis? I'm just really beat tonight, and this martini didn't do a thing to help," she said before downing the last of the potent liquor.

Examining a cuticle, Justine considered the tennis invitation. "You know what? Morning is no good. Let's do an afternoon match, and afterward we'll have lunch. . . . We can meet here at, say, around twelve thirty? Is that good for you?"

"Twelve thirty's fine. I'll see you then. Bye for now. You take care, Roger."

They exchanged hugs and handshakes before Tracy and Reginald made their grand exit, headed for home.

As HER PARENTS stood outside The Ivory Estate awaiting their car, Valerie was awkwardly scrambling up the stairs, thanking God with every step that she had beaten them home. Her head felt woozy and her body was sore, but she would not have traded the night's events for a million dollars!

What she needed now was a nice warm bath to soothe her aching muscles, and then she'd get Lydia on the phone to share all the glorious details. She had to tell someone or she'd burst, and Olivia was no doubt locked away in her room, as usual, oblivious to anything going on in the rest of the house.

Wait until Lydia hears this!

She had given her virginity to Joseph Ellison.

LATER THAT NIGHT when they were in bed, Tracy held Reginald's head to her breast after they had made love; tunes from their favorite soft-rock CD filtered through the room, faint background music.

Reggie brushed his lips lightly across the curve of her breast. "So, what was it you wanted to talk about?" His voice was low, and she knew he was minutes away from falling asleep.

With a prayer to God in the back of her liquor-hazed mind, Tracy decided to simply say what needed to be said. She took a deep breath. "Before I say this, I want to make a point of saying that I really do understand your concerns, Reggie. I mean, about the girls, and how working in Orlando hurt your relationship with them. I get it, so I can understand your being so disappointed."

"I know you understand," he replied. "I know you were listening that night at the bowling alley. That's why I love you. You understand *me*." He softly kissed her breast again.

"This is precisely why I need to tell you what's going on with Olivia.

I must say that I had considered against it, but I've realized that—despite her objections—you have a right to know. You *need* to know." Alarmed, Reggie attempted to raise his head, but she tightened her hold on him, discouraging it. "Now, honey, just listen. . . . Olivia is pregnant."

Silence. Only the soft, mellow music disturbed it.

Tracy waited for a reaction—patiently.

Then, slowly, Reginald made another attempt to raise his head. Again, Tracy discouraged it. "I know it's a shock, Reggie, but please keep your cool. She doesn't want anyone to know. It's all under control. We have an appointment on Monday to take care of it."

Applying more force this time, Reggie pulled out of her arms and sat in the bed, frozen. Silence reigned for several minutes. Finally, he asked, "She doesn't want *anyone* to know? Or just not me?"

Rising to a sitting position, Tracy touched his broad shoulders. "Reggie, you know she doesn't want you to know. Let's not act like that's in question. For reasons that escape me, she just has so much coldness toward you. Believe me, I've tried to talk with her about it. . . . To get to the bottom of it, but it hasn't worked at all."

Reggie shook his head. "I can still see her as a pretentious little ten-year-old. She was so self-confident, even then. And she loved me so much." He paused. "How pregnant is she?"

"She's about six weeks now. But believe me when I tell you that she *can't* have this baby. Not now. Everything points to it. Not to mention that this Sean is nobody she needs to be tied to forever."

"Sean . . . that's the one you were telling me about the other day? Comes to pick her up all the time?"

"Uh-uh, that's him. But he's just a boy, and he's put poor Olivia through more hell than not. He's still wrapped up with his ex. I had to scare him away from here the last time."

"I can't believe she's pregnant." Reggie left the bed and slowly walked to the bathroom.

Tracy lay back against the pillows, relieved that she had gotten it off her chest. Now she just hoped he wouldn't make an issue of it with Olivia. After all, the problem would be solved on Monday.

When he returned to the bed, Reggie asked, "How long have you known this?"

"Since . . ." she hesitated. "Since she first found out. She came to me almost immediately." After a pause: "If you don't mind too much, Reggie, I think it best to keep this just between us. Don't approach her with it. I think that in time, the ice will melt and she'll share this experience with you when she's comfortable."

Reggie held Tracy close as they settled in for sleep. He didn't know what disturbed him more: the fact that at twenty-one, Olivia didn't want him to know about the goings-on in her life, or knowing that had he been around, she would have come to both him and Tracy together—which was as it should have been.

18

SHE HAD AWAKENED that morning feeling a slight lift in spirits. The summerlike Miami morning was bright and welcoming.

As she approached the towering glass building in North Miami, she had a little more faith in her recent decisions—she'd made quite a few overwhelming choices. Dressed in an elegant, but cool cotton strapless dress, the woman was the picture of allure, and it escaped no one's notice as she entered the building. To avoid recognition, she donned a broad-rimmed summer hat and her dark, impenetrable shades.

Scanning the directory, she said aloud, "Dr. Ulysses Berenger . . . Suite 315." She moved swiftly to the elevator, hoping to ride alone, but was followed by several people that seemed to have appeared out of nowhere. The woman kept her head low and avoided making eye contact with anyone, in spite of her shades.

When she reached Suite 315, she entered and announced her name and appointment time to the young, cheery receptionist. "You're a bit early, ma'am, but Dr. Berenger shouldn't be much longer with his current appointment. Please have a seat through that doorway"—she pointed beyond the woman's shoulder—"and I'll call you when he's ready, okay?"

So she entered the spacious waiting area and admired the lavish decorations. The décor was quite contemporary, but with portraits of famous stars from classic movie scenes. The woman admired them all. There was Vivien Leigh, vowing never to be hungry again in *Gone With the Wind;* Judy Garland's frightened face as she waited in the Wicked Witch's castle in *The Wizard of Oz;* Audrey Hepburn perched in a window, singing "Moon River" in *Breakfast at Tiffany's,* and several others from equally well-known films.

The woman took a seat, enjoying the classical music that hummed softly from hidden speakers around the room. The music, as intended, acted as a mind-soothing balm. In only a few minutes, she was so relaxed that the receptionist had to call her name twice when the doctor was ready. Still, she now approached his office feeling a little uneasy.

After they had exchanged introductions and greetings, Dr. Berenger took his seat, facing her where she sat on the sofa. In his early fifties, he was a sturdy-looking man of average height, with a shock of silver hair. Without preamble, Dr. Berenger began his mental probe. "What would you like to talk about today?" His voice was soft and comforting, in an attempt to help her relent, to gain her trust.

She hesitated. *Where will I begin?*

Sensing her uncertainty, Dr. Berenger said, "Why don't we begin this way. Share with me your feelings upon waking this morning. What was on your mind when you got up just this morning?"

"Well," she began, "the first thing I thought was how much better I felt knowing that I had this appointment. I really believe that discussing all this with someone who can be objective, and offer good advice based on that, will be of great help to me right now."

"Your belief is correct, and it is good that you can recognize that. It says a lot. Now, why did you choose me? Why not a friend or a family member?"

"Like I said, I need someone who can be objective, and my friends and family won't be. . . . Complete objectivity is what I need in this matter. They're too close to me."

"I see. Any particular reason they couldn't be objective enough in your mind? Have you done anything you should not have done?"

"Oh, no, Doctor—it's my husband."

"What has your husband done?"

"Well, I discovered that he has a whole slew of women all over the country." She struggled to remain calm, although the very thought brought the anger to a slow simmer.

"So he's being unfaithful."

"Yes, he is. And I've known for quite some time but I . . . I guess I needed hard proof of it. So I hired a private investigator to get it for me."

"Okay, some of my questions may seem fundamental, but please understand that they are only to facilitate complete understanding." The woman nodded. "Good. Now, how do you feel about these infidelities? How do you *really* feel?"

She thought of the best way to express it without sounding like a cliché. After all, men cheated on their wives every day. "I feel like . . . I feel like I've been living in a farce for the past eighteen years. Like everything we've ever shared was all one-sided . . . as though I've been alone in what I thought was *our* relationship. I feel like . . . like he's ruined my life." Her words were spoken quietly, yet with a certain desperation that expressed their need to be spoken.

"You've been married eighteen years, and in the whole of those eighteen years, how long have you suspected infidelities?"

"Well, you know what they say about hindsight being twenty-twenty." After a pause, she continued. "I think I've known all along, from the week we were married. And I know you're wondering why I've stayed, then, for eighteen years—correct? Well, it's simple. I was living life with rose-colored glasses on. I think I *chose* to ignore his deceptions. I loved him. . . . I still love him. And that's why I'm here."

"No, you're incorrect on that. I think you're here because of what exists at the root of your uncertainty when I asked what you wanted to talk about today." He let his words sink in before he continued. "Think of that hesitation and why you hesitated. . . . Why you couldn't just say, 'I would like to talk about my husband's infidelities.' Or something of the like. You couldn't just come out with that because . . . ?"

"Well, I just didn't know where to begin. I didn't know how to . . . to bring it up."

"Yes, but there is a reason or several reasons for that. Can you think of what they could be?"

"Nothing more than a lack of words, I suppose."

"Let me see if I can help you see why." Dr. Berenger leaned forward and rested his elbows on his knees. "There must be great pain and uncertainty in what you're feeling right now regarding your husband. You knew what you wanted to discuss today, but when asked directly, you didn't know how to express it without being led up to it. Now, with that in mind, think of how it indirectly applies to the eighteen years of marriage you've lived through."

What the hell was he talking about? "I'm not sure I follow, Doctor," she said, puzzled.

"You just said, and rather simply, I might add, that you are here because you still love your husband, right?"

"Yes, I love him, and that's why it's been so hard to break away. That's why I need guidance in dealing with this situation."

"So easily said now, but couldn't be expressed quite so simply at the beginning of our discussion . . ."

ONE HOUR AFTER her arrival, she left Dr. Berenger's office with more insight than she could have imagined. He helped her acknowledge the weakness that had given her a false sense of security in a precarious marriage.

Armed with her newfound wisdom, the woman realized an irony in the fact that she had actually been *helped* by the shrink, which was so much more than she had expected to get from the compulsory visit.

19

REGGIE AND FRANKLIN HAD plans to meet at the gym bright and early Saturday morning. Waking at six, Frank left a sleeping Theresa in his bed and threw a gym bag together for the workout.

Despite the fact that he was getting more than his fill of sex, there was a problem with Frank's sex life—Tracy had left it.

She had chosen Reginald over him.

It was a slap in the face, seeing her now. An embarrassing ache for her filled him whenever she was in his presence.

He recalled the Sunday afternoon about two weeks ago when he had visited to shoot pool with Reggie. She had been breathtaking. Frank had had no idea where she was going, but she was dressed in a shimmering, soft pink blouse with long sleeves and an upturned collar, a black wraparound miniskirt complementing it. He had covertly observed her slip on chic sunglasses, wave her good-byes, and leave the room. She was as beautiful as any movie star in Hollywood. Ironically, Tracy hadn't changed; she had always looked that way. But she'd never been more attractive to Franklin.

He resented the intimate looks that he saw pass between her and Reggie. The very looks that caused him to grin mischievously two months prior were now grating his nerves like sheets of sandpaper. Even more, he hated the loss of anticipation—that he no longer had anything to look forward to. In the past, when Reggie was there, they both knew they had a certain number of days before they could get together again. But that was all over with now, and Frank found anger and bitterness consuming him—all channeled toward Reginald.

FRANKLIN ARRIVED AT The Ivory Estate in a foul mood. Once inside the sophisticated fitness facilities, he realized that, as usual, he had beaten Reginald there. It did nothing to help his sour mood.

There were a few other men and women running on treadmills and pedaling bikes. They listened through earphones or watched the large-screen monitors that hung from the ceiling of the workout room. Reginald arrived just as Frank finished stretching and began lifting for upper-body strength.

"Hey," Reggie said, joining him.

"Hey," Frank deadpanned, not looking at him.

Reggie immediately began filling him in on the situation at home, oblivious to Frank's mood. Given his response, hearing about Olivia's pregnancy was not half as surprising to Frank as hearing that she was going to abort it.

"You mean she's *agreed* to get rid of it? Hell, I thought she was head over heels for Sean—"

"You mean you know him? You know this Sean?" Reggie's movements stilled.

"Yeah, I've seen him over there a couple times. But Olivia told me how she felt about him. She was enamored, said he treated her really well and all that stuff. So I'm a little shocked that she would agree to an abortion. . . ."

Reginald fell silent. Had Franklin been looking, he would have witnessed the sting that filled his eyes.

They lifted in silence for several minutes until finally Frank spoke. "So, I bet Tracy's the one who's pushing for the abortion, huh?"

"Well, I wouldn't say that she was pushing it. I just think she's making the best decision for Olivia under the circumstances. Besides, from what she tells me, this guy is no match for Olivia."

"Well, I must admit he does have that dime-store-hood look about him. So how did Trace get Olivia to agree to this abortion?"

"Apparently, Sean is involved with someone else. . . . Some ex-girlfriend or something. Lord, Frank, if you only knew how badly I want to talk to her about all this! I'd love for her to share it with me, let me help her. . . . Be included, you know?"

"Yeah, I know. But don't worry. You just have to give her some time. She'll come around."

"I know, I know. Time."

AFTER THEY SHOWERED and changed, they had breakfast in the dining room. Frank decided to explore another area of Reggie's eventful life. "How's everything with your sister and that Valerie-Debbie team-up?" He watched Reggie carefully.

"Thelma's need for drama far supercedes her capabilities for sound reasoning. She loves to cook up trouble where there is none—you know that. When I first got back, she and I had a long talk about that whole fiasco, and I think she got the picture. I won't stand for her being some sort of catalyst to threaten my marriage with Tracy. You know they never really got along, and all Thelma needs is Valerie's insinuations to set her off."

"Regg, have you ever . . ." Franklin hesitated and took a sip of his black coffee before continuing quietly. "You ever consider the possibility that it might've been true?"

Silence.

Frank looked across the table; a flicker of anger had crossed Reginald's face. Frank could not understand. The son of a bitch was incredible. For years he'd left his wife and kids, choosing to go play man of the house in Orlando, and now he had the nerve to be outraged that Tracy could be fucking someone else.

Just then, Lila, a veteran waitress at The Ivory served their breakfast of cheese omelets, bacon, and muffins.

"Why would I think that it was true?" Reggie asked when Lila stepped away. "Do *you* suspect Tracy was seeing another man?"

Frank's eyes turned cold. For full effect, he said, "Well, you know what they say, Regg, about asking questions you don't want the answers to." He proceeded to spread apple jelly over a fluffy English muffin.

Reginald watched Frank's movements as he bit into the bread. Could it be possible that Franklin knew who Tracy had been seeing? Reggie cleared his throat before saying, "Are you trying to tell me that you knew about this and never mentioned it to me?" He held his breath unconsciously.

"No, no . . . I'm not saying that. All I mean is that you *were* gone a lot, Reggie, and I don't think it should surprise you or anyone to learn that Tracy may have been . . . you know. If she did indeed do it, I think it would be understandable."

For the very first time, it occurred to Reginald that the time Frank had spent with Tracy and the girls over the years had given him an advantage of insight into their lives—an advantage that he, Reginald, had denied himself. After all, hadn't he always asked Frank to look out for them while he was away?

Suddenly, without warning, Reginald experienced a shard of envy so strong it threatened to pierce his chest.

He sipped apple juice and attempted to remain composed. Frank was right, and so words escaped Reggie. To avoid saying anything that would come out sounding egotistical, he opted to comment no further.

The two men ate in loaded silence. Dozens of patrons joined them in the dining room, many visiting their table to offer greetings. Within minutes, the room's atmosphere was filled with animated chatter. The early morning crowd began to annoy Reggie, who just wanted to be alone, to mull over his conflicting emotions.

"So, I take it that all has not gone as expected on the home front." Frank used a napkin to wipe his mouth, finishing the last of his omelet.

"I don't know what I expected. . . . To come home and turn into the goddamn Brady Bunch, I guess. You know, where every problem could be solved in half an hour."

"Well, forget about the past, and focus on the future, Regg. I mean, face it. If Tracy was seeing somebody, there's nothing you can do about it now, is there?"

Reggie thoughtfully sipped the last of his coffee. "You're right. I know Trace loves me—that's essentially all that matters—and we'll be fine, especially now that Orlando is virtually over. But I'm not quite as confident about Olivia. I just don't understand this . . . this extreme aloofness. I mean, it's like she truly doesn't see me. She's even planning to move out, and I'm sure it's all because of my being home now."

Lila appeared and refilled their cups with steaming coffee. "Can I get you gentlemen anything else? Some fruits, maybe?"

"No, we're fine, Lila. Thanks," Frank replied. Once the waitress moved away, Frank continued. "Like I said before, Olivia will come around. Give her some time and space. Even if she moves out, so what? Maybe that's what she needs."

What used to be welcome advice and support now bounced off Reginald's envy like springs. Embarrassed by his jealousy, Reggie kept his feelings under control.

It wasn't Franklin's fault—it was his own.

AFTER PLAYING SEVERAL sets of tennis on The Ivory's vast, lime green tennis courts, Tracy and Justine had showered and changed, and were now seated for lunch in the dining room. Incidentally, they'd been placed at the same table Frank and Reginald had occupied a few hours earlier. Lila mentioned the coincidence prior to taking their orders.

At hearing Frank's name, Tracy cringed. She wondered how much longer it would be before the mere mentioning of Frank's name had *absolutely no* effect on her. A year? Maybe two?

Justine noticed the change in Tracy's mood. She wondered if she knew about Reginald's woman and kid in Orlando. She'd wanted to tell her for years, but Roger had sworn her to secrecy, threatening her very life if she ever breathed a word of it to anyone.

The women chatted lightly about inconsequential matters as they awaited their turkey sandwiches—which couples were to be married; who was robbing the cradle; whose mistress was pregnant or trying to become pregnant; who'd just bought new cars, houses, yachts, and so forth. Finally, Tracy broke the blasé dialogue. "Justine, I can trust you, can't I? I mean, if I needed advice on a delicate matter, I could rely on you?"

Justine scrunched her face. "Tracy Brooks, I can't believe that you have to ask me such a thing! Of course you can trust me! Really, now!"

Glancing around, Tracy reassured her, "Please don't take offense, Justine, it's just that this is a very sensitive issue for us and I'd really like to get a trustworthy, objective opinion on it. I fear confidants that are closest to me won't be as objective as they should."

Suppressing a knowing smile, Justine said seriously, "Spill it. I'm as objective as you can get—I promise."

Tracy began in a low voice, face full of concern, despite the boisterous chatter that surrounded them. "Well, it's about Olivia. . . . She's pregnant, and my first instinct was that she should have an abortion, and Reginald agrees. However, my mother said some things that actually have me second-guessing myself. . . ." Tracy went on to explain that Olivia, too, wished to have the abortion, and that everything pointed to it as a logical option.

Justine listened to Tracy's reservations, and after careful thought she replied, "Hon, I think it would be for the best, too. I mean, if she were my daughter, I'd want the same thing. If this Sean is as useless as you say, then what's the point of weighing herself down now with a baby? I agree with you and Reginald. Your mother's heart is in the right place, but I think she's still stuck in that old-fashioned mentality. Besides, from what you've said, the pros outweigh the cons." When she discussed it later with Roger, he would be in agreement on the matter. Olivia was a young, beautiful, and bright girl. There was just no sense in stifling her potential with a baby.

"Well, I must say that I do feel a whole lot better about it now. I mean, I felt it was the right choice, but I suppose I just needed some reinforcement. A thing like this would be a lot to regret later on down the road."

Justine reached over and patted her hand. "Ahh, don't fret about it another second. You're making the right decision. You'll see—it's for the best."

Throughout the remainder of their lunch, Justine found herself studying Tracy. She wondered about her life with Reginald. She wondered about the renewed happiness that she and Reginald seemed to have found.

But Justine also found herself wondering how long it could last. . . .

VALERIE AND LYDIA were at the Miami Pines Mall, shopping for lingerie on Saturday afternoon. The minute she had gotten out of the bathtub the night before, Valerie called Lydia with all the awesome details of her first sexual experience. Naturally, Lydia had drowned her with all sorts of questions; some of them even embarrassed her a bit. "Was he big or small?" she had asked. "Did it hurt? Where did you guys do it? How long did it take him to come? Did he act like he had done it before? Did he go 'downtown'?" Embarrassment notwithstanding, she had answered each question excitedly. When they'd finally gotten off the telephone, a gritty-eyed Valerie looked at the clock—it was after four in the morning, hours after she'd heard her parents come home.

Now, as they perused the merchandise of Victoria's Secret, Lydia was still at it. "But, Val, I still can't believe you spread on the first date!" Lydia chuckled while holding up a red lace thong. "You think Ron's gonna like this? He loves red—it's his favorite color."

Valerie lowered her shades. "Forget Ron. What about Joe? Think he'll like these?" She held up a shocking pink pair of the same style. "I don't know what his favorite color is yet, but I like the pink ones."

"Since when do you wear thongs, milady?" Lydia laughed.

"Since last night!" Valerie replied, raising her hand for a high five.

The girls exited Victoria's Secret and headed for the food court. Once they had their meals and managed to find an empty table among the crowd, Lydia said, "You didn't answer my question. How come you did it with him on the first date?"

Smiling from ear to ear, Valerie said, "Girl, I don't know what happened! All I know is that I probably would've done anything he told me to do. Joe is so incredibly sweet! He's just . . . he's just so different from those other guys, I guess. It just felt right, you know? Besides, don't you think I've been a virgin long enough? I was getting tired of you and Ron having all the fun!"

"Yeah, I guess it *was* about time. But Ron and I didn't do it the first time we went out. We didn't start having sex until, like, a month later. . . ."

"Well, I couldn't wait a month! Say no to Joe Ellison for an entire month? No way! I'd die." Valerie wiped her mouth and sipped Coke.

"So I guess it's safe to say you're gonna do it again tonight, right?"

Smiling, Valerie said, "But of course! Whatever Joe wants, Joe gets, my dear." She had to laugh at herself. She sounded so silly. . . . But in a good way.

"Listen to you!" Lydia said, chewing an onion ring. She cocked her head to the side. "Well, have your fun, girl, but just don't get pregnant, okay? Or worse. Okay? Did you make him use a rubber?"

"What? Of course he used a rubber! And I didn't even have to mention it. Joe had it all under control. Isn't that great? He's like a real man—he takes care of his business," Valerie bragged confidently.

Though Lydia had no cause for suspicion, had she observed her friend closely, she would have seen the truth. Joe hadn't used any protection.

Condoms had never even crossed Valerie's mind—until now.

20

THE TWO-BEDROOM TOWN HOUSE was brand new. After viewing the model late Saturday afternoon, the real estate agent, Jenny Parker, had agreed to meet Olivia the following day to show the home that was now on the market. Having spent most of the morning and afternoon with Olivia viewing homes from North Miami to Fort Lauderdale, Jenny had explained that she had other appointments later in the day.

Olivia was grateful that the sun was out and brightly shining on this Sunday morning. It was a good day for her to get a nice view of the area the house was in. A friend at school had referred her to Jenny, and she hadn't wanted to waste any time before starting her house hunt. Timing was everything to Olivia now. She had to get out of her parents' house.

Now, as Jenny walked her through the Tilula model, she pointed out the brand-new Kenmore appliances, tiled floors, full-sized washer and dryer, walk-in closets, oversized bedrooms, and all the other niceties that the spacious home offered. As Jenny continued, Olivia's mind wandered. . . . She was very excited about getting into a place of her own, but she still had an unpleasant feeling in the pit of her stomach, and it was more than just the awareness of the baby. It was loneliness. Nothing seemed to fill the void that Sean's absence left in her life, in her whole being. How did one deal with loneliness? Who, if anyone, could she speak with about it?

Jenny Parker said something to her regarding the variety of colors available for the plush carpeting, but she had to repeat it before Olivia was even aware she had spoken. That was happening to her a lot lately. It was as though she were living in a glass cocoon, and life was normal for everyone else on the outside—but not for her.

BEFORE OLIVIA KNEW it, Monday morning had arrived and it was time. The time had come to rid herself of her mistake. She was extremely grateful for her mother's presence, and that she didn't have to go through with it alone.

As she sat filling out the plethora of paperwork required for the procedure, Olivia knew she was doing the right thing. She wasn't ready to have a baby. As much as she loved Sean, in spite of her better judgment, the baby had to go. Now was just not the time for her to make such a commitment, and Sean was simply not the kind of man she envisioned as the father of her children. She would be extremely selective in choosing a husband, because if all went well, that man would be her husband forever, and she had high expectations in that regard. Sean certainly didn't meet any on the short list. Olivia would ensure she married a man that would be a good father to their children, one that would never be a disappointment. . . .

She felt even more secure knowing that her mother was on her side and agreed that this was the best thing. It made it easier, so much easier. If she'd had to do it alone, she probably would have decided to tell Sean, and that was something she never wanted to do. Telling him was completely unnecessary. Olivia wasn't certain what his opinion would be on the matter, but she wasn't willing to risk it. What if he objected to the abortion? No. She wouldn't take the risk.

In the end, no one but her mom would ever know. Telling her mother was the same as telling no one at all. Of course, Tracy would more than likely talk it over with her mother, Beverly, but that was a given.

Olivia clipped the papers back onto the clipboard, returned them to the receptionist, and picked up a pamphlet near the window that read PREGNANCY OPTIONS. Once she had returned to her seat, Tracy adjusted the lapels on her coat and reached for a copy of *People* magazine.

They were both deeply engrossed in their reading material by the time the nurse opened the door, calling Olivia's name. Replacing the pamphlet, Olivia unconsciously took a deep breath and followed the nurse down a long corridor where she was weighed, had her blood pressure checked, and her temperature taken.

Outside in the waiting area, Tracy sent prayers to heaven. She prayed for forgiveness for encouraging her daughter to kill her first child. She prayed that Olivia would be all right when this was all over. She realized that the removal of the baby didn't mean the removal of the problem as a whole—not by a long shot.

"I THINK WE should go to New York," Tracy said that evening as they were running around the block. When Reginald was in town and the weather permitted, they liked to go running in the evening at sundown.

Reggie looked over at her. "Why New York? I was thinking the Caribbean—you know, Jamaica or Saint Thomas . . . something tropical. And much more romantic than New York!"

Tracy laughed. "Oh, please! You can create romance anywhere. Besides, we haven't seen Mervena in over a year, not to mention all the shopping I can do in Manhattan."

"How come your family never comes to Florida? Whenever we see them, it's always on our dime. Mervena's never even been to Florida, has she?"

"No, she hasn't, but don't get technical, Reggie. That's just a ploy because you don't wanna go to New York—and we both know it."

Reginald grinned. He did not want to go to New York. He wanted to go to the tropics, where they could rent a lavish bungalow on the beach, make love in the Jacuzzi, laze around in the shade, and dance in the nightclubs. He just wanted to be alone with his wife and try as best he could to put a great distance between the present and all the clandestine events of recent years.

"Regg, can't we go just for a few days? We can always go to the Caribbean afterward and take the girls, can't we? Hey, slow down. I'm beat." Tracy slowed to a jog and wiped her forehead with her towel.

"Yeah, I suppose we could do that," Reggie said, reducing his speed. "What are the odds of Olivia coming with us?"

"Not good," Tracy said heavily. "You know, today in the doctor's office, I prayed for so many things. I prayed that nothing would go wrong in there. I prayed she would get over this Sean idiot. I *really* prayed that she wouldn't live to regret aborting the baby. And most of all"—Tracy breathed deeply as she jogged—"most of all, I prayed that she would get over this wall where you're concerned. It just breaks my heart, Reggie."

"Well, you know that it bothers me, too. I've been able to think of little else since I got home—" Reggie was interrupted when their neighbors, the Ledfords, drove past, calling out to them. "Hey, did you remember to send a get-well basket or something over for the grandmother?"

"Of course. Don't you remember I told you Olivia and I dropped it off one evening?"

"You did? Hell, I don't remember. I guess my mind's been too cluttered."

"Yeah, we took it over weeks ago. Mrs. Ledford's doing much better now, by the way. I think she only spent a few days in the hospital, at most. But, anyway, back to this trip. . . . I think we'd better just leave Olivia alone for the time being. If she doesn't want to come, leave her alone. We can only hope that this funk will run its course and work itself out. Let's hope she'll realize that she's just wasting energy, you know?"

"Yeah, I suppose. But, I don't like it, Tracy. I don't like it the least bit. I think the time's coming when I'm going to have to sit her down and force her to have it out. The bottom line is, I'm her father. She can't ignore that forever. She can't go on ignoring me forever."

They slowed to a brisk walk then, making their way back to the house, reminiscing about years past, when Olivia and Valerie were children and so much easier to control.

And for a moment—albeit a brief moment—it was as if Reginald had never been to Orlando.

WHEN THEY GOT back into the house, Tracy jogged straight into the kitchen and grabbed two bottles of Zephyrhills from the fridge. The phone rang just as she tossed one to Reggie, where he sat on the barstool. She moved to glance at the caller ID box in the stationery nook.

"Hello?" Tracy said before taking a drink of the cold water. She heard dead air. "Hello?" she said again. Then the line was disconnected.

"What did the ID say?" Reggie asked when she shrugged and replaced the receiver.

"Out of area . . . it's probably one of those credit card companies again, or some place like that. Come on, let's go get a shower before dinner."

The phone rang again before they made it to the stairs. "I'll get it. You go on up." Tracy went back into the kitchen and quickly glanced at the caller ID. Once again it read OUT OF AREA. "Hello?"

She heard someone briefly clear her throat and then say, "Hi, can I speak to Reginald Brooks, please?"

"Sure. May I tell him who's calling?" Tracy rolled her eyes as she took another sip of water, thinking, *I knew it was just another damn card company selling something.*

"Yes, my name is Renee Jameson."

"Uh . . . Renee Jameson of . . ." She waited for the name of the creditor.

"I don't think I follow."

"Ms. Jameson, what company do you represent?" Tracy was losing patience. She was hot and sticky and needed a shower. She didn't want to be bothered with these pesky solicitors.

"I don't represent any company."

The tone in the woman's voice brought Tracy's hand to a halt as she was about to take another sip of water. "Oh, I'm so sorry. I mistook you for a solicitor. Please forgive me. What did you say your name was again?"

"Jameson. Renee Jameson."

"Please hold, Ms. Jameson. I'll see if Reginald's available." Tracy placed the call on hold and jogged up the stairs to the bedroom.

SHE FOUND REGGIE in the bathroom with the tweezers. He was pulling the few gray strands that had invaded his head of dark hair. She made eye contact with him in the large mirror. "The phone is for you."

"Yeah? Who is it? Can I call back?" He examined his hairline for other grays.

"I guess you can. It's a woman named Renee Jameson."

It would later occur to Reginald that if he had just had some kind of warning, a hint or a premonition of some sort, he may have been able to hide his shock at hearing Renee's name come out of Tracy's mouth. Unfortunately, he was caught *completely* off guard, and Tracy saw the shock register in his eyes before the tweezers hit the marble sink—and most importantly, before he could recover.

Slowly, Reggie picked up the tweezers and resumed his search for gray hairs, then said, "Tell her I'll return the call from the office in the morning."

"Sure." Tracy went out into the bedroom and picked up the receiver. "Hello, ma'am, are you still there?"

"Yes, I am."

"Reginald says he'll call you back tomorrow morning from the office."

"Okay, that'll be fine. Thank you."

Tracy replaced the receiver. Her eyes shut.

She felt a strange fluttering sensation in her stomach. If she questioned Reginald about the call, it would surely mark the end of the incredible relationship they had begun to rebuild.

Besides, who was she to cast the first stone? Had she herself not been living in a glass house?

21

DANA PETREL INCONSPICUOUSLY observed her boss as he dictated details regarding a trip he and his wife, Tracy, would be taking to New
York. She noted that his appearance was customary this morning, no
different than any other morning. He wore a perfectly fitted suit with
a blue tie and the usual cuff links.

Dana knew, priding herself on being an extremely good judge of
character, that Reginald Brooks was a man of impeccable distinction.
Where business or personal affairs were concerned, no detail could ever
be missed or overlooked. All of his instructions had to be followed to
the letter; all bases had to be covered. She admired those qualities in
Reginald Brooks. In fact, she admired them more than she had ever
admitted. From the day she was hired, she'd found it difficult to keep
her attraction to her boss under wraps. He was a dreamboat, one of the
most magnificent-looking men on the planet. If he had ever asked her
out, she would've quit the next day in favor of dating him. Alas, he had
never asked her out.

Over the years, Dana had learned that following his lead was the best
way in which to keep the atmosphere calm and serene at Hart-Roman.
She had also learned that it was the best way in which to maintain her
employment.

As such, she was careful not to appear too observant of her boss's demeanor this morning, so she half observed, half listened to his instructions. He wanted round-trip, first-class tickets, a suite at the Plaza

Hotel, tickets to a Broadway musical, and a rental car awaiting them at the airport. As she scribbled the information down, Dana tried to pinpoint what it was that disturbed her today about her boss. Was it a professional issue, or was it a personal one? She watched him for a few more minutes and decided—personal.

To anyone who didn't know him well, the troubled tone of his voice would've gone unnoticed. The extra effort that it took for him to remain focused on what he was saying would have been overlooked. But Dana knew him well. She knew him well enough to know that on this morning, the well-polished and poised exterior of her boss concealed tension underneath.

ONCE DANA HAD left his office and closed the door, Reggie tapped his pen on the desk and took a deep breath. It would do no good to explode on Renee.

Just as he reached for the telephone to call her, Dana buzzed him with a client on the line. He spent more than fifteen minutes pacifying the gentleman on a matter of miscommunication, then proceeded to place his call to Renee. She answered on the second ring.

"Hello, Renee."

"Reggie! I've been worried sick," she said with exasperation.

"Renee, you *cannot* call me at home. Are you crazy? How did you get that number?" Reginald rose from his seat and faced the window. He commended himself for remaining calm.

"Home?" Renee paused. *"At home?"* She hesitated before saying, "You say that as though you live there."

"Well, I've been staying there for the past few . . . for a while. You know, for Valerie's sake." The lies weren't coming as easily as they used to. "Anyway, it's nothing for you to worry about. I sleep in a spare bedroom. Why did you call there?"

"I told you, I've been worried! I've left several messages on your cell phone and at your hotel, and we haven't heard from you in a while, Reggie. What's going on? How's Valerie doing?"

"Well, she's been . . . she's been hanging in there." The words were like sawdust in his mouth. "How's everything up there? Denise okay?"

"Yes, she's fine. Everything's fine. All we need here is you. So, you still have no idea when you can get away for a visit, huh?" Her voice was desperate.

"Oh, I wish I could get away right now, but I can't. Between work and keeping my focus on this whole situation, I'm rooted for a while."

"I miss you! God, I miss you so much. We both do."

"I miss you guys, too." Reggie sat back in his chair and sighed. "I'll tell you what. . . . I'll try my best to get up there in the next few weeks. But it'll have to be a very brief trip, okay? And, Renee, please don't call the house again. If you need me, call the cell phone, and I promise I'll call you back as soon as I can. It won't do for Tracy to find out about you. Do you understand that if she knows, she'll hang me out to dry when we split up?"

"Yes, I do understand about that, Reggie. I promise I do. I'm sorry. I just need to hear from you and know that everything's okay. Promise you'll call me every day?"

"I promise. I'll make it a priority, since I know you're so worried, all right? Now you kiss my little girl for me and tell her Daddy loves her."

"I will. I love you, Reggie."

"Me too. Bye."

Reginald hung up and laid his head on his desk. He felt sick.

Something had to give—but what?

MILES AWAY IN Orlando, Renee squeezed her eyes shut and blindly placed the phone in its cradle. She remembered the sound of his wife's voice. Confident. Self-assured. And very, very comfortable.

Renee wondered about the current Mrs. Brooks. How did *she* feel about Reginald? Did she want things to work out between them? Did she want him back? Did she believe that having him in the house would bring them closer together? What was her story?

THE FOLLOWING EVENING, Reginald invited Franklin over for dinner, and when he arrived, Tracy was prepared. She was less haunted by the fact that they were both bound by this massive, deceitful secret. After all, Frank had always been a constant in their lives, even before the girls came along. She couldn't very well throw a tantrum whenever his name was mentioned, could she? So Tracy fought to accept the reality, and whenever guilt threatened to consume her, she recited the serenity prayer: *"Lord, help me to accept the things I cannot change, the courage to change the things I can, and the wisdom to know the difference."*

It seemed to be working.

She could not change the fact that she'd had an affair with her husband's closest friend. She couldn't change the fact that Reggie had taken that assignment in Orlando and had been gone as much as he'd been at home. She also couldn't change the fact that he had obviously met a woman up there. A woman? Or several women?

It didn't matter. He was here now, they were together, and they both had absolute control over what happened in their marriage going forward.

Sure, they had almost lost their way—at least she knew she had almost lost her way—but everything was back on track now. This line of reasoning enabled her to behave more and more naturally in Franklin's presence. She certainly cringed less at the mere mention of his name.

THAT NIGHT, SHE MANAGED to convince Olivia to come down for dinner. Tracy was not sure if it was her coaxing that did the trick, or the fact that Olivia would have a chance to observe her and her Uncle Franklin in the same room together with her father. Whatever the motivation, she had agreed to join them.

Now, as they all chatted easily and passed bowls and saucers around the table, Tracy felt as close to normal as she thought she ever could under the circumstances.

"So, Liv, how's school coming along? How'd that Marjory Stoneman Douglas paper turn out?" Frank asked, as he took in a mouthful of mashed potatoes.

Tracy saw Reginald flinch.

Olivia smiled as she told about the ups and downs of writing on a woman as intriguing as Stoneman Douglas. "Yep, I learned a lot about her. I even learned that she stopped having sex at, like, twenty-three years old or something like that."

"What?" Valerie joined in. "How old was she when she died?"

"She was in her eighties, I think."

"What? Gosh! That's, like, sixty years!"

*   *   *

AFTER DINNER, THEY all hung out around the pool, talking until Olivia announced that she was going inside.

"Hey, I'm gonna head home now, too," Frank said. He moved to throw his empty Budweiser can in the trash. "Why don't you walk me to the car and tell me more about this house hunting you're doing? I know some good Realtors, if you need one."

Olivia's eyes brightened as she said, "No, I've already found a place, Uncle Frank. It's in Weston."

"Weston?" This from Valerie and Tracy.

"Weston's so far north, in Broward County. Why so far?" Tracy asked.

"That's where I found the best deal. You'll love it as much as I love it! It's great. Just wait until you see it at closing."

Then Frank and Olivia left the pool area, chatting, with Valerie trailing behind.

Reginald turned to Tracy. "Well, I guess she'll really be gone soon, huh?"

She stepped into his arms, and they held each other.

22

ROGER ROMAN THREW BACK the last of his bourbon and returned to the bar for a refill.

"How come I didn't see this coming? Am I getting that goddamn old?" He paused. "Honey, you can't be serious. A divorce? You want a divorce? For God's sake, why?"

Justine sipped her own cognac and said indifferently, "Roger, really. We've been drifting apart for years. You're never home anymore, and when you are, all we seem to do is gossip about other people or butt heads about issues that are of no real consequence. Let's face it, our marriage died years ago." A mental bell sounded then, reminding her of her shrink's recommendations. Though she respected the good doctor's counsel, this was one issue upon which she could not take his advice.

She would never allow Roger to see her pain.

For the past two weeks, she had kept several appointments with Dr. Berenger. Those sessions had proven to be more advantageous than Justine could have ever dreamed. Everything was in the right perspective now. She no longer had thoughts of ending her life to halt the pain and humiliation. Her future looked bigger and brighter than it had in years. All she had to do now was teach this manipulative blackguard a lesson. And it would be a painful lesson, one he would not soon forget.

Roger moved toward the chaise that she occupied, attempting to touch her arm.

"Roger, don't." She pulled her arm away. "It won't do any good. It's over, and I want a divorce."

"Justine, you must know that I'm no fool. Where is this coming from?" He reached behind the chaise and pulled out a footstool. Taking the armchair alongside her, Roger perched his feet and took another sip of bourbon. "Come on, speak up. What's really going on? Have you met another man? Or more importantly, a *younger* man?"

Justine's blue eyes bulged. "Roger, please don't be silly! There is no other man. I just don't feel close to you anymore. We've lost that special something that we had when we met." After a pause, she added, "And I think you feel it, too, Roger. You must."

Roger stared at his wife. She was just as stunning as the day he met her in that church all those years ago, the beautiful nineteen-year-old daughter of Deacon Dressler. He had wanted to make her his trophy, and he had. No man could have been prouder of a wife. She entertained, she hosted and impressed with seemingly little effort at all, just as a society wife ought to.

Now, after eighteen years, she wanted to divorce him, make a laughingstock of him, prove right all the insolent predictions of failure. All the hypocrites and gossips that had said she would eventually tire of him, meet a *younger* man, and leave him. How dare she? After all the effort he expended trying to satisfy her every desire in life, she would dare talk of leaving him? It was ludicrous.

"Justine, I think what we need is a vacation. You know, some time away, time to reconnect and get to know each other again. I can admit that we've been a bit disconnected. I mean, it's never occurred to me before, but we do actually spend more time discussing the lives and feelings of others than we do our own. So let's get away, huh? What would suit you . . . the Mediterranean? Sardinia? I'll tie up ends at the office, Brooks can oversee things while we're away. It'll be perfect. Just what the doctor ordered."

"Roger, have you not heard a word I've said? It's over—over. The reason we spend so much time discussing others is simply because we don't want to face the reality of what's happening in our own lives and our own home. Please, let's make this easy on both of us." She rose and went to the bar for another drink. "I've decided to move," she said, pouring another drink. "All the arrangements have been made. I'll start packing tomorrow. I hope to be gone by the end of the week. You'll hear from my attorney shortly thereafter."

Roger was astounded. *She's found another place to live? Hell, she's fucking serious!* "Justine, you're going to stop all this nonsense right now! We both know that you're not going anywhere."

Rounding the kidney-shaped bar, drink in hand, Justine made her way up the curved staircase, head high, shoulders straight. Once she reached the top, she turned to look down on her husband. "It's over, Roger, and there isn't a damn thing you can do about it now. It's too late."

FORTY-FIVE MINUTES AFTER her well-planned confrontation with Roger, Justine spun her Mercedes into the driveway of her new home. She was glad that she had beaten Tracy there. Tracy had agreed to meet her after one of her committee board meetings at United Way of Dade County, where she did countless hours of volunteer work.

For her first residence as a single woman, Justine had spared no expense. The three-bedroom home was located in the Enclave Estates of North Miami, one of the most exorbitant in the vicinity. Roger didn't know it yet, but he had sprung for it. He had paid for the silk curtains at each and every window, the Italian marble on the floors and counters, and the tasteful yet lavish décor throughout.

Inside, she went to the stereo and put on a favorite Judy Garland CD to sweeten the atmosphere. Justine swayed back and forth as the vibrant music filled the house from every direction. She felt fabulous! The look on Roger's face had been priceless. Though on more than one occasion, she had been filled with an overwhelming apprehension. It would be so easy to give in to him, to acquiesce. But at what cost? Eighteen more squandered years of her life?

Her heart ached when she thought of the reality of what she was doing. It would not be an easy feat, severing all ties with the only safety net she'd ever known. It wasn't effortless, but it was also not impossible. It was a necessary action that she had to take in order to regain her emotional integrity. Dr. Berenger had taught her that.

Now as she waited for Tracy's telephone call from the front gates, she hummed along with Judy, went into her bedroom, and proceeded to unpack some things. Unbeknownst to Roger, she had already moved half her things from their penthouse. *Just goes to show how much attention he's really been paying in recent years,* she thought resentfully. Just then, the phone rang and she answered, pressing 9 to open the front gates when she heard Tracy.

She was adjusting her shoe rack when the doorbell chimed. Running to the door, Justine flung it open and greeted Tracy with an enormous smile.

Smiling hesitantly, Tracy asked, "Justine, who lives here? What's going on?" Tracy stepped into the foyer as Justine stepped aside to let her in.

Sitting on her oversized white leather couches, Justine gave Tracy a condensed version of the recent roller-coaster ride she'd been on. She had adjusted the volume of the music so that it hummed softly throughout the house.

"My goodness! Why didn't you tell me about all this sooner?"

Justine brushed her long hair away from her face. "Oh, I just had to get through the mess before I could discuss it with anyone, you know?"

"I guess so," said Tracy. "So you're actually leaving Roger? Unbelievable. You two seemed so good together, always in sync with each other—or so it seemed." Tracy shook her head in disbelief. "I can't believe he's been so outright with his affairs."

"Believe it, Tracy. You know what the sad part is? I really believed that he loved me. For years, I just settled into the easy life. In a way, I let Roger buy my trust. All I had to do was give the slightest hint that I wanted something, and poof, it was there—like magic."

"So when did you decide to hire the PI?"

"Well, it was something that I considered doing myself at first. But then I thought better of it, since I needed good proof to use against him in the divorce."

"Well, if it's any consolation, I believe that Roger loves you. I mean, you can see it in the way he looks at you, Justine."

"You mean despite the fact that he's fucking the entire U. S. of A.?" Justine looked at Tracy pointedly.

"Yes, in spite of that . . . just because Roger sleeps with other women doesn't mean he doesn't love *you* . . . in his heart."

"But, Tracy, how can you say that? This isn't just one woman we're talking about here. By the way, do you want something to drink? I can't believe my manners!" She laughed, heading for the kitchen.

"What do you have?" Tracy said, following her.

"Anything you want. The kitchen is gloriously stocked! But you know what? I feel like eating pizza. You hungry?"

"Yeah, pizza's good. Off my diet, but what the hell!"

AN HOUR LATER, they were sitting around the coffee table in the den, watching a *Three's Company* rerun. Justine bit into her second slice of pepperoni pizza and threw her head back, saying, "You know, I feel really good about this! A new life, a fresh start. I might even meet someone else sooner than I think." Justine winked.

Tracy laughed. "Are you seriously going to put yourself back on the market so soon? Can't you at least wait until the ink's dry on the divorce papers?"

"Look, it may not be the safest way to put Roger out of my mind, but it is a guaranteed way, and I'm ready. Don't worry," she added when she saw the look on Tracy's face. "I'll be careful."

Tracy swallowed and took a sip of Pepsi. "Just be sensible, Justine. I'm happy for you, though. Only you know what's going to make you happy. If Roger's not doing it for you anymore, more power to being a single woman."

"Thank you. That means so much. The support is really needed right now. I don't know that my family's going to feel the same way, but that's another story. It doesn't matter what they think, right? Because in the end, it's me who's living my life." Justine raised her Pepsi can.

"Amen to that," Tracy said, tapping her can against Justine's.

"Okay, enough about me. How's Olivia doing? Did everything go smoothly?"

"Yes, thank God, it went very well. She's okay. I think she's stronger than any of us really know. She'll pull through this experience with something learned, and that's the best she can get from it."

"That's true," Justine said, downing the last of the Pepsi.

Tracy had an idea. Pride made her hesitant to broach the subject with anyone, even Justine. They sat in silence for a while, both enjoying the companionship.

The seed had been planted weeks before, when the woman with the reticent voice had called. Renee Jameson. Tracy wondered if that was her real name or if it was just a cover. Curiosity got the best of her; she bit the bullet.

"Justine, could you give me the number to your PI?"

Justine stared at her, confused for a few moments before realization set in; then she sat up. "Tracy, just because it was the right thing for me to do doesn't mean it's the best thing for you. I mean, Reginald really loves you. What the two of you have is so far superior to the farce Roger and I had that it's ridiculous."

"Justine, a woman called the house the other day, said her name was Renee Jameson. I need to find out about her. I need to find out how she fits into Reggie's life. I mean, I wouldn't even confront him about it. I just need to know, you know?"

"You believe he's got someone in Orlando, don't you?" When Tracy nodded, Justine continued. "Why wouldn't you confront him about it?"

Tracy shook her head. "Because of the circumstances. I mean, he's spent an awful lot of time in Orlando over the years and . . . I *know* that he loves me. I think that's the important thing. He loves me and the girls and he's here now, giving us his all."

"Well, if you feel that way, why bother with the investigation? It could only bring about pain. You must know that?"

Tracy placed her Pepsi can on the coaster in front of her. "I need to know, just to pacify my selfish curiosity."

"But if you know they've had an affair, what else do you think there is to discover?"

"Who is she? What does she do? Where does she live exactly? How long has he been seeing her?" Tracy paused. "I just need to know. Don't ask me to explain why, because I'm sure I can't." She relaxed into the soft cushion of the sofa. "So will you give me his number, or do I have to find one of my own?" Tracy chuckled.

Sighing, Justine shrugged. "I'll give you his contact info, but please remember to take your own advice. Be sensible. Was it or was it not you who just said that to me not five minutes ago?"

"Don't worry. I know that if you go looking for snakes, you shouldn't be shocked if you're bitten. I'm not expecting to be *overjoyed* by what's uncovered about this Renee Jameson, but I can handle it. I'll have to handle it."

After filling Justine in on their upcoming plans to fly to New York, Tracy helped her clean up before coming back to the original discussion. "You know it's pure courage that led you to this point," she said, "and now I'm going to need a lot of it myself. Wish me luck."

The women hugged each other.

PERHAPS THIS WILL *be for the best,* Justine thought a few minutes later, waving after Tracy's Cherokee. At least Tracy would find out about the little girl, which had always been something that Justine felt Tracy should've known about years ago. Her loyalty to Roger, however, had prevented her from enlightening her friend.

Well, now Brent Stone would do the same for Tracy that he had done for her—confirm what she already knew to be true. *Well, not exactly,* she thought. Tracy would be making a much-unanticipated discovery—a six-year-old discovery.

Justine hoped that Tracy would turn to her for support when she needed it. There was no doubt whatsoever that she would need someone—and soon.

23

THE EDGY SOUND OF Lenny Kravitz blared from Olivia's car speakers as she and Valerie headed to her new house in Weston.

She was grateful, having just closed and moved in the previous week, that Valerie was willing to help her unpack the rest of her belongings. All the furnishings and household items were brand-new, save for an armchair, a couple of barstools, dining ware, and a few other items donated by her parents.

Despite the relocation, Olivia's step toward happiness was still incomplete. Lenny was responsible for her melancholy mood this afternoon. The CD belonged to Sean, who had been MIA since yesterday.

Since their parents had gone to New York on a minigetaway, they had agreed to let Valerie stay with Olivia. Surprisingly enough, Olivia welcomed the company. "So, tell me more about this Joseph," she said, turning the volume down on the radio. She needed to kick this semi-depressive state and Lenny Kravitz wasn't really helping, so she decided to shift the focus away from herself and settle it on her little sister. "How'd you two meet?"

Valerie popped her bubble gum, smiling. "I told you, he goes to my school. Lydia's boyfriend had weight training with him last semester." It was mid-August, and school was out for summer recess. In that time, Valerie had pulled nearly every trick in the book to get away and spend time with Joe—lots of movies, sleepovers, and trips to the skating rink or the arcade with Lydia. If her parents were suspicious about the increase in her outings with Lydia, they never mentioned it. Valerie assumed that they felt bad about keeping her holed up in the house for nearly a month without her phone or television.

Olivia pulled into her garage. "So, is he cute? How come you've never brought him to the house—you know, introduced him?"

"I don't know, Liv. I wanna wait awhile. You know, put some space between all that crap with me and Debbie. Then I'll feel better about bringing a guy home."

"Are you sure there isn't something wrong with him that's stopping you? I mean, he isn't some hoodlum or anything, is he?" She reached for her purse in the backseat and got out of the car.

"Olivia, he's not a hoodlum!" Valerie said, shutting her door and rolling her oval eyes. "He's, well, you'll see when you meet him."

Once inside, Valerie dropped her bags in the spare bedroom, used the bathroom, and then joined Olivia in her room. She was sitting on the bed, checking her voice mail messages. "I wanna invite him here. Can I?" Valerie asked, flopping on the bed.

"Sure," Olivia replied, "but if I even pick up one itty-bitty scent of a low life, he's outta here."

"Speaking of lowlifes, what's this doing here?" When Olivia looked over at Valerie, she was holding up a Miami Heat knapsack.

It belonged to Sean.

"Olivia, don't tell me you moved out of the house *just* so you could take Sean back without any of us knowing! That's so pathetic," Valerie said, dropping the bag in disgust.

"Look, Valerie, don't start. Yes, I took him back. If you don't like it, then just mind your own business. I don't want to hear any negativity about *my* own choices. Especially before I get to size up this Joseph person." With that, Olivia headed for the kitchen. "Now, please come and help me unpack the rest of the dishes."

24

THE FAST-PACED LIFESTYLE of New York City never ceased to amaze Tracy.

Settling into the leather seat of their rental, she relaxed, drinking in the midmorning crowds as Reginald skillfully maneuvered the car through the sea of cars and pedestrians. They expected the ride from LaGuardia Airport to the Plaza to be about twenty-five to thirty minutes.

After landing, they had gotten their luggage and visited the rental car desk in record time. All Reggie wanted to do now was get some sleep. In preparation for his absence, he had been up late the night before, tying last-minute loose ends with Roger. "You won't mind if I catch up on my sleep before we go to Mervena's, would you? I'm bushed," he said around a yawn that spoke for itself.

"No, honey, you can take a nap. . . . I'll just do some sightseeing after we check in. I'll call Mervena and tell her we'll stay in tonight and come over tomorrow."

ONCE THEY HAD checked into their suite, Reginald tipped the bellhop and closed the door behind him. The front desk called to inquire about their satisfaction, and as Tracy assured them that everything was fine, Reginald headed for the bathroom for a quick shower before his nap.

Though the shower lasted no more than five minutes, when he emerged from the bathroom, a cloud of steam behind him, Tracy had already gone. His disappointment was immediate. He had hoped to come out and find her waiting to make love to him before he fell asleep.

Though he hadn't really allowed himself time to ponder it, as of late, he sensed a change in Tracy's presence. He allowed himself to think about it now, just before falling asleep. His insides knotted as he thought about the other man she had taken as her lover. He drifted into a troubled sleep, wondering whether or not her affair with this man was indeed over.

DONNING A CHIC but casual pantsuit, Tracy set out to see Manhattan. Getting off the elevator, she decided her first stop would be the Plaza's gift shop. She admired a few things, made some purchases, and arranged for them to be delivered to the suite.

Outside, horse-drawn carriages moved leisurely along, and joggers and business people moved swiftly about their way. The beautiful greenery of the trees in Central Park beckoned to Tracy. Needing time to think, she considered walking across the street to the park, but opted to go shopping first. She decided a walk through the streets of Manhattan would be more pleasant than driving the rental. Initially, Tracy moved swiftly with the crowds, rushing toward the shopping district of Manhattan. Then slowing down, she lingered at the windows of Chanel, Gucci, and Tiffany, appreciating this morning's window displays.

Standing at the Tiffany display, admiring an elegant wristwatch, her mind drifted to the troubles at hand. By the time they returned home, Brent Stone would have a full report on this Renee Jameson woman. Tracy didn't know how she truly felt about launching that whole investigation. Fear of damaging their reconnection stopped her from questioning Reginald directly about this woman. *But hasn't that happened already?* she thought as she entered FAO Schwarz a few minutes later, deciding to buy toys for her nieces and nephews for when she visited tomorrow.

In the past few weeks, the change in atmosphere had not gone unnoticed. There were too many heavy silences, concealed emotions, words left unsaid, and too many strained behaviors to ignore. Could they remedy the issue without discussing the relevant problems? And if they discussed the issues, how could she berate him without being a traitor as wretched as Judas himself?

Tracy knew the answer to both questions—no. If she tore into Reginald about infidelity, she herself would be left wide open for interrogation. And how could she be certain that he hadn't been curious about Valerie's suspicions? Could she be certain that he hadn't suspected anything, anything at all? Especially following the embarrassing episode with Valerie and Deborah . . . why *wouldn't* he become suspicious?

WHEN TRACY FINALLY made her way back to the Plaza, it was in a taxi. After the courteous driver helped her unload her many packages, two bellboys carried them upstairs to the suite. Tipping them well and thanking them graciously, Tracy dropped her purse, shrugged off her coat, and rushed into the bathroom. She was truly exhausted from walking all afternoon. Her only desire was to shower and go the way of her husband, who at a glance was still sleeping peacefully in the middle of the large bed.

WESTON, FLORIDA

VALERIE LOCKED OLIVIA'S front door behind Joe at exactly five seventeen in the morning. He had come over earlier that afternoon to meet Olivia, who had no clue he'd been spending the last three nights with her at the house. He stayed until the wee hours of the morning, when the alarm on his wristwatch buzzed. Then he'd wake Valerie up for a quickie before he tiptoed through the house to the front door, walked to the Stop & Shop at the end of the street, cranked his car, and drove home.

After she quietly secured the chain at the top of the door, Valerie hurried to the bathroom to wash up. The intercourse with Joe hadn't been too painful last night, but this morning it was all she could do to keep from screaming in pain.

She sat on the toilet and spread her legs. Ripping a piece of toilet paper from the roll, she carefully wiped her vagina. The slimy residue of Joe's semen appeared no different than usual. Slowly, Valerie raised the paper to her nose and sniffed. Oh, no. Something was definitely wrong with this picture.

A bit panicky, she stepped into the shower and washed herself thoroughly. When she finished, she used her washcloth to wipe and smell herself once again. What was going on?

Don't tell me I have a yeast infection or something, she thought, getting dressed. She quietly left the house and hurried to the corner store at the end of the street.

THE TALL, LANKY man behind the counter looked up from his Tom Clancy paperback when a young girl rushed into the well-lit store. He watched as she quickly scanned each aisle. Observing her agitated state, he wondered what her story was. He couldn't help wondering what had caused her to come out to the corner shop at five thirty in the morning, behaving as though she were about to jump out of her skin, her dark, shoulder-length hair pulled into a severe ponytail.

The man's curiosity was further piqued when she apparently found what it was she was looking for and rushed up to the counter, clutching two boxes.

FIFTEEN MINUTES LATER, Valerie was back on the toilet, following the instructions on the box of Summer's Eve douche formula. "Oh, God," she prayed aloud. "Please let this work."

After a few minutes, she began to bleed. Her heart jumped as a stab of fear shot through her. Blood. She was bleeding, and she knew it couldn't be her period. Her skin crawled. Tears of panic sprang to Valerie's eyes and she shot from the bathroom like lightening.

Running into Olivia's room, she shook her sister awake. "Olivia! Wake up. I'm bleeding!"

"Bleeding? Bleeding where?" Olivia's voice was laced with sleep.

"Down there, Liv. It's bleeding! What should I do? What's happening? Why am I bleeding?" Valerie was crying now, and it clearly panicked Olivia.

Olivia threw off the covers, then reached up and turned on the bed-side lamp. "Wait, Val, let me see. When did it start?"

"See? What is there to see? I just told you, I'm bleeding! There's blood coming out!" After a pause, she said, "It started after I used a douche." She wiped her cheeks.

"Douche? Why are you douching?"

Valerie covered her face with her hands and said in embarrassment, "I smelt something funny. It had a funny smell, so I went out and got a douche."

"A funny smell?" Olivia hesitated. "Why would you have a funny smell? Have you been having sex?"

Valerie said nothing, only sobbed behind her hands.

"Are you having sex?" Olivia said, "Tell me the truth, Valerie."

"Yes! Okay? Yes! I've been having sex with Joe. But he's it. I've never done it before! Oh, God, Liv, please take me to the hospital! I'm bleeding!"

Olivia became uneasy then, as if she didn't really know what to think. "What would be causing you to bleed *and* have a funny odor?" she mused, more to herself than to Valerie. "Okay, what have you done? Did you put a pad on? Is it heavy bleeding? Like your period?"

Valerie hugged herself so tightly her muscles ached. "I . . . I put toilet paper . . . it's not really that heavy. I just saw spots of blood. . . . And then it wouldn't stop."

Olivia motioned toward her bathroom. "Come on, let me give you a maxi, and then I'll call Dr. Gabriel when the office opens and we'll go see him."

"Why don't we just go to the ER? I mean, I'm bleeding!"

"Valerie, look, nine times out of ten, you probably went and caught an STD, so I'm sure it won't hurt to wait a couple of hours. Besides, we'd probably end up being at the hospital all day long, anyway."

After she finished in the bathroom, Valerie joined Olivia in the kitchen, where she was making tea. "Liv, I'm scared. What's wrong with me?"

Olivia shook her head and said, "Did you make him use a condom?"

Just then, Valerie had a moment of déjà vu. Lydia had asked her the very same thing. . . . And she had lied. She wasn't about to lie now, though.

As Olivia handed her a steaming cup of mint tea, she said, "No. He never used anything."

NEW YORK CITY, NEW YORK

A FEW DAYS after their arrival in New York, Reginald suggested they go for a stroll in Central Park. That morning, they had breakfasted in silence over croissants and eggs. And it was at that time, as he sipped coffee and took in their surroundings, that Reginald decided something had to be said. They should be enjoying themselves, should they not?

Here they were in New York City, sitting in a beautiful and elegant suite with mauve silk on the walls, drinking piping hot French coffee from Italian coffeepots, and practically behaving as strangers. That afternoon, they had gone down to the Plaza's café for a late lunch that was as quiet as their breakfast had been. It was ludicrous. There were no credible alternatives to confronting the problem once and for all.

LATER, STROLLING IN the park, with its multitude of colors brightening their path, they walked in silence for several minutes before Reginald stopped and suggested they sit on a nearby bench. Joggers and brisk walkers swept by them as they made their way over to the long seat. Both were uncomfortably aware of the awkward energy flowing between them, even here in New York City.

When they'd visited Tracy's sister, Mervena, they had spent the majority of the time in separate areas of the house. Tracy and Mervena had relaxed on the porch, catching up on activities and goings-on in each other's lives, while Reginald had spent the time in the den with Mervena's husband, Sam.

Now as they sat alongside each other and evening bore down, they lingered in a momentary silence before Reggie worked up the courage to say words that he knew would bring the tension to a head.

Shaking off all doubt that there was any other alternative, Reginald faced his wife. "Tracy, I think it's pretty evident that a lot of things need to be said between us. There's obviously a problem, and I'd like to try talking about it so we can move on."

Pulling her collar up around her neck, Tracy half turned to face him. "Reggie, I . . . don't really know what to say."

"Come on, Trace, let's not do that."

"Do what?"

"Avoid the problem. Behave as though there's nothing going on. Obviously, something's come between us, and I want to know what it is. Things were going fine when I first got back, and now suddenly there's . . . something's come between us," he said, shrugging.

"What?" Tracy asked, raising her shoulders. "What exactly has come between us, Reginald?" Taking a deep breath, she said quietly, "The answer should be obvious. . . . Don't you think?" It was clear from the look on her face that she wanted to take that back.

Reggie remained silent. He only stared her in the eyes, forcing her to continue.

"Who is Renee Jameson?" she said finally, the same apprehensive look on her face.

Reginald's eyes left hers. He looked out across the park before replying softly, so softly that Tracy strained to hear his deep voice. "As soon as you tell me about the man you've been seeing, I think I'd be more than willing to tell you about Renee."

Tracy's eyes glazed over. "You know, it's a bit of a shock to hear you actually say that. I've been afraid that you've suspected that all along." She paused before adding slowly, "It also hurts to hear you acknowledge this other woman's existence." She took a deep breath. "So, you did believe Valerie's accusations, then?"

Reginald laughed bitterly. "Why do you ask? Is there any truth to it?"

Tracy literally swallowed her pride. "Yes." She looked at him pointedly. "But it's over now. Can you say the same?"

"Of course I can. Why do you think I've been breaking my back to make up for the past ten years? Believe me, I'm well aware that this is my fault."

"Okay, that's fair. But why, then, is this woman still calling you?" Tracy asked, tilting her head. "Why did she call you the other night? And more importantly, what did you say to her when you called her back?"

He watched as Tracy swiped tears from her face. Could he tell her?

In that moment, Reginald made the choice. He turned on the bench, facing her fully. Parting with his fear, he asked, "Are we agreeing to be brutally honest in this discussion? I mean, this could make or break us, Tracy."

Unable to look him in the eye, her gaze fell from his eyes to his mouth.

"Say something . . . please."

"What do you want me to say? That it's okay for you to ruin my life? Our lives? It's okay to tell me all about this woman? Well, it's not!" Tracy's voice rose involuntarily, and a jogger turned to look, but he quickly averted his head. Tracy lowered her voice. "Reggie, this is . . . this is very hard for me. I'm having a hard time figuring out how we got here. I mean, where did the years go? How did we end up getting involved with other people?" She pulled a Kleenex from her pocket and dried her face, tormented by whatever was going on inside her head.

Spreading his long legs, Reggie rested his elbows on his knees. His heartbeat quickened. He had no idea what was going to happen next, and that scared him to death. "Tracy, believe me when I say I don't want to hurt you. But I'm beginning to see that I'm doing more damage to us by trying to hide my transgressions. So I've decided to throw my cards on the table and hope we can work through it. Can you do the same? Because if you can, then it'll make it a lot easier for me to say what I have to say."

Tracy stood. She looked at him and trembled. "You're scaring me."

Reginald reached for her hand and pulled her back to the bench. "You wanna go back to the room and finish this?"

She shook her head vehemently. "No, no. We've already established that there have been other people in our marriage, right?" When he nodded, she continued. "So if the affairs are over, what else is there to admit to?"

Suddenly, Reginald became aware of where they were—in Central Park, on a bench, having the most detrimental conversation of their lives. For a moment, he considered staying quiet about Denise. But how could he now? How could he just go on pretending he didn't have another child? One that he wanted to care for and help raise? No, it had to come out now. He had thought the guilt would end completely when he came back home for good, but only now did he realize how wrong he'd been.

Apparently annoyed by his silence and frightened by his disposition, Tracy rose once again. "Reggie, we're never going to leave this park if you don't say what you need to say." Her demanding tone belied the tension written all over her face. "Just say it. Whatever it is, I'm sure we can deal with it."

He looked her directly in the eyes, while his own filled with regret. "There's more than just Renee, Tracy. There's also Denise."

Tracy drew a sharp breath. "I suspected that, too, you know. I suspected that there was probably more than one woman."

Encouraged by fear, Reginald considered twisting the truth, allowing her to believe that Denise was just another woman. However, his next words were forced out by a desperate need to be free of carrying the burdens of the last six years. "Denise is not another woman. She's my daughter—a child I have with Renee." He couldn't look at her then, so he focused on a sleek white limousine pulling into the Plaza across the street. He saw Tracy in his peripheral view. She was frozen.

"What?" The question was uttered so quietly that neither of them was quite sure she had made a sound. "You . . . you have another child? *Another daughter?*" Fresh tears pooled in her eyes. "Another child." She slumped down to the bench.

He turned to face her directly. Her head was bent, and she appeared to be staring at the leaves beneath her feet. "Tracy, I don't know what else to say, except it doesn't change anything for me as far as you and I are concerned. Of course, I want her to be a part of my life, and maybe one day you and the girls can accept her, too, but I would never force the issue."

Tracy raised her head and looked at Reginald. Tears were standing in his eyes and they sparkled under the glare of the bright park lights. "How old is this daughter?"

"She's six," he said. Tracy's eyes shut. "She'll be seven in March."

"Six years, Reginald? You've had another child for six years and you never squeaked a word?" After a pause, she said, "Well, why should you have? You weren't home enough for it to make any difference to us, I suppose."

"Tracy, that's not fair." Reginald's voice hardened. "I'm not the only one that's guilty of this. It just so happens that you were lucky enough not to get pregnant with your lover's baby." Reggie paused, apparently reining in his anger. "God, my blood boils at the mere thought of you in some other man's bed."

Franklin's name rang in Tracy's head like a brutal bell of shame. Guilt hit her like a ton of bricks then, and it caused her body to begin racking with sobs, as though she were trying to shake off a shameful cloak.

How could she tell him that the other man's bed belonged to Frank? *Could* she tell him? The shaking intensified as she imagined his reaction.

Reginald resisted an overwhelming urge to reach for her, to comfort her as her body shook. He knew she would be devastated. "Trace, talk to me. Let it out. We can talk through this. Just tell me what's going on in your head right now. . . . What're you thinking. You said before that we could deal with anything. Is that still true?"

Minutes went by and neither spoke. Finally drying her tears, Tracy rose from the bench and put both hands on her head. "I think I've had all the brutal honesty I can stand for one evening, don't you? I have a headache now. Let's go back." She turned toward the street.

"Screw the damn headache!" Reginald practically yelled. The power in his voice brought her to an instant halt. "This is our *life* we're talking about, Tracy! Our lives together. You can't just get up and walk away at a time like this. No. No, we're not leaving here until we know exactly where we stand with one another!"

"Reggie, lower your voice. People are staring," she said, returning to the bench.

Dropping his voice slightly, Reggie said, "I don't care about those people, Tracy. All I care about right now is you and my girls and our family. . . . And our future."

Tracy looked at him. "All three of your girls?"

"Yes, damn it, all *three* of them! No, I can't deny that it was wrong to create this situation, but damn it, Tracy, we either deal with it now or we call it quits later."

"What do you want from me, Reggie? What do you want me to say?"

"I want you to say that we can work this out. I love you, Tracy—you know that. I don't want to lose my wife. You and the girls are my life. I want to hear you say that we can get past all these mistakes—the mistakes that we've both made—and start making a better life together. And I want you to mean it."

Tracy's conscience urged her to lay her bad hand on the table. *Tell him now. Tell him that it was Franklin.*

But she couldn't. She didn't dare.

Later, she would question herself as to whether it would've made a difference if she had confessed it then, right there under the New York City skies. But she just could not bring herself to say the words: *It was Franklin.*

She just couldn't do it, so . . .

The opportunity passed.

25

JUSTINE HAD JUST replaced the receiver after having a satisfying conversation with her attorney, when the phone rang almost immediately. *Roger couldn't have gotten the news that quickly,* she thought, glancing at the caller ID. It was the gate.

She moved to the stereo and adjusted the volume. It was always kept blaring to fuel her with energy, no matter where she was in the house. It was an expression of freedom for Justine, a way to celebrate her new life, her independence.

When she opened the front door a few minutes later, she was totally unprepared for Tracy's bereft state. Seating her on the sofa in the living room, she took in Tracy's distraught appearance. Her lovely face was void of makeup, her usually full and bouncy hair was roped into a chignon at the back of her nape, and her eyes were puffy from crying. "Tracy, my dear, whatever's the matter?" she asked, face full of concern.

"Justine, I had nowhere else to go. I'm sorry," she said, as Justine drew Kleenex from a gold ceramic box nearby and passed it to her. "I just had to get out of the house, and this was the first place I thought it safe to come to."

"Oh, honey, don't apologize! If anyone knows about needing just the right person to talk to, it's me. Now, take your time and tell me what's happened." Justine feared that she already knew *exactly* what had happened.

"I'm overreacting, I know I am, but I'm sickened by guilt. . . ." Tracy paused. "After all that's happened, I guess it should have crossed my mind, but it never did—I swear it *never* did, not even once!" She stuck her forefinger up for emphasis.

"Tracy, I think I already know what this is about." When Tracy's eyes crinkled in confusion, Justine continued, "I know about the woman. . . . And the little girl."

"What do you mean, you know? How could you?" Realization dawned on Tracy then. Roger. Who else but Roger? "Reggie must've told Roger." When Justine nodded, she said, "How long have you known?"

"Oh, Tracy, I'm so sorry. I've known for years. Roger swore me to secrecy, and I just thought it best to keep out of it, as well. After all, who wants to be responsible for the disintegration of a family? But when you asked about Brent Stone, I figured it was for the best that you found out that way. . . . I guess you won't need his services now, though, huh?"

Tracy was nodding her head. "I decided to go ahead with it. He called to inform me that he was ready to make his report and I was about to tell him to cancel it, but then I thought, Why not find out about this woman? Why not? I mean, for the last ten years, she's had as much of a life with my husband as I have, hasn't she? Curiosity got the best of me, so I'm meeting him later today. Besides, he'd already completed the job, and I'd have to pay him regardless."

"Well, tell me what happened. What brought this about?" Justine slid down to the floor and hugged one of the cushions from the sofa.

"New York. I don't think I'll ever be able to go there again and not remember this awful time. We went to New York to visit my sister, Mervena, and do some shopping. Things had been sort of tense between us because of that phone call from . . . her. So I guess it was too much for him to bear, and he confessed. . . . He confessed everything. . . . He just confessed. . . ." Her voice trailed off.

"Isn't that something? I never would've figured Reginald Brooks for the confession type."

"Well, I know him pretty well. And I know that when something's bothering him, it doesn't take long before it erupts like lava. I guess this just started bothering him. And it erupted in Central Park, and let me tell you, Justine, the thought of him having another child with another woman . . ." Tracy gulped the lump in her throat. "It's just . . . eating me up inside. And I can only imagine what it's gonna do to Valerie and . . ." She broke into fresh tears.

Justine moved to the couch and put her arms around her. "Oh, Trace. I know it must hurt. I know."

Tracy wiped savagely at her face. "But that's not even the worst of it. Guilt is what's really compounding it! I feel like a criminal! I mean . . ." She faltered, seeming hesitant to continue.

Justine knew that sometimes offering too much comfort could open floodgates of tears at a time like this. She knew that all too well. So she returned to her seat on the carpet. "It's okay, honey, take your time. Would you like something to drink?"

"No, no. Thank you. I can't eat, I can't drink, I can't sleep. I can't do anything. It's been hell, pure hell." After a pause, she continued. "I have all this guilt inside because I had an affair of my own. I had an affair. . . ." She broke off, unable to continue. When she finally spoke again, she said, "It's really difficult to admit that infidelity to anyone, especially now, when I'm carrying the guilt like a heavy, corrosive sin."

Justine remained silent, not judging, and waited patiently for Tracy to continue. She would not press her to continue. It was much easier if she spoke at her own pace.

"I had an affair," Tracy continued. "He assumed it, and I didn't deny it."

"Tracy, it's not the end of the world. I can understand why you would've turned to another man. Perhaps you were even entitled, you know? I mean, Reginald was gone an awful lot. Don't let that weigh you down too much. It's time to think about mending the wounds in the family now."

"I was entitled, you say? Really?" Tracy slightly cocked her head. "Did you ever cheat on Roger?"

"No. But I'm not you, and you're not me. We're different people. Different women with different needs at different times."

Tracy looked at Justine. Did she know what kind of mending it would take to fix the fact that she had had a four-year relationship with her husband's oldest and closest friend? Pride kept those words safely lodged in Tracy's throat.

"Well, we're trying. I told Reggie in New York that we could work through it, and he thinks that all my tears and heartache are because of the existence of that little girl."

"But Tracy, there's something I don't understand. If Reginald knows about the affair and he's willing to forgive it, why are you so consumed with guilt? I mean, the truth's out, isn't it?"

"Oh, Justine, you wouldn't understand. I've contributed to the disgrace. Don't you see? It's not all his fault. It never should have happened. I've played a role in the possible ruination of my own family—it's so shameful."

"My only advice is that you get help. Seek professional help to find the best way to work all this out. When you're ready, let me know, and I'll recommend the doctor that's helped me. He's excellent, and I think he could possibly help you and Reginald, as well."

"You . . . you saw a counselor?" Tracy asked.

"Yes, I did. Originally, it was for the purpose of the divorce—you know, to show the extent of my distress caused by Roger's affairs. I had no intention of actually seeking real help, but I've truly benefited from seeing Dr. Berenger. I'm not as dismal and broken as I was before I walked into his office that first day. He helped me put all this in the best perspective, and I'm one hundred percent better for it."

"Well, do you really think he could help us? I mean, as a family?"

"I have no doubt whatsoever."

Nodding, Tracy said, "Yeah, that might be what we need right now. Could you give me his number?"

Justine went into one of her spare bedrooms and returned with a distinguished card of gold embossment. She handed it to Tracy. "Let me know how it goes."

As Judy Garland crooned softly from the stereo speakers, they sat and drank Chardonnay for the next hour, only speaking occasionally.

Justine offered to accompany her to Brent Stone's office, and Tracy readily accepted. After borrowing a few things from Justine's makeup kit and having another glass of wine, Tracy felt normal again. Though she and Justine had been acquaintances for years, it wasn't until this very day that Tracy knew she had found a true friend in the other woman.

THERESA GOT A whiff of Reginald's cologne as he stopped in front of Franklin's door. It made her nauseous, which was unusual, since she usually loved Reginald's scent.

"Hello, Theresa."

"Hi, there, Reggie. How are you?"

"I'm well. And you?" Reggie was slightly winded, having jogged up the two flights of stairs to Frank's apartment.

"I'm good. I'll see you later, though. Gotta run—planning a little surprise for Frank's birthday on the seventeenth." She put her forefinger against her lips. "Shhh, don't breathe a word, okay? Say hello to Tracy for me."

"Will do," he said as he turned away to ring the doorbell.

WHEN FRANK LET Reggie in, he was wearing only a towel wrapped around his waist, having just gotten out of the shower. "So, let me get this straight," he said, tossing Reggie a beer. "You told Tracy *everything*?"

"I told her everything. All about Renee. All about Denise." He went on to explain the circumstances with which it occurred while they were in New York. "And you know something? I never imagined it would all come out in the open and I'd still be standing to talk about it. But as I expected, Tracy's taking it pretty hard. She's really cut up about it. But I don't regret telling her. It's out now, and I don't have this awful deed hanging over my head any longer."

They left the kitchen and sat in the living room, sipping their beers. Frank was astounded that Reginald actually confessed everything. "Well, shouldn't this be good news? I mean, didn't we both assume she'd leave you high and dry if she ever found out?" Frank felt a twinge of . . . of what? He didn't know what he felt. Annoyance? Envy? Desperation? Was he upset that they appeared to have survived the worst? Or had they?

"You know, it *is* good news. . . . It really is. We're gonna beat this. I know we are." He paused, and then said, "You remember the conversation we had at The Ivory? Well, she, too, admitted to seeing someone else."

Frank's eyebrows arched in surprise and interest. "Really?"

"And I'm not really sure exactly how I feel about it, either. I just know that I love her, and we have to get our marriage back on track."

"Who was the other man?"

"I don't know. And guess what? I don't care. I don't think it matters who it is, Frank. All that should matter is that it's over now, right?"

"She told you that? That it was over?"

"Yes, and I believe her. But I was fairly certain of that before New York."

"Reggie, I don't understand why you don't want to know who it was. I mean, I'd give my eyetooth to find out." Frank wasn't sure what he was doing; he only knew that he didn't like the way things were unfolding.

"If the truth be told," Reggie replied, "I am curious. But knowing a name isn't important. What difference would it make to know the name of some faceless guy? It would do nothing to help the state of my family. It's not relevant, Frank. What's important is moving forward and getting my house in order. . . . Back to the way things were before that whole situation happened with Renee."

"Well, I disagree. I think it's *very* important that you get her to tell you who she had the affair with. It could be someone you know."

"No way. Who in the hell could that be? No, it's nothing like that. It's of no consequence. I just need to work on helping my wife get beyond the fact that another woman had my child, and focus on repairing the damage—however long it takes. If I hadn't let Renee into my life, that other man would've never gotten to Tracy. I broke it, but we'll fix it together. We'll fix it together as a family."

A familiar and overwhelming urge enveloped Franklin. He wanted to ruin Reginald. He wanted to see him suffer for a change—really suffer. "What about Renee? Let's not forget that she's up there believing that crap you fed her about Valerie being sick." Why the hell were the gods always smiling on Reginald Brooks?

"Yeah, I've given that a lot of thought. I talked about it with Tracy, and we decided it would be a good idea for me to write Renee a letter, tell her the truth."

"Oh, you and Tracy talked about it, did you? So you really are trying to work through all this, aren't you? Trying to make an honest man of yourself?"

"Yeah, we both are. It's not gonna be easy—not at all—but I have faith that we can work through it and be stronger in the end."

"What do Val and Liv have to say about all this?"

"Well, we haven't spoken to them about it yet. I told Tracy we didn't have to rush it. We needed to give ourselves time to absorb everything. I don't anticipate things going too well with them. I'm sure it's gonna throw Valerie for a complete loop. And Olivia . . . well, I can only imagine." He set his beer on the table and ran his hands over his face. "As if things aren't bad enough with Olivia."

"And what about Denise? Did you and Tracy talk about her, too?"

"Of course. Tracy's still in shock about Denise, though, so I thought it was best not to press the issue. When the time is right, we'll work something out with Renee." After a pause, Reggie clasped his fingers, saying, "Frank, I cannot possibly explain to you what a relief it's been, dropping this burden! I'm not sure what exactly came over me the last few months, but I thank God it did. It's over. Now the healing can begin."

"Well, it seems like everything's gonna work out, then."

"Yeah, it does. And you know what?" Reggie chuckled. "I have to thank you, Frank, for putting up with the insanity for all these years. I mean, it's now that I clearly see the absurdity behind all those ridiculous conversations we've had over the years. I hate to say it, but if the truth be told, Denise shouldn't even exist. Even if I was unfaithful to Tracy here and there, she's always been my wife, and I should've been much more responsible. Protecting my family should always be my first priority. It should've been from the start."

"Should've, would've, could've . . . it makes no difference to cry over spilt milk. It's already spilt."

"You know, I realized that it's all about development. It's about how much of it I lacked when this problem first arose. I had a choice to make—a very important choice. I made the wrong one, Frank—*I made the wrong one.* I never should've misled Renee and set up a home life with her. Since she decided to keep the baby, I should've flown home immediately to tell my wife."

Reggie paused, staring through the window. "I have to be accountable for what happened, for the choice I did make. I've been a man for years, but only now do I feel like a decent man." He grabbed his beer then and took a sip, looking at Frank. "There's nothing more freeing than a clear conscience."

Franklin rose. "Well, Regg, I don't want to cut you short, but I've gotta get going. Theresa and I are going out, and I have to pick her up. It's great to hear that everything's working out for you. I'm glad. Just make sure you don't spill any more milk from here on out, eh?"

Reginald stood. "Thanks, buddy. I'll be in touch."

DRIVING HOME, REGINALD felt less relaxed than he usually did after a tête-à-tête with Franklin. . . .

Frank had been . . . he'd been different. Was there something going on with him?

BRENT STONE TOOK a sip of cappuccino, pulling the file for his next appointment from the cabinet. The folder tab read BROOKS, TRACY. He recalled that she was the new client referred by the beautiful mystery woman—the woman that had nearly caused Brent to compromise his treasured code of ethics.

On several occasions in the past weeks, Brent had come dangerously close to contacting Mrs. Justine Roman, tempted to pursue his interests. The company of his current lady friends had done little to erase the indelible impression of her in his mind.

As he sat reflecting on the morning she had walked into this office, Brent could still smell the spicy scent of her perfume. He recalled the large but elegant hat she'd worn, and the dark shades that had concealed her eyes, which he imagined to be blue and luminous.

A soft knock at his office door brought him out of his reverie. It was Lola, his sixteen-year-old niece whom he'd hired as a much needed secretary. "Hey, Uncle Brent, two ladies are here. Are you expecting them?" Brent rolled his eyes. One would think she didn't have a record of his appointments staring her in the face all day on the front desk. He would have to find time to give Lola some proper training.

"Two women? Who are they? I'm expecting a . . . Tracy Brooks," he said, consulting his docket.

Lola turned, and he heard her ask, "Is one of you Tracy Brooks?" He heard voices, and then Lola turned back, saying, "Yeah, she's here. You ready for her?"

"Yes, send them in." He wondered who was with her.

He opened her file as they walked in. The first one to enter was a strikingly gorgeous woman, who Brent assumed was Tracy Brooks. The second caused Brent's eyes to widen in pleasant surprise. It was her—the mystery woman, Justine—without the sunglasses. He'd been right—the eyes were blue . . . and beautiful. "Good afternoon, ladies. Please come in and have a seat."

Tracy extended her hand to him before sitting. "It's a pleasure, Mr. Stone."

Next, Justine extended her hand, and as he took it, he looked directly into her eyes and said, "It's wonderful to see you again, Ms. Roman." He was tempted to raise her hand to his lips, but he resisted the urge. At that moment, he decided he'd take a gamble, figuring that honest and direct was the key to this lady's bed. And there was no doubt that that's where he wanted to be.

Justine was immediately aware of the telepathy traveling from Brent's gray eyes to hers. "Thank you. Likewise." Over the next few minutes, as he discussed his findings with Tracy, Justine realized that she liked it. Why hadn't she noticed him before? As he spoke, she sat in silent observation. Her eyes fell to his lips, full and very capable, masculine-looking lips. His dark hair was cropped and had a blue-black sheer tone that Justine found extremely attractive. Was it just her raging hormones, or was he really interested?

"And that's basically the extent of the information you requested, Mrs. Brooks—" he was saying.

"Please, you may call me Tracy."

"Okay, Tracy . . . that's the extent of it. She was working as a store-front clerk at a local Mobil station when she met your husband. Sources say they dated for months until she became pregnant. Mr. Brooks proceeded to purchase a town home several months into the pregnancy—the street address is in the file if you're interested—which is where she and the child still reside to date. I was quite thorough, as you requested, so the file is very detailed. From minute details of Miss Jameson's pregnancy to the private school the child currently attends—it's all there."

Tracy wasn't sure how she felt. Save for the lunchtime traffic in the streets below, the room was silent once Brent completed his summation. She only knew that her heart was heavy with grief that wasn't justified. Renee Jameson was a total stranger to her. . . .

Franklin was no stranger to Reginald.

Brent spoke again. "Would you like a copy of the file, Tracy?" Ever respectful of his clients' emotional state while in his office, Brent spoke quietly, although Tracy Brooks looked anything but in need of consoling. She appeared quite relaxed in the armchair, sitting with her shapely legs crossed, head resting between her thumb and forefinger. If she was in any way affected by what she'd just heard, there was no indication.

"As a matter of fact, yes. I'd appreciate a copy of the file."

"Very well." Brent rose. "Please excuse me while I have Lola prepare one for you. It'll just be a few minutes."

Justine relaxed as the door closed softly behind Brent. She wondered how she had missed such a powerful attraction on her previous visit.

"Justine, I knew this would only make me feel worse, so why did I go through with this?" Tracy sighed. "Just had to satisfy that old curiosity. . . . The same one that killed the cat, I suppose."

Justine placed a gentle hand on her shoulder and said, "Tracy, just remember that the most important thing now is getting your family back on track. Every family has its ups and downs, but that's why family is so sacred, because you fight to get through them." Her gaze fell to the floor and she fought back tears. "I wish I had trusted mine more. . . . Then maybe I wouldn't have gotten into a mess named Roger Roman. But you know what? I'm a better person for it, and you will be, too. Trust me." She gave Tracy's shoulder a pat. "Go see Dr. Berenger."

"I plan to. I just hope I can get Reginald to agree to it without too much protest." Tracy turned to Justine then and said in a stage whisper, "Now . . ." She looked to the door before continuing. "Is it me, or did this Stone guy get an instant hard-on the second you walked through the door?"

Justine fought to contain the laughter that bubbled in her chest. "Oh . . . my . . . God! You mean, you noticed it, too? I thought it was just my sex-starved ego."

Laughing, Tracy said, "My goodness, I mean, the man looked as though he wanted to have you on the desk right here and now!" Tracy covered her mouth to muffle her girlish giggling.

"Well, I'm definitely available so, maybe I'll ask *him* out. What do you think about that?"

"Are you sure you want to jump onto the dating scene so soon? I mean, the divorce papers haven't even been drafted yet!"

"Oh, how wrong you are. They've been drawn up and are being de-livered as we speak—if they haven't been already."

"Well, Roger isn't going to be a very happy CEO today, is he?"

Just then, Brent returned with the two files. He handed Tracy the copy and filed the original back in his cabinet. "Well, I believe that con-cludes our business," he said, as the cabinet clicked shut. "I trust every-thing was done to your satisfaction?"

"Oh, most certainly, Mr. Stone. Thank you so much." They shook hands, and the two women rose.

"Excuse me, Ms. Roman, but may I speak with you alone for a mo-ment before you go?"

Justine stopped halfway to the door, her back to him. For the briefest moment, she made eye contact with Tracy and winked. "I'll meet you downstairs, Trace," she said before facing Brent.

Brent fixed his gray stare on Justine as the door clicked softly behind Tracy. "I want you to have dinner with me." His eyes coaxed . . . com-manded her to consent.

A raging tornado couldn't have dragged her eyes from his as she said in a firm voice, "I want me to have dinner with you, too." Her stom-ach quivered.

Brent resisted an urge to walk over and touch her. "Well, please, Ms. Roman, name the time and the place, and I'll be there."

Justine smiled. *Think?* He wanted her to think at a time like this? When she knew with delicious certainty that *dinner* was a synonym for *sex.*

Like a sleek panther, she moved over to his desk. Breaking the intense eye contact, she reached for a pen and jotted her new address on a Post-it pad.

Her blond hair fell over her shoulder as she tore off another sticky-paper, writing: *My place, this evening.* She paused for effect, and then scribbled, *And come prepared.*

Just then, her cell phone rang.

26

ROGER ROMAN SLAMMED his fist into the elegant marble of his credenza, causing several of his prized Lalique crystals to tumble to the floor. "Goddamn it! Justine, you can't do this to me!"

The divorce papers had arrived ten minutes earlier via messenger. After reading the pertinent clauses, he immediately picked up the phone and punched in Justine's cell phone number.

Hearing it ring twice, he hung up before she answered. What the fuck was he going to say to her? *Please don't sue me for 50 percent of my life?* She'd laugh in his face.

Roger threw off his glasses and rubbed the bridge of his nose. She knows. Somehow she found out about the women, and this was her way of gutting him like a fluttering fish. It was all in ink—signed, sealed, and fucking delivered!

Frustrated beyond belief, Roger grabbed the phone again and dialed Reginald's secretary, Dana. Knowing he was probably loud enough to cause permanent damage to her eardrum, he barked, "Is Brooks back from lunch yet?"

"Yes, Mr. Roman. Would you like me to transfer you?"

"No, thank you." He slammed the phone back into the cradle.

In less than a minute, Roger barged into Reginald's office, slamming the door behind him. "Brooks! She's trying to ruin me!" He tossed the papers onto Reginald's desk. "Half! She wants half of all assets and holdings! Christ, Brooks, how the hell did this happen? *When* the hell did this happen? One day, everything's perfectly normal, and the next, Justine's suing me for divorce and wants to take me for damn near everything I'm worth!" His face was flushed as he paced the length of Reginald's spacious office.

"Are you serious? *Justine is leaving you?*" Reginald's eyes quickly scanned the documents now in front of him.

"Leaving? She already left! I thought it was just some extensive cry for attention, but damn it, she's serious! This is no goddamn plea for attention!" Roger's forceful voice bounced off the walls of the office.

"All right, calm down for a minute. I'm sure the entire floor can hear you. Calm down, and let's just talk about it." Leaving his desk, Reginald settled into a leather armchair near the window. "Sit. Let's talk about this." Roger took the armchair opposite him and ran his fingers down the length of his face.

After a lengthy pause, he finally said, "Christ, Reginald, she wants to ruin me." This time his voice was so low that Reggie strained to hear it. "I can't believe it. She found out. . . . And she's pissed enough to try and stick me where it hurts. That's the reason for all this." Roger stared out the window at the lake across the street. "What the hell am I gonna do, Brooks?"

"Well, not that I'm the one to be handing out advice at this point, but I think you should try talking to her. Try to work it out with her. I mean, at least you don't have an outside kid to bring home."

Roger took a deep breath and exhaled heavily. "I don't know, Brooks. I mean, you should've seen her the day she left. She didn't even want me to touch her, let alone talk it over. I suggested a romantic getaway, you know, seclusion so we could reconnect. She wouldn't even consider it!"

"When did she leave?"

"Nearly two weeks ago."

"Justine left you two weeks ago and you didn't tell me? Why the hell not? Especially since I've been so on edge about Tracy. It would've done me some good to know you were miserable, too." Reggie half-smiled.

"I told you I didn't think it was anything significant. I figured I'd give her some space, you know, some time to think this foolishness over." Roger sighed again. "I guess that was a bad idea. . . . Well, I'll take your advice and go see her. If she wants to leave, she can leave. I won't fight her, but I'll see her in hell before she gets *one cent* more than I see fit to give her!" he said, slamming his fist into the chair's soft cushion.

Reginald offered a word of caution. "Just try to remember to keep your cool with her, though. I mean, the objective is for a resolution, right? So, don't run off half-cocked and add insult to injury."

Roger left the office ten minutes later, still fighting to control his rage.

Reginald raised his hands toward heaven. *Thank God I'm not in his shoes.*

LESS THAN AN hour after leaving the office, Roger drove up to the gate of the Enclave Estates and rang for Justine. She answered on the second ring, and Roger kept his voice steady as he said, "It's me. I got the papers. We need to talk."

He heard no response as the gate lifted and he was granted admittance to the community. That, at least, was something. She hadn't slammed the phone down and just left him sitting there.

I wonder where the hell the money came from for all this, he thought as he drove through the affluent neighborhood to the address he had jotted down in haste. *Where the hell else?* Justine hadn't worked a day in her life, thanks to their marriage. And now she had the gall to try and leave him!

ONCE THEY WERE face-to-face in her living room, Roger was clearly making every effort to retain his composure, while Justine silently prayed for this to end peacefully.

Roger loosened his tie. "Now, what's going on, Justine? Why exactly are you doing this? You pick up and move out of our home with no notice—you've obviously had the intention for quite some time since you had prearranged living arrangements—and now I get notified of divorce proceedings with your intent to sue me for fifty percent of everything." Roger sat back against the fluffy pillows of her sofa. "Please just tell me what this is really all about."

Justine rolled her eyes, annoyed. "Roger, I fail to see the problem. I explained how I felt the other day at the house. We've grown apart. Given your actions, you know it's your own fault and you can't make me love you again. It's too late for that. As for the money . . . I'm entitled. After all, I've invested eighteen years of my life—eighteen good years of my life. I'd say I was due a damn good return. Besides, you can more than afford it, dear."

Roger sat up. His eyes pierced hers. "And just what power on Earth do you think is going to make me agree to these terms, Justine? I admit that there have been other women, but you've always been my wife. You've always *reaped the benefits* of being my wife. I was just thinking to myself as I drove in here that you've never worked a day in your life!" His voice rose high above Justine's music from the stereo. "You fell in love with life down on Easy Street, didn't you? But now suddenly, I'm not good enough? Why? Because I've screwed a few other women? Get over it, Justine. All the other wives do. . . . Take Tracy Brooks, for example."

Something snapped in Justine then and she felt her composure slip away. "*A few women?* You bastard! You've got women all over the goddamn globe! And I have proof." Her eyes blazed as she lashed out, reliving the humiliation she'd felt. "Your whores are in Denver, L.A., Boston, Reno, London, Atlanta, Long Island, Manhattan—even Toronto!" Tears pooled in her frosty blue eyes. "Shall I go on? Or perhaps tangible proof is what you need. Is that it?" She spun around, leaving him gaping after her like a stunned animal.

After a quick trip to the bedroom she returned, crying openly and toting a thick manila envelope.

Roger knew instantly—of course—that he had lost the war.

27

"YOU HAVE TO INFORM this Joe person about the situation, Valerie. He probably doesn't have a clue that he has this disease, and he'll just continue to spread it," Olivia said.

They were sitting together in Valerie's room, waiting for Reginald to get home from the office. Their mother had informed them that they all needed to have an important family discussion, and they were both very curious, to say the least.

"Olivia, I can't. I don't wanna have anything to do with that scumbag. I don't care if he doesn't know. . . . Serves him right." Valerie lay back against her pillows and curled into a fetal position. It seemed she couldn't get herself to stop crying. Ever since she'd awakened from her sedation on that horrid morning . . .

The morning Olivia had taken her to see Dr. Gabriel had proven to be one she would not soon forget. After giving her a thorough examination, he diagnosed her with one of the many forms of the human papilloma viruses, a.k.a. genital warts. The warts were internal and had developed on her cervix. He explained that the douching had been a good thing, as it caused the bleeding, which may not have occurred otherwise. He also clarified that although outbreaks could be treated, this was indeed a virus for which there was no known cure, and flare-ups were unpredictable and irregular. He then mentioned a few drugs used to control such outbreaks. Valerie listened in a daze as he talked about methods of removal. From a great distance, she heard the words *burn, freeze,* and *preferred method of treatment.*

Since she had been in no position to make any decisions, when they got out to the front desk, Olivia set up an appointment for her to return the following day. The procedure took less than an hour, and Olivia had lingered nervously in the waiting room, thinking how easily it could've been her lying in there with that problem.

Going through this experience with Valerie sobered her to the fact that Sean could easily bring something awful to her. Then what would she do? After all, she had gotten pregnant, hadn't she? And nothing about him had changed. He was still disappearing for days and feeding her bullshit stories about where he'd been and why he hadn't returned her phone calls.

Yes, Olivia had definitely learned from the experience. And she, too, would never forget it. Almost overnight, Sean Johnson and all he symbolized officially became American history.

Now as Valerie refused to do what she insisted was the right thing and contact this boy, Olivia reached over and shoved her hip. "You have to tell him. Do you want someone else to go through what you did? Valerie? You must tell him. You have a moral responsibility to tell him."

Valerie rolled her eyes, heaving a submissive sigh. "Fine. I'll tell him. I'll call him tomorrow. You happy now? Geez." She had no intention of doing any such thing. Deep down, she imagined the experience would be far too humiliating. If she could help it, Joseph Ellison would never hear her voice again.

"Good. The last thing he needs to do is keep having sex and spreading that stuff." Olivia softened when she saw new tears on Valerie's face. "Oh, Val . . . I know this has been rough, but it'll smooth out. Cry if you have to, but try to remember that if we don't learn anything from this, then we'd *really* have something to cry about."

Just then, there was a knock at the door, followed by Reginald's voice announcing his arrival. Valerie ran into her bathroom and splashed water on her puffy face. The way she felt, the last thing she needed was questions from her parents. As it was, she wished like hell that she could somehow grow a new body. She was utterly disgusted with herself. Olivia gave her a few more words of encouragement before they slowly opened the bedroom door and descended the stairs.

"I WONDER WHAT this is about," Olivia said as they headed for the den. Valerie just shrugged. At this point, she didn't much care.

When they sat down, Olivia said, "So what's this all about? Daddy going back to Orlando again?"

Valerie remained silent but sent a venomous look her way. Olivia's attitude about their father obviously still annoyed the hell out of her.

"Olivia, this is serious—" Tracy began, a glance at Valerie causing her to break off. "Val, what's wrong? Your eyes are red and swollen. Have you been crying or something?"

Feigning a yawn, Valerie said, "Crying? No, I was asleep."

"Oh . . . well." She returned her gaze to Olivia and said in a firm voice, "Your father's not going anywhere, but there is a matter of great importance that he has to share with the both of you." Tracy turned her eyes to Reginald, as if to say, *They're all yours.*

Reginald cleared his throat and kept an air of confidence about his words, but they all still strained to hear him. "You both have a baby sister." He watched for their reactions.

At first, shock registered simultaneously on their faces. Olivia's face then became hard. Valerie's filled with pain and disbelief.

"She's six years old and her name is Denise," he continued. "Your mother and I have disc—"

"Another daughter? Daddy, you can't be serious!" Valerie said, wide-eyed. But she seemed to know from the looks on her parents' faces that he was serious—very serious. "With who? How did that happen!" Her already saturated eyes suddenly filled with fresh tears. "A little girl? Oh, my God . . . how could that happen?" Her hand flew to cover her mouth as she searched her parents' faces.

Reggie opened his mouth to respond, but Olivia interjected. "Well, well. I can't say that I'm even the *least* bit surprised." She folded her arms across her chest and looked out the window. "So, do we happen to have *any more* siblings we should know about, or do you plan to spring them on us every six years or so?" Her tone was sharp as she looked back at her father.

Reginald raised his hand, face full of confusion. "Wait a minute . . . what is this? You moved out of the house, and suddenly you earned a ticket to be insolent? I am still your father." His face changed then; he became very matter-of-fact as he pointed a finger in Olivia's direction. "No more—do you hear me? I've had enough. Enough of this ridiculous father beseeching daughter for forgiveness. I—am—your—father, damn it! And I will not allow my own child—my firstborn child at that—to insult me in my own house! You may not live under this roof anymore, but whenever you enter through that front door, you *will* have respect. Whether you like it or not, *I will always be your father.*" Reginald's anger boiled. The more he had coddled her, the more she had shied away.

They all watched mutely as his anger pooled. "For years I've been jumping through hoops to make you happy. . . . Bending over backwards to make a good life for you, to make up for not being here. But obviously none of it's ever been good enough. Hell, maybe I deserve some resentment." He spread his arms wide and then let them drop. "I don't know, maybe so. . . . But I do know this: You disrespect me again, and I promise you, it'll be the *last* time you do it while under my roof!"

Her dad's eyes bored into hers. Olivia was momentarily dumbfounded, and it was all over her face. Reggie was sure she couldn't remember the last time he'd spoken to anyone—much less her—with such raw emotion, good or bad.

Tracy watched the pivotal scene. Fighting to control her own emotions, she said, "That brings us to the next reason for this meeting." She kept her voice calm, ever the conciliator. "I want us—the four of us—to go see a family counselor. I truly believe that . . . well, that we'll really need it to help us get through everything that's happening."

A hush fell over the room then for what seemed like an eternity. They each tried to assemble their thoughts. The creeping minute hand on the marble grandfather clock seemed to echo throughout the room like a freight train, hitting and dismantling the family with each tick.

Valerie's eyes locked momentarily with her father's. She couldn't believe that he actually had another daughter, another child besides them. What did that mean? What was going to happen to their lives together now that this other kid existed? Why did this have to happen? Was it really happening? Did her parents really call them downstairs for this? She thought she heard the telephone ringing off in the distance, but she couldn't be sure. . . .

Olivia stared unseeingly at the space in front of her. She wasn't sure how she felt just then or how she wanted to react to all that had been said in the last five minutes. Her mind kept replaying her father's pent-up frustration. Obviously, he'd been suppressing those feelings. . . . And Olivia was ambivalent about how to react to them. What should she say?

Tracy struggled with the urge to shut down all the carefully running facets of her self-control and just cave in, right there in front of them. She didn't know how she could stand the myriad of emotions running through her. She heard the invasive ringing of the telephone, but who cared? How did one handle such awful things? Especially when they were happening to your own family? How did one handle finding the love of your life at such a young age, creating two extraordinary new lives out of that love, only to have it all turn into a scene such as this? She crossed her arms over her chest and squeezed herself.

Reginald shook his head slowly. Was he really responsible for all of this? Had he really been the catalyst?

Yes, he had. To the point where they all now needed to go see a shrink. But hadn't he always known that someday he'd have to pay a price for years of pretending to be someone he wasn't? Beleaguered by his fault, Reginald slowly lowered himself into a nearby lounge chair.

Renee had only been a warm body, nothing more, nothing less. Just a warm body. Unfortunately, she had become pregnant. And what had he done? He allowed Franklin to convince him that living in make-believe would be the best thing for everyone. He created the illusion that he was an available and unattached man. He had grossly misled her.

Simultaneously, on the other end of his life, he had pretended to be a faithful, hardworking husband and father, a man who deserved the love and respect of his children. He had grossly misled them, as well.

By the time the fog of false pretense had lifted, he'd come home to find that his wife had been left to seek solace in the arms of another man, and his little girls were now women that he knew next to nothing about.

At that very moment, the essential, harsh reality of what he had done settled around Reginald. There were at least *six* lives that would've gone down roads better traveled had he not lost his head in a mist of pretension. And sadly enough, that pretension had lasted nearly seven years. This was the result.

Finally, Olivia broke the saturated silence. She took heed to control her voice so that it wouldn't be offensive. "I just want to say one thing before I go get my purse and leave." She rose and moved toward the entryway. "I'm glad that I don't live here anymore. I couldn't bear living around such a scandalous mess. Good luck with the new kid . . . and the shrink."

"You hold it right there, Olivia." Tracy rose from her chair. "Just where do you think you're going? You may not live here with us anymore, but you are *still* a part of this family and we have to see our way through this 'scandalous mess,' as you so suitably phrased it."

"How? By going to see a shrink, like we're all crazy? No, thank you. It would be so embarrassing. I can handle my own problems. I'm not going to some . . . some *psychiatrist,* like a nutcase."

"And just how are you handling *this* particular problem? By walking out? Pretending that we all don't matter? Well, I've got news for you, young lady, we do matter. We're your family. I am your mother; I gave birth to you. He's your father." She motioned toward Reginald. "He was there. Neither one of you would be here, living and breathing to express yourselves this way, if it weren't for the two of us.

"We're not perfect—I'm not suggesting that we ever have been—but if we hadn't done right by you, neither one of you would be as bright and intelligent as you are. Nor would you be able to think for yourselves as you do now."

Tracy took a deep breath. "Now, you may be of age and you may live on your own and you may think you're all grown up, but I'll tell you *both* that you'll *never* be old enough to have the right to turn your backs on us. We happen to be parents who don't deserve that from their children. You were raised to be more sensible than that.

"Now, we all just found out that there is another child in the picture.

Reggie and I decided that we could work through it. We've both made mistakes"—she looked pointedly at Valerie, who quickly looked away—"but we've loved each other for a long time, long before either of you came into our lives. But in order to have the best chance at a better life, we need help. There's nothing wrong with that, nothing to be ashamed of in seeking professional help."

Olivia shrugged. "I'm sorry, Mom. I'm not going. I can't . . . I just can't." She began walking away.

"Olivia!" Tracy's tone was sharp. Olivia stopped in her tracks and spun around to face her mother. Tears filled Tracy's eyes, but her words were firm. "If you leave this house and refuse to join us in this fight— *a fight for each one of us*—you've turned your back on this family and on any hope for us to live well with each other. She whispered the next words. "If you do that, stay away. You won't be welcomed back—and you certainly won't get any more financial help. . . . Not even to buy yourself an aspirin."

Olivia and Valerie gasped.

Reginald, feeling broken, looked from Tracy to Olivia, anticipating her response.

Olivia stood frozen. Her mind rejected her mother's words. *Stay away, you won't be welcomed back?* She couldn't be serious!

But . . . what if she was?

"Mom, you're not for real—you can't mean that!" Olivia stepped back into the room. "Just because I don't want to go see a shrink?"

Tracy said nothing. She simply dried her cheeks and stared at her daughter. Olivia was well aware that it ran deeper than that—much deeper.

Valerie, still crying herself, watched the scene play out as though it were all just an elaborate dream. This simply couldn't be happening. . . . Why was this happening?

Finally, eyes filling with tears of frustration, Olivia caved. "Fine! I'll go! But I resent that you're forcing this on me!" With that, she stormed off toward the staircase.

They were all sitting in silence when she came back down, carrying her purse.

Without a word, Olivia purposefully strode out the front door, closing it quietly behind herself.

28

JUST A FEW HOURS after her exhausting confrontation with Roger, Justine opened her front door to Brent Stone. A shard of apprehension shot through her when their eyes collided. What was she doing? She didn't know this man from Adam! And she hadn't had sex with anyone but Roger Roman in more than eighteen years. Was she ready to do it now?

Brent took in her attire, his eyes leisurely sweeping over her. It was obvious—pleasurably obvious—that she had dressed for the occasion. She was ready. She was ready indeed.

The blue spaghetti-strap dress—if you could call it a dress—came up short, just below her buttocks, and grazed them just below the flesh. It looked as if a light breeze would leave her *quite* exposed. Brent liked it. . . . He liked it so much, he began growing deliciously hard. He was ready.

"You're here." She stepped aside and let him in. This man had such a presence! His fragrance filled her nostrils, and she smiled. She felt like a schoolgirl, like a virgin again. And her body begged to be deflowered by this impressively virile man. Justine ached for him to take her into his arms that very second, as he took a seat on her sofa. She sat beside him, leaving a polite distance between them. The soft sounds of her smooth jazz CD elevated her fervent state.

For a moment they simply stared at each other, both aware of the high-voltage power in the attraction going on between them. The circumstance under which they met crept its way into Justine's mind, but she quickly pushed it away. She wanted this guy, and she didn't care how she had come to meet him. She could think about that later.

Brent assessed the lady and obviously liked what he saw. She wanted to be dominated. She was the type. She didn't need coaxing or persuasive speeches, as most did.

"Would you like a drink?"

He didn't respond, nor did his eyes leave hers as he slowly moved over her, pushing her onto her back. He kissed her hard then, and Justine felt an instant moistness gush between her legs. Why had she wasted so much time pining for Roger?

Brent slid his tongue into her mouth and parted her thighs, slipping his fingers under the dress. When he discovered her bare and dripping, he lost control. A needy groan escaped him and he quickly got rid of his pants. Justine felt him hard and pulsing as the tip of his penis pierced the lapels of her sex. She closed her eyes and inhaled.

Then he was inside her, he was riding her, and it was intensely delicious. Between her cries and Brent's groans, they drowned out the saxophones and pianos coming from the speakers.

WHEN IT WAS over and they had drifted from their high, they laughed at the picture they made on her sofa. She, spread-eagle with her blue mini rolled up under her arms, and he, crammed into her and bottomless, still wearing his silk shirt, which was now damp with sweat.

Much later, they lay entwined, sipping Möet as the music played and they talked. Brent admitted his immediate attraction to her and how he'd dubbed her "the beautiful mystery woman." Though Justine was flattered, she was careful to guard her thoughts. Roger had known her heart and soul through and through, and it had done more harm than good for their marriage. She would not wear her feelings on her sleeve for any other man, even if he were the irresistible Brent Stone.

"So, what's the story with your friend Tracy?"

"Hmm?" Justine felt deliciously sated. Her body had been yearning, and it had been more than satisfied. It was bliss, pure bliss.

"Tracy Brooks. Is she leaving her husband?" Brent gently stroked her gorgeous blond hair.

"I don't think so. She's in a rough place right now. But I do know that they love each other. I just hope they can work it out."

"And you? Are you leaving your husband?" Brent's hand stilled. "Because I'd hate to have an affair with a married woman."

She smiled against his chest before she said, "So does that mean you plan to do this again?"

"Oh, hell yes." His expression was serious. "There's something about you that seems to draw me in. . . . Just like the moth and the flame." His eyes suggested that the appeal was more than just sexual.

She told him about her visit with Roger earlier that day, and about its success. After having a look at the glossy photos that featured none other than Roger Roman himself, Roger had chosen to pay her off instead of fighting her in court. When all was said and done, Justine would never have to work a day in her life. . . . Befitting compensation under the circumstances.

Now as she lay in the arms of this extremely attractive and available man, Justine relaxed for the first time in years. She knew with absolute certainty that she could survive without Roger, that she would be happy. She no longer needed to rely on anything for reassurance.

Making love with Brent Stone was simply the beginning—the beginning of the rest of her life. A life that would never again include Roger Roman.

29

As Thanksgiving Day approached, Tracy busied herself helping her mother make arrangements for their traditionally huge feast. Each year they alternated between her parents' house or Reginald's.

She and Reggie had agreed to hold off on their family therapy until after Thanksgiving. Tracy began to wonder if that had been such a good idea. The situation in the house had become more strained than she could bear.

Several weeks had passed since their memorable family meeting, and Olivia had been scarce. Tracy only glimpsed her on the few occasions she came to take Valerie out. Olivia would drive up, blow the horn, and wait for her sister to rush out to the car.

It was tearing Tracy apart.

She missed her. Their relationship had always been such a close one. But there had been no alternative to giving her the ultimatum. The time had come for Olivia to brush that ridiculous chip off her shoulder. After all, her father had provided her with all she ever wanted or needed her entire life. Hell, did she forget where the money had come from to buy that town house? Olivia's job would never pay the rent.

Yes, the time had come to take a stand, show her what really mattered in life. Even so, Tracy had no idea what she would've done had Olivia called her bluff. She didn't even want to think about the possibility.

Valerie, on the other hand, had begun spending much more time with them, with her mother in particular. When Tracy was cooking dinner in the kitchen, Valerie was usually there, offering to help. Whenever she was going out to run errands or grocery shop, Valerie wanted to accompany her. In her heart, Tracy was joyous about the transition. Still, she couldn't help wondering what sparked the sudden attentiveness. . . . Could it be because of the news of Denise? Perhaps Valerie, too, sensed the need for togetherness at this pivotal time in all their lives.

Reginald, as expected, had been going the extra mile to bring them closer together. Never had he been more determined or more sincere in his efforts. And the more effort he put forth, the farther it seemed to push Tracy away.

Even though he had no way of knowing, Franklin dwelled between them like an air pocket. Each time Reginald surprised Tracy with a special gift when he came in from work, or caressed her in their bed at night and whispered tender words in her ear as they made love, she was haunted by her secret. She was suddenly unable to get it out of her mind, and she lived with a foreboding that she never would. And what was worse? Frank seemed to be around constantly nowadays, and he had a serious attitude problem. Even Reginald had commented on it.

On several occasions, he'd made efforts to get her alone, but Tracy refused. What was there to talk about? Her conscience was eating her alive as it was. She found herself wishing now that he would just disappear from their lives all together. . . . And she sensed that Frank was fully aware of her discomfort.

Tracy realized that eventually, she would have to find some way to put the guilt behind her. She wished she had someone to talk to about it, but whom? Shame barred her from revealing such a thing to anyone. . . .

It was funny how different things were now. When Reginald was away, she had taken great pleasure in her affair with Frank; now that he had come home to her and confessed his own wrongdoing, she felt as if she should be burned at the stake for treason.

One thing was for sure: Confession was out of the question.

Or was it?

*   *   *

THE DAY BEFORE Thanksgiving, Tracy was sitting at her vanity table, blow-drying her hair, when Reginald entered their bedroom with a long white jewelry box. Tracy felt the familiar cringe at the sight of yet another gift. God, he was doing so much. And though she loved him for it, it only made the shame fester. . . . A vengeful monster within her.

She watched him walk over to where she sat; so tall, so handsome and capable. She'd spent all of her adulthood loving this man. He was the father of her babies. . . . The love of her life.

And she had slept with Frank.

"This is for you." Reginald placed the box directly in front of her.

Catching his eye in the mirror, she said, "You know, you don't have to keep doing this. I'm okay. We'll be okay. I know where your heart is."

Taking off his coat, Reggie sat next to her on the ottoman. "Open the box."

Smiling slightly, Tracy removed the box's lid. Inside lay two platinum necklaces against gold cotton. Both had diamond-encrusted pendants that read T & R, NOVEMBER 25, 2004. Her eyes flooded with tears.

They both already had necklaces that read T & R, APRIL 18, 1982, which they used to wear faithfully while they were dating.

"Today marks the beginning of the rest of our lives together. Tonight, I want us to *officially* put the past behind us and start writing on a new page in the book of our life together." He reached for one of the necklaces and placed it around her neck. "And I want us to wear these just like we used to wear the old ones all those years ago. . . . To sort of benchmark a revival."

Tracy slowly reached out and folded her arms around his neck. She squeezed her eyes shut and held him close. *How much of this can I take?*

"Trace? Can you do that? Are you ready to put this whole mess behind us and truly move on? I know we have Denise to think about, but are you sure you can handle it? Because I need you to be sure." He pulled away from her and his eyes searched hers, seeking reassurance.

"Reggie, I'm not going anywhere. You know I'm not. I've made mistakes, too, but like you said in New York . . ." Her gaze fell before she continued. "Just because there wasn't a child as a product doesn't mean the possibility didn't exist. . . ."

He placed a quick kiss on her lips before he rose and got something out of his briefcase. "I have another surprise." She saw him pull a CD from a plastic bag. "Nat King Cole. You love him so much, but"—he held it up so she could see it—"you don't have this one." He smiled.

Tracy's eyes widened. "Oh, thank you, Reggie! That's so thoughtful! Thank you so much. Put it on!"

"I knew *that* would put a smile on your face." Reggie slid the CD into the stereo, and when the smooth melody of "The Very Thought of You" filled the room, he turned back to her. "Now, there's something I wanna ask you to do for me, but I'm not sure what you'll think about it—"

"What?"

"I'd like for you to write the letter to Renee."

"What? Me? Why should I write it?"

"Well, I'll tell you what to write, but I want you to be a part of it. I don't want to do it without you. And also because your handwriting could help her realize that this is not just another fictitious story. . . ."

Tracy did not feel comfortable writing the letter, but she agreed to sit with him while he wrote it himself. They went downstairs to Reginald's home office, where he labored over it for nearly two hours. It was an arduous experience for Tracy. She still found it difficult to believe that Reggie had another offspring out there. . . . A child she hadn't mothered.

Once they were both happy with the final draft, Tracy sealed the envelope and promised to mail it for him right after Thanksgiving.

THANKSGIVING DAY WAS uneventful. Olivia was a no-show, despite the fact that Valerie practically begged her to join them, and they each felt the emptiness of her absence. Nevertheless, they all went through the motions as expected, but their minds were elsewhere.

Reginald watched football with Tracy's brothers, but his mind was only partially tuned into the game. He sensed a strange resistance in Tracy. Though she said and did all the right things, something wasn't right, and Reginald spent the better part of the day thinking about it. Had the news about Renee and Denise been harder to swallow than she was letting on?

Tracy busied herself, as usual, at her mother's side. Though Beverly made several attempts to talk about the issues at home, Tracy was reticent in her responses. As time progressed, her guilt about Franklin was only increasing, and it was all she could do not to wear it plainly on her sleeve for the world to see. The last thing she wanted to do was discuss the unpleasant goings-on with anyone—even her mother. She just couldn't yet.

Valerie stuck close to her mother and grandmother, despite the fact that her cousins were there and encouraged her to mingle with them. She worried about the new course her life was taking. She worried about her condition. . . . About the possibility of another outbreak of warts . . .

It was a solemn day, and in their own unique ways, each of them found it difficult to be thankful, given the sequence of events that had led them to their present individual situations.

CURLED UP ON her sofa and watching the parades on television, Olivia spent Thanksgiving Day completely alone. Her phone rang several times, but she never even bothered to check the caller ID box to see who was calling.

30

ORLANDO, FLORIDA

HER BROTHER, JOHN, stared down at her; his eyes were blazing as he laughed. Her mother and father sat together on a see-through sofa, shaking their heads in disappointment. Her sister, Helen, was reaching for Denise, whom she held firmly in her arms.

"Denise goes with me!" Renee hissed as she stepped backward. She looked down quickly and realized she was barefoot. "Wherever I go, she goes."

Helen stretched and grabbed for Denise's feet, but Renee pulled away, stepping backward farther and farther until their sniggering faces seemed to finally be fading. But she could still hear the laughing. They were laughing at her, her own family.

"Renee!" She heard Helen's voice. "Renee! Come back! She's only six years old. . . . Bring Denise back! We'll take care of you—both of you! Come back!" Helen's voice became desperate, but all Renee heard was the laughing.

She held Denise with a firm grip, hanging on to her for dear life. Denise was her only hope.

"Mommy?"

She heard her daughter's voice above all the laughter as she continued to step backward. Renee was afraid, and she glanced behind her to see where they were going, but she could see nothing. Nothing but darkness lay before them.

"Mommy? It's dark down there. Where are we going?"

"Be quiet now, Denise. I need you to be quiet so Mommy can think, okay?" Renee continued to step backward into the darkness.

"But, Mommy, I'm scared. It's dark over there. Let's . . . let's go back to Aunt Helen." She felt Denise's small hands tighten their grip on her shoulders.

"Renee!" Helen's voice reverberated throughout the darkness. "Renee, you fool! You're such a fool!" Then she began to laugh again. "You stupid fool! You have to come back—you have no place else to go now! We told you, you fool! We told you!" Helen's forceful laughter pierced her, a sharp, evil stab. She looked down.

Her hands were bleeding.

Renee turned around now and began running into the darkness. She had to get away from them, all of them. She ran even though she could see nothing.

She secured her grip on Denise, and she ran.

HER BODY JERKED, awakening her from the awful dream. Renee bolted to a sitting position in the bed and realized that her silk nightgown was plastered to her heaving chest, soaked in sweat. She'd begun wearing her sexiest attire to bed, hoping that Reginald might return and surprise her late at night or early in the morning. Alas, he had not yet returned.

As usual, as reality slowly settled around her, her body slackened with relief and she breathed deeply. She was safe in her bedroom. She'd had another dream.

The dreams had been happening a lot lately. Always the same piercing laughter. Always her holding Denise and running into the blackness. And always ending with her waking up soaked in sweat, feeling so frightful, it gnawed her soul.

What the hell was all the laughing about?

IN THE MONTHS since Reginald had left to care for his sick daughter, Renee had been living in torment.

There was no consoling her; there was no making her happy. Nothing anyone said or did took away the emptiness. She wanted Reginald back, here at home with her and Denise.

Renee felt as though she was lost. . . . And she wouldn't find herself again until Reginald returned to her. . . .

SOMETHING WAS WRONG with her mommy. Denise didn't know how she could fix it. How could she make Mommy like her again?

One evening, her mommy had set her bath and left her in the tub to give herself a washing with the soap and water. Since she had never done it before, she had tried her best with the big bar of soap. She did what she saw her mommy and her Aunt Helen do; made bubbles with the water and rubbed them all over her body. They always said to wash under your arms and privates really good. Denise made sure she washed hard, so that maybe Mommy would see how good she did it and she would like her again.

But no . . . all she did was come and dry her off with her big Barbie towel and pull her nightgown over her head. Then she told her to stay in her room and go straight to bed. How long was Mommy going to be mad at her? What did she do to make her mad? Denise wished she knew so she could stop doing it. She didn't like doing her own wash in the tub. She wanted her mommy to give her baths.

Denise also wanted her daddy to come back home so that she could stop missing him now. She wondered if Mommy would be happy again if Daddy came back home from his long time at work.

Now as she lay in her bed, snuggled under her Barbie comforter, Denise closed her eyes and said her prayers. She told God to bless Mommy and Daddy, to make her a good little girl so that her mommy would like her again, and to make her daddy come back home so he could help her make Mommy be happy again.

AS WITH NEARLY every morning of late, on Thanksgiving Day, Renee had to force herself to open her eyes when she awoke. A look at the bedside clock told her it was early, only seven thirty.

She heard the chatter of a television and realized that that must've been what had awakened her. Getting up, she made her way down the hallway and opened Denise's bedroom door. She wasn't there. The television was on, however, and Renee turned and made her way downstairs.

She came up short when she entered the kitchen. Denise was standing on the counter in her nightgown, reaching on top of the refrigerator for the box of Lucky Charms cereal near the edge. One of the wooden chairs was pulled out from under the table and had been perched by the counter.

"What are you doing?" Renee stomped over to the counter and pulled her down. "Are you crazy? Suppose you fell off there." She slammed Denise down on her feet and shoved the chair back under the table, the hind legs making an awful screeching sound. "And why do you have that television so loud this early in the morning, Denise? It woke me up!" She bore down on her daughter and slapped her hard across her cheek. "Get your little butt upstairs and turn that TV off right now!"

Denise's hand flew to her jaw to smother the stinging. Tears pooled in her eyes. "But, Mommy, I'm hungry. I just wanted some cereal, and you didn't wake up yet, so I was trying to get it by myself."

Renee backhanded her exposed jaw. "Did I not say get upstairs? Get upstairs and turn off that damn television—now!"

Denise held in her wail as her small body shook with a moan. The tears fell as she covered her mouth to avoid making her mother slap her again.

She knew better. . . . This was becoming a habit.

HELEN WAS WASHED with pride as she withdrew the turkey from the oven. No one, not even her mother, could make a turkey as well as she did. It was always tender and succulent. Yes, her turkeys were the best.

As she and her mother, Bea, prepared the food for serving, Renee and Denise arrived. As usual, Denise came running in to them with a big smile. Helen wiped her hands on a dishcloth and bent to scoop her up.

Her eyes widened in alarm when she saw her face. The child had four well-defined fingers printed out on her left cheek, just under her eye. Both sides of her face were slightly swollen and red.

"Renee, what the hell happened now? Mom, look at this child's face!" Helen held her up toward Bea.

Bea's face hardened as she spun on Renee. "What in Christ's name is going on? Why did you slap the poor child in her face like that?"

Helen clutched Denise to her and said, "I'm gonna go put something on these welts. Oh, my God!" She shook her head as she carried Denise off to the bathroom upstairs.

Renee rolled her eyes as she addressed her mother. "Listen, she woke me up this morning with the television blasting, and when I went downstairs, she had climbed up on the kitchen counter trying to get the cereal off the top of the refrigerator! Now, Denise ought to know better than that. She could've fallen off and broken her neck."

"No more than you whacking her across the jaw so hard it left your handprint on her face!" Bea took a deep breath. "Renee, I don't think anyone has to tell you that you shouldn't have slapped the baby on her face like that! Why not slap her on her butt or on her legs? Why on her face? Did you see what you did to her face? That wasn't necessary, Renee!" Bea slammed a large serving spoon down on the counter. "I'm sick of you beating and yelling at the poor child as though you're some god-awful tyrant and she's a little devil. She's not! She's a good little girl."

Her brother walked in. John was of medium height and though he was thirty, he didn't look a day over eighteen. "What's all this going on in here? We can hear you all from the den!"

"Renee's gonna beat that baby to death, you hear? Every time I turn around, there's a new mark or something on the child." Bea looked at Renee, hard. "What's happening to you, daughter? What's really going on with you?"

"Look, you all need to just back off. Leave me alone. Children need discipline. Denise is no exception. I'm not breaking any bones. I just have to let her know when she's doing something wrong, that's all."

"It seems the poor child can't breathe for fear of doing something wrong, Renee!" Bea said, slamming her hand on the counter once again. "Can't you see that?"

John stepped over to his mother. "All right, calm down, now." After a pause, he said, "Renee, why don't you let Denise stay with Helen and the kids for a while? Maybe that'll help. . . . For a while at least."

Renee's head swung to face him. "What? Stay with Helen? No, that's not necessary. I can take care of my child, thank you, John." She couldn't do that. What would Reginald think?

"Denise tells me that she's been washing herself, as she puts it!" Helen said, storming back into the kitchen. From the sounds of play coming from the den, she'd apparently left Denise with Ashley and the others. "Renee, please tell me that you haven't been making the little girl bathe herself."

Renee rolled her eyes again. "I haven't been making her bathe herself. Come on. I've been teaching her how to bathe properly on her own, but I still bathe her myself. Geez, would you all get off my case? I'll take Denise and go home if this is how we're spending our Thanksgiving Day!"

Bea pursed her lips tightly, grabbed the spoon that she had discarded, and resumed serving the steaming rice into a large dish.

No one said another word.

"SOMETHING HAS TO be done about this situation before it gets worse," Helen said later, when Renee had gone. "Is it just me, or isn't it obvious Renee's losing it?" She dried the last casserole dish and handed it to her mother.

Bea absently took the dish and gazed thoughtfully through the kitchen window over the sink. "I think one of us ought to get in touch with Reginald."

Sitting at the table, her husband, Ben, cleared his throat and reached for a toothpick. "What's he gonna do? He's the reason her head's all screwed up now. In all my born days, I never knew I'd live to see such a pass. She just let that man go straight to her head!"

"Oh, come on, Daddy. Mom's right." Helen joined her father and brother at the table. "If Reggie knew what was happening with Denise, I'm sure he'd be on the next plane leaving Miami. Everybody here knows that he loves that little girl. . . . Regardless of everything else."

"I just can't understand how she could've changed so much in the last few months," John said, crinkling his forehead. "I mean, to actually be abusing Denise like that . . . it's unbelievable. What's really going on in her head?"

Ben let out a harsh laugh around the toothpick. "I'll tell you what's going on in her head: Reginald, that's what. The man up and left her and went back to Miami to his wife and kids, and she can't handle it, so she's taking the frustrations out on the only person around, and that's the child—*his* child at that."

"Ben, do you think she might somehow resent Denise or something?" Bea asked, taking the remaining seat at the table, across from her husband. "Like, what if this is more than her simply venting frustration?"

"Well, venting does make sense, doesn't it? I mean, she never treated the child that way before, right? Even when the man was out of town all the time, she never put bruises like that on Denise."

All four sat in silence then, thinking. Something had to be done to help Renee and to spare Denise any more abuse. For months, the family had watched Renee slipping deeper and deeper into herself. She became extremely edgy and unusually quiet, and at a moment's notice would take off anyone's head without much provocation. Just about anything said or done aggravated and annoyed her, and of late, the aggravation ended up as a vivid bruise on Denise's body. They had to do something. They had to do something soon.

Helen broke the silence. "So, who's gonna call him? Who has his number in Miami? Because I don't."

"I got it for Renee a few weeks ago, after she hounded me for the favor," John said. "But I told her she was a fool. Really, how honest are his explanations if he can't even give her a number to reach him at?"

"Your friend Kenny still works for the phone company?" Helen asked. John nodded his head. Helen said, "Good. Get the number again, and I'll call Reggie. He needs to come down here and talk some sense into this girl before somebody gets hurt, because I swear if I see *one* more bruise on that little girl, I'll give Renee one to match it! Did you guys hear me? Blood pressure be damned. I'll flatten her."

"Oh now, Helen, let's hope this doesn't get that bad. I don't know if I could stand the thought of you two fighting like a couple of strangers." Bea patted Helen's shoulder.

Ben stood. "Come on, Beatrice. Let's get on home before it gets too late. This day has worn me out."

WHEN HER PARENTS and brother had left, Helen went about straightening the den before heading upstairs to shower and go to bed. Brian and Ashley were already asleep, and the house was finally peaceful after all the day's hustle and bustle.

Though she didn't want to alarm her mother and father by admitting it, Helen had a terrible sense of foreboding about everything going on with Renee and Denise. The poor child was suffering for . . . for what, really? The fact that her father was gone, perhaps for good? Or was it more than that? Was it because she was his child, but that she wasn't enough to keep him in Orlando? Was that the *real* truth at the core of Renee's reckless, impulsive behavior?

Helen slowly climbed the stairs, heading for the bathroom. Her heart was so heavy, worrying about her precious little niece. She prayed to God that Denise went safely to bed on this Thanksgiving night. . . . Without any fresh bruises.

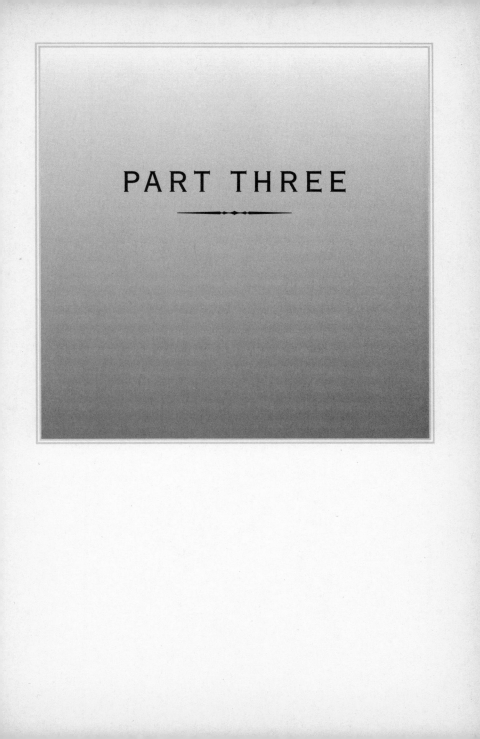

PART THREE

31

MIAMI, FLORIDA

FRANKLIN STOOD STARING into the refrigerator for far longer than was necessary. His mind could not have been farther from the roast beef and mashed potato dinner Theresa had prepared and left for him.

His life was virtually unrecognizable.

Weeks ago, Theresa had informed him that she was pregnant. What the hell else could go wrong?

The day following his last discussion with Reginald had proved to be a red-letter day in the life of Franklin Bevins. He and Theresa had gone to a house party the night before, and she spent the entire evening complaining about every scent she smelled, even mentioning how Reginald's cologne had sickened her the previous day. The thought of pregnancy had never even crossed Frank's mind. He told her she might be coming down with something. . . . Little did he know that something was a mini Franklin.

When she broke the news, his first instinct was to deny, to question that it was positively his child. But alas, even he was above such malicious conduct—he was nearly 100 percent sure it was his baby. Anyone who knew Theresa would know it had to be his baby.

In the end, though, he inflicted just as much damage as if he had denied it. Theresa had practically begged for him to "see the light," as she put it. With hope in her eyes and urgency in her voice, she begged him to realize that this was a sign; a sign that they should've married years ago, when he left her. He had been cold and distant, telling her that he didn't want a kid right now and that she'd better think about an abortion.

Frank closed the refrigerator door as he recalled that dreadful evening in his study. He would probably never forget it, since it had been his birthday and Theresa had planned the perfect evening for two. He had been at his desk, replying to e-mail, when she arrived. Her reaction to his suggesting abortion had taken him aback. Theresa had flung her imitation Louis Vuitton handbag directly at his head. Luckily, he had ducked before it hit its target, but it landed on his desk instead, knocking the lamp to the carpet. She proceeded to rant and rave about how she had spent years being his showgirl and sex slave. And for what? To end up pregnant and alone! Theresa had shown more emotion that one day than she had in all the years he'd known her.

He remained at his desk and said nothing throughout her tirade. Frank had even found himself hoping that maybe she'd get mad enough and have a miscarriage or want nothing more to do with him, at the very least.

No such luck.

For reasons he didn't think he would ever understand, she'd ended up apologizing for the things she said and asking *his* forgiveness for ruining his birthday. If he thought he couldn't get rid of her before, it would be damn near impossible now that she was having his baby.

A fire truck wailed in the distance, snapping Frank out of his trance, and he realized that he hadn't taken a thing from the fridge. He opened the door again and pulled out the food Theresa had prepared. How dumb was she? He had seen some silly women in his day, but Theresa topped them all.

Though he had been refusing to accompany her to the doctor visits, refusing to even talk much about the damn baby, she still came by nearly every day and cooked for him, saying he'd come around one day and accept that they belonged together.

Despite the recent developments in his bizarre relationship with Theresa, Franklin's mind was cluttered with something else. . . . With *someone* else. Someone that had been haunting him for weeks, when he should've been worried about Theresa and her damn baby.

Tracy.

And Frank would be damned if he could understand it.

He had actually lost Tracy . . . to Reginald.

32

OLIVIA MADE USELESS ATTEMPTS to calm her frazzled nerves as she spun into the three-story parking garage of Dr. Ulysses Berenger's office building. She'd been circling the building for more than ten minutes, searching unsuccessfully for a parking space. "I sure hope *all* these people aren't here to see the shrink," she said aloud. Olivia had to admit that the elusive parking spot had little to do with her annoyance.

The day had finally come. The day that she had been dreading for weeks. Time to go sit in front of the shrink and play stupid. She was dressed casually in a brown cotton dress under a black knit cardigan that she'd left unbuttoned, yet she felt utterly stifled.

After circling the first floor of the garage with no luck, she spun up to the second. To her relief, she immediately spotted an elderly couple walking away from the elevators toward the row of cars on the right. She drove up, putting on her indicator, because the last thing she needed now was to have some jerk come and rob her of one of the closest spots to the elevators.

After parking, Olivia consulted the card that her mother had given her the night before. SUITE 315, ULYSSES BERENGER. She stepped out of the car, smoothed her dress, and half slammed the door.

She was not thrilled about having to be there. Olivia did not expect things to go well at all.

VALERIE SLID HER feet into her Chanel slip-ons and ran a brush through her hair. Her mother had said they'd be leaving in about fifteen minutes.

How did she feel about going to the psychiatrist's office? Valerie wasn't sure. She was almost certain that things couldn't get much worst at home. Their entire world had been diced to pieces. She was no longer Daddy's little girl. Daddy had a new little girl now—named Denise.

At the thought, Valerie felt that weird sensation in the pit of her stomach, the same sensation she'd felt when her father's words had seeped into her mind and rang true. For reasons she could not explain, after that awful and strange day in the den, the need to be close to her mother became overwhelmingly great. She felt the pain in her mother every time their eyes met. This had really devastated her, and Valerie sensed that her mom was trying hard to hide it. . . . Perhaps a bit too hard.

There was a knock at her door. "Val? Let's go. We're ready."

"SHE SHOULD'VE GOTTEN that letter by now," Reginald said. They were in Tracy's Jeep, riding along I-95 toward the doctor's office.

Tracy turned her gaze from the window and glanced at him. "You're worried about that, aren't you?" When Reggie gave no verbal answer, only met her eyes briefly, she sighed. "What do you think she'll do? What do you anticipate her reaction to be?"

He shrugged. "I don't know." After a brief pause, he added, "I just hope for the best. . . . Once she digests it all, you know?"

Valerie sat in the back of the Jeep and kept quiet. She watched the people in the cars riding alongside them. *Look at that girl,* she thought, as a young Asian woman drove by in a gray Honda. *I wonder what's going on in her life.*

When the next car pulled alongside them, there was a black woman at the wheel, bobbing her head to music, and Valerie thought, *I wonder if she's ever been to a psychiatrist. . . .*

33

Dr. Ulysses Berenger welcomed the Brookses into his office at precisely eleven o'clock that morning. His secretary efficiently closed the door behind them, and it was then time to begin.

As the family took seats and politely greeted him, giving their names, the silver-haired doctor made quick assessments of each. He was immediately aware of the palpable anxiety in each of them, though all four hid behind facades of ease.

Dr. Berenger smiled kindly and began the session in his soft and comforting tone. "Well, I am quite eager to find out what a lovely family such as this has to discuss with me." He smiled warmly at each of them. "Which of you would like to begin?"

Valerie gazed out the large window behind her father. She could see the tall buildings across the street and she wondered about all the people in those buildings. Had any of them ever been to a psychiatrist?

Tracy took her eyes off the doctor and glanced at Reginald, who just stared back at her; he had an uncertain expression in his eyes. Where should they begin? Just as she opened her mouth to speak, Olivia interrupted.

"Doctor, it's very simple, I think. We're here because my mother thinks we can't handle our family problems as a *family*. She seems to think we have to seek help from a stranger in order to solve them." Olivia, crossing her legs, swung her eyes to her mother.

Before Tracy could respond, Dr. Berenger said, "Would it be a safe assumption that you don't agree with your mother, Olivia?"

"Yes, it would, because I don't think we need to be here."

Dr. Berenger turned to Tracy. "Why do you feel the family should be here, Mrs. Brooks?"

Tracy hesitated briefly before saying, "Doctor, there have been several occurrences over the last few months that have greatly affected our family, and because of the way we've been affected, I thought seeking professional help was our best hope for dealing with it." She cast a heavy glance at Olivia. Why was she making things more difficult? Why couldn't she just cooperate?

Tracy continued, "We've just recently learned that . . . that Reginald has another child, an outside child with another woman."

"Is this true, Mr. Brooks?" Dr. Berenger addressed Reginald politely.

"Yes, she's six years old." Reggie shifted in his armchair. "She lives in Orlando with her mother." He cleared his throat. "I just recently disclosed this to Tracy and to the girls, and as you can imagine . . . we haven't been doing all that well since."

Just then, Olivia sighed heavily, drawing everyone's attention. Dr. Berenger looked to her. "Olivia, tell me how this has affected you . . . specifically." He clasped his hands in front of him atop his desk.

"Dr. Berenger, I can't sit here and do this," Olivia said, uncrossing her legs.

"Do what, dear?" the doctor asked gently.

"Do *this*." she waved her hand in front of her. "Sit here and be a character in this farce. This isn't going to help—if anything, it'll just make things worse. Coming here today is only a matter of going through ridiculous motions."

Dr. Berenger smiled. "Well, I don't know why you feel that way, Olivia, but please believe that I have the best interest of this family at heart and I will try my very best to be of whatever help I can. Why do you feel this is a farce?"

Everyone was staring at Olivia, with the exception of Valerie, who appeared to be studying the mauve vase on the doctor's desk. Finally, Olivia said in irritation, "Why am I here? Why did I even bother to show up?" Then she looked at her father and said, "He knows it's a show. Mom seems to think coming here can somehow fix things, but *he* knows better. You don't hide a kid for six years and . . ." She trailed off, appearing too offended to continue.

Reginald straightened. "Olivia, this attitude of yours . . . your reluctance to forgive is part of why we *need* to be here. Can't you at least try meeting me halfway . . . even now?"

Dr. Berenger interjected, "I gather, Olivia, that you are particularly upset about your father's other daughter?"

Olivia hesitated before answering stubbornly, "You know, I don't know if I could *respectfully* express my feelings about what my father's done—especially in this setting."

Reginald flinched.

Dr. Berenger nodded. "It is understandable that you are angry, Olivia. I feel you are all entitled to your emotions under these particular circumstances, and I suspect that you'll get no argument from your father about that. However, there should come a time for forgiveness and progression, don't you agree? You are a family, and the mere fact that Reginald is here now shows that he cares a great deal about setting his family back in order. Would you agree with that?" He sat back in his chair.

"No, Doctor, I can't say that I would agree." Olivia gave a harsh snort. "*If* he had cared, we wouldn't be in this situation in the first place. If he cared and really wanted to fix things with us, he'd have come into this office and began honestly with you. Instead, he does what Reginald Brooks always does: He plays a part—he *acts*. That's what he's done for as long as I can remember."

Reginald's eyes widened, struck by the relentless hostility from Olivia. He looked at her long and hard in the brief silence that followed. "Have I really alienated you this much?"

"Olivia, let me ask you this," Dr. Berenger said. "Did you know about your father's other daughter? I mean, prior to him telling the family?"

In curiosity, Tracy and Valerie swung around to face Olivia.

Olivia looked confused. "No. Valerie and I found out at the same time."

"I only asked because there seems to be something more, something in addition, surrounding this mere incident for you."

Olivia smiled sweetly at the doctor. "That's my point, Dr. Berenger. Like my mother said before, a lot has happened to cause these problems. There's a lot more to it than just this kid and Daddy's sitting there, acting like there isn't. You heard what he said about things not being 'all that well' since we heard about his other kid. My point is, things haven't been 'all that well' for years. In fact, I wasn't the least bit surprised about this other child. I've grown to expect nothing better from my father."

"Olivia, pipe it down a bit, okay?" Tracy's tone was clipped when she finally found her voice. She was appalled by Olivia's bluntness in the short ten minutes that they'd been there.

A glance at Valerie showed that her anger was rising with every word that flew from Olivia's mouth. Despite what had happened, it was obvious that she still felt a great need to defend her father from Olivia's ridicule. She looked as if she was itching to retaliate, but the fact that they were sitting in a counseling session must've humbled her.

Reginald spoke then. "Olivia, don't you think I realize how my being away so much—for so long—has affected you? All of you? I know that it's driven us apart and onto separate paths." He turned to Dr. Berenger, his face rigid, determined to be understood. "Doctor, for the past ten years or so, my job has required me to travel back and forth between here and Orlando. Every month was split between here and there—two weeks here and two there."

"He's basically had two separate homes," Tracy said. "I know that, as a little girl, Olivia grew to resent that fact almost right away. She would cry constantly when he had to leave or whenever he missed her birthday or a graduation. I think that's why she's had all this pent-up anger to this day. She's just missed him."

"I think Olivia recognizes her father's desire to reconcile all the troubles his absence has caused," Dr. Berenger said. "However, it seems to me that there's a desire to reflect pain. On some level, you want your dad to hurt just as you're hurting. You want to make sure he *understands* what he's done by being away all these years. Could that be true, Olivia?"

"I don't want him to hurt. I want him to stop pretending. He needs to recognize that the acting can't last forever. For years, he's been basically living two lives, and I've always felt it. He stopped being my daddy the first day he left for Orlando. And now we all know why."

Reginald spoke in his defense. "I have come to realize that my family is what's most important to me." He looked at Dr. Berenger and continued. "I feel a great need for everyone to understand how I feel. . . . I began to realize that I didn't know my daughters. One day, they were little girls, and the next day, they were grown young women that were practically strangers to me."

"And this realization is what led you to admit to having another child, and then ultimately to this office today, at this point in time?"

"Yes," Reginald replied. "But not only that, Dr. Berenger. There's a great deal of time that needs to be made up for here. I've tried to reach out to Olivia, to get to know her as she is today, but she's hell-bent on keeping this wall between us." Reggie hesitated. "My biggest grievance is that recently she's been going through a lot, and if it were left up to her, I wouldn't even know the half about what's been going on in her life."

Olivia's head snapped up. Her eyes flew to her father, then to her mother.

Somewhere far away she heard Dr. Berenger begin to babble something about her being comfortable with the anger toward her father, and having a fear of letting her guard down. She barely heard him. She trained bitter eyes on her mother.

Her father knew about the baby?

She had told him!

Olivia raised a palm in front of her. "Wait a minute, Dr. Berenger. I think we should back up just a little bit." She glared at Tracy. "What is he talking about? What wouldn't he know if it were left up to me?"

Before Tracy could respond, Reginald said quietly, "I know about the baby—your mother told me, and she had *every* right to do so." His eyes bore into hers. "I am your father, and I do have an interest in your well-being."

Olivia's mind reeled. She had not taken her murderous glare off of

Tracy. *"You told him?"* The words were frozen in ice as she squeezed them through her teeth.

Her mother swallowed. "Olivia, I couldn't keep it from him. He's your dad, and he cares about what happens to you. You have to know that."

Valerie spoke for the first time. "Baby? What baby?"

Olivia felt the anger leaking out of her, flowing around like hot lava. Her voice boomed through the room. "How dare you tell him about that? I thought I could trust you—you're my mother! You dared to tell him about the most embarrassing time in my life, after you promised me you wouldn't?"

"Olivia, just calm down—" Reginald began.

"Calm down? Calm down? Calm down, my ass! Mom, you had no right!" She was now perched on the edge of the chair as if she was going to lurch at someone.

Reginald's voice rose now, as well. "She had every right! Contrary to what you have grown into thinking, I *am* still your father and I *do* have an interest in the things that happen to you—especially something of that nature. We came here for a reason, and that's to get help. And as you pointed out earlier, if we're gonna do that, we have to be open and honest about the real issues. I'm willing to do it. I'm *trying* my best to do it."

"Olivia, he's right," Tracy said, looking into her eyes.

Olivia stared at her mother. The open hostility undoubtedly set off warning signals in the back of Tracy's mind. Anger washed over Olivia in sea waves. *All hell's gonna break loose in here today,* she thought.

She sat back in her seat, appearing to relax.

The doctor addressed her mother, "Tracy, I think you were justified in deciding to seek counsel for your family. There are obviously several issues that need to be addressed before the four of you can progress as a happy, healthy family. Of course, it will mean a commitment on everyone's part. The first thing I would like to do is meet with you all individually, prior to the next family meeting."

"There's nothing I want more than to set things right with my family and move on, and I'm willing to do whatever it takes to achieve that," Reginald said firmly.

"Well, if we're all supposed to be *open* and *honest* here about the is-sues," Olivia interrupted calmly, "why don't we do that, then? Let's dis-close all of our issues. . . . For the benefit of the family, of course," she added sweetly.

Tracy stiffened. Unconsciously, her back lifted from the chair. "Olivia?" She said her name as a warning, but it came out as a question. *She wouldn't,* Tracy thought, feeling the air in her stomach dip.

"Knowing all the facts will put you in a better position to really help us, Doctor, right?" Olivia kept her eyes on Dr. Berenger, as if no one else was in the room.

Before he could respond, she continued. "Let's see. . . . So far you know that Daddy's been unfaithful and has another child as a result. You also know that I've been pregnant, and I'll be up-front about that. . . . I had an abortion because the timing and the man weren't right. I'm not ashamed of it. I did what I felt was best for my life, and I took counsel from my *mother,* thinking she was the only person I could trust." Her voice hardened. "Unfortunately, I was wrong. It seems she's no longer the same person she was while Daddy was away much of the time. . . ."

She swung her eyes to Reginald. "Why didn't I tell my father? Or anyone else?" she said, glancing briefly at Valerie, who was gaping at her in shock. "It was a private and special time for me, and my father hasn't been a part of those times for years. He's right—he doesn't know me, and I don't tell virtual strangers such private details about my life. My father only comes around and *acts as if* he's the perfect husband and loving father we think he should be."

Reginald said, "Okay, I think that's enough. I know how you feel about me—we all do. What I need to know now is this: What can be done about it? Are you saying that, ultimately, you can never get past this and pardon me for not being there for you over the years? In spite of my willingness to make up for it now?"

Olivia raised a hand. "Wait a sec. I'm not finished. We'll get to the fixing part in a minute. Let's continue being *open* and *honest* until the doctor has it all on the table."

"Olivia." This time, it was a warning. Tracy's heart was racing. Her fingers tightened on the leather handbag in her lap.

"He knows about you"—she pointed at Reginald—"and he knows about me," she said pointing toward herself. "But what about Mom and Val?" she said, pointing to them cheerfully, as if she were discussing their favorite things. "Who wants to go first? Be open and honest about the issues. Mom? Or you, Val?"

"Olivia, stop this!" Valerie said forcefully. "What's wrong with you? What are you trying to prove with all this?"

"Come, now, Valerie, tell them about your . . . you know, the problem. It's time for honesty—the doctor wants to help us."

Tracy's eyes closed briefly. Was she just going to sit there and let her own child do this to her? "Olivia, stop it." Her voice was calm. "This isn't going to help anything. You're just lashing out at your father. Why? Because he loves you and wants to make up for lost time?"

"And you, too, Mom. Why don't you disclose your secrets? Be honest about—"

Tracy shot from her chair. "Olivia! Stop it! Now!" She moved toward her.

Reginald stood, as well, his face full of confusion.

"—Uncle Frank," Olivia continued quickly, as though her mother hadn't said anything. "Why not tell the doctor about your affair with him—"

Tracy's fist slammed into her daughter's face. Olivia's head flew back against the high backing of the chair—thwack!

"Oh, no! Mrs. Brooks, please!" Dr. Berenger exclaimed, jumping out of his chair.

Olivia's hand flew to her mouth. She felt blood.

Tracy's fist was about to land another blow, but Dr. Berenger grabbed her arm and pulled her back. "Mrs. Brooks, please!" he said again, moving to stand in front of her.

Tracy's eyes never left Olivia's, pinning her with a violent glare. When Dr. Berenger seemed sure she would strike no more, he let go of her arms and said, "Are you okay?"

"Of course she's not okay," Olivia said in her gleeful voice. "Her husband just found out that she's been having an affair with his best friend. How could she be okay? But that's what honesty is all about." She drew in her lower lip and swallowed her blood. Her lip began to swell.

Then, for the first time, Olivia's eyes flew to her father.

In a fog, Tracy pictured Reginald standing by his chair, staring at her back as she stood, glaring down at Olivia.

She heard Valerie jump from her seat. "*Uncle Frank?* Mom, you were sleeping with *Uncle Frank?* Oh, my God." She covered her mouth with her hand, swinging around to look at her father.

"Tracy?" Reginald's voice was eerily calm. "Tracy, turn around."

Her chest heaved and her eyes shifted briefly from Olivia. She felt like jumping out the window, fleeing the stifling humiliation that was quickly sucking all the oxygen from the room.

He knew.

They all knew.

The room was dead silent.

Reginald stared at the back of Tracy's head.

A searing heat began creeping through his neck.

It was true. . . . He knew it. Tracy's silence was louder than a supersonic boom.

The image of her head began to blur as she slowly turned around. Reggie began seeing through a red hue. . . . And the heat was now in his eyes, seeping up into his forehead.

Tears instantly stung the backs of his eyelids as reality violated his psyche. Suddenly, as he stood there, he began seeing images, and everyone just stood staring at him. . . .

He saw images of Franklin and Tracy talking at the dinner table, talking at the barbecues, talking at The Ivory Estates, talking . . . touching . . . fucking.

And the heat was seeping from his ears now.

He remembered Frank's attitude whenever they would discuss Tracy's possible affair. . . .

Before anyone could stop him, Reggie flew from the room. He rounded the sitting area in a flash and was out the door.

"Mr. Brooks!" Dr. Berenger called out.

But it was too late.

He was gone, leaving the four of them speechless, staring after him.

Tracy watched in horror as Reginald tore out of the office. It was several moments before she regained control of her motor skills, standing in shock from all that had just transpired.

Suddenly, without thinking, she grabbed her purse from the chair she had occupied and rushed out the door after him. Olivia and Valerie were right on her heels.

They all ran out, leaving Dr. Berenger staring after them.

34

HE FLEW DOWN the interstate as if demons were after him.

If someone had asked him where he was going, he would not have been able to say. His mind had taken a backseat to his heart.

And in his heart, he knew exactly where he was going.

THE UPS CORPORATE office was a great place to work. Though the policies were strictly enforced, Susan Dooley had always enjoyed her job as executive assistant to Franklin Bevins.

However, this morning was not one of her better days. She'd had a fight with her boyfriend, Steven, earlier in the week and had refused to see him ever since. It had been only three days since their argument, and already the separation was causing Susan to fall apart. She missed him.

At around twelve thirty, she crossed the hall and tapped on her boss' door to let him know that she would be leaving early for lunch. She normally went for lunch at one, but today she wanted to catch Steven on his lunch hour and give him a chance to beg her for forgiveness.

Just as she retrieved her purse and locked the drawer, she saw Mr. Brooks making wide strides toward their suite from the nearby stairwell. He was dressed in black and looked like a sleek panther as he strode through the hall. She was immediately shaken by the fierce expression on his face as he blew past her without even speaking, which was highly out of character. Susan got a weird feeling in the pit of her stomach as she watched Mr. Brooks throw open her boss' door without preamble.

Forgetting about her lunch plans, she unconsciously sat back in her chair in lieu of following him into the office to find out what the problem was.

Just then, she heard Mr. Brooks say somewhat calmly, "If you can't look me in the eye, *right now,* and tell me that you haven't been sleeping with Tracy, I am going to kill you."

Susan saw that Mr. Bevins had been on the telephone when Mr. Brooks arrived, the receiver still at his ear. She read his lips as he spoke into the phone, "Let me get back with you on that later." Then she watched him slowly replace the receiver.

Uh-oh, Susan thought. *He found out about them.* She sent a quick prayer to heaven for her boss. Mr. Brooks outweighed him by at least twenty pounds. She had a feeling that the odds were not going to be in his favor for too much longer.

"OH MY GOD, you guys, what do you think he's gonna do?" Olivia was speeding down the interstate toward Ives Dairy Road, Tracy and Valerie in the car with her. Once Tracy had raced down the stairs, she'd come to an abrupt halt when she realized that she had no vehicle in which to chase after Reginald. In a state of panic, she had turned to Olivia and demanded that they follow him.

Now her mother sat in silence while her insides were undoubtedly twisting like noodles. "Shut up, Olivia, and just drive. What the fuck do you think he's gonna do?" She spun on her. "You just make sure you know *you're* responsible for whatever the hell is about to happen!"

"*I'm* responsible?" Olivia kept her eyes on the road. "We both know that's not true." She flew past a line of cars and dangerously cut in front of another as she manipulated her way over to the exit.

Her mind was reeling. She had been stirred when she looked into her father's eyes a few minutes ago in that office.

Her father had been gravely wounded. She had seen it in his eyes.

FRANKLIN SLOWLY REPLACED the receiver and returned Reginald's intense stare. "Come on, my friend," he said, his tone pleasant. "You seem barely able to control your surprise." He smiled, but it didn't reach his eyes. "So you finally figured it out, huh? I guess the time has finally come." He snorted. "Quite frankly, I was beginning to wonder if I was gonna have to send you an anonymous letter or something."

Reginald took threatening steps closer, approaching the desk. His fists clenched and his jaw tightened. He bore down on Franklin as his mind raced through the many ways in which he could stop a human being from breathing.

"Big, bad Reginald Brooks," Frank said, rising from his chair. "For years, I've put up with you. For years, I took a backseat to the almighty and the all-powerful Reggie Brooks. I mean, all women did was step over me to get to you." An arrogant smile curled the edges of Frank's lips. "So after all those years of being second best, of always being the one losing and giving—losing in the name of you—can you really blame me for having a little fun with Tracy?"

SUSAN WATCHED FROM behind as Mr. Brooks stepped farther into the office. She heard Mr. Bevins say, "So you finally figured it out, huh? I guess the time has finally come." A pause. "Quite frankly, I was beginning to wonder if I was gonna have to send you an anonymous letter or something."

Why is he taunting him? Susan wondered. *He should be thinking of the best way to get out of that office in one piece.* Just then, Mr. Bevins was saying, ". . . was step over me to get to you." Another pause. "So after all those years of being second best, of always being the one losing and giving—losing in the name of you—can you really blame me for having a little fun with Tracy?"

Without warning, Mr. Brooks grabbed her boss and flung him up against the glass window behind his desk.

Susan screamed.

WHEN OLIVIA PULLED up to the circular drop-off and pickup driveway in front of the lobby, they immediately saw Tracy's Cherokee abandoned there. Tracy didn't think her heart could pump blood any faster—but it did.

Ignoring the NO PARKING sign as Reginald obviously had, the three of them jumped out of the car and raced into the building. The security guard on duty called out to them as they raced unobstructed past the receptionist's desk. "Excuse me! You ladies must sign in! Who are you here to see? You can't just go up there! Hey!"

Tracy was the first to reach the stairwell and her daughters followed. They didn't have time for the elevator. God only knew what Reginald was going to do. Feeling as though a stone were in her chest, Tracy took the stairs two at a time until she reached the third floor.

They heard the crash before they reached Susan's desk.

Susan Dooley's scream ricocheted through the entire third floor as they raced past her.

REGINALD WOULD NEVER be able to tell anyone exactly what happened in Franklin's office that day. His mind had completely shut down, his heart propelling the actions.

Tracy, Olivia, Valerie, and Susan watched in absolute horror as Frank slid from the broken window frame and slumped to the floor behind his desk. They heard shards of glass hit the sidewalk below them outside.

Reaching to grab a paperweight from his desk, Frank moved to stand up, obviously intending to throw it at Reggie as he charged, but he did not reach it in time. In one swift motion, Reginald kicked him back to the floor, and with the heel of his Timberland boot, began brutally stomping Frank's head.

Franklin screamed.

"Oh, my God, he's gonna kill him," Tracy said as she ran over to grab Reginald's arm. She glanced down at Franklin just in time to see deep red blood spew from his nose.

"Reggie, stop! For God's sake! You're gonna kill him!" She grabbed his left hand and tried to pull him toward her. "Reginald!! Stop it!"

"Don't you dare come in here and try to protect him!" Reginald shouted, before propelling her backward and off his arm. Tracy stumbled into Olivia, who was right behind her.

He continued to pummel Frank's head and chest, anywhere his foot would land. "You dirty son of a bitch! I'm gonna kill you!" Reggie yelled with each and every stomp. It was blind rage; a bright red hue illuminated what he saw.

Olivia glanced down and saw all the blood. It was quickly splattering everywhere.

Valerie shook as she watched blood splash the desk and the walls. She couldn't believe this was actually happening. She hovered just inside the door, in fear of what would be next.

Susan Dooley shakily reached for the phone and pushed the button for an outside line as she saw Buzz, the security guard, emerge from the stairwell. His chest was heaving from exhaustion as he made his way toward her.

The suite was quickly filling with onlookers from around the floor, who heard the commotion. Susan carefully punched 911 as her gaze shifted back to the motionless figure of her boss lying on the carpet behind his desk.

Buzz flew by her and brushed past Valerie. When he took in the scene, he rushed over to Reginald, attempting to grab hold of the taller man's arms. "Sir, you've got to stop this! Sir!" But the silver-haired man was no match for Reginald. He was tossed off just as Tracy had been.

And Reggie continued to stomp. They could hear Frank's bones as they cracked under Reggie's boots.

Tracy was screaming for help now. "Susan, call an ambulance! Somebody call an ambulance—now, now, now! Oh, my God! He's killing him!" She tried again to grab Reginald.

"Tracy . . . get . . . the hell . . . away . . . from me!" Reginald yelled between blows. *"How . . . dare you . . . come in here . . . and try . . . to help him."* The words were forced through clenched teeth.

"Daddy!" Olivia's screech bounced off the walls. "Daddy, stop it! You're gonna kill him! Look what you're doing to him! Look!" She pointed at Frank's unrecognizable face. "Stop, goddamn it! Stop it now!" Her hands flew to her head in shock, pure shock.

Then Reginald's foot stilled. He spun his head around to look at them . . . through the red hue. His chest was heaving. He couldn't see a thing.

There was no movement from Frank.

Buzz seized the opportunity to reach once again for Reginald's arms, and this time there was no resistance. Reginald's chest continued to heave in rage; his eyes blazed as, unconsciously, he allowed himself to be led out the door.

Tracy and Olivia rushed to kneel beside Frank. His face, like a death mask, looked up at them. His nose appeared to be nonexistent, as they stared at him. His entire head seemed to be oozing blood and his shirt had been torn, exposing a ghastly tear in his upper chest that was white on the inside.

"Did somebody call an ambulance?" Olivia said, frantically looking at Valerie, who was clutching the doorjamb. "Holy shit, Val, he looks like he's dead."

"Susan, did you call the police?" Tracy said, racing toward the door.

"Yes," Susan replied, fixing a bitter stare on Tracy. *This was all her fault—the slut!* "They're on the way."

35

DENISE PULLED OUT a light-blue crayon from the box and colored in her daddy's tie. She tried hard to remember exactly the way her daddy wore it. She was afraid she was forgetting her daddy, so she decided to draw pictures of him to keep him remembered. When he finally came home, she would surprise him with them, and he would scoop her up and kiss her and call her his little angel.

She wished Daddy would hurry up and come back home. How come he was staying gone so long? Didn't he say that she wouldn't have to miss him too long? Denise knew that her new mommy was mad all the time because Daddy was gone so long. . . . And she missed her old mommy.

Her old mommy used to watch cartoons with her in the nighttime and tuck her in bed with one of her favorite bedtime stories. The new Mommy didn't do that anymore. The new Mommy was mean. . . . Really mean. Denise wished she could go stay with her Aunt Helen until her daddy came back, because Aunt Helen didn't like the new Mommy either. Denise heard them arguing all the time about her.

She changed crayons again to color in her daddy's dark hair. It was supposed to be a picture of all three of them, but when she thought about drawing Mommy, Denise got mad. She didn't want to put her mommy in the picture, so she drew herself in her daddy's lap, with a big smile that stretched all the way across her face.

When her picture was done, Denise realized that she had to go to the bathroom. Lately, she had made a habit of holding it, in order to avoid going out into the hall and making any of the noise that always made the new Mommy mean to her.

Taking one tiny step at a time, Denise went to the door and slowly turned the knob to open it. She peeked out into the hall and listened for the new Mommy. She heard shuffling coming from the kitchen downstairs and was glad the new Mommy was down there, instead of in her room down the hall.

Being careful not to put her little feet down too hard on the plush carpet, Denise sprinted across the hall and into the bathroom. With her heart pounding against her chest, she rushed to finish and wash her hands.

On her way back to her room, she glanced down and saw her mommy curled into a round thing on the floor just outside the kitchen. Denise wondered why the new Mommy was lying on the floor like that, but she didn't dare go down there, so she continued running back to her room. She knew what could happen if the new Mommy saw her out of her room or heard any of that noise that made her so mad.

She would get beat up again.

RENEE HAD JUST finished washing the dishes when she forgot that she hadn't checked the mail that day. That had been happening a lot lately. She was forgetting almost everything. Drying her hands, she opened the front door and ran out to check the mailbox.

In the days since Thanksgiving, Renee's temperament had only grown progressively worse. Every morning, she awoke telling herself that this would be the day Reginald would call to say he was coming home, or this was the day that he would simply show up. However, it had been weeks since he'd promised to try to fly in for a few days, and he had yet to fulfill the promise. When he called, she heard the detachment in his voice. He was no longer focused on her. It was slowly killing Renee.

Shuffling through the three or four envelopes that she'd pulled from the mailbox, Renee took Reginald's usual seat at the dining table, as she did every night to read the mail. When she came upon a rose-colored envelope with a sophisticated foil label in the upper left-hand corner,

Renee's hands stilled. It was from Reggie. The names on the label read TRACY & REGINALD BROOKS.

Renee wasted no time in grabbing the letter opener and dragging it through the top of the thick envelope. As she opened the two-page letter, her heart fluttered with anxiety. She blew out a deep breath and began reading. . . .

Dear Renee,

I hope this letter finds you and my little angel well. I am writing to confess something that I should have told you a long time ago—before leaving Orlando. The time has come for me to be 100 percent truthful about my intentions toward you and Denise. Things cannot go on as they have been. I have not been fair to you. . . . I can barely write this because I feel so ashamed of creating this situation and lying to you, and to my wife and family. My wife, Tracy, is sitting here with me as I write this letter, since I have quite a bit of cleaning up to do with her as well as with you. It's important that she be a part of this.

The explanations that I gave you before I left for Miami need to be clarified, since I must shamefully admit that it was only half the truth, and the other half a complete lie. First, I must take this opportunity to beg your forgiveness, although I could understand it if you never wanted to see my face again. I truly would understand. I actually wouldn't even know how to tell you the truth if I couldn't do it on paper. I guess I'm a coward. Nonetheless, the truth is this. . . . My wife and I have never been separated and our daughter Valerie is not sick, as I told you. I invented that situation to keep from telling you the truth, once I realized that I no longer belonged in Orlando.

The words on the page blurred under Renee's vision as tears poured into her eyes. She was shaking as she swiped them, but she quickly read on.

The truth is that I love my wife and kids, and they have suffered tremendously due to my absence in the last ten years. I made a mistake in thinking that it was okay to pretend to be someone I wasn't.

I wasn't a free man when I met and started a life with you, and I wasn't a faithful husband whenever I came home to my family. I've realized that my mistakes were very self-centered. . . . Now I'm committed to doing all that I can to make it up to everyone concerned.

Tracy and I have decided that we can give our life together another chance. She now knows about Denise and agrees to accept her as my daughter. You see, Renee, I'm not totally dishonorable. I love Denise, and I know that my obligations to you both are very real. But of course, I cannot return to Orlando to live.

I know that you will be very hurt and very angry when you get this letter, but I also know that you are a strong woman. Please apologize to your family for me. I know that they'll be equally as angry and grieved by this.

I'll be in touch once you've had a chance to absorb this letter. Please believe that taking care of Denise and having her know me as her father is my number one priority right now. I have a responsibility to both of you, and I intend to fulfill it. When next we speak, I pray that we can find a common ground on which to share responsibilities regarding Denise.

Again, I'm so very sorry for entering your life and giving you false hope when there actually could never have been a future for you with me. I have no doubt, however, that you'll meet a man who deserves you and will also be extremely lucky to have you.

If you feel you're ready to speak to me before I phone, please feel free to call me so we can begin making arrangements regarding Denise. I guess you already have the phone number to the house.

With the deepest regret,
Reginald

Renee quickly flipped the cream-colored pages over to see if there was anything more. Perhaps a note saying it was a joke. She slowly rose from the table, in a trance, and moved toward the entryway. Her shoulders began shaking heavily from sobs that could not find their way to her mouth. Tears stung her eyes and soaked her face as she clung to the column of the doorway. She was trembling violently now.

She didn't know how, but somehow she sank to the tile and curled herself into a fetal position, trying to squash the ache in her chest.

What would her family say?

That's what the dreams had been about! Her face crinkled as emotions knifed her.

Lips trembling, a small sound escaped her then, like a wounded animal about to be put out of its misery.

Then a slow whine squeaked out and she began to rock slowly back and forth to the rhythm of the pain as it surged through her. Her stomach hollowed out, her head began to tighten. Her whine turned into a series of choked moans. And she sobbed.

Renee remembered the piercing words from the cream-colored page: *I love my wife and kids. . . . Tracy and I have decided that we can give our life together another chance. . . . Taking care of Denise and having her know me as her father is my number one priority right now. . . .*

And she wept bitterly, staring unseeingly at the whimsical design of the kitchen tile.

MORE THAN AN hour later, Renee wearily pulled herself to a sitting position and leaned against the column of the kitchen entryway.

Something was broken.

She reached up to push her hair out of her face, but her hand froze in midair.

Reginald wasn't coming back. *He was not coming back.*

All he wanted now was to talk about his future with Denise. How could she explain this away? How could she live knowing that *her* Reginald was never coming home, never going to hold her or sleep in the same bed with her or make love to her again? How could she stand that their life together was *over*?

Her life was over.

It was all over.

Renee squeezed her eyes shut. . . . And summoned death.

36

REGINALD WAS ARRESTED and charged with assault and battery. Accepting the statement of Franklin's secretary, Susan Dooley, UPS executives decided against pressing charges of their own against him.

Within an hour, Tracy arrived at the police station, prepared to post his bail.

Franklin had been rushed to the hospital and his condition was listed as critical but stable, which had worked in Reginald's favor as far as the criminal charges were concerned. He had barely escaped attempted manslaughter.

Olivia and Valerie had insisted on staying with Frank until they could be assured he would be all right, that he would live. Despite all that had happened, he was still their Uncle Frank; the Uncle Frank who had been there for them as children and had watched them grow up, the Uncle Frank who never came to the house without a gift or small trinket, the Uncle Frank who had really been like a father to them both for as long as they could remember.

TRACY SLOWED THE Jeep as she sped along I-95, heading home. She knew she would crash if she didn't slow down. She was crying so much, the tears were blurring her vision. Reaching for the glove compartment, she pulled out her box of Kleenex, wiping her nose and face.

Reginald was gone. He was actually leaving her.

His face had been that of a heartbroken man when he was released from the jail. Gone was the raging anger of a few hours before when he had beaten Frank to a pulp. Tracy still could not believe that it all actually happened.

She and their attorney, Richard Love, had rushed over to his side. "Reggie, are you okay?" She'd said urgently. "Rich did his best to get you out of there as soon as possible."

"Get away from me." Reginald's face had been like granite as the desk sergeant handed him a see-through plastic bag with his few belongings. "I *cannot* talk to you right now." He turned to Richard then, and the pair walked off and left Tracy standing in front of the desk sergeant.

Outside, Tracy rushed after them. "Reggie, we *have* to talk now. Let's just go home and—"

Reginald kept walking toward the parking lot, ignoring her.

Richard touched her shoulder. "Just give him time. Whatever it was that occurred, it's probably just best to give him space to cool off. You can try tomorrow, when you've both had time to calm yourselves and think things over." He paused. "In the interim, let's hope Mr. Bevins doesn't hold a grudge. From what you've told me, he's pretty banged up and could have permanent impairments." Then he turned and followed Reginald into the parking lot.

She watched them get into Richard's Range Rover and drive off.

Now as Tracy remembered the harsh look on Reginald's face, the blatant scorn in his eyes, she gave up trying to drive altogether and pulled over to the shoulder of the road.

And there she just cried.

What had she done to her life?

37

HER MOMMY WAS back! Her *old* mommy!

Denise raced through Toys 'R' Us, picking up all her favorite toys. Her mommy had said that they were going away on a long trip and she could take all the toys and games she wanted.

"Where are we going again, Mommy?" she asked when they were back in the car.

Renee smiled sweetly. "I told you, honey, first we're stopping at Grandma's and then we're going far away, where your daddy can't find us."

"But why don't we want him to find us again? I miss Daddy," Denise said, her face turning sad.

Still smiling, Renee laughed. "Don't worry, Pooch. When we go away, I bet your daddy will be so upset that he'll forget everything else and come after us. Then he'll realize how much we mean to him, and he'll never leave us again. Just remember that this is our little secret, Pooch, okay? So don't say anything to Grandma. If you tell anybody, Daddy won't come after us."

Her mommy was even calling her Pooch again! Denise's eyes brightened as she said, "Daddy will come get us and never leave again, right? And he'll always bring me ice cream, right?"

"That's right, honey. Daddy will do whatever we want." Renee kept smiling.

Denise brushed the glistening hair of her new Tropical Barbie and smiled. "I hope he finds us quick so I don't have to miss him so long anymore. See, Mommy, I was always right about Daddy. He *can* keep his promises, and he promised I won't have to miss him too long."

Pain flickered through Renee's eyes as she tried to remain focused on the road. "I miss Daddy, too, honey. . . . But Daddy doesn't visit us anymore, and we have to teach him a lesson." Her face hardened. "A brutal lesson."

BEATRICE JAMESON WAS watching *The Price is Right* when Renee arrived with Denise.

Renee's smiling face made Bea's heart flip with a private joy. Things were back to normal again. She knew that smile. God had answered her prayers, and Renee had found her way out of that dire phase. Even Denise seemed happy again. Gone was the heartbreaking gloominess in her eyes. Beatrice praised God.

Renee went to the kitchen and poured herself a glass of water. "Mom, I'm gonna need you to watch her for me for a little while. I have a couple errands to run and I can do them faster if I'm by myself." The last thing Renee needed was to alarm Denise and make her start asking any more questions.

"Sure, dear. You go ahead. Denise and I will be fine." Bea turned to her granddaughter. "Denise, are you hungry, child? Grandma can make you some hot dogs! I know how much you love hot dogs with ketchup and relish."

Denise jumped up and down, holding her Barbie tightly. "Yeah, hot dogs with lots of ketchup and lots of relish, too! Can Mommy have some, too, when she comes back?"

"Sure, honey. We'll save some for her, if she wants."

"Okay, Ma, I'll be back in a while," Renee said, leaving.

OUTSIDE, RENEE REVVED the engine of her Eclipse and turned up the radio full blast. She had a lot of work to do.

LYLE BENNETT, AN administrator at Forrester Academy, smiled when he saw the young woman walk into the office. She was wearing tight blue jeans and a form-fitting green T-shirt that had the letters DKNY sprawled across the front.

What a body! Lyle thought. *If only she were a tad better looking . . .* "Good morning. How may I help you?"

"Good morning," the woman said cheerfully. "I need to withdraw my daughter. We're leaving the area."

RENEE'S NEXT STOP was the post office. She walked in feeling freer than ever. She smiled to herself as she picked up the change of address card and began filling it out.

Reginald had hurt them for the last time. She was through being a fool. All along they'd been right! Her mother and father, Helen and John; they'd all been right. She had even alienated all of her friends when they expressed suspicions about Reggie.

Well, she wasn't gonna stick around for the gloating "I told you so" speeches. She didn't think she could stomach even one. And if Reginald thought he was gonna live happily ever after with *wifey*, folding Denise into their neat little family, he had better think again.

After completing the card, she dropped it into one of the blue mail-boxes lined up outside and got back into the car. Unable to contain her exhilaration, she laughed out loud and blasted the radio even louder than before, as she sped out of the parking lot. She had one more stop to make, then they'd be gone.

For the first time since she had met Reginald Brooks, Renee Jameson was in control.

RENEE WAS RELIEVED to see that the First Union bank wasn't crowded. She signed in at the podium and took a seat next to an elderly lady. The lady was busy scuffing a Florida lotto scratch-off card. Renee silently wished the old woman luck.

As she waited, patrons shuffled all around, moving through the bank, going about their financial business. Her mind drifted as she sat there. . . . She thought about when she first met Reggie. This tall, deliciously handsome man that she had succeeded in attracting. No other man had ever been his equal. And she'd wanted no other man since.

Then she thought of all the years she had spent with him since; all the years that he'd been making a complete fool of her.

Two weeks in Miami. Two weeks in Miami. *Those damn two weeks in Miami!*

Her imagination wandered as she imagined what those two weeks had represented. A wife and two daughters. A whole other life. He'd come home and make love to her so sweetly, and he'd tell her he loved her, but in reality . . . those damn two weeks in Miami!

Renee's mind drifted to the days just before he had left. He'd been so distant, so . . . gone. She remembered how he rushed their sex in the shower, how he'd hurt her. He had already gone back to *her*. The wife . . . Tracy. His letter said that he loved her.

He loved her.

His letter also said that Denise was now his main concern. . . .

On the verge of tears, Renee kept them at bay with a smile. She found that she was able to do that a lot now, and it felt really good to have confidence and be able to smile again.

It was a feeling she prayed would be lost to Reginald once he realized his precious Denise was gone.

After about fifteen minutes, one of the financial counselors, Warren Hutton, bid his patron good-bye and consulted the sign-in sheet at the podium. "Renee Jameson?" he called out, scanning the row of waiting customers. Renee raised her hand and rose, following him to his desk.

Once they were seated, Warren said, "Good morning, Ms. Jameson. You'd like to close an account today?"

AFTER LEAVING FIRST Union, Renee went home. She had a telephone call to make.

She dropped her purse on the counter and headed for the desk in the living room. Picking up the phone, she dialed Reginald's cell phone number.

38

THE SOFT MELODIES of pianos and violins seemed to be coming from somewhere far away. Reginald heard it but fought to keep it from disturbing his sleep. Where the hell was it coming from, anyway?

Finally awakened, he raised his head from the pillow and realized it was coming from the alarm clock on the nightstand. He sleepily rubbed his swollen eyes, bringing the large, red digits into focus. It was half past one in the afternoon. Why the hell would anyone set an alarm clock to go off at this hour? He reached over and slammed his hand on the small radio.

After leaving the county jail the night before, Reginald had wearily asked his attorney, Richard Love, to drop him off at the Fontainebleau Hotel. He checked in with nothing but the clothes on his back, his cell phone, and the money in his pocket. Thank God for credit cards. He would need to buy new clothes and toiletries, because only God knew when he would ever set foot in that house again.

Reginald had spent most of the night crying. He could not recall when in all his adult life he had ever cried so much.

He wondered if anyone would ever know how this shit hurt. Never before had he felt an ache quite like this—never.

Tracy . . . and Frank. The thought filled his eyes with fresh tears.

His Tracy. He had taken her virginity. He had been there when she gave birth to their children. *His* Tracy.

And Franklin. He cringed to think of how much amusement Frank must've had, watching him struggle over the years. He had confided *everything* to Frank, everything and anything that mattered. His best friend. He could not remember a time when Frank hadn't been a part of his life.

And he'd been sleeping with Tracy.

Hindsight was twenty-twenty. And what made it worse was that Tracy hadn't denied it once. *Not even once.*

He wondered if they had laughed together behind his back. Had they lain together late at night after hot, passionate sex and laughed at how ignorant he was? The anger brewed in Reggie's chest at the thought.

He rose from the bed and went to the bathroom. A look in the mirror told him that his face looked like hell. His eyes were puffy around the lids, and his nose had a reddish look and was slightly swollen. He could hardly believe that he had spent the night crying. . . . Like a sap.

Crying in the dark.

His eyes fell to the necklace. . . . He stared at the reflection as it shimmered in the mirror. He wearily pulled it from his neck and tossed it into the wastebasket.

He used the toilet and decided to call his sister, Thelma. He needed a soft place to fall, and he could rely on her. She would certainly take good care of him.

Just as he was dialing her number, his cell phone chirped. He hung up the hotel phone and checked the cell phone's display to see who was calling—he was certainly in no shape to talk to Tracy.

When he saw that it was the Orlando town house, he took a deep breath and answered the call.

"Hello, Renee." He sat down on the bed.

"Hello, Reginald. I got your letter."

Reginald's eyes fell shut. *The letter.*

Was he a victim of the boomerang effect? You know, what goes around comes around? Was this God's way of punishing him for what he had done to poor Renee?

"Did you hear me? I said I got your letter."

"Oh, I'm sorry. Yes, I heard you." Reggie was at a loss for words. "I'm sorry." What was he supposed to say to her? Everything had changed so quickly. He was clueless as to where his life was now heading.

"Don't be sorry, honey. That's why I'm calling. We do need to talk about Denise and what kind of custody arrangement we can agree on."

Reggie began shaking his head. Damn it, he didn't want to deal with this right now. "Well, we don't have to discuss all that so soon. I mean, I'm sure this has all come as a shock to you, so, you know, we can give it some time."

"No, Reginald. No time like the present." Renee paused. "I'd like you to come and see us. It won't take long—I promise. I just need to get this whole situation squared away so I can get on with my life. I think you owe me at least that. . . . Some peace of mind."

Reginald fell back onto the fluffy pillows. What the hell; why not? He hadn't planned on doing anything but hole up in this hotel room for the next few days, anyhow. Besides, he had caused Renee enough misery. The least he could do was make things as easy for her as possible from here on out.

"All right," he half-whispered. "I'll be on the morning flight up."

39

SMILING BRIGHTLY, Renee replaced the receiver and immediately picked up her pen. She proceeded to write two letters.

She knew this would crush her family, but she hoped they'd come to understand why she had to go. No, she *knew* they'd understand. It would just take some time, that's all. Her letter would help. They would come to understand that in the end, this had nothing to do with them.

It was all for Reginald. They were leaving for Reggie.

ONCE THE LETTERS were complete, Renee stuck one in her purse for the mail and placed the other carefully on the kitchen counter, where it was sure to be seen. Then she went upstairs to her bedroom.

For the last time, she went toward the walk-in closet and slid open the mirrored doors. Stepping in, she walked along the sides, slowly running her hands all over the clothes, both hers and Reginald's.

Next, she went into the bathroom. She leisurely touched all of the towels and the toothbrushes and the washcloths. She hadn't moved any of Reginald's things since he left, and they hung exactly the way he had left them. She then went back out into the bedroom and opened each and every drawer, touching and examining each garment as though she had never seen them before.

Finally, she lay on their waterbed. She thought of all the nights he'd held her and made love to her in this bed. She remembered how it felt, how *he* felt. Renee began running her hands over her body as she became lost in her memories. . . .

SOME TIME LATER, when she finally left the house to get Denise from her mother's, Renee felt more empowered than she had in months. Everything was prepared.

Reginald's betrayal stung like a venomous wasp. However, she was in control now—and nothing could possibly feel better than that.

She had *claimed* control—and the son of a bitch would soon be made well aware of it.

"SO, DID YOU get everything done?" Bea asked when she closed the door behind Renee.

"Oh yeah, Mom. Thanks a lot for watching Denise." She bent and gave Denise a loving kiss on the cheek. "Were you a good girl for Grandma?"

"'Course I was, Mommy. I'm always a good girl. We left hot dogs for you in the kitchen. I ate mine!" Denise giggled, rubbing her tummy. "Grandma put mustard and ketchup and relish, and I ate it all up!"

"That's a good girl." Renee relaxed. She was sure Denise hadn't said anything about them leaving to her mother.

"You hungry, Renee? I've got some food, some real food, if you are."

"Oh, no, Mom. Thanks. We're gonna head home now. I've got a few things to get done around the house before it gets too late." Renee paused. "Where's Daddy?"

"Oh, he's upstairs taking a nap. He's been asleep all afternoon."

Renee reached for her mother and gave her a solid hug. Would she ever get to hug her again? She kissed her on the lips and looked her in the eye. "See you, Mom."

BEA WATCHED THEM drive off.

But it wasn't until the Eclipse had completely disappeared around the bend and was out of sight that she wondered why Denise had not been in school today. . . .

40

ORLANDO, FLORIDA

AFTER LEAVING GRANDMA'S, Denise realized they were going home. Her mother had both of the car windows down, and the breeze was making her ponytails bounce. Denise liked that. "Mommy, are we going back home to get our clothes?" She asked, her eyes animatedly bright.

Mommy smiled. "No, sweetie, we're not taking anything Daddy bought for us, except your toys, so you'll be happy when we go. It should make Daddy want to come after us even more when he sees we didn't take anything, right?"

Denise grinned mischievously. "Yeah, Mommy. Daddy's gonna be really wondering! Then he'll never leave again, right?"

"That's right, sweetie. He'll never leave us again."

Denise looked at her mom. She was always smiling now. She loved Mommy's smile. She was so glad that the new Mommy was gone. . . . The one that was really mean. Her old mommy was back and everything would be normal again when they went away, and her daddy came to find them.

WHEN THEY ARRIVED home, Renee quickly drove the Eclipse into the garage, nearly hitting the barbecue grill, and climbed out. "Come on, Pooch," she said hurriedly, as Denise ran to catch up with her at the door. "You have to go upstairs and make sure you haven't left any of your favorite toys." Renee closed the garage door with a quick press of the button alongside the door that led into the house.

Denise ran toward the stairs, her pigtails bouncing on her shoulders. "Mommy, I didn't leave anything. We checked and checked before we left, remember?"

"I know we did, Pooch, but I just want to check one more time, just to make sure, you know?" Renee was smiling. "Don't you wanna make sure you leave with all your good stuff? Now, you go ahead, while Mommy gets us some water from the kitchen."

Denise giggled as she jogged up the stairs. "Let's hurry up, Mommy. 'Cuz the quicker we leave, the quicker Daddy will come find us, right?"

"That's right, Pooch."

When Denise was out of sight, Renee stepped quickly into the kitchen and got the water from the refrigerator.

As she went back toward the entryway, the letter she had placed on the counter caught her eye. She squashed the doubts it roused before they could overwhelm her.

Denise was padding down the stairs. "See, Mommy, I didn't leave any toys." Stopping in front of her mother, she said, "Are we ready now?"

Renee stared down at her strangely. "We'll go as soon as you drink this glass of water, Pooch, okay? Drink up for Mommy like a good girl."

Denise frowned, confused. "But, Mommy, that's not my Barbie cup. I can't drink outta that, it's too big. . . ."

"Well, Denise, just this once you're gonna have to use it, because your Barbie cup's already in the car, remember? It's coming with us." She lowered the tall glass to inches away from Denise's lips. "Now, come on, be a good girl and drink some water so we can go. I'll help you hold the glass."

Hastily, Denise gulped every drop of water. Swallowing the last mouthful, she said, "Okay, can we go now? Please?"

Renee gave her another eerie stare. "Yes, Pooch . . . now we can go."

It was time.

She lifted Denise, and they made their way toward the garage.

"Mommy, you forgot to tell me where we're gonna be going,"

Denise said excitedly. She began twirling one of her pigtails, as Renee carried her.

"We're going far, far away, baby. Far away. We can't make it easy for Daddy to find us now, can we? No, no, no, that would be too good for him."

She heard Denise giggle. With each step, Denise's excited chatter seemed to be coming from farther and farther away.

When she reached the door, she turned to stare at the living room, then back toward the kitchen. She had so loved this house. But now she hated it more. What was left to love?

Finally, Renee held Denise tightly and went into the garage. Securing the door behind them, she gave Denise a quick kiss on the cheek and put her on her feet. She was still chatting excitedly, and Renee wasn't sure if she answered her or not when Denise asked something about the smell of the grill in the garage.

Second thoughts. She was having second thoughts. . . .

Maybe running from this wasn't the best way to get back at Reginald. Maybe she and Denise should be there waiting for him when he came from the airport; waiting to make him see what a mistake he was making by deserting them for his wife and kids.

But as the pills began to take effect in Denise's body, Renee knew that if there had been any room for doubt before, it did not exist now. It was too late to go back.

Or was it? What if she left for the hospital right now? Maybe . . .

No.

No way. Reginald Brooks was through calling the shots. It was time for *him* to look like the fool; time for him to *be* the fool.

Let him come looking for his precious Denise. She'll be here, all right.

Denise was already in the car. "Mommy? Come on," she whined impatiently around a massive yawn. "Why are you just standing there? We have to go already. . . ." Dazed, she mumbled, "I'm so sleepy now, Mommy. I have to take a nap while we drive. . . . Okay . . . ?"

Within minutes, Denise snored peacefully.

Very slowly, Renee moved to the car door. She opened it and got inside. Turning to the body of her sleeping child, she reached for her, saying, "Are you happy, Pooch?"

As she stared at Denise's sleeping face, from far, far away, Renee clearly heard her animated little voice answer. . . .

And so she replied, "Me, too, Pooch . . . me, too. It's time to go."

41

"WE HAVE TO CALL them, Olivia," Valerie said, as they drove back to Olivia's house from the McDonald's down the street. "Mom's already left us four messages, and I'm *so* worried about Daddy."

Olivia made no reply until they got back into the comfort of her house. Taking her Big Mac from the bag, Olivia began shaking her head stubbornly. "I'm not calling either one of them," she said. "But that doesn't mean you can't call, Valerie. Why don't you just go ahead and call? Just do it—like Nike." She grabbed her soda, flopped on the sofa, and turned on the television.

Valerie had not moved to join her. She stood at the table for a moment, staring down into the McDonald's bag. "Olivia, don't you care about what happened?" she asked quietly. "How come you just never really seem to care . . . about how any of *us* might be feeling?"

Olivia bit into her burger. It was like biting sawdust. Tears sprang to her eyes as the memories came flooding back. If she had ever wanted to hurt her father, there was little doubt that she had now succeeded.

But why had she done it? Why had she pushed to see him hurt so much?

Olivia's heart dipped. Did she really *hate* him?

The room fell silent until she said softly, "Did you see his face?" That look had tormented her ever since. She would never forget the look in his eyes. He had really been . . . *hurt.*

"I know. I still can't believe it. . . . All along it was Uncle Frank," Valerie said, shaking her head. "I mean, *Uncle Frank.* Mom should've known somebody would get killed if—"

"I made a huge mistake!" Olivia said, suddenly wiping the tears on her face. "I wasn't thinking straight! My God, what *was* I thinking?" She began sobbing. "All of this is my fault, Val! I never hated Daddy. All I ever really wanted was just to have him here like normal people's dads, at home with us."

Valerie looked up from the bag and saw tears on Olivia's face. Her own eyes filled then. She did not know what to do. Should she go over to her? Should she yell at her for nearly embarrassing her beyond belief? Valerie just wasn't sure what she felt like doing.

Slowly, she went over to sit next to Olivia. Olivia looked up, and Valerie saw her eyes squeeze shut. She opened her mouth to speak, but Olivia shocked her again by saying, "And I'm sorry, okay? I'm sorry! I never should've even thought about telling them about what happened to you! I'm so ashamed, Val. . . . Look what I've done."

Valerie stared out the glass door and her own tears came fast now. "How come you never told me that you were pregnant?" Her voice was choked.

"Oh, Valerie, give me a break. I didn't tell anyone but Mom." She paused. "I was too embarrassed."

Valerie stared at her sister, a bit mystified. Then she understood. She reached over and hugged her. They held each other, both of them crying, draining the fullness from their hearts. The phone rang suddenly and Valerie said, "Answer it, Liv. You know it's probably Mom again."

Valerie rose then and went back to the table to start eating. She wondered what was going to happen now. What was going to happen to her life? To the family?

Olivia attempted to regain some composure as she reached for the phone. She dried her face. "Hello?"

She heard her mother breathe a sigh of relief. "Olivia, why haven't you returned my calls? I've been calling constantly. Is Valerie there with you? Is she okay?"

"Yes, she's here with me, Mom. She's fine." She paused. "Mommy . . . I'm so sorry about what happened. I wasn't thinking. . . . But you had no right to tell anyone!" Her voice choked up. "You had no right. . . . Because I trusted you."

"I know you don't agree, Olivia, but he had a right to know. I was wrong when I agreed to keep it from him. Did you see how upset he was about it? It really hurt that you wanted to keep something like that a secret from him."

Olivia fell back against the sofa. "I know, I know. Where is he now? Is he still in jail?" She held her breath.

"No, luckily, it was early enough for him to get bail, and I posted it." Tracy's voice faltered. "But I have no idea where he went. He hasn't come home. He just got in the car with our lawyer and drove away. . . . He didn't even look at me."

"Well, that's expected, isn't it?"

"You know, for a while I literally could've killed you. But I was up the whole night with my conscience and . . . this isn't your fault. I know better. It would have come out sooner or later, I suppose. And Frank would probably have ended up in the same place, anyway."

"Well, they said at the hospital that it was too soon to tell about his face. He definitely needs plastic, or maybe some type of reconstructive, surgery. Plus, he's got cracked ribs. . . ." She faltered as her thoughts swung back to her father. "You know, we were just talking about calling Daddy, because we need to at least make sure he's okay."

There was a pause. Then Tracy said, "You really do care, don't you, Liv? I think you've always loved your father very much, but it's just been easier for you to stay angry rather than open up and risk being let down. Right?"

Olivia started to cry again. "Oh, Mom. I do love Daddy. Of course I do. And I think Valerie and I need to stick close to him now—now more than ever."

Olivia pictured her mother sitting at a barstool in the kitchen. In her big, empty kitchen. "Yes, he will, Liv. He's gonna need you two very much. . . . And you should *both* be there for him."

*   *   *

LATER THAT EVENING, Tracy awoke to find that her eyes were glued shut. . . . She could not open them.

With careful steps, she stumbled toward the general direction of the bathroom, bumping into the loveseat along the way. Once she got through the door, she felt around for her washcloth and used warm water to slowly wash open her swollen eyes. One look in the mirror, and she cringed. She looked awful.

She had literally cried herself to sleep after talking to Olivia, unable to recall when she had fallen asleep. And now she was paying for it—big time. Her head felt as though it were ten times its actual size. She could barely stand holding it up.

She thought about calling Justine. . . .

Crawling back into bed, she reached for the telephone and called her mother.

Beverly Russell answered on the third ring. "Hello?"

"Mom, it's me." Tracy's voice cracked as her throat filled with the overwhelming need to bawl more tears.

"What's wrong, Tracy? Honey? You sound terrible. . . ."

After an apprehensive pause, Tracy said, "Come over, Mom. . . . I need you to come over."

THE FACT THAT he was possibly breaking the law by flying to Orlando never occurred to Reginald until he was halfway to the airport that morning.

It didn't matter. He was going, anyway. He would be back shortly, and no one would have to be the wiser.

His cell phone rang just as his taxicab was turning into Miami International Airport. He checked the screen. It was Olivia.

Reggie answered quickly, tucking the phone between his ear and shoulder. "Hello, Olivia."

Initially, there was silence as Olivia hesitated, apparently not sure of what she wanted to say. "Are . . . are you all right? Where are you? Mom's really worried."

The cab pulled over to the curb and Reggie stepped out. "I'm fine, thanks. And don't call again for your mother. I *do not* want to hear any reference to her—not right now." Setting his overnight bag on the curb, he pulled out his wallet and paid the driver.

"I get that, Daddy, but we didn't call just for her. We're worried about you, too, me and Valerie. . . ."

Reginald was certain of what he heard in her voice. . . . She cared. And in that moment, he was sure she always had.

"Listen, I'm going up to Orlando right now to try and work something out with Denise's mother. Hopefully, everything will go smoothly and I should be back tomorrow. I'll be in touch then, okay?"

"Wait a minute—Valerie wants to talk to you." There was shuffling as Olivia gave Valerie the phone.

Valerie audibly hurried to swallow her last bite of whatever she was having for breakfast. "Daddy, are you okay? Where are you?"

"I'm at the airport, sweetheart. Olivia will explain. I'll call you guys tomorrow. Don't worry about me. I'm fine."

Heading into the airport terminal, he disconnected the call. For the first time since the awful scene in Dr. Berenger's office, Reginald felt the desire to smile. . . . And he did.

REGINALD LANDED AT Orlando International just before noon. The sun was beaming down when he got out of the airport and hailed a cab. He hoped Renee was okay. He remembered how desperate she had been the last time he'd seen her. He remembered the lies he had fed her, and shook his head in shame.

"Where to, sir?" The middle-aged cab driver asked.

Reginald gave him Renee's address (it was funny how he now thought of it as *Renee's* address), and giving a brief nod of affirmation, the cabby moved out into the steady flow of traffic.

AFTER PAYING HIS cab fare, Reginald slowly walked up the winding sidewalk to the front door. He stopped for a minute and stared at the town house. This had been a home to him for so many years, yet as he approached, he felt like such a stranger. Could it be because he had spent all these years simply pretending Orlando was his home?

Letting himself into the house, Reggie walked toward the stairs, dropped his bag, and called out for Renee, announcing his presence.

Hearing nothing, he jogged up the stairs and headed for the bedroom. Glancing into Denise's room, he noticed that most of the stuffed animals were missing, which was odd, since the colorful bears had always been at every corner of her room. He went into the bedroom he had shared with Renee and checked the bathroom. It appeared she had gone out.

Going back downstairs, he decided to call the office and make sure his corporate apartment was still available for the night. He would have to make other arrangements if the lease had already been terminated. Staying in the house might only serve to give Renee false hope. . . . Reginald had no intentions of taking such a risk. The pretense was over, and going forward, he intended to be nothing but forthcoming with Renee and her family.

He went into the kitchen to grab a soda and immediately spotted the envelope on the countertop. Renee had left him a note. Good. At least he would know when she'd be back. His name had been neatly written across the front in capital letters: REGINALD.

Reaching for the letter, Reginald arched an eyebrow in curiosity and broke the seal. There was only one slip of paper inside, and it was definitely Renee's handwriting. It read:

Dearest Reginald,

You were right. I was extremely angry and deeply hurt when I read your letter. Even though you said you know I'm strong, I think you underestimated just how STRONG I actually am. Well, you're about to find out, because now I've taken control.

I've decided to leave and to take Denise with me. You claim she's your number one priority now, but you don't deserve her, and I'd rather die than have my child be anywhere near your wife and kids! What? So you can all live happily ever after with your perfect little family while I'm left alone to drown in a sea of humiliation for losing you—the way they all said I would?? You'll see me dead before that EVER happens!

Your letter also asked me to apologize to my family for you. You said you knew they'd be angry and grieved. Well, since I'm in control,

I leave you with the responsibility of apologizing to them yourself for their anger and their grief.

I hope you can sleep well at night after that.

From a heart that was always yours,
Renee
P.S. If you'd like to say good-bye, we're still in the garage.

Breathing a sigh of relief, Reginald headed for the garage. Renee wanted to scare him into thinking she was going to run off with Denise! He shook his head as he reached the garage door and turned the knob.

The smell hit him the minute the door was opened. Charcoal. Reggie saw the grill sitting in front of the car. What the hell was it doing burning in the garage?

His eyes stung as he stepped through the doorway.

"Renee?" he called out. He squinted as he walked toward the car. What in the world was she doing? "Denise?"

Reggie opened his mouth to call her name again. . . . But that's when they came into focus.

He froze.

His mouth fell open.

There, in the front seat of her Eclipse, was Renee. Her eyes were closed and her head was slumped forward, bent to the right.

Sprawled out in her arms, appearing to be no more than asleep on her mother's shoulder, was Denise. Their skin was a bizarre, abnormal color that Reggie's near-paralyzed mind couldn't even begin to identify.

He moved forward, mystified. His brain could not compute what he was seeing. As if dreaming, Reginald flung open the door and attempted to pull Denise from the car. "Holy shit . . ." he whispered, dazed. Her arms clung to her mother. . . . They were stuck.

Rigor mortis had long since set in.

Managing to clumsily dislodge her, Reggie ran with the little body into the kitchen, put her on the floor, and began blowing his breath into her stiff mouth. "Jesus Christ . . ." he said, still unable to make sense of what was happening or even what he was doing.

He felt for her pulse. But of course, there was no pulse.

Reggie's eyes suddenly glazed over. He knelt there so long that the tears ran down his face. . . . And splashed onto Denise's corpse.

Finally, in a state of absolute shock, Reginald raced for the telephone and dialed 911.

ON DECEMBER 2, 2004, the murder-suicide of twenty-nine-year-old Renee Holly Jameson and six-year-old Denise Rose Brooks made both local and national news.

It wasn't everyday that a woman locked herself in a garage with her child and waited for death to claim them . . .

The Jameson family was devastated.

THE FOLLOWING DAY, Beatrice Jameson received a letter in the mail. There was no return address. In it she found a cashier's check from Renee's bank. It was in excess of seventy-eight thousand dollars.

Engulfed by what her daughter had done, Bea collapsed on her front lawn, sobbing under the rays of the insultingly bright sun. A startled neighbor saw Bea and ran over from her front porch to help her back into the house.

REGINALD STAYED AT the town house until it was no longer a crime scene, having been officially cleared by police investigators. He immediately phoned his Orlando Realtor to put it on the market.

It had been nearly one week since he arrived to find Renee and Denise dead in the garage, yet he could still see them. He saw them just as they had been: a daughter with her arms around her mother . . .

He had allowed himself contact with no one, opting to seclude himself in that place; the place in which he had created a home for a woman and a then-unwanted child.

Who could have guessed, in their worst nightmare, that it would come to this? That sweet, innocent little girl was gone. Gone.

Denise was dead. The toxic fumes had filled her small lungs, and just like that . . . she was gone forever.

And he was responsible.

Reginald wondered. . . . Would he ever again close his eyes and not see her face? Would he ever again lie down to sleep without her image behind his eyelids—haunting him?

But of course he wouldn't. . . . Renee had given her own life to guarantee it.

RENEE KNEW WHAT she had been doing.

In a calculated and vile act of vengeance, she had sacrificed her own life in order to take the life of Reginald's child.

Revenge would be hers for all eternity.

THE ENTIRE JAMESON family struggled to recover from Renee's death.

Her mother and father suffered the most through the funerals. Beatrice withdrew into an emotional cocoon, leaving Benjamin utterly confused—and desperate to comfort his wife. He did not know how to help her when he himself needed so much consoling.

As time passed, Helen and John visited their parents daily, but they both needed just as much comforting as they had come to offer.

Things were made even worse when Renee's mail began showing up in her parents' mailbox. . . . When they all swallowed the extent to which she had gone, the premeditation, the planning. . . . It was just too much to bear.

They eventually turned to their church, seeking counsel to cope with the grief. Still, it was anyone's guess when true healing would begin. Accepting what Renee had done, the incredible pain she'd left behind . . . it would be a long time coming.

REGINALD BROOKS RETURNED to Miami with Renee's legacy floating over him—a black, chilling cloud that blocked all sunlight.

Taking a condo near his sister, Thelma, he went through the motions of living within the darkness of the cloud. And for months, he could not return to the work he loved; a clear head eluded him.

His world had been eternally dimmed, and he no longer believed he deserved to have a normal life. . . . The kind of life he had begun to crave.

VALERIE FINALLY BUILT up the courage, Olivia's insistence notwithstanding, to send a brief letter to Joseph Ellison, alerting him to his condition, but she also made it clear that she had no interest in communicating with him further. Joe must have shared her feelings, for he never attempted to speak to her when they saw each other in school.

Valerie focused on forgiving herself for screwing up, getting over the feelings of self-disgust and humiliation, and for as long as they needed her, she would be there for her parents until . . . until their family was whole again.

IN KEEPING WITH family values, Olivia clung to her little sister and to her parents. Making sure they knew she cared became a habit she passionately fulfilled, even as she kept busy with school. She never got around to voicing the feelings to Valerie, but she nursed dreams of their parents reconciling. . . . She recognized the desires her father possessed when he'd come home from Orlando that last time.

Though it was painful to see them apart, Valerie and Olivia rallied around their parents. They worried that without them, their mother and father would sink deeper and deeper into their own forms of depression. . . . And they were not willing to simply stand by and watch that happen.

Maybe at some point, they could all go back to see Dr. Berenger. They both hoped that one day they would get there.

TWO THINGS BROUGHT Franklin bittersweet amazement.

The first being that throughout his convalescence, Olivia and Valerie made it a point to stay in contact and visit with him. Though wounded in more ways than the obvious, he was grateful that they had not turned their backs, in spite of the disgrace, as quickly as Reginald and Tracy had. He told himself that they were the reason he didn't go the distance with Reggie in court. . . .

The second surprise was that, in spite of finding out about his relationship with Tracy and the obvious results, Theresa Parker refused to leave the picture. As her pregnancy progressed, Franklin found himself wishing more and more that something would happen to make her miscarry; then he would be free.

After all, Tracy was now free. . . .

* * *

WHEN SHE GOT news of Renee Jameson's death, Tracy tried desperately to offer Reginald comfort, even flying to Orlando to attend the funerals, but he found that he could barely stand the sight of her. He could not ignore, though, that the need to be with her overwhelmed him at times; the need to have her reassurance and her comfort . . . as only Tracy could provide them.

However, when he looked at Tracy, he saw Franklin, and humiliation pricked at him like thorns. So despite her persistent visits to Thelma's home for sympathy, despite her apologetic voice mail messages, with a broken heart he'd had Richard Love serve her with divorce papers, citing irreconcilable differences.

Tracy was devastated. He knew it—he *felt* it. Her mother, Beverly, was staying with her at the house, and sometimes Olivia spent the night.

Were it not for the presence of Valerie and Olivia, Reginald himself would have rotted away. He would have succumbed to the haunting that threatened to take over his very existence. The cloud of disgrace would have gotten the best of him, suffocating him forever. . . . And for months it nearly did. He struggled to keep his head above the guilt. He felt doomed to carry Renee's legacy like a second skin.

When people looked into Reginald's eyes, they saw it there. As if he would be forever tainted . . . scarred by the penalties of being the greatest pretender of them all.

EPILOGUE

Six months later, as June 2, 2005, neared, Reginald decided he needed to return to the town house. The evening prior, Roger arranged for him to fly out on the Hart-Roman jet.

As he boarded the plane, someone called out, "Reggie, wait . . . I'm coming with you!"

He spun around at the sound of Tracy's voice. He had not spoken to her since the night she bailed him out of jail.

"How long are we gonna go on like this?" Tracy held her breath. . . .Waiting for his answer. They were airborne, bound for the airfield in Orlando.

Minutes ticked by in silence.

"Reginald?" she said desperately.

He would not even look at her. Reginald busied himself reading Hart-Roman proposal drafts and memos.

They flew in silence for the entire hour of the flight to Orlando.

When they landed, Reginald rented a car and drove to the Embassy Suites ten minutes away from the home he had shared with Renee and Denise.

They checked into separate suites, and the next morning, Tracy rose before dawn to wait outside his door, ensuring he would not leave without her.

*   *   *

AFTER A STOP at Blossom Bloom, he drove to the town house. He parked across the street, and leaving Tracy in the car, got out and crossed the road.

Standing on the sidewalk, Reginald took in the house. He remembered all the nights he had driven into this driveway with flowers, walked up the path to that front door. . . . Opened the door to the sparkling eyes of a happily anxious little girl, just waiting to throw her arms around her daddy . . . that little girl would never grow up now.

A new family lived here today. . . . An authentic family.

He stood rooted to the sidewalk and stared at the house. . . . Remembering his sins . . . and also making his peace.

IT WAS NOT until they were standing over the graves, carefully laying the flowers, that Reginald finally spoke to her.

"How did you know I was coming up here?"

Obviously caught off guard, Tracy cleared her throat. "Roger called me." She paused. Then she said softly, "Reggie, this has to stop. We have to talk. . . . You can't keep me shut out forever. Even Roger sees it. You need me. . . . Just like I need you."

Reggie fell silent. He knelt beside Denise's marble headstone and closed his eyes, praying. Once he was finished, he gently kissed the bare marble and then laid his cheek upon it.

Minutes later, when they were walking along the path back toward the car, Reginald stopped. He turned to Tracy, and for the first time in six months, he looked her in the eye. "I thought it didn't matter who it was. Tom, Dick, Harry. It didn't matter. I could live with it because *I* was hiding a child." His eyes never left hers. The emotions of the day were playing in them. "But, Franklin? *Franklin Bevins,* Tracy?"

Tracy reached for his hands. "I'm sorry." Her eyes filled. "I'm so sorry. If I could undo it all, I would. I . . . I can't defend it, Reggie. I can't defend it, but I don't even know where to begin explaining why it happened. All I know is, you'd been gone, and he was in pursuit. It's no excuse, but . . . that's how it happened. I—"

"No," Reggie said, stopping her. He gently removed his hands from hers. "No. I can't hear any of that right now."

"Okay," she said, wiping her face. "But please don't shut me out anymore. At least move back into the house, Reggie. *Please.* We can see Dr. Berenger, but we have to start somewhere. You can stay in the guest room, but please come back home. I know you want to. . . . I can see it in your eyes. . . . I can feel it bouncing off you. You *want* to come home. You still need me just as much as I still need you. . . ." Tracy wept.

He broke eye contact and glanced around. Except for them, the cemetery was empty. Their path was shaded by tall, looming trees overhead. Out on the street, he noticed there was a car in the intersection waiting to enter the graveyard. Who did they have buried here? Certainly not a six-year-old angel. . . . Or a heartbroken and desperate mother . . . surely he was the only one who had such an ignominy as *that* here.

He turned to Tracy, and once again, he looked into her eyes. They were full of tears. She was begging him to come back home. . . .

Wordlessly, he put his arm around her. Together they walked back to the car, both feeling a wave of nostalgia. They were teenagers again, a new bud of love on the brink of blooming.

And when Reginald returned with her to Miami, for the first time since he had found Renee and Denise . . . there was a break in the cloud.

THE
GREAT
PRETENDER

MILLENIA BLACK

A CONVERSATION WITH MILLENIA BLACK

Q. What was your inspiration for writing The Great Pretender?

A. I was very intrigued by the idea of a man who was the head of two separate families, but neither of his families knew the other existed. I wanted to explore the possibility that this man could pull this off successfully for several years and then have various factors make him want to stop . . . only by then, it would be impossible to end it without all hell breaking loose one way or another—for all concerned.

Q. How has becoming a published author changed your life?

A. I have an optimism and drive that wasn't there before. Writing a novel is a great, personal accomplishment, and the journey of offering that work to all readers makes for a very motivating and worthy challenge.

Q. What have you learned through writing this book and becoming a published author?

A. I was actually very surprised to learn that there is an intensely palpable and unjust racial divide dominating the literary world.

Q. What is your greatest aspiration as an author?

A. I aspire to have a boundless appeal—one that could incite the eternal extinction of the racial inequality that still exists in a society of "equal opportunity".

Q. Is there still room for novice writers hoping to get published?

A. Yes, always. I believe there is room for anyone who is willing to make room for themselves. It takes good material, earnest determination, the patience of Job, and that lucky break every first-time bestseller gets to make big goals come to fruition.

Q. Thank you very much for your time. Is there anything else that you wish to add?

A. Yes! Readers can visit my Web site at http://www.milleniablack.com to request book club chats, enter the contests, etc. I've written an article, '7 Smoke Signals Your Man Is Living a Double Life', also posted at the Web site. Visitors may also join my announcement list and the 'Ask Millenia' newsletter where I respond monthly to questions from visitors who think their mate could be cheating or living a double life . . .

QUESTIONS FOR DISCUSSION

1. Discuss the central characters—Reginald, Tracy, Franklin, Olivia, Valeria, Renee, and Denise. Discuss the secondary characters—Justine, Roger, and Brent. Did you have any favorites? Least favorites? What are your thoughts on each of them? What were their individual motivations? Discuss their judgments and behaviors throughout the story.

2. Tracy and Reginald were married for two decades. Do they really love each other? Their family? Discuss how they both turned outside of the marriage to meet needs. What were those needs? Were they met?

Discuss their time in New York. Reggie revealed all of his secrets. Should Tracy have been completely honest about Franklin at that time? Could that have saved Frank's face? How might things have turned out differently if she had been as forthcoming as Reginald? Discuss the relationship between Tracy and Franklin by the end of the story. How had it changed?

3. When did you know who the "mystery woman" was? Who had you suspected before her identity was revealed?

4. Justine Roman referred Tracy to Dr. Berenger so the family could get help. Discuss the result of the first and only session. Should they have listened to Olivia and not gone after all? What were your feelings when it was all over?

5. In your opinion, what was the relationship between Reginald and Renee about from beginning to end? Do you think Reginald actually loved Renee? What did Reggie mean to Renee?

Reginald chose to confess all to Renee in a letter. Did you agree with this? Could he have possibly prevented her death, and Denise's, had he chosen a different way to communicate the truth to her? Discuss Renee's state of mind after reading this letter and what she proceeds to do to guarantee an eternal revenge. Was her action foreshadowed?